Glass Hearts

Lore Olesya

Copyright © 2025 Lore Olesya

All rights reserved.

No part of this book my be reproduced, or stored in a retrieval system, or transmitted into any form or by any means, electronic, mechanical, photocopying, recording, or otherwise, without express written permission of the author.

ISBN: 9798284975732

Cover art by EnchantedWhispersArt
Book design by Lore Olesya

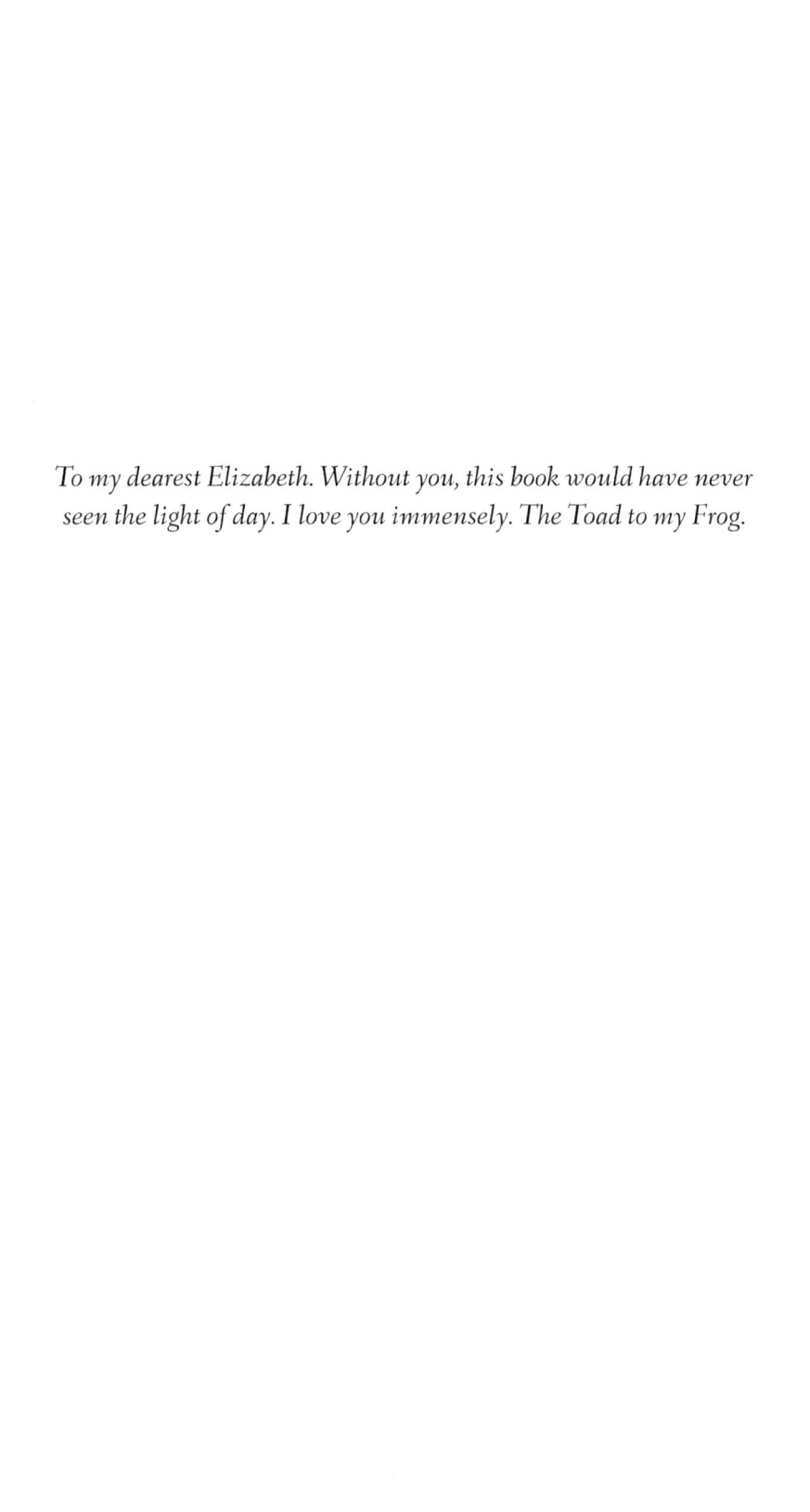

To my dearest Elizabeth. Without you, this book would have never seen the light of day. I love you immensely. The Toad to my Frog.

Prologue
Evrardin

Amongst the Lyre Shores of the Sun Kingdom, August the first, 593 A.G. (After the Gods) Sixteen days prior to the Summer Solstice

THE SUN GLAZED over the sandy shores, the auburn foliage filtering the morning light, making it gleam the same crimson sheen it bore centuries ago after the War of Lyres. Bodies strewn amongst the seaside, blood soaking deep into the grains and staining the sand a ruddy beige for over a year. Now, that battle lived only in memory, a tale spun to keep the fear of the fae rooted within the people of Kairth—to blame the sinking city on another kingdom.

The Captain of the Royal Guard looked out beyond the steep of Kairth's graveyard, over the beachy waters, letting the rising sun warm his groaning bones. He gazed at his hands, tainted in blood, the same carmine shade as the trees surrounding him. The innocent soldier's pulse thrummed in the center of his palms. Flashes of bloody spurts gurgling from the arteries of the solitaire knight, seeping into the cracks of the sun emblem embossed on his copper chest plate, haunted him. The magnificent sea could not erase the image of the knight sitting helplessly on his knees, his arms flailing up to his neck in prayer as he tried to stanch the overflow of cascading blood.

It wasn't just this knight—or this one time—all of his victims' faces were plastered across his vision, forced to remember what he unjustly stole. Ruefully, he knew it was a mirrored fate for those innocent men that plagued him—they, too, would be ingrained with the captain's face as he robbed the life from their bodies. He would never be free of this torment, of these ghostly memories. The terror on their faces—realization, confusion, betrayal—followed the captain like a wraith. He loomed behind his victims, always in rumination about the ancient tale of being endlessly intertwined with the last thing you saw before you crossed over. He didn't want to be inadvertently hindered by these men, yet his soul was tethered to their grueling purgatory.

He let that solitude wash out of him momentarily as he loosened a breath. He climbed the sandy gravel, his hand wrapped tightly around the sword sheathed at his hip as he traipsed back toward the castle. The castle's halls were peaceful this early in the morning, glowing from the sun, the air not yet warm enough to cause discomfort in his long-sleeved tunic. He strolled into the prince's chambers, unsurprised to find Lord Alfson speaking tantalizing whispers into the prince's ear.

"Captain," Lord Alfson greeted when he finally laid eyes on the intruder.

"Evrardin," the prince said with a sly grin growing on his lips, "pack your things. We shall be attending the welcoming of the Summer Solstice in Wrens Reach this season."

Evrardin adjusted his stance, the metal buckles on his boots rattling, his curly hair spilling over his face and slicked to his sweaty skin. He thought the prince would be nose-deep in affairs here in Kairth, too busy to consider leaving. "We will?"

The prince glanced at himself in his floor-length mirror, the sun shining in such a way that it reflected off the surface and cast a halo around his inky hair. "The Glass Princess is looking for a suitor." He turned to Evrardin. "A well-paired match."

Evrardin took a moment to process his words. "And... you suppose you're that match?"

"I must be," he insisted. His eyebrows relaxed, serenity coating his features like a glaze. "She does have a glass heart, after all—though, I do wonder how tempered it will be."

"You're so certain you can waltz into Wrens Reach and secure her hand just because you're a prince?"

"A Sun Prince," he corrected. He wasn't just another crowned prince, but one with the power of the sun growing within.

Evrardin scoffed. "The southerners are a surly lot. I wouldn't be so convinced they'd graciously accept someone of such balmy blood."

"Ah, you doubt me, old friend?" The prince tugged on the leather gloves he had left on his armoire. His lips quirked in a brash tilt like he knew something the captain didn't. "I plan to make her mine whether she agrees to it or not."

Evrardin laughed. "That whole house has lost its magick. No one's glassfaired in almost a century. You do not want her bound to you."

"Are you so sure about that?" Lord Alfson interrupted. Evrardin had the sudden urge to wrap his hands around his neck.

The prince's words unthreaded his sharpening snarl, calling the captain's attention back. "So they've said. But I don't believe they're telling the truth."

Evrardin raised his brows. "And you think she's worth the risk?"

The prince nodded. "I know she's worth the risk."

Chapter One
Mara

Wrens Reach of the Glass Kingdom, August the tenth, 593 A.G. Seven days prior to the Summer Solstice

The castle's stained-glass windows let in a waterfall of light that melted over the oakwood floorboards, swirling like a pot of brewing tea leaves.

The Glass Princess' steps echoed softly in the quiet morning as she stealthily moved down one of the many halls of Venmore Castle, windows flanking her, the morning glow illuminating her path. She slid up to a familiar steel door, shadowing it in darkness, the warm light wafting behind, not treading this far down the corridor. She placed her fingers against the cool metal surface and slid the key she had stolen from her father's chambers out of her skirt pocket.

She did a quick sweep over her shoulder, paranoid someone might be tempted to follow her, before unlocking the door. The room was swathed in bright light, the curtains ajar and tangled with dust. *Everything* was tangled with dust. It had been years since her parents' room was filled with life, the space confined to those last sparks of time before it was abandoned, everything left how it was the day *she* died.

The last time the princess saw her mother flooded her mind just as it did most mornings. It was something she couldn't scrub from the dark side of her eyelids. The image of her mother—prone on the floor, her body torn in unnatural ways, blood pooling around her—scarred her memory. Her father's haunting scream as he cried out her name, "Meredith!"

She blinked back tears as she appraised her mother's old rooms. Her bed was still ruffled as if she had been sleeping in it just moments ago, the velvet fabric a sage green—her mother's favorite color—and embroidered with golden flowers and insects. When she stepped on the matching sage carpet, her foot left a ghostly print in the dust.

She'd been expecting this horror, but it still unsettled her when she saw the vast array of scattered mirrors in her mother's chambers. Once such a common instrument that seemed to fuel Wrens Reach, now an outlawed relic, most shattered and left to rust in one of the adjacent woodland valleys. The few that remained, like the one in the princess' room, were covered in drapes at all times.

She knew that her mother's room would still have its mirrors, but she couldn't stop the disquietude from settling within her. While Wrens Reach had been one of the last kingdoms to lose their abilities gifted by the now absent gods—the other being Solstrale—their power had finally completely drained. And her mother paid the price. As she stepped through that mirror fourteen years ago, knowing her abilities had weakened, her connection shattered, and she was split in two. Her father banished all mirrors, the Glass Court pretending to have never possessed any magick abilities at all.

She held back her panic, shoving it down deep within her, and darted out of her mother's chambers, locking the door behind her. She collapsed against the door and sucked in wild breaths of air in an attempt to compose herself. She shouldn't have done this today, of all days. Determined that this would work, that visiting here would grant her the reprieve she craved, dark retribution filled her.

She ran her fingers along her nightdress, smoothing out nonexistent wrinkles, forcing herself to appear presentable before making the trek back to the living side of the castle. When she entered the west hall, thinking she had managed to elude her handmaidens, a feminine voice called out to her. "Mara!"

The princess scrunched her face in annoyance before spinning to face the gilded young woman who scurried to her side.

"There you are," her handmaiden said, relieved. "I've been searching the halls for you. You know we only have so long to prepare you."

She cringed at the idea of having to be primed for hours solely for the ogling gazes that saw her as nothing but decor. Mara rolled her eyes and shifted paths, now trailing back to her apartments. "Apologies, Jessamine. But you can imagine my lack of enthusiasm."

Jessamine gave her a sidelong look, their shoes clinking off the floorboards in sync. "Such a cynic. A well of hope would do you some good."

"Oh, like you?"

"Yes. Exactly like me. You could learn a thing or two from following in my footsteps, don't you think?"

Mara stifled her laugh and nudged her handmaiden on the shoulder.

When the two women made it back to the princess' chambers, Jessamine began smoothing out the furs of Mara's daisy and silkworm comforter. Mara's friend was all gold: golden locks that spun out of her head, golden skin that had been kissed by the ever-chilling sun in the south, and golden eyes that glittered whenever the light refracted off them.

When Jessamine had finished fussing over her unkempt bed, she made her way to the windows, ignoring Mara's dramatic faces. She tore open the drapes, letting the icy morning light spill into the room completely, reducing Mara's vision to a squint.

"Does it please you to torture me?"

"The king wants you ready so you can greet the guests," she said, her voice a decibel too loud for someone as irritable as Mara in the mornings.

Both women knew Mara wasn't about to waste the first half of her day politely greeting strangers who pretended to care about her natal day. Jessamine bit her lip. "I'm not forcing you to do it, but just let me do what the king requested of me, at least."

Mara huffed, moving closer to Jessamine, and lifted her hands so she could begin to remove her night attire. "I just don't see how you're not more upset by this."

Her friend gave her a sympathetic look, tying a clean chemise around Mara's waist, the weather warm and calling for a light undergarment.

It was early August by the time Mara's first and twentieth birthday rolled around. Ladies were usually married off by sixteen, especially ones of such nobility. Mara eluded marrying for a time; King Björn Faintree so engrossed with his firstborn's affairs, Azor, that he didn't press his daughter. But now she was turning twenty and one, and she still wasn't wed. She was a scandal waiting to unfold.

She was aware it was seen as something shameful to have an unwed princess left to wander the kingdom at her leisure, but what she didn't see was why it mattered so much to others. And while the desire to conform bothered her, the more pressing issue was how she could be used like a piece of property—*which she technically was under the law*—bartered off to unite powerful alliances and prevent wars.

Thus, today's birthday ceremony was also a life sentence. *Don't be so dramatic*, her father had chided her, which swiftly became *Enough! I've had it with the theatrics, Maralena. You are to be married and that's final!*

Mara sank into her vanity chair as Jessamine brushed through her hair. The drape that usually covered the single skinny mirror clung to a hook on the side of the frame, revealing Mara's drowsiness in the reflection. Her chestnut-blonde hair hung along her back in loose waves, its length reaching close to her lower back. Her underdress slid off her shoulder, revealing sun-splotched freckles. She sighed.

"Just think about all the young princes you'll get to choose from. One of them ought to catch your eye."

Mara didn't comment on the fact that Jessamine referred to them as *young* when most of her options were likely to be middle-aged men—and that was if she was lucky. "You're just happy because if I get married, that means you get to leave this place, too." Mara winced at her own words, recalling the fact that Jessamine would be free of her debt when Mara married, able to return back to Throneskeep to be with her family, while Mara would be on a journey to some other kingdom to marry a stranger...alone.

"Is that so wrong?"

She had to remind herself that at least Jessamine, her closest friend, would get something worth celebrating out of this political congregation, even if it meant the separation of the two women. Mara mirthlessly laughed. "It is when it means your closest friend has to suffer for it!"

Three other handmaidens entered Mara's room and began to

do their duty, cleaning up the mess Mara left behind. She knew it was part of their designation, but she still hated how little privacy she was often granted.

"Such hysterics," Jessamine said, playfully rolling her eyes. "It's all young ladies' duty to marry. You're not the first to go through this, you know?"

"And just because other ladies endure the same misfortune, that means mine will bear any less pain?" Mara's voice cracked as she spoke, the facetiousness gone, her anxiety finally building up enough to explode out the seams of her teeth like a rag doll. She had done her best to stow her fears deep within her gut, but today it seemed to all be coming undone. She glanced in the corroded mirror at her shocked friend with an apologetic look. "Sorry. It's just..."

"I'm only trying to help." Jessamine's hands paused where they were buried in Mara's nest of hair. "Would you rather me let you wallow in self-pity? Pointing out all the dreadful details you've been complaining about for months?"

"I only wish I could be free like my brother."

Jessamine's eyes dropped; the silver brush that stroked through Mara's hair faltered for a moment. It wasn't her place to agree—she would be speaking out of turn if she validated all of Mara's concerns. The world was a terrible place, and Mara managed to avoid the brunt of it all being born into such a powerful family. But, at the end of the day, she was still a woman. And women had one duty: to serve the men around them—marry them, make them happy, bear their children, and act as pretty decorations at social gatherings.

Jessamine gave Mara's shoulder a light squeeze. "Just think about all the things you'll see traveling to a new kingdom." Jessamine looked like she was caught in a reverie. "I hope you choose someone from the Faelands." Her eyes sparkled as she thought about the inhumanly perfect fae that resided on the other side of Junefell, off along the coast of the northern shores.

"You would enjoy this far more than I ever will," Mara chuckled. She could already picture Jessamine pointing out all the handsome nobles to Mara, taking it upon herself to solidify Mara's dancing itinerary.

"If you didn't have such a stick up your ass, you could enjoy it too!"

Mara's lips ticked upward.

"And the ball tonight," Jessamine squealed. "You're going to look amazing in your dress." Jessamine's fingers dexterously braided Mara's hair. "And the tournament! Think about all the knights fighting in the tournament! You'll get to choose from them, too." Jessamine's eyes rounded, lost in a daydream of handsome gentlemen. "It's like they're all fighting for your hand."

Mara glared at her friend. "Oh, you're going to have a wondrous time. I'll be sure to pass the men off to you once I'm done."

Jessamine smiled, not taking the jest. "I heard the Sun Prince will be there." Mara's lack of enthusiasm didn't seem to deter Jessamine from gossiping. "At least he's closer in age to you. I think he's eight and twenty—oh, no wait. That can't be right. When was the last Summer Solstice?" Jessamine didn't notice Mara flinching as she tugged too hard at her hair while she thought. "Maybe he's older than that. Well, never mind the specifics, he's plenty young."

"The Sun Prince?" Mara felt like her eyes might get stuck in the back of her skull if she kept rolling them so harshly. "He's done nothing but caroused in his father's shadow."

"Less work for you that way. You have to be logical, Mara."

"Do I really want an unambitious drunkard for a husband?"

"Nothing will satiate you."

Jessamine was probably right. Mara was bound to find a flaw in every man she met tonight.

"I still say you should go for one of the fae," Jessamine said, wiggling her eyebrows at Mara in the reflection of her decrepit mirror.

One hand trailing along the rough stone wall for support, Mara descended the cobbled steps with a grimace, her eyes set on the emerging lance yard. She had managed to escape her several relentless handmaidens and was making her way to the dueling grounds—granted, the tournament wasn't until later this evening, but Mara wanted to scope out the competitors beforehand.

Mara loved the brutality and sport of fighting, predicting the victor of countless dueling competitions, her triumphs lining her purse with an effortless ease. Azor always complained that she was cheating; she would smirk with pride knowing she could outwit her brother which did nothing but drive a silver thorn under his skin, and she was happy to hammer it in further. She had often gone into town, hidden in her cloak, and watched the various brawls that unfolded in the back of seedy taverns, placing bets, and winning more times than not. She had thought about running away with her earnings on the rare occasion, but the fleeting idea would never come to fruition.

The clattering of iron swords and the smell of sweat and horse shit infiltrated the breeze that blew through Mara's hair. She peered off the castle's parapets, rewarded with a perfect view of the knights. With her elbows on the edge, she leaned her weight and pushed onto her toes to watch the pride-hungry men jousting down below.

She recognized a few from prior years. There was Sir Orion, whose shaggy blonde hair had grown considerably in length since the last time she saw him. He darted forward, thrusting his sword toward another knight, laughing boisterously as he went.

Beside him, facing his squire, was Sir Roe from Throneskeep, a member of the High King's Court. As much as she didn't want that to intimidate her, it sent a shiver down her spine. Was he here to revel in the festivities or did he hear that the Glass Princess was looking for a suitor?

Dread shrouded her mirth. There was something so unnerving about watching proper knights stripped of their armor and jousting around like boys.

"Scoping out a winner?" a voice said from behind her.

"I'm doing no such thing," Mara replied without turning to face her brother.

Mara could hear the smile in Azor's speech as he leaned against the stone wall. "Picking out a husband, then, perhaps?"

Mara's eyes darted to Azor's and narrowed. It wasn't completely unwarranted. These knights were amongst the pool of possible suitors she'd have a choice between, most of them having families in high rankings. It would please her father plenty for her to accept one of their hands.

Mara shook her head and Azor nudged her shoulder. She set her eyes back on the men below, wanting to forget about the agonizing events of tonight's celebrations.

"It's not so bad. Lots of them are handsome enough," Azor teased, just in time for Sir Hector from the Icewoods, representing House Ceaytr, to turn into their view. His pudgy face, half frostburnt from an incident last winter, on full display. *Shouldn't the winter people know how to protect themselves from the frost by now?* Mara thought, gritting her teeth.

"It's only amusing because you don't have to worry about any of this happening to you," Mara whined with a hint of envy. Her voice was a whisper in the wind, her throat tensing up every time she thought about the fact that soon she'd have to spend the rest of her life with a stranger.

"You know that's not entirely true." Compassion dusted across Azor's soft features. "I'll still have to fulfill my marital duties."

Mara turned to face her brother. The gentleness of his countenance mirrored hers, both of their noses rounding at the tip. His jaw was far sharper than hers, but other than that, no one could doubt their likeness. They both shared olive-toned skin and light-brown eyes. Mara's complexion was kissed with freckles whereas Azor's was smooth and silken. He stood a good six inches taller than her, always making a point to emphasize that he had to look down to meet her stare. They both had soft features and rounded faces, creating an air of warmth around them wherever they went.

Mara slouched against the flagstone. "Yes, but you don't have a sundial tethered to you—following you around, reminding you of how rapidly time is passing, your womb still empty."

"Do you always have to be so vulgar?" Azor asked. Mara glared at him. "I already tried speaking to Father," Azor added after taking a deep breath. His arms rested on the stone, his eyes finally shifting to hers.

"And...?" Mara urged after too long of a pause.

Azor averted his eyes. "Just be glad you get to choose a suitor. Not many princesses have that luxury."

"*Luxury*," she muttered under her breath in disappointment, her eyes wandering over to the wet wood on her flank, various weaponry leaning against it. Her lips parted.

Someone was looking at her.

The stranger clutched a long sword languidly enough that it

gave him an air of overconfidence. It rested on his knee as he sat and wiped it down, his armored plates lying haphazardly beside him. His inky hair was in disarray, loose pieces hanging down to frame his sweat-covered face. A bit of blood bloomed around his jawline. He grinned at her before looking back at what he was doing, his mouth moving as he responded to one of his counterparts.

"Who is that?" Mara asked Azor.

"Uh," Azor began, his eyes squinting as he tried to get a better view of the man. "If that's his armor on the ground etched with a sun, he must be from the Sun Court."

"The Sun Prince? I thought him above traveling to the southern lands, I didn't think he'd actually show."

"Can't be. The prince wouldn't risk his life in a silly tourney."

Mara settled her features. "Regardless, I think he'll be our winner."

Azor cracked a smile and shifted to face his sister fully, his boyish mischief somewhat of a solace to the stress Mara carted around. "You willing to wager that?"

Mara pulled a small sack that clinked with coins out of her dress pocket, giving her brother a shit-eating grin. "Always."

The wind howled against the castle, mulberry flags flapping in the breeze. Mara and her brother shared a moment in silence as they watched the men, though Mara's mind had wandered elsewhere.

Mara thought of her mother. How much she wished she was here right now to reassure her everything would turn out how it was supposed to. As much as her brother was someone she could rely on, he'd never completely understand the torment and indignation that brewed inside her knowing the very meaning of her life was to become someone's wife.

Her brother would be King of Wrens Reach one day. That alone was no small feat. What would become of Mara? Her marriage might help unite her house with another kingdom, but beyond that, she would be used as a placeholder at gatherings and balls. She'd be forced to mother sons who would one day become more powerful than she ever would.

Her mother's round eyes and strawberry hair were still vivid in her memories, but her likeness had begun to fade. Mara sucked in a deep breath.

"Everything will be just fine," her brother reminded her before pushing himself off the parapet to make his way below to speak with the guests.

Chapter Two
Mara

Mara smoothed the wrinkles on her dress, the soft purple of it complimenting her slightly tanning skin. She had been sitting in the sun these days, reveling in the beginning of summer, glad to soak up the warmth after the long winter had overtaken the south, her skin becoming as pale as milk. Light cast through the sheer gossamer around the shoulders, tightening at the wrist, breaks in the fabric exposing the freckles along her arms.

She pushed back the curtain and looked at herself in the ornate mirror, her lips forming a tight line as she scanned her body. The dress fitted perfectly to her every curve, molding to her, the skirt flowing outward at the end of her bodice, a long slit displaying white lace. The bottom was mostly muslin, outlining the shape of her legs beneath in an opaque shadow. Purple flowers were splattered on the tulle of the dress and climbed up the seams. Her chestnut-blonde hair was pulled back out of her face and sat in loose curls along her exposed back apart from two long tendrils that swirled on either side of her head, reminding her of an unfurled flower. Long curling strands of matching fabric bled from the crown of her head and disguised itself within the braid of her hair. She donned royal purple sugilite earrings, and a tight golden torque with a sugilite gem plastered in the middle.

She felt like a doll.

She felt silly, like she was pretending to be someone she wasn't.

"You look beautiful," Jessamine encouraged.

Mara huffed. "Of course he would want me to wear *this*." The dress accentuated her curves, the corset exposing much more of her décolletage than she typically liked, her breasts appearing far fuller with the fitted material, her legs visible beneath the sheer fabric. She was the embodiment of an elderberry tart, warm and waiting for the noblemen to devour at the feast. Her mistress of the robes had made it clear to the tailors that she wanted Mara to look as sultry as possible while still looking elegant and regal. She knew the king needed this night to end in an engagement.

"Nonsense," Jessamine said as she fixed the hem of Mara's dress.

"He's practically whoring me out," Mara mumbled.

Jessamine shot her a warning glance in the mirror, urging her to move.

Mara had to make herself present at the ball—it was *her* natal day after all—and she was already running late, but her feet wouldn't budge. They were nailed to the floorboards, keeping her in place like a marbled statue. In stiff movements, she left her chambers, escorted by a guard clad in the violet colors of Venmore Castle, to the Great Hall.

Mara wanted to reach out and claw at the stone walls, heaving herself away from the guard that would surely grip her waist in rebuttal and drag her to her father's feet.

She reluctantly found herself entering the grandiose affair, spotting her father as he sat on his throne, a long stretched-out table before him, intricately carved chairs adorning his side. Her father had on a sinuous cloak lined in white fur, the velvet of it a deep cerulean blue. His glass crown reflected the light, tiny opals dotting the tip of every point. His chestnut-blonde hair was pulled back, threads of white peppered above his ears, his beard cut short, highlighting the sharpness of his chin. Her father had more angular features than both his children who favored the softness of their mother.

Mara went up the steps and curtsied to her father who smiled at her. "Daughter," he hummed. Mara went to step around and sit beside her father. "No, don't sit. Go." He gestured his hand in a wave. "You have many suitors who are waiting to dance with you." Mara went to open her mouth, but her father was already standing up, his glass of wine shaking on the table as his thighs hit the wood in a sense of apathy.

"My daughter, Princess Maralena Faintree," he boomed. The swarm of nobles went quiet, turning to face the king. Her father looked sidelong at her. Mara stepped forward and gave a tight smile to the crowd of courtiers before striding down the steps of the dais. The cacophony of noise returned and a heckle of eager men approached Mara as she made her way to the parquet floor engraved with swirls of the wind.

The king had a sly grin on his face as he watched his daughter. Mara couldn't help but wonder if the king had ulterior motives for tonight, beyond that of finding his daughter a suitor. He never seemed to keep her in the loop, and she feared he saw too much of her mother in her to truly face his children.

A hand reached out and gripped hers just as she descended the final step. She faced Sir Orion, much to her dismay. Mara matched his height as she hovered on the last step, debating if she would be able to trek back up them before Sir Orion could force her to dance. His eyes flicked upward, and he grinned at her, his lips puckering slightly before he spoke. "My Princess," he said bowing, her hand still trapped in his.

Mara curtsied in correspondence.

"Shall we?" he implored, though his words didn't sound like a request, but rather a demand. The group of men surrounding them groaned and dispersed, clearly irritated that Sir Orion had stolen her to dance first. She was sure they would think they stood no chance against him. He was incredibly wealthy. His kingdom housed an expansive army at least twice the size of Wrens Reach, and he was set to inherit Branwen, a large city in the Icewoods.

It was a match made in perdition.

Mara couldn't find the strength to fake a smile as Sir Orion led her into the throng of dancing guests. His large hand engulfed her own, cold against her palm—she wondered if that was an attribute of all the Ice People. She looked up at him as he yanked her into his chest, a hand resting on her lower waist, the tips of his fingers brushing over her exposed skin where the back of her dress cut down her spine. Mara's cheeks warmed and her heart twisted uncomfortably. She wasn't keen on the way Sir Orion felt against her.

He gave her a wicked smile, all his white teeth sparkling through his parted lips. "You look beautiful tonight, Princess."

Mara's lips tightened as she attempted to not look as repulsed as she felt. "You flatter me."

Sir Orion spun her around, making her gasp when he abruptly caught her waist again. "I was just telling the Glass King how I'm set to inherit Branwen sooner than expected. Uncle isn't... right-minded lately." He spoke like everyone in the room was listening, dying to know his next word. It made Mara stifle a yawn.

"I'm sorry about your uncle," she responded, though she wasn't sure he was even looking for a retort.

"Yes, thank you," he said tersely. "Soon, I'll take my place on the throne of Branwen. And I'll need a wife."

The throne of Branwen, she thought, wanting to chide him about his use of the word throne. *Lords subject to the crown don't really sit upon a throne, now do they?*

His fingers tightened, sending a wave of repugnancy through her. His devious smile made it seem like he thought he succeeded in seducing her. "Someone to give me golden-haired babes. A son to precede me."

Mara's gut twisted, faking a jovial grin. His cornflower eyes gave him a frosted appearance and she broke his stare out of sheer perturbation.

As Sir Orion spun her to the woodwind instruments, he leaned in, only a mere kiss away from her ear. "Your father has all but granted me his blessing to marry you." He pulled back to look at her, her eyes expanding.

"Sir Orion, I'm flattered, b—"

"Yes. I thought you might be. Only a few matters to straighten out before it's official," he affirmed, but surely, he was just fooling her into subduing his proposal. "Shall we go ahead and practice, then?" Mara stared at him blankly. "For our wedding night, I mean," he added in a sultry voice, making her shiver in dread, though Sir Orion likely took it as overflowing lust.

She pushed him away, straightening her dress as he raised a brow. "I apologize, Sir Orion. I seem to be feeling faint. I...I think I'm going to step out for a moment. Fresh air and all that," she stammered.

He gripped her hand, bowing, and placed a wet kiss on the back, smirking at the thought of Mara being so overwhelmed with his proposal she had to take a minute to calm herself—to collect her decorum. Mara had to restrain from recoiling from his touch by wiping her damp hand on her dress—she'd wait until she was out of sight to do that.

When he finally let go, she turned and scoured off toward the courtyard. On her way to the grandiose glass doors that led out into the dark chilled night, the knight she spotted earlier in the lance yard looked across the room and caught her gaze. She almost halted in her step, feeling an intense weight as he surveyed her, something sickly swimming in his gaze.

She shyly broke her eyes away and tried to slip out the door without anyone noticing—well, apart from him. She hoped he wouldn't alarm one of the king's guards about her disappearance; Mara just wanted to be left alone to sulk. She was about to be fated for life to someone she didn't know, the least she could be granted was the ability to spend her remaining moments alone.

Chapter Three
Mara

Mara shivered against the cool breeze. She knew she wouldn't be able to stay out here long, but just breathing in the crisp air gave her some semblance of reprieve from the domineering Great Hall. She laughed at herself for already feeling the need to escape. This was going to be a tortuous night.

Sir Orion's touch lingered on her skin and it made her want to take a scalding bath.

Mara passed two guards as she strolled through the keep's gardens, their eyes following her closely. She thought back to Sir Orion's words; he had already been speaking to her father, telling him about his rise to Lord of Branwen. Her father had reassured her she would decide whose hand to accept, but nonetheless, dysphoria coursed through her.

Mara wished she could see Jessamine. Maybe she'd be able to sneak down to the kitchens to see her friend who'd be busy at work. She genuinely considered it, contemplating if upsetting her father by disappearing would be worth it.

The sweet scent of bread wafted out of one of the open doors, the feast beginning. She spent several additional minutes turning about the garden before she was ready to walk back. As she went to approach the castle, she realized how far she had strolled beyond the vision of the sentinels. It was much darker this late, being so far from the candlelight inside.

As she approached closer, she spotted a figure under one of the jutted merlons beside the stationed sentinels. When Mara squinted, she recognized the blonde mop of hair as Sir Orion scanning the gardens for her.

Shit, shit, shit.

The last thing she wanted was to be trapped outside alone with him. It was one thing to be forced to converse with him in a room filled with people, but alone in the dark gardens...

Mara quickly shifted her body behind one of the tall sculpted bushes, hoping he didn't see her. Her heart raced, booming loudly inside her chest, making her feel ill, her hands tremulous. This was finally becoming real. She was going to be forced to take a suitor and swept away to his residency—a custom of the southern people.

This was real. It *was* real.

Mara turned, trying to peek out beyond the hedge, and she was faced with a tall lean body. *Gods be damned.*

"What are you doing all the way out here, little princess?" Sir Orion asked her.

"I needed to step outside for a minute. I told you—"

"In the night-covered gardens? Alone?" He eyed her, a malicious smirk quipping on the edge of his lips as he cut her off.

Mara had to tilt her head to look up at him, taking a small step backward, her heel sinking into the soft ground.

"It's not safe out here, who knows what could be lurking in the shadows."

Mara wanted to sneer but she restrained herself with great difficulty. The only thing lurking in the shadows was him.

"If I didn't know better, I'd think you were inviting debauchery to your fingertips."

"I—I…" she stuttered. "I must have wandered too far in the heat of the moment. I just needed to feel a cool breeze. I'll be sure to meet you back inside, Sir Orion. I thank you for checking on me."

Mara tried to take a step around him, but he grabbed her arm, forcing hers to lace with his. "You don't have to pretend with me, Princess. If you wanted to meet me alone, there is no shame in that."

His cool smile made her body rack with tiny angry sparks, her face contorting into a scowl. What she would give to be able to stomp as hard as she could on his foot right now without the repercussions of assaulting a knight. Though, maybe she could get away with it. He wouldn't want the shame brought on by admitting to being bested by a *little princess*.

"Sir Orion, I think—"

"Princess Maralena," a sudden voice alerted both of them to the right. "Your brother is asking for you." The stranger's words were like decadent honey to her ears. Mara took the man in, instantly recognizing his fair features, but unsure from where. His eyes narrowed in on Sir Orion's grip. "He asked if I'd escort you myself." He looked at Sir Orion imperiously. It seemed as though the man knew Sir Orion would immediately insist on taking Mara, but with such authority in his timbre, bluntly spoken and relaying his orders to take her, Sir Orion was sure to concede. It didn't hurt that the man had an imposing sword strapped to his person.

Sir Orion's jaw clenched as he looked down at Mara and forced a smile. "Princess," he muttered, bowing slightly at her, and then making his way back into the castle.

Mara followed the stranger, waiting until they were inside the castle to ask, "What does my brother want, Sir...?"

The man stopped, shifting his gaze to Mara, her figure only up to his shoulder. "*Lord* Cofsi. And nothing of value. You just looked like you were in need of saving. In fact, I don't think I've even seen Prince Azor yet tonight." He gave her a small smile.

"Lord Cofsi," she said hurriedly, "my apologies, I hadn't recognized you."

He held up a hand. "Nonsense. You were just a child last time I was here for the Summer Solstice."

She remembered Lord Cofsi, as faint as that memory was. He was much younger then, too, probably only just becoming a man. And he lacked the *lord* honorific—he must have taken his father's place on the Duskwood throne back in The Shadowed Isles since then, now deemed the Dusk Lord.

He hovered above her, his hands now behind his back. His suit was a silver blue, the buttons sparkling in the candlelight. His ashen-blonde hair was styled back, granting him a sharp and dignified appearance. His face was clean-shaven, lacking any imperfection apart from the faint scar that ran across his cheek. His pale blue eyes were full of warmth, making her feel at ease. She thought him rather limpid for a person of the Dusk Court.

"Well, thank you," she said demurely. "I've felt rather suffocated all night it seems."

"Of course, Princess. I can only imagine. Well, you look stunning, if it's any consolation."

Mara blushed.

"I'd love to stay and keep you from your other obligations..." he mused.

"Oh, of course!" She shook her head at her absentmindedness, not wanting to keep him. "Thank you for your assistance. You've done me a great kindness."

"You should get back to the celebration," he added after Mara

Glass Hearts

stood there silently, clearly not in any rush to retake her spot in the Great Hall.

"I'm just going to stop by the kitchens before I return."

He nodded in understanding, giving her an impish look. She was rather surprised the Dusk Lord could be so languid about her evasive escapade, though she appreciated it greatly. He gave her a curt bow, his lips turning in a polite grin. Then he uniformly marched off. Mara was glad it was Lord Cofsi who had been the one to rescue her—not that anyone else would have—pleased to know some saw her as worth the effort.

Instead of heading for the kitchens, Mara set off toward the alcove down by the back terrace that wouldn't be closely guarded. There wasn't much there, apart from the marbled statue of her mother. *Stars*, she missed her. Mara tried to picture her mother's face; her long wavy hair; her round, wide eyes; the soft curve of her nose. Her evocation was a wash of oil paints on a damp canvas starting to bleed together. It had been so long since she'd seen her mother in the flesh, her likeness fading.

Soon, I'll take my place on the throne of Branwen. And I'll need a wife.

Sir Orion's words rang in her head. Mara's hands came up and combed through her hair, tugging to try and dampen the sound of Sir Orion's gut-wrenching voice. She wanted her mother. She wanted to collapse into her lap and have her tenderly stroke her head, telling her everything would be just fine.

Someone to give me golden-haired babes. A son to precede me.

The thought of becoming Sir Orion's wife and giving him children made her body spiral with sickly gooseflesh.

She hadn't wanted to think about how she was to leave her kingdom, to go live wherever her future husband resided. It was something she had tried to suppress thinking about, but now Sir Orion's threat lingered in the traces of her mind, reminding her that she would be alone in a foreign land. She'd have to leave the one place that carried her mother's spirit, her presence still permeating the halls.

Sir Orion's home resided in the Icewoods, meaning her days there would be far more chill-inducing than in Wrens Reach. At least they saw sunlight and warm days here. In Branwen, the ice and snow were a year-round affair.

Lost in thought, one of Mara's heels got stuck in the cobblestones, and she tripped, catching herself on her knees, her palms splayed out under her. She heard a crack, her foot falling loose, making her topple forward. She turned behind her, the tip of her heel caught between two stones, completely severed from her shoe.

"What have I done to upset the gods?" she cursed.

Mara's head hung loosely as she stared down at her hands that just barely held her up. She couldn't move. Everything that had been bubbling up had finally decided to boil over. Hot tears welled in her eyes, waiting to cascade down her cheeks the moment she blinked. Her vision blurred, the liquid wetting the gray stones beneath her.

This really was it, wasn't it? This was going to be Mara's fate. She had lived in a fairy tale her whole life, and now she was being threatened off the safe confines of stained parchment, forced to perform her duties, marrying and having babies. That was what was to come of her. She'd become nothing more than breeding stock.

She sat back on her haunches, still not standing, wiping her face roughly with her fingers.

Boots echoing on the stone corridor caught her attention, instinctively making her look up. A large figure approached her. It seemed the figure noticed her at the same time she did, their footsteps halting briefly, surprised, before sauntering closer to her. Mara continued to stare as the sizable man came into view, his face stoic and unreadable.

She raised a brow through her blurry tears, the man appearing to have been coming back from her mother and father's old wing, exactly where Mara was headed.

"Are you all right?" The deep baritone of his voice startled her.

Mara's head tilted to follow him as he got within an arm's length, her eyes encasing the enormous man towering over her contorted one.

"Yes, I..." Her words abandoned her. The man arched his brow, waiting for her to find her tongue. "Where were you coming from?" She didn't recognize him or his leathers—not that she'd know the face of every Venmore guard, but he didn't dress the part either.

The man didn't try to hide the lie in his voice. "Never been inside Venmore Castle before. Lost my way."

"Lost your way?" she scoffed.

"Do you talk to everyone you meet this disrespectfully?"

Mara pulled back, taken by surprise at his blunt speech. "Only when they're a stranger in *my* home, blatantly lying to my face."

His lips quirked at the side like he was holding back a smile and Mara gritted her teeth. "Apologies," he said flatly. He stuck out a hand to assist her, and Mara winced, looking at the offering. His eyes narrowed, his presence creating a tense mist in the air; she wasn't sure any guards were close enough, that if he tried anything, they'd hear her screaming. Perhaps she would have rather been in Sir Orion's tedious company over that of a stranger.

His hand fell back to his side, grunting as if this was routine and he didn't care at all but was only being chivalrous because she a lady and he a man.

She was aware her discount was rude, and she opened her mouth to apologize, but she lost balance as she tried to stand, tipping sideways as her foot fell back without its heel to hold her in place. The man swiftly reached out and grabbed her arms in the same spot Sir Orion had gripped her earlier. Except this stranger's hold felt gentle on her skin, a sharp contrast to his daunting exterior.

"Care to tell me what you're doing down here instead of galavanting in the Great Hall?"

Mara shoved away from his grip, stumbling but keeping herself upright this time. She wanted to laugh. "I find that's none of your business, Sir." Her fingers swept down her dress, smoothing the fabric out.

"No? I'm supposed to allow a rogue princess to resolve to hiding on the ground so far away from the festivities? Away from her guards?"

Mara swallowed, the threat clear in his tone. She pursed her lips. Mara shifted, leaning down to take off her other shoe. "I was avoiding Sir Orion."

"That blonde prick?" he asked casually, his eyes looking out beyond her, scanning the halls as if Sir Orion might turn a corner and stumble upon them.

She never heard anyone speak of a knight as prominent as Sir Orion like that beyond her friends, especially someone of lower standing. "Are you a knight, too?" she asked him, struggling to hide her smirk, knowing he couldn't possibly be one.

"Something like that."

His eyes met hers. The shadows from the flickering sconces illuminated the features of his face. She could see freckles speckled beneath his beard, his eyes dark, almost black. His skin was deep brown, making her think he spent all his time in the sun. His hair a dark umber curly mess, long enough to be pulled back, small strands stuck around his forehead from sweat and others curling behind his ear.

Her eyes drifted down to his large chest, unnerved by his cast on her, his broad shoulders and taut muscles visible beneath his shirt. Mara fisted her two shoes in her hand, realizing she'd have to return to her room to get a new pair.

The man was burning holes through her. Now that she had told him why she was down these abandoned halls, she curiously wanted him to return the gesture. "Are you avoiding someone, too?"

He thought for a brief moment. "Court dramatics don't particularly interest me."

It hadn't occurred to her until right now that he could be a bachelor up for her hand. Suddenly, her cheeks warmed.

Mara scrunched her nose. "Court dramatics?"

"I don't know half of these lords and ladies, especially not unjustly-arrogant cunts waltzing around like their knighthood admonishes them from upholding any sort of decency."

Mara's eyes widened, speaking in disbelief. "Sir Orion?"

"Sure, if that's what you prefer to call him." He had a scowl on his face—it suited him. She thought it might be unsettling to see him smile.

"He is wretched, isn't he?"

"Most of them are."

"Well, that's not very encouraging," she sighed, her mouth tightening into a thin line. He looked at her with a bit of confusion tainting his permanent snarl. "My father insists I choose a suitor tonight. And that it's one of the noblemen."

"And that's the bastard he picked for you?" he asked in disapproval. His voice was sonorous, flustering her while he brazenly spoke.

Mara shook her head, picking at her fingernails. "If they're all really that awful, I just won't pick any of them."

The brooding man sneered, his shirt going taut over his toned chest as it rumbled in mirthless laughter. Mara's eyes shifted to pinpoints. "What?" he asked her incredulously. "You don't actually believe you have a choice in all this?"

An unspeakable rage began to settle in Mara's veins where anxiety once lay. What did he know about her betrothal? Fire circled within her tiny frame, begging to escape. He found it amusing enough for his lips to tick.

Mara all but stomped her foot in a tantrum. "Are you always this distasteful?" she said exasperated, lost for words to curse him out.

His face only grew more sinister. "Not used to being talked to like this, *liten rev?*" His accent on his final words slid up her spine in a spurt of embers.

No, actually, she wasn't used to being disrespected *like this.*

Mara decided she'd rather be sweating in the Great Hall surrounded by spoiled assholes than have to waste any more time talking to this knave. After scrunching her face, she spoke quietly, the fire lacing her words no less potent. "I have a revel to attend to."

She turned to leave, but the man grabbed her arm roughly, hauling her backward so she almost collided with his chest. She gasped, her throat tensing. "I heard you're a betting woman," the man all but whispered. "How about I make a bet? By the end of the night, the Sun Prince will steal your hand whether you like it or not." He paused. "Should be an easy win for you if you have as much say in the matter as you claim."

Her heart stuttered. "What's in it for you?"

His breath was warm where it fanned over her neck. "I get to see the look of horror on your entitled face."

She turned her head so she could see him out of her peripheral vision. "Fine. And if I win?"

He laughed and let her go, pushing past her to make his way toward the Great Hall.

She stood stunned in his wake, shaking her head like she might have imagined this entire encounter. Mara's eyes welled. She tried to shove back the scoundrel's piercing words: *You don't actually believe you have a choice in all this.* Of course she did. Her father told her she could choose, just so long as she got married.

Her affirmations didn't calm her. She prayed to the stars that the disdainful something-like-that of a knight wasn't right as she scurried back to her room to fetch new shoes.

Chapter Four
Mara

After what felt like hours of sitting in the ostentatious Great Hall picking at her plate, she arrived outside the lance yard. The large, encased arena had been scattered with melting candles, the glow from the setting sun the only natural source of light. The crowd grew as people began taking their seats amongst the grandstands. A billowing breeze danced over her exposed skin, the sheer fabric doing nothing to warm her.

Plenty of guests reveled in the drunken political atmosphere of the ball, but a much larger portion were seething with anticipation for the tournament. It was the official start of the Sundance. Weeks before the actual Summer Solstice, grand events took place in all eight kingdoms. Venmore's most notorious soiree being the jousting tourney.

Guests coming here were fully aware they'd have a better opportunity to dance and feast all night long when Mara was married. They didn't come just for her betrothal; they came for the violence. The bloodshed.

She wondered if the brooding man from earlier was here to joust. She would bet everything against him purely out of spite.

Lost in her macabre daydreams, she hadn't noticed the knight from the Sun Court approaching the stands. Mara looked at the grounds as she made it to her seat near the king and found the man peering up. He lept against the railing, taking purchase effortlessly, and spoke directly to the king. Her father chuckled at whatever he was saying. Her neck began to sweat despite the cool chill rising inside her, slowly putting pieces together. Could this knight actually be the Sun Prince?

She watched with wide eyes, open in surprise at his hardihood, speaking to her father like they were well-acquainted equals. She took notice of his sharp profile from this angle, his face free of any hair. He reminded her of the fae, but his ears were rounded just like hers. His lips were quipped up like a sly fox, making Mara's heart race.

For the second time that night, he turned to look at her. It was subtle enough that his attention was still centered on the king, but Mara knew he had caught her staring. She tried to suppress the crimson blush that was surely blooming across her face in embarrassment, hoping the candlelight would disguise her features enough, preventing him from making out her bashfulness, her arms crossing against her chest in tune with the sweeping wind.

He hopped down, his knees bending as he caught himself a solid five feet below, turning on his heels and strutting down the arena.

Mara bit her lip and caught sight of a beige skirt by her feet. Jessamine carried a tray of sugarberry scones to set before the lords and ladies waiting to be entertained. She gave Mara a nod, clearly having spotted the knight and Mara's rapt attention on him. Jessamine's lip quirked in a subtle smirk making Mara playfully roll her eyes.

As Jessamine set the tray down before the king, he stood up, silencing the crowd. Jessamine continued to set the tables with scones as another maiden filled their cups with red-mulled wine.

"As you all know, tonight marks the beginning of summer and the Sundance celebrations, as well as the first and twentieth birthday of the Glass Princess.

"During our grand competition of chivalrous knights jousting for not only the esteemed credit they will grant to themselves but the people of the kingdom. Usually rewarded in the golden color of summer. Instead, the winner this year will be granted my daughter's hand in marriage. A jewel far more valuable than any sum of coins."

Mara felt the whites of her eyes nearly cover her entire face. Her hands went cold, a hard breeze cooling the heat of her cheeks. Her heartbeat calmed for a moment, then vibrated rapidly when she let her father's words sink in.

She heard gasps in the audience, a quick flow of whispers before her father evinced, but the rest of her father's introduction fell silent on her ears, nothing but rambling that echoed through her clouded brain. *He promised.*

Mara knew she had too many faces studying her to allow herself to cry. She knew if she tried to say something to her father, the tears would come in a cascading avalanche.

As if this moment wasn't terrible enough, her mind wandered back to *him*. To the self-assured knave she met in the halls. She wanted nothing more than to punch him repeatedly in the chest for being right—perhaps taking her anger on her father out on this stranger. As much as she enjoyed jousting and the fighting ring, she never reveled in the bloodshed. But now, she prayed that the knave was part of the tournament, willing to watch him bleed out on his knees before his superiors—*before her.*

She had been foolish. A stupid, silly girl who thought she might foresee a future that broke way of the tight and rigid boundaries princesses usually followed. To choose her own suitor. While not unheard of for a princess to get to select a husband from a pool of approved options, she shouldn't have been surprised that the men in her life could control her fate with something as blithe as the victor of a jousting tournament.

The loud clapping from the audience woke her, the tournament beginning in a rumble of clamor. She looked over at her father who felt her regard. "Not a word," he asserted. Mara's chest tensed in shock; her father wasn't the most agreeable man, but he was more detached than usual. He had spoken to her like he would chide a servant.

She couldn't help but think how unlike her father this was. Always so particular and calculated—the reason Wrens Reach was allied with all the kingdoms—she couldn't understand why he'd do something so insouciant as to marry his daughter off with an uncharacteristically blasé attitude.

A loud, rhythmic pulse echoed in her ear. She shifted her fingers, finding one of her gold bands, and twisted it around and around. She swallowed her tears, turning her head and watching the tournament like a statue, unwavering apart from her trembling lip.

She spotted a knight approaching his horse at the right end of the track, taking his jousting stick from his squire. His short stature surprised her, his face obscured behind his silver helm. Down at the other end, Sir Orion mounted his mare. He was dressed similarly to the other knight sans the head covering. Mara wondered if it was because he didn't want to hide his golden hair and chiseled chin. He knew all the ladies of the court would be watching and fawning over him.

As the men prepared to begin, it hit Mara that Sir Orion stood a chance at winning. Her stomach flipped. There's no way she would let him marry her. She would kick and scream if she had to. However, Mara knew that no amount of resistance within her could recant a proclamation of the king.

The men sat on their steeds at either end of the grounds, shifting between their feet in pent-up energy as they waited anxiously to parade their prowess. Her father stood beside her and slowly raised his hands, the crowd growing eerily silent. Finally, he clapped, only once, and the crowd awoke again. The knights charged at one another, their horses galloping at a speed that made Mara wonder how they were even able to concentrate on what they were doing.

Sir Orion was far taller than his opponent, the difference noticeable even atop their horses. As they neared one another, the building apprehension inside her flourished. She didn't want to look, and yet she never once shifted her eyes away. Sir Orion's joust slammed into his opponent's armored chest and flung him off the back of his horse. Mara winced as the knight landed with a generous thud, bouncing off the ground before laying still. She stood with a gasp. The crowd cheered as Sir Orion rode around in a victorious loop, waving at the audience. The knight on the ground slowly began to move, standing up and lacing his arm over the shoulder of his squire. In relief, Mara shifted her gaze to Sir Orion who was looking at her with a wicked grin.

Mara's hands grew moist, nervously wiping her palms on her dress. Now, she only prayed someone could beat Sir Orion to the cessation. But that meant a random knight was going to own her hand by the end of this.

Mara stifled her cries, her breathing making her lightheaded.

Glass Hearts

An hour ticked by and Mara grew tired, but her attention refused to slip from the knights as they knocked each other off their horses, claiming victory. Her head rested on her hands as she leaned forward, trying to keep her eyes from watering.

That's when she saw the knight who seemed to transcend normal sense, picking her out of the crowd with ease. Mara's face automatically flushed again despite her will to dampen the heat. His armor gleamed a dark obsidian, a stark contrast to Sir Orion's ivory attire, with a large sun imprinted into the front of his chest plate. Swirls and spikes lined his legs and arms, making him appear predatory. He was smaller than Sir Orion, at least in stature, but it only made him more serpentine, lithe, and sleek.

"Prince Acastus. Sun Prince to the Solar Sect and Prince of Solstrale," the herald rattled. "Sir Orion, honored knight of Branwen of the Icewoods."

Mara's hands gripped her seat, so focused on the prince that she didn't even notice the brooding man beside his squire. His eyes had landed on her, her slippers now a silvery color replacing the broken violet heels he had seen her with earlier. His face flashed with disgust. The man loomed so far in the distance though; her cynicism could have been playing tricks on her. Maybe she wanted him to look at her with smug authority, to allow her anger to brew in his name instead of her father's—the man she desperately desired to trust.

Acastus stretched his arms as Mara looked at her new adversary. Mara returned the knave's gaze, her eyes shooting daggers, pissed that he was standing there with the knowledge that he had been right. And there was no hiding it, the king announced it loud enough for all to hear. She expected him to smirk, to taunt her in some way, but he solemnly looked away and said something to Prince Acastus as he mounted his horse.

Acastus sat upon an ebony steed that matched his armor, a caparison draped over its back with a sun in gold. His garniture was a gray, steely color, complimenting his dark hair. She couldn't see the ladies off to her right, but she heard them giggle as they watched Acastus prepare for his turn.

He took position on his side of the tilt, placing his lance in the arret that protruded from his breastplate.

Clad in shining armor that had never seen a day of wear, Sir Orion spurred his steed, determination gleaming in his eyes as he set forth toward his opponent, lance at the ready. The thunder of hooves echoed through the arena as he charged, ready to prove his valor to the king.

With imperturbable composure, Acastus rode toward Sir Orion, both of their lances missing each other by a thin hair. The crowd simultaneously held their breath. She prayed Sir Orion wouldn't win.

But did she want Prince Acastus to win instead?

That would mean a lifelong commitment to the Sun Prince

Her last bit of hope in the gods rose as she silently prayed for a better outcome than any of this. But Mara's desolate daydreams were cut off as the roaring stampede of the two knights' horses took off, heading toward one another again.

It all happened so fast that Mara could barely make out the course of events slotting into place in front of her and the other few hundred people watching. Acastus leaned forward, his smile menacing as he notched his lance in the throat of Sir Orion, knocking him off his horse. When Mara looked back up at the victor, she gasped at the blood splattering across his chest and face. He looked feral with violent victory. Her eyes flickered back down to Sir Orion who lay convulsing on the dirt ground, blood gushing out from around his neck, his hands ineffective in their attempts to stop the bleeding.

The crowd seemed to mirror Mara's reaction, but in mere moments they were clapping and cheering. She—obviously—never liked Sir Orion, but watching him shake and choke on the ground, no one around to kneel beside him as the light faded from behind his eyes, she felt pity. She wouldn't wish him dead, at least not in such a gruesome way. Her eyes were locked on Sir Orion, his body gently coming to a halt, but the blood never seemed to cease. She wanted to turn away, to be sick, but she stared at him like a sentry, entranced as a man leaned down and scooped his body up. Through tears that she hadn't realized began to fall, she identified the man as the knave.

So, was this his job—scut work? Is that what he was here for? To attend to the motionless corpses that no respectable person would want to clean up?

Her vision blurred as she watched the large man sling Sir Orion over his shoulder, burgundy blood showering him, and marched away behind the stands. With the crude insults he had thrown at Sir Orion when Mara stood alone with him, she could only imagine the sadistic joy he got from holding his lifeless body.

Once he was out of sight, she turned to her father who was clapping and admiring the victorious prince as he rode around the track on his horse, waving. She was startled by the droplets of blood on his face and armor like he was decorated in red stars as he collected a laurel crown from a lady stretched over the balcony. When he put it on his head, a rush of fear made her heart beat erratically. He looked terrifying as his eyes slowly met hers.

It was more uncommon for such esteemed knights to die at one of these events, most of their knighthood seemed to be purely for show. Usually, the blood would tumble from the veins of lower-ranking attendants, even squires who were forced to defend their knight's honor. There, in the hands of inferiors, the blood would bleed. Sir Orion's death was likely to spark wildness throughout the kingdoms, especially at the hands of someone like Prince Acastus.

Chapter Five

Evrardin

Evrardin stood silently on a sickle-leaf rug of white and gold as Prince Acastus smiled in the ornate mirror before him. A drape in the color of Wrens Reach lay crumpled in the corner, ripped from the mirror's frame by the prince, now a violet pool on the floor. Acastus' lanky fingers tentatively reached out and stroked the melted silver surface of the mirror, sighing.

"Anything?" the prince questioned Evrardin, making eye contact through the mirror.

Evrardin's fingers anxiously fiddled with the sword strapped to his hip. "Queen Meredith's effigy confirmed it."

"What did it say?"

"Where light meets shadow, her reign echoes in our reflections."

Acastus hummed, clearly agreeing her vague inscription hinted that she died glassfairing, something the prince already suspected. He turned to face Evrardin who still had blood crusted around his neck and hairline from Sir Orion. "Thunder and Runes, Ev. See to your washing; you're a right mess."

"Cas, I urge you to think about this. The princess is not the most agreeable—"

Cas held his hands up to stop Evrardin. Ev immediately locked his lips, waiting for Cas to speak. "She'll have to do. I need a glassfairer. I don't care how agreeable she is... You'll make sure she stays in line."

"But her mother died glassfairing—" Ev added.

"Yes. Her mother's death might indicate the Glass Court's depleted divine connection, but if the girl is bound to me, I expect her prowess to be lifted," Acastus reasoned. "Solstrale is the last kingdom to possess such powers. Now, go wash and be cleansed of your filth—you're leaking all over my carpets," he spat through gritted teeth.

Evrardin's fist clenched around the hilt of his sword. He had the puerile desire to remind Acastus that these weren't technically *his* carpets, but he kept his mouth sealed like the envelope he carried in his pocket. He took in a breath, knowing there was nothing he could do to prevent what was bound to happen.

He turned to leave and Acastus began pacing in his room, mumbling to himself about there not being enough time. Evrardin looked at his palm which was now not only blanketed in dried blood but had encrusted imprints lining it from the chasings on the hilt of his sword.

Evrardin wasn't convinced the Glass Court had much prowess left. Almost all the kingdoms had severed connections, losing all divine magick. However, the gods in Solstrale and Wrens Reach had been the last to leave, lingering amounts of power still tingling their fingertips. But with the Glass Queen dying as she crossed through a mirror, Ev worried the Glass Princess would not be able to hone the power Acastus needed.

And Evrardin would have been glad to watch Acastus reap his consequences if it wasn't Ev who would have to clean it up.

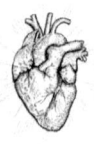

Evrardin scrubbed the blood from his face and changed his clothes, standing in his small guest quarters with the letter unfolded in his hand. His eyes darted back and forth across the page, his demeanor unwavering as he read.

> *The dusk settles faster than it ever should. I'll be in Kairth for the wedding... As for the mirrors, I'm afraid I know no more than you do. I'll leave you with that, keeping you in the dark as you asked.*
> *— C*

He tossed it in the fire before him.

Ev strolled down the hall. It was late now, likely edging toward midnight. He tried to swallow the events of today, sweeping through the scenes in his mind as he passed two open double doors. Inside laid rows of shelves stacked high with books. Tables with tomes left open, parchment rolled up and stacked. But what caught Ev's eye was the small ember tittering in the air like a flamefly. Attached to the small flame was a woman. She held a candle in her hand as she scanned one of the shelves, two large books already clutched in her other arm.

The princess. The one Evrardin stumbled upon in the cobblestoned hall of Venmore, sprawled out on her hands and knees, cursing to herself like a mad woman.

Intrigued, he leaned against the doorframe and watched her.

Maralena, unaware of his looming presence, tilted her head back. She glared at the tomes like she was swearing in her mind. She seemed to want one on the higher shelves where the neglected grimoires were shoved. She looked around her feet and settled on laying the books in her hand on the floor before scurrying over to the bookshelf traverse, pushing it to where she needed it.

She climbed the rungs, her hand gripping the candle tightly as she inched upward. Once she made it to the top, she craned her neck to get view of the tomes and the ladder wobbled beneath her. A gasp left her lips as she abruptly leaned forward and caught herself on the shelves with a thud.

Evrardin hadn't realized his feet began moving closer to her as if on instinct.

Mara released her hands once she steadied herself and let her finger drag along the spine of the tomes until she landed on the one she had been searching for. She pulled it into her arm, careful not to disturb the other books packed tightly on either side. She held them securely under her arm, her other hand squeezed around the candle, and she glanced down.

Mara leaned forward to keep her balance as she slowly stuck a slippered foot out to land on the rung beneath her. The tip of her toes slid against it, her eyes widening as she began to fall. Mara tried to grab out for the ladder, but with occupied hands, she plummeted toward the hardwood floor. "Shit—*argh*," she tried to curse midair but instead spouted nonsense, everything happening so fast.

He moved without thinking, reaching out for her, his arms outspread, pulling her against his chest.

Mara opened her eyes and turned her head to meet his gaze. Her back pressed against his chest, his arms wrapped around her upper arms and across her torso. The candle had fallen to the floor and extinguished with a wave of smoke, but the tome was still clutched in her grip. He glared at her, neither of them speaking.

Mara shook her head finally and wiggled. "Put me down!"

"That's no way to thank someone who just saved you," he grumbled, releasing her.

Mara stumbled away from him, picking up her candle and straightening her nightgown. He appraised her, her chemise a soft cream color that did little to shield the shadow of her body beneath. Mara's cheeks and chest pinked, embarrassed.

"I didn't ask for your help," she grunted.

"So, next time I should just let you break your neck, then?"

"There won't be a next time," Mara refuted, picking up the two other books she left on the floor.

"Mmm," he hummed. "Your betrothal says different." No, Evrardin would be seeing a lot of her now that she was to marry Acastus.

Mara spun around so fast to face him, he thought she might snap her neck. "You insufferable prick!" she spat.

Evrardin's eyes widened in brief shock at her outburst—her forwardness. Then he slowly grinned. "Ah, yes. I was right, it is rewarding to see your face scrunched with vexation."

She snarled. "What did you do? I know you did something to"—she waved her hands around, lost for words—"force my father into changing his mind! You made it so the Sun Prince would win my hand."

Evrardin scoffed. "You think I hold such power?"

She appraised him, her face twisted with disgust.

"No, you know I hold no such power. You think I'm beneath you." Not a question, but a fact. "You hate that I'm right. That I foretold your future better than you could."

Tears began to well in her eyes and she spun around. "You're awful."

"I never claimed to be otherwise."

"You got what you wanted. Now, leave me be."

He shook his head even though she wasn't facing him.

She finally turned around when he remained silent and she gave him a sour look. She shoved past him to leave. When she made it to the doors, she looked over her shoulder and jumped; he was right behind her. "W-What are you doing?"

"Escorting you back to your room."

Mara furrowed her brows, gesturing around her. "As you can see, no guards escorted me here, so I certainly don't need one to get back."

"The halls are dark at night. And with so many guests here, it's not safe for a princess to be wandering all alone. Especially dressed like that," he said, gesturing his head at her.

Mara blushed again, pulling the books to her chest to block his view. "Is that a threat?"

"Only if you want it to be." Mara went to open her mouth, the indignation brewing over her features, but he cut her off. "You can argue till you're red in the face. I'm walking you to your room whether you like it or not, *liten rev*."

Mara's face went from pink in embarrassment to crimson in fury. She pursed her lips then turned on her heels and marched away, making him smirk as he started to trail behind her.

After a few moments of stomping down the halls, he broke the silence. "Evrardin."

Mara looked over her shoulder. "Hm?" She glazed over his form like she was only now noticing how he finally wasn't covered in dirt or sweat. His hair was slicked back from being washed, a few curled pieces hanging in front of his face. His eyes were heavy from all the monstrosities he had borne witness, and the way he carried himself screamed self-assured. He was certainly older than her, but probably only by ten years or so.

"My name. I'm sure you've been calling me a slew of crude monikers in your head. But that's my real one."

Mara rolled her eyes then looked back in front of her. "Maralena," she mumbled.

Of course, Evrardin already knew that. Mara slowed, letting Evrardin match her stride. He hated that he wondered what she was thinking—probably about how Knave suited him far better. She looked over at him, his eyes already on her, making her awkwardly refocus her attention on her feet. "Do you really have nothing better to do than harass me?"

"I told you why."

She raised a brow in exhausted irritation. "Do you truly expect me to believe you're concerned about my well-being inside the familiar walls of my home? After you swore to see my demise, even going so far as to bet on it?"

Evrardin paused for a moment, a loud screech cutting off his thoughts.

"What in the seven hells was that?" Mara asked, her eyes wide, halting as she looked around. It was hard to tell where it came from.

The sound of something large crashing into the walls echoed down the hall. Stomping and thumping in a rampage.

Ev nudged her to keep walking. "Told you. Lots of guests around tonight. It's not safe."

Mara begrudgingly kept moving, but not before calling him a crude name under her breath.

"Quite the colorful tongue for a princess," he mumbled.

Mara ignored his remark. "What could have made that sound?" she queried.

Evrardin stayed silent beside her.

"So, enlighten me. Are you the prince's manservant?" she goaded after some beats of silence.

Ev shot daggers at her and spoke through gritted teeth. "Something like that."

"*Something like that*," she mocked, "and also 'something like that' of a knight. Do you ever speak plainly? Or do you thrive on irritating discourse?"

When he didn't answer and they continued in silence, Mara's demeanor shifted, her fingers digging into the tome's leather-bound skin. "What's he like?" she asked quietly.

Ev noted the change in her tone, from aggressive and fiery, to solemn and soft. He decided he liked it better when she was cruel. "Regal."

"Regal?" Mara scoffed.

Evrardin glanced at her. "What? Do you want me to list every minuscule vice and malevolent compulsion the prince possesses? Would that truly make you feel better?"

Mara frowned.

"Doesn't matter what he's like. Either way, you're stuck with him."

"What tragedy has made you so sadistic?" she asked, her tone sharpening again.

"I'm not sadistic. I just don't have the patience to comfort a spoiled princess over the fact that she's marrying a prestigious prince who—*let me remind you*—is not a decrepit old man like half the pricks competing tonight; desperate to procure the accordance of a young princess like yourself into their beds." He paused his chide, but only briefly. "Though, come to think of it, they'd likely prefer it if you went unwillingly." Mara's eyebrows rose and Evrardin got sick satisfaction from stumping her. "Should I tell you what my duty to the prince is?"

Mara's lips tightened into a straight line. They rounded the corner to Mara's room, a guard stationed outside. "Princess Mara?!" the guard said, confused. "How—When did you leave your chambers?"

She walked up to the large wooden door, pausing to face Evrardin. "Thank you for escorting me. Good night, Evrardin." Her words unctuous.

Mara slammed the door behind her like a child. His lips quirked at her pompous disposition. Evrardin nodded at the still-stunned guard and ambled back the way he came.

Chapter Six
Mara

In the morning, Mara made her way to the gardens, her father there to greet her. Annoying tradition called for the prince to properly propose engagement to the princess before her father would let them depart for the prince's region in Solstrale. That entailed a small walk with each other, chaperones hovering in the distance. The prince would have to ask her father for his blessing, which her father would grant, blessing the gift Acastus would then bestow onto the princess. It was all a fussy convention Mara didn't care much for.

She showed up in an ivory-colored dress, its satin material clinging to her. It had long sleeves that were embroidered with green vines. The same vines began at the end of the skirt and faded as they crawled to her waist. Her hair was pulled into a long braid, emerald jewels woven amongst it.

This was the first time since the tournament Mara had seen her father. She hurried to him, his eyes catching her rabbit-like form. "Princess," he greeted, though, more as a question.

"Good morning, Father."

Thousands of thoughts she craved to shout corroded behind her hazel eyes. He sighed. "Out with it, then."

She tried to suppress her burning anger that had all night to brew as she spoke. "You told me I got to *choose*."

"And I am the king, am I not? And the king has changed his mind." Mara's face sank. King Björn reached his ruddy hand out and stroked his daughter's cheek. "This is all for you, my dear. Prince Acastus is a respectable man. Young. Handsome. You'll be happy with him." Her father's voice was soft as he spoke to her. She leaned her face into his hand further, always craving her father's affection which she so rarely was rewarded since her mother's passing.

"I just don't understand. Why would you tell me I got to choose my betrothed, just to change your mind and let something as silly as a tourney decide my fate?"

The king wiped away a stray tear that trickled down Mara's cheek. "I'm sorry," he whispered. "Solstrale is an invaluable ally. You must trust me." Something odd laced her father's words, almost like he spoke without his natural lilt.

"Did you know?"

"Know what?" her father asked.

"That Prince Acastus would win?"

"You know I wouldn't have let you get swept away by just any noble." He gave her a faded smile. "You would have picked him at the end of the day."

She looked up at him, his down-turned eyes appraising her countenance. His face was aged from time spent as king, but his features still sharp and regal like he always had been. His green eyes shifted between hers, secrets swirled in their dark starbursts. The crown on his head gleamed from the morning light that entered through the floor-length windows looking out onto the intricate gardens. He gestured his head to the prince waiting behind her.

This was nothing but a political arrangement, she told herself. Her marriage was going to be no different than the countless ones before her.

"Go," her father crooned.

Mara took another glance at her father, pleading with her eyes not to make her do this, but he had already looked away, staring at the approaching prince and the courtiers behind her. She let out a breath and turned to Acastus.

"My Princess," he bowed, taking her hand in his and placing a kiss upon the back of it. He was far more handsome up close. Mara's breath lodged in her throat. His high-collar black shirt was lined in gold, drawing her attention to his face. His hair was pushed back, exposing his clean-shaven and elegant facial features. His dark eyes had a silver tinge that she found breathtaking as they narrowed in on her, making her sweat under his scrutiny. He stood back up, taller than her, but not as much as her father or Evrardin.

Regal. Evrardin was right, that was the best word to describe him.

"Shall we?" he asked with a grin that lit up his face. He reminded her of an oil painting with the way his skin had a faint sheen to it that made him look simultaneously otherworldly and trapped behind a guise. Like a wilting flower that still had its vibrant petals. He didn't seem to have a flaw anywhere on him. She nodded, accepting his arm, and followed him as he guided her out to the gardens.

The air was warm this morning, the breeze sweeping past her feet and through her hair. She smiled. No matter how bad things got, she'd always have this. It didn't matter where Acastus swept her away to, there would always be the beauty and idyllic comfort of nature. She hadn't realized she closed her eyes, absorbing the sun, until Acastus spoke, shaking her from her reverie.

"We have a magnificent garden back in Kairth." His voice was smooth like melted silk. She looked down at where her arm intertwined with his, finding it hard to keep his regard. She noticed he donned gloves that crept under the sleeves of his shirt, not an inch of his skin showing apart from his face. "The salt of the oceans makes for interesting arability. Curious how something as haunting as the abysmal sea can create such serene beauty." He seemed lost in thought as he spoke.

"Will I be able to visit them?" Mara asked.

"Of course," he tittered, his intonation making Mara's chest spark. "You'll be free to do whatever you please. I have no plans to treat you as a prisoner." His eyes danced between her own. "I think you'll like being so close to the ocean. It's a welcome comfort with such blazing heat. Have you ever been to the sea, Princess?"

Mara shook her head and Acastus smiled as he guided her further.

The sound of their steps on the gravel was comforting as they waltzed deeper into the gardens. She could see her father and a few of his advisors when she glanced over her shoulder. Just behind them, she spotted Evrardin, his eyes already on her. She regretted not letting him tell her what his relation to the prince was, curious as to why he was here amongst Acastus' other courtiers. She swallowed her nerves then turned her attention back to the prince.

"I'm aware this is all so sudden"—he looked down at her—"and you're no doubt dreading having to leave your home to live with a stranger," he added empathetically. "My father insisted I finally marry. Threatened he would surpass my birthright onto my brother if I didn't claim a wife." Mara shuddered at his word choice, *claim*. "While you're beautiful and probably as sweet as you look, I had no say in the matter. I thought you might find comfort in the fact that I plan on letting you decide the pace of our relationship. I think we'll enjoy each other's company, but I wanted you to know that I'm just as apprehensive about this as you likely are."

She thought it an odd way to pick a wife, through a form of competition, for someone as prestigious as the Sun Prince.

He spoke like he was answering her thoughts. "I had no interest going through a line of viable ladies, picking one out based on ranking and resources their father could provide. When your father announced that the winner of the tourney would have your hand, I let fate decide my future. Perhaps this was meant to happen."

In a lot of ways, his forthright verbiage did comfort Mara. And in other ways, it scared her. He spoke about fate so casually, but she knew it meant more to him than it did to her. The Sun Court was far more pious than some of the other courts, including the Glass Court. While the fact that her marriage with Acastus was sure to be more spiritual than she was used to—the Glass Court didn't consider their high priest as part of the court like every other kingdom did—she didn't fear it. She wondered if she'd be forced to join the Solar Sect. Regardless, she smiled at Acastus.

"That does bring me some comfort. Thank you. I appreciate your sincerity, My Prince."

He nodded, his free hand coming over to cover her own that gripped his bicep. They waltzed through the gardens, stopping to admire this season's blooms, halting before a bush of lyre flowers, his finger tracing their soft petals reminiscent of a bleeding heart. "We don't have these in the north." He looked over at her. "Ironic, isn't it? The thing we get our name from is now a foreigner to our land."

Mara knew he was referring to the city the Sun Court resided in, Kairth, which was known as the Coast of Bleeding Hearts. Hundreds of years ago, a time in which only the fae remember now, a tragic battle had broken out along Kairth's shores. The blood soaked in the sand and waters, turning the tides pink for weeks on end. Where the blood had rooted deep into the sand, bleeding heart flowers began to rise all around the forgotten bodies, blooming in elegies. Such an atrocious and violent war that ended in far more deaths than they ever anticipated had resulted in beauty with blush-colored waters and blooming carmine flowers.

"They're my favorite," Mara added, hoping saying so wasn't insulting. He picked one attached to a sagging stem and slid it behind her ear. Mara blushed as his knuckles ghosted her cheek.

"Then I'll make sure they're imported. Your room will always be stocked with them."

Mara gave a melancholy smile at the gesture.

Once they circled the gardens and made it back to the court of onlookers, Prince Acastus approached her father, asking for her hand. He pulled out a necklace from his pocket, holding it for the king to evaluate. It was obscured by his fingers and Mara couldn't get a glimpse at it.

She watched her father agree and place his hand on the necklace as the priest beside him hovered his hand above the other two men. Mara shifted uncomfortably on her feet and tried not to look over to Evrardin who she could feel staring at her. Her father muttered a blessing, the air around her thickening. This was truly happening.

Acastus turned to Mara and gestured for her to spin so he could lock the necklace around her neck, sealing the engagement. She bit her lip, irritated that none of this revolved around her consent, it was all about the men and their decisions. Still, she turned and moved her braid for him. She felt her hackles stand as his fingers dusted across her skin while he fiddled with the lock.

Once it was on, she pulled the charm down in her hand to look at it. It was an anatomical heart, three small rubies dangling off of it, mimicking blood. It was strange and not at all what she expected, but it was gorgeous. She turned to look at the prince then smiled at him. But her contentment was short-lived, Evrardin appearing at Acastus' side, glaring at her, something dark in his eyes as he shifted his gaze to the prince who leaned over and whispered in his ear.

Mara stood awkwardly as Acastus pulled at his gloves, securing them tighter, even with the warming weather. Acastus reached out and took Mara's hand, leaning over and placing a kiss on the back. He grinned as he stood to his full height, but there was something painful in his expression.

"My heart swims valiantly knowing you are my bride-to-be." Mara flinched at his words, giving him a docile look. Acastus' hand still held her own, the leather of his glove cool against her. "I have a few obligations to settle, Princess." He finally dropped his hold and turned to Evrardin. "Evrardin will be taking my stead at the celebration dinner. I'm sorry I can't be there, but my hands are tied. My inept council requires more pressing matters for me to attend to," he said with an air of sarcasm.

"No need to apologize, My Prince—"

"Cas," he corrected.

"Cas. I'm sure Evrardin will be a worthy guest." She gave Evrardin a quick impish grin. Evrardin refrained from shaking his head at her childish behavior.

The prince left along with all of his courtiers, her father already gone, likely dragged away to the throne room for tedious political matters.

Mara glanced at Evrardin. "You do not need to babysit me."

"I've been instructed to stay by your side."

Mara quirked a brow. "I have my own guards for that." She gestured to the sentinels stationed around the building, some even strolling through the gardens. "I relieve you of your duties," she said wryly.

Evrardin didn't respond. For some reason, that irritated Mara far more than any snub he could have made.

Mara huffed and headed toward her rooms, Evrardin immediately following behind her like a lost pup. She should be more annoyed with Acastus for commanding Evrardin to stalk her, but all her anger laid misaligned with her new guard dog.

Back in her rooms, Evrardin took perch by the doorway, leaning back against the wall. He watched as she stood upon a fitting pedestal, the royal dressmaker fiddling with the hem of a mockup. If Evrardin was to trail around her, she was glad he would at least succumb to boredom as bespoke garments that met Mara's specifications were discussed and she was sized for.

Mara would mostly be taking dresses she already possessed with her, but the king said she should have a few gowns expedited for special occasions. Anything Aurora, the royal dressmaker, didn't finish with would be sent by courier to her in Kairth.

She had one day to prepare herself. One day. She held back the tears welling in her eyes, turning to face the windows as Aurora measured her waist for the third time, hoping Evrardin wouldn't see the distress inside her. He'd only think her pathetic for getting upset over this—he made that much clear.

Dinner was quaint, nothing of note. Evrardin had taken a seat to her right where Acastus would have sat if he had attended.

It certainly was odd having a celebratory dinner for their engagement and half of the party was not in attendance.

A few of Acastus' courtiers sat around the table, amongst the closest members of the Glass Court, and the king. Mara scowled at Evrardin when he sat down, and he shook his head in annoyance.

The dinner involved mostly her father discussing details with Acastus' representatives, boring matters Mara tuned out.

"Isn't that right, Maralena?" her father boomed.

Mara glanced up, straightening her spine and nodding politely, a smile plastered on her face, to a conversation she had not been following. Her father turned back to the men at the table and carried on the discussion, the attention to her superficial.

Mara slouched back and looked at Evrardin as she twirled her spoon in her soup. "Why couldn't the prince attend?"

The rest of the table paid no attention to the two of them. Evrardin glanced at her but didn't do her the decency of turning his head when he spoke. "Nothing important."

Mara scoffed, dropping her spoon noisily into her dish. "It feels like it should be rather important, given that he's missing his own dinner."

Evrardin appeared bemused. "Feisty little thing, aren't you?"

Mara shied away at his words, a blush creeping on her cheeks. "Only with you," she muttered, not intending for her words to sound so suggestive.

Evrardin shook his head slightly. Mara let out an exasperated breath and leaned on the table, wanting to go back to her room.

"You should probably learn to like me," Evrardin added, tilting his body closer to her so only she could hear him.

"And why would I do something so strenuous?"

"Seeing as I'm the captain of Acastus's guard, he's entrusted me with the duty of protecting his *wife* when we get back to Kairth."

Mara blinked a few times, digesting his words. She looked over at him with surprise, expecting him to have a sly expression, but he looked just as he always did: bored and irritated.

Mara figured Evrardin was one of the prince's advisors, but she hadn't considered the fact that he might be Acastus' top choice. He wasn't even a knight. She swallowed hard like a dagger being forced down her throat. The idea of Evrardin guarding her was livable, but the way he referred to her as Acastus' wife made her—without being so melodramatic—dizzy.

"And I don't suppose the prince is one for negotiations?" she asked, hiding the indignation from her voice.

It was Evrardin's turn to scoff. "No, I don't suppose he is. At least not when it comes to you."

"What does that mean?"

"I fear he's already grown protective." He said it like it was a bad thing.

Mara tried to accept Evrardin's words, praying he was just being puckish and the prince wasn't actually placing her at such a high value.

"Why did the prince want to have my hand so desperately that he would compete for it? I know he said something about his father wanting him to marry, but he's the Sun Prince—he has the pick of the land when it comes to a future consort."

"He needed a noble-born lady. What better than a pretty princess."

Mara swallowed the urge to tease him about inadvertently calling her pretty, but her heart was too jittery at his other words to even consider being playful. "Yes, but why *me*? There are far more worthy princesses amongst the kingdoms. I've seen the Fae Princess—the eldest one—she would unite Solstrale and the Faelands. I would think that'd be of far more use to him than

Wrens Reach. And she's ethereal. I'm just...a human girl. The prince is so handsome, I don't compare in the slightest degree." Mara heated realizing she was rambling. She tended to do that when she was nervous.

"Quite the political assessment." Evrardin's face turned sour as if he wanted to say something he shouldn't. But then his countenance went back to being brutish. "It's not me you have to convince not to marry you." His words were coarse, like this conversation was teetering on painful for him.

"Thank you for your wise counsel. I feel much better," she said sarcastically.

"I wasn't trying to make you feel better."

"Clearly." Mara crossed her arms, quiet for the rest of dinner, only speaking when spoken to.

Chapter Seven
Mara

"Write to me, won't you?" Jessamine mumbled into Mara's neck. Their arms clung around one another, tears welling in Mara's eyes as she breathed in the soft walnut shampoo that lingered in her friend's hair.

"Only if you promise to pester Azor in my absence," Mara responded. "At least until you leave for Throneskeep."

Leaving Jessamine behind weighed heavily on Mara's chest, but she knew she couldn't ask her friend to come with her to Solstrale. It wouldn't be fair to Jess, who had been homesick for as long as she had known her. Jess belonged in Throneskeep, which she would set out for soon after Mara left, no longer obliged to attend to the princess. Her family's debt to the crown would officially be paid.

The women pulled back from one another, their hands still clutching each other's shoulders. "I'm gonna miss you wildly," Jess said. "Maybe I'll find a husband of my own in Throneskeep," she tried to add on a lighter note.

Mara gave her a lopsided smile. As much as that filled her with a spark of happiness—the idea of her friend finding love—it pained her knowing she wouldn't be around to watch such things unfold. Jessamine wouldn't come gushing to Mara about the man courting her; not when Mara was so many kingdoms away.

"It's an unparalleled journey we're headed on," Jess said, trying to disguise the fact that she was wiping her tears rather than brushing an eyelash from her cheek. "New and scary, but journeys usually are. This is good for us"—she grabbed Mara's arms, pleading—"the world is finally opening up and allowing us in. You'll be able to live out your silly fairy tales just as you always dreamed. And just think, in a few days' time, you'll finally touch the salted sea for yourself." Jessamine had hearts in her eyes as she got lost in a reverie, thinking of the wide expanse of the sea that the two of them had only ever read about.

That prospect gave Mara the jolt of energy she currently lacked. She had been reeling about how soon she was going to see the open ocean and she tried to use that to drown out her other wallowing emotions. Her mother always said the sea was her first love, and Mara longed to feel the treacherous, thrilling waters for herself. Being away from her mother's statue was leaving a piece of her behind in Venmore, but maybe the waves along the coast of Kairth would bring her the same warm blanketed hug she felt when she talked to her mother's marbled effigy.

"When did you get so poetic?"

"I've been trapped with Master Wistmore for too long. Him and his scribes are starting to corrupt me," Jess teased.

With a sense of newfound, terrifying excursions, the air around her suddenly smelt so enticing. The potent scent of horse shit, baking bread, and wet stone never appealed to Mara, but at this moment, it was the most comforting smell in the world. She didn't want to move; she wished time could crumble around her, morphing into the stillness of a painting, trapping her in this very moment with her friend's arms wrapped around her. She never wanted to leave.

Her brother came up beside her and squeezed her sides, making her yelp. Mara turned and swatted his chest. "I'm most certainly not going to miss that."

Azor smiled. "You say that now, but in two months, you'll be wishing I was haunting you with my antics."

Mara's face sank at his words. "I'm really going to be gone for that long," she said, more to herself than anything.

Azor's face cringed.

"Don't think like that," he said, bumping her shoulder. "I'll see you soon enough. You'll just appreciate me that much more with our time apart."

"Promise me. Promise me you'll visit as soon as you can."

"Promise," he said with a grin, pulling his sister into a hug.

Mara awkwardly wrapped her arms around her brother, wanting to feign disgust, but she collapsed into him, wishing she never had to leave his arms.

Azor looked around before releasing Mara. "Is father not here?"

Mara kicked the dirt beneath her feet. "He said goodbye this morning."

She would have thought her father would be a sobbing mess as he watched her depart, finally carted off to be married. Maybe that's why he didn't show—he wouldn't want the courtiers to see him an emotional wreck.

"I trust father," Azor began. Mara found it hard to meet his eyes. "He wouldn't be forcing you to marry someone if he didn't think it right. Solstrale hasn't unionized with any other kingdom in some time, their alliances weakening. This will be good for Wrens Reach."

Mara sucked in a breath. "I know. I know. And I want to do my duty...It's just..."

Azor tugged her closer. "I wish it didn't have to be like this either." His hand rubbed patterns on her shoulder in comfort. "You'll settle in Kairth soon enough—befriend new ladies, fall madly in love with your husband. Everything will be okay." He shook her so she'd look at him. "Okay?"

She nodded, a swell of relief mixing with her erratic heartbeat.

With a big gulp of air, and a final goodbye to her friend and brother, Mara turned, clutching the skirt of her dress in her hands like she used to do as a child, and faced her destiny, which happened to be a large wooden carousel of carts that lined the road before her. Several horses pulled at the reins; unlike anything she had seen before. Usually, nobles traveled in a wagon or a litter; she had never heard of an array of small house-like boxes connected to make a string of moving carts. The Royal Procession, the maid had called it.

The bag at Mara's side shifted as she headed toward the cart, one of the guards on her flank, unwilling to let herself cry. She didn't want to seem weak or to give *someone* the satisfaction that she was, indeed, a spoiled princess who felt sorry for herself.

As if summoned, her eyes caught sight of a tall man bobbing his way between the caravans up ahead. His hair was pulled back into a low bun, several tendrils spilling around the framing of his face—she wondered why he would even bother tying it up.

Mara didn't want to let Evrardin catch a glimpse of her wavering, proving he was right in his assumption about her. Women got carted off to marry strangers all the time, at least her betrothed was a handsome prince; not all women were afforded such a luxury. Mara wasn't a child, she was a grown woman who was ready to perform her duty.

She followed a stout fellow as he escorted her into one of the caravans painted a deep burgundy. The interior seemed too expansive for its outward size, completely foreign to anything she had ever traveled in. She tentatively took a seat on one of the benches lined with red and gold upholstery, sitting as close to the wall as she could so she'd be able to stare out the window and watch her lands that she loved so much roll past. One of her handmaidens came in and sat beside her, awkwardly patting her skirt down, not knowing what to say to the upset princess.

Chattering caused her to turn, taking in the sight of three women stepping aboard, greeting her in a polite curtsy, before settling in across from her. She assumed these would be her ladies-in-waiting. She wasn't much in the mood for talking so she was glad when they kept to themselves, only speaking to Mara's handmaiden, letting her sulk in the corner.

At least she would have a few bits from home, even if it was just in the one handmaiden and a handful of guards.

It seemed like the caravans were ready to leave as Mara heard shouts that resembled orders and the tightening of reins, when the cart tilted to the left, drawing all the women's attention to the derivation. A familiar brooding figure stepped into the confinement and Mara let out an annoyed grunt.

"Lovely to see you too, Princess," he quipped. The other ladies looked between them, extremely inconspicuous in their stares. Evrardin took a seat diagonally from her, shifting his sword as he sat. The carts immediately began moving, leaving Mara to assume Evrardin was waiting until the last possible second to board.

"Have you come to harass me?" she asked, irritated.

"I want to be here far less than you think, but Cas wanted someone to watch over you."

"What? So, you're chaperoning me before we even get to Kairth? Am I a sheep to be shepherded?"

Ev brought his foot up so his boot sat lazily across his thigh. He nodded at her, already bored of the conversation. He wore relaxed attire, his cotton tunic hanging loosely from his chest, the sleeves pushed up to his elbow. He sported a sword, but no other forms of armor or protection.

"Why do the gods keep punishing me?" she asked with spite at the ceiling of the cart.

The ladies looked at her with wide eyes. "Princess, he's the Captain of the Royal Guard," one of the women chided in a hushed tone.

Ev had a smirk on his face as he watched Mara struggle between keeping face or cursing him out further. "Of course, my apologies," she said, unsuccessful in restraining her rolling eyes.

"Careful. Keep that up and they'll get stuck that way."

Mara stuck her tongue out at him like a petulant child. She heard him chuckle in his chest and that only made her more irate. She knew how pathetic she must be in his eyes, but when she thought about being taken away from her home against her will, she didn't care for manners. Mara looked out the window, her body simmering with sparks of fire.

Several hours passed, the sun slowly sinking in the west, when they came to a stop. Evrardin sat forward, looking away from his exhilarating nail picking, and stood, hunched so as to not hit his head on the ceiling as he peered out the window. "What the fuck are they doing stopping here?"

"Where?" Mara asked, mimicking him by looking out her own window. They appeared to be in a forest, a thicket surrounding them. When she saw the dark shadows, it dawned on Mara where they likely were. "Are we in the Sandwoods?"

Evrardin grunted as he tore the door open wildly before

turning around and glaring right at Mara. She had seen him brooding and exasperated, but never enraged. She felt small all of a sudden, his eyes piercing her.

Sand might not sound frightening for a forest, but it coined that name because its woods separated the Glass and Sun Courts. Where heat and sand make glass. It's where things went to die. To get lost forever. It was borderline forbidden, though, most still risked trekking through it otherwise they'd have to suffer the long way. If one stayed on the path and did not stray, all should be fine.

"Do not leave this fucking cart. Do you hear me?"

"Oh, and I'm supposed to do whatever you say?" She shouldn't have questioned him. Not when he was being so serious. Ev stalked toward her. *Oh, she really shouldn't have said that.*

Evrardin rested both hands on either side of the backrest, caging Mara in between his arms as he loomed over her like a storybook villain. She kept her eyes locked on him, refusing to cower away in challenge, but still feeling small in comparison. "You think just because you're royalty, you can say and do whatever you please. That you're above everyone else." His voice was low, only she could hear him. She gulped. "It gives me great displeasure to disclose this chivalrous obligation,"—Evrardin didn't try to hide the sardonic tone of his voice—"but I am the one who will fall on a sword for you—*for the prince*. It's me who will protect you from harm's way. Unfortunately, your extensive training in being a pain in the ass won't do you any good out here. So, when I tell you to stay in the cart. You stay in the fucking cart."

His eyes searched hers and she wondered what he was looking for. Compliance? Fear? Mara could feel the warmth from his breath as he spoke, and she prayed he'd be attacked by a wild bear when he left the cart.

"I know you'd love to see my blood streaked on the trees out there because of your own adversity." He gestured his head toward the open door. "I even bet that's what you're picturing right now, but at least wait until we arrive in Kairth. You can torment me with that smart mouth of yours all you want, but you'll do as I say while we're stuck in these forsaken woods. The *prince* insists on it." His mouth contorted into a snarl, his words a vibration that twirled up Mara's spine.

Any sense of leverage she thought she possessed being betrothed to the prince evaporated. Mara had a plethora of snarky remarks lined up in her head, but all she did was nod, daunted by the rogue guard who seemed to have defiance written in red at the top of his code of chivalry. Evrardin gave her one last stern look before pushing off her chair and exiting the cart. Mara's hands pressed against her flushed cheeks, trying to cool her chagrined blood rush.

She sat back in her seat in defeat, looking at the ladies in front and beside her, giving them a reassuring smile. The ladies seemed to not care to acknowledge Evrardin's urgency, immediately going to gossip in his absence. Mara wasn't about to complain.

"Handsome, isn't he, Ternia?" one of the younger women said, her cheeks pinking. Mara looked at the blonde and smiled softly. She couldn't have been any older than she was. It made her think how vastly different their lives were.

"A handsome face that is ruined with all his sulking," the older woman retorted, relaxing her hands on the lap of her skirt. Mara snickered. *Good*, she wasn't the only one who thought Evrardin's macabre outlook a tedious affair.

Ternia responded to the younger girl's first question. "Don't be stupid, Herra," she said, nudging Herra with her elbow. "You shouldn't talk about the captain like that, especially in the presence of the prince's future wife."

Herra's warm eyes rounded, terror crossing her gentle features as they flashed over at Mara. "It's okay," Mara reassured, smirking at Herra. "He is handsome. It's rather irritating, actually."

The brunette girl, Ternia, likely a few years her senior, spoke. "It must be some stipulation to work for the prince." Mara quirked an eyebrow at her in question. Ternia spoke in a low tone. "You'll see once we get to Kairth. All of Prince Acastus' courtiers are dreadfully gorgeous. The men and women alike. It's terribly inconvenient."

"How so?" Mara asked.

The older woman gave Ternia a look as if scolding her for gossiping, but Ternia didn't pay any mind. "The lords and ladies already get their way with just the flick of a finger. But with them all being so young and handsome... it makes it impossible for anyone around to refuse a request."

The eldest woman's eyes traced along Mara's fingers as she played with her rings anxiously. She didn't know how she'd fair as a newcomer. And taking the hand of such a handsome prince, being so bland and unremarkable herself, she was sure to face scrutiny. "That's enough," the eldest reprimanded, silencing the two women who couldn't help but giggle.

Mara gazed out the window, the dust in the air twinkling like shards of glass, making the dark forest look like the night sky. She wondered why they stopped here so abruptly and why it had upset Evrardin so much. She knew the woods weren't safe, but as long as they didn't stray from the road, she didn't see why this would be an issue. She wondered if he'd get reprimanded for leaving her unattended. A small cynical smirk played on her lips at the idea.

Mara shook her head. Gods be damned, she was becoming just as bad as Evrardin. She wasn't usually such a miserable, sadistic person. She decided she might try to restart her relationship with Evrardin—perhaps become amicable acquaintances. She sighed then stood up, reaching out for the cross-hatched door, the woods eliciting a silent thrum like they were calling out to her.

"Princess Mara, the captain requested you stay here," her maiden said to her.

Mara gritted her teeth before collapsing back on her bench. As time ticked by, she became more anxious, ready for the carts to begin moving again. She reached for the door handle again, ignoring the women's protests. "I'm just going to relieve myself. I'll be right back." Before she could hear their responses, she slipped outside. She stood along the dirt road, examining the caravans up and down. Silence.

She carefully trekked farther down the litter, searching for the source of their stop. A growling sound echoed in the woods causing Mara to freeze, turning to face the tree line. After several beats, she thought she had made the noise up in her head. The moment she moved her feet to keep walking, the coppice shifted, sticks rumbling, and Mara stood stunned as silvery orbs glowed behind the trees—a set of eyes.

She stumbled back, collapsing against the caravan, her heart racing in terror. The creature slowly emerged, feathers sprouted along its lithe body. Even though it was midday, the forest was dark, shadows cast along the path. She struggled to make out the inky creature, but she could at least tell it had feathers and was rather tall. It made a low gurgling noise, reaching for her, its claw brushing her cheek. She winced, her eyes shutting, her hands digging into the wood of the caravan.

Her lips parted, and before she could cry out, Evrardin sprung from the tree line and moved swiftly toward the creature, his sword drawn and face sweaty. The creature recoiled back, but not before its claws tore along her cheek. Blood tickled a path on her skin and Mara gawked in surprise, not pain.

Evrardin turned to her. "Get inside!"

She looked between him and the creature then turned and

sprinted into the caravan. The woman gave her concerning looks as she shook, sitting back in her seat, her eyes plastered open in horror.

She stared at the door, everyone remaining silent, waiting for Evrardin to either cry out in agony, or to storm in. After a few dreadfully long minutes, Evrardin climbed back into the caravan, out of breath and huffing for air.

Mara stood at his sudden intrusion, his eyes locking on hers. She thought he might march over to her to scold her. To berate her for disobeying him. A cold breeze fluttered in through the door he left agape. He took the few strides to reach her and grabbed her shoulders. She gasped at the contact. She expected him to shake her, to call her a madwoman. Instead, he appraised her face and then trailed his eyes down her dress. "You're hurt," he finally said, more out of obligation than genuine concern.

She gulped and shook her head, taken aback. "What was that?"

She could tell he was staring at the cut along her cheek. "You're bleeding."

"So are you. And far worse than me, might I add."

He ignored her, stepping away and digging through one of the nearby baskets for clean linens.

"Ev, I'm fine. It's barely a scratch. You should—" He waved her off and she hated how easily his shortened name tumbled out of her mouth.

He tossed the clean cloth at her, urging her to wipe her face of the blood. "Next time, listen to what I say, *liten rev*." Evrardin's voice was strained and not as full of aggression as she expected it to be. He sounded exhausted. Like he was miserable having to babysit a spoiled princess who was making his life harder than it already was.

She watched him without moving or showing any acknowledgment that she heard him. His lips tightened in vexation, then he stepped out of the caravan, the door slamming behind him. She saw a trail of blood on the wooden floor where he had just been.

    She crashed back into the red chair, letting one of the maidens guide her as she cleaned the cut along her face.

Chapter Eight
Mara

A FEW MINUTES LATER, Evrardin stepped back into the caravan, the concession moving once again. His shirt had been soaked along the collar with water, his face now free of blood.

He sat back down silently, and Mara twiddled her thumbs. "Tell me what that was," she finally said.

He didn't move or speak, just kept glaring at the floor.

"Fine. Keep your secrets," she began flippantly, "but I've read about the Sandwoods and have never seen anything about a creature—"

"There are no *secrets*," he grumbled. "Not everything important is in dusty old books. In fact, many things are not written out in physical form—things not meant to be shared."

"*See*," she dragged. "Secrets."

Evrardin blinked back his rage momentarily to look at her with what she suspected was only a minute drop of concern—but it was concern, nonetheless.

"Do you have a death wish? You cannot waltz around like the

coddled heir you are, doing whatever the hell you please. In the middle of the fucking Sandwoods, of all places."

Mara felt the anger culminate in her spine and simmer its way to her mouth, her lips twitching, begging to curse him out. She knew the woods were scary, but she hadn't thought a bloody creature would attack her!

Instead of admitting that, to apologize, she said, "And whose fault was it that I was left unattended to my own devices, able to do *whatever the hell I please*? Should I have sat around like a lap dog, waiting with my tongue out for you to return?"

Evrardin's jaw clenched. "My patience is waning, *liten rev*."

They arrived in Kairth at midday, the sun warming the once crisp morning air. She spent the entirety of the trip thinking back to the creature and the gnawing sounds it made as it slithered closer to her. She shivered at the memory.

The castle sprouted out of the sandy ground, most of the sandstone walls weathered from the raging sea as it crashed against the exterior. Towers jutted up in an incongruous array, some short, others so tall they looked like they might ascend into the clouds, appearing without any rhyme or reason. Sea ivy crowded the crevices and gaps, climbing up through the stones like it was holding the structure together, flame flowers blossoming sporadically and creating a soft orange glow. Mara marveled at the ethereal disposition of Kairth, its sandy structures and crystalized mirrors making it seem like the castle had bloomed from deep within the ocean. It was unlike anything she had ever seen...but something dark lingered in small corners and backends. A shadow cast where sunlight clearly poured over. The celestial fortress shrouded in a looming darkness that unsettled the princess.

Once they made it inside, Evrardin disappeared, leaving Mara with Lord Alfson—the self-proclaimed Hand to the King—but Cas had introduced him differently. "I see you've met the Puppet Master." Lord Alfson's face turned red with embarrassment. She heard him mutter something under his breath as Cas departed and Lord Alfson took her to her chambers.

He was rather old, his head absent of hair, but his short beard entirely gray. His skin was dark and his face had only a few wrinkles, but it was easy to tell he had aged faster than most, his back hunched slightly as he moved. One of his eyes was shrouded in a smokey cloud, the other a deep brown. She assumed he was blind in that one clouded eye. His robes were dark, like steel, dull silver threads etching Solstrale's sigil. "The king and queen would like you to join them for dinner, Princess Maralena."

"And when is that?"

"A few hours from now."

She nodded like she was supposed to, the salacious timbre of Lord Alfson's voice doing nothing to settle the homesickness she already began to feel. Mara, as well the two guards from Wrens Reach that trailed her, followed him up a winding set of stairs. Large stained-glass windows stood taller than Mara, stretching up the side of the building, letting in an opulent array of colors. The shape of an anatomical heart sat in the middle of the windowpane where the gods were said to look through to watch over their subjects.

"It's so beautiful," she marveled.

Lord Alfson strolled silently ahead of Mara, the clacking of his shoes the only sound between them as he led her down a never-ending route of corridors. By the time he stopped in front of her chambers, Mara was lost. There was no way she'd be able to find her way back to the entry hall, let alone the dining hall where the king had requested her.

Lord Alfson stared at her expectantly.

"Oh," Mara mumbled, quickly going to move through her open door, passing a stoic guard who was plastered to the exterior wall of her room. She slipped into the apartment and marveled at the luxurious furnishing. She grew up as royalty, so she was well versed in the ostentatious displays of wealth, but she had never had a room like this. The windows were gilded in gold, sheer curtains making the sun shine in and create a pool of honey along the wooden floorboards. The bed was large and layered with far too many pillows, all with intricate embroidery and tassels, a soft gossamer canopy decorating the bedposts. There was a decadent rug that spread out across the underbelly of her bed. Several wardrobes lined the back wall, an assortment of shining dresses out on display. Though, the ornate mirror that extended the entire length of the wall was what really caught Mara's eye. It was wrapped in golden trim that resembled the likeness of a tree branch, butterflies and flowers engraved along its edges. She wasn't used to seeing mirrors revered.

"Captain Konungrsson will be by shortly to escort you, Princess." Alfson's voice shocked her out of her ogling, blinking several times to wash the eye-burning beauty from her vision. The idea of Evrardin being the one to escort her set a rock sinking into her stomach.

"Surely my own guards are capable of taking me to dinner. I wouldn't want to bother the captain." She added in the last line abruptly so as to not sound disdainful.

Lord Alfson's expression was unmoving, a soggy frown on his wrinkled face. "Apologies, Princess, but the prince has requested the captain specifically."

Mara's shoulders sank, but she gave him a smile. "Of course."

Lord Alfson wasted no time leaving; orienting Mara about

the intricacies of the Sun Court and layout of the castle clearly beneath him. She'd have to ask her ladies-in-waiting and base her judgements on her readings of Kairth.

Mara twirled in her room, marveling at all the intricate details, her thoughts lingering to the captain's surname. *Konungrsson*... Son of the King. He was a bastard of the north, then. He had a slight accent so she knew he wasn't from Solstrale. And he certainly was no fae. So perhaps he was a bastard of the king in the Wastelands.

She shook her head and forced her thoughts to focus back on her room and away from Evrardin's history. She couldn't believe this would be her room—at least until she was to share one with the prince. It was over twice the size of hers back home.

Home. She supposed this was her home now.

She startled when a knock sounded at her door. Faint, but she was positive she heard it. One of her guards opened the door and she expected to find a brooding knave, but instead she had to tilt her head to lock eyes with a much shorter boy. The prince and him shared unmistakable features. His hair was dark and curled, his eyes gleaming gold, similar to how Acastus' looked in the sun. This must be the brother Acastus' had mentioned.

"So, you're really here," he began, leaning over to look past Mara into her rooms.

"And who are you?" She held back a smile at the curious boy.

He righted himself as if switching into his regal persona. "Prince Aevum."

"Princess Maralena," she said, giving him a slight curtsy. "Younger brother to Acastus, I presume?"

He nodded. "I didn't believe it when they said Cas had chosen a bride." He twirled his hands together and Mara noticed he was wearing leather gloves, just as Acastus did. "Thought she might be magical if she had caught his eye." The boy was hesitant to look up at her, but when he did, there was a rose blush across his round cheeks at the rude implication of his words.

"I'm afraid I'm none of that."

"I'm sorry, I didn't mean..." He shifted his tone. "No matter," he said, waving his hand. "I think I'll like you just the same." He gave her a toothy smile and Mara's heart lurched.

"Did you want to come in?" Mara asked him.

"I..." He looked at the sentinel outside her door and then shook his head. "I have to get back to my lessons. I just wanted to see my new sister."

"Well, if you're sure. I wouldn't mind some company while I unpacked."

She could see the desire within the boy bubbling up. He desperately wanted to stay. She wondered if he had many friends.

"I really can't. I'll see you at dinner though!" he beamed.

Mara nodded, unable to repress her grin as the prince skipped off back down the halls, turning to give her a timid wave.

Once he was out of sight, the guard outside her compartments announced her luggage had arrived. She busied herself by putting her things away; taking the dresses and shoes she brought, placing them in the wardrobe, hanging up her dresses. She wanted to do anything but think about being trapped here for the rest of her life.

Mara waited alone in her rooms. She edged closer to the mirror, her hand extending to stroke its

silvery surface. Her fingers danced across the cool glass, its face so heavy and smooth that it looked like pools of liquid rippled out from where her fingertips touched.

A man cleared his throat from behind her, making her jump. She spotted Evrardin by her door through the mirror. "Seven hells!" she gasped, the annoyance already setting in as she peered back at him in the reflection.

Her eyes roved over his large stature, stoic as he mimicked her, appraising her outfit succinctly. She begrudgingly turned on her heels to face him, fiddling with the rings on her fingers.

Evrardin noticed her silence, likely already accustomed to the abundance of words that often spewed from her mouth. "Nervous?" he mocked.

Her eyes darted to him, the fire within them rising like he had already seen so many times now. Oh, how easy it was to start the princess.

Mara pursed her lips and stormed over to him. "Let's just get this over with," she muttered as she slipped past him and out the door.

"That's the attitude." He closed her door before passing her in two easy strides. She was about to march her way down the halls in front of him, knowing very well she had no idea where anything was located in this castle, simply on precedent of not wanting to ask the way.

"This way," he said, gesturing his chin over his shoulder. She hesitated before abandoning her idea of going down the wrong corridor and decided to drag her feet behind Evrardin.

As they approached a grand set of stairs she didn't remember seeing earlier, she pointed down a long hall dressed in shadows. "What's down there?"

Evrardin followed her line of sight. He grunted as they began down the stairs. "The prince's quarters."

"It's so dark," she thought aloud.

"It'd be wise of you not to wander down there unchaperoned," he scolded.

Mara's chest warmed, her cheeks pinking, understanding the implication. She didn't think he'd care about her reputation.

Lost in thought, she stumbled on the last step, her dress catching on her shoe, and she tumbled into Ev's back. She quickly righted herself, withdrawing her hands from where they caught between his shoulder blades.

She expected his reprimand—chiding her clumsiness at the very least. But all he did was clench his jaw and continue forward.

He is such lovely company, she thought. She preferred him when he snapped at her—ironically, she could feel the hatred pool off of him more when he wasn't speaking.

Mara hadn't realized they entered the dining hall, her eyes busy tracing every surface they passed, taking it all in. "Princess Maralena," she heard the captain say. She looked at him, coming back to reality, her presence now within the grand hall where the tables were set elegantly, the king, queen, and princes already seated and looking at her.

She quickly curtsied, forcing a wide smile as she introduced herself to King Acanthus and Queen Darla.

The king's hand extended, gesturing for her to sit. "Pleasure to finally meet the princess who caught my son's eye."

Chapter Nine
Mara

Mara tensed, her back rigid as she slid into her seat, her eyes nervously flickering between her hosts. She gave a curt "Thank you," to the servant who tucked her chair in, fumbling with her words. Her heart settled slightly when she met Prince Aevum's eyes across the table, giving him a tiny wave.

"Wondrous, isn't she?" Acastus exclaimed.

The princess who caught my son's eye.

Mara had barely interacted with Acastus in the three days they'd been acquainted—certainly not enough for her to gain the attribute of *wondrous*. Acastus' dulcet tone hinted to her that he had simply told his father how much he adored her for appeasement. The prince quirked a brow at her, smiling, amused at the situation. Acastus' tacit to please his father was something she understood far too well.

"She certainly is very beautiful," the queen spoke softly.

"She's only beautiful because there aren't powerful enough words to paint the radiance she casts," the prince added.

Mara blushed even though she knew this was all a farce. Everything in royal families were acts purely for political gain. Every courtier a pawn to be moved and played right. She wished she had more of a chance to speak with Cas alone. He seemed to always be in such a rush, darting off somewhere more important.

Mara examined the queen as the king spoke to her. "Beauty isn't everything, darling."

"No. But it helps, does it not?"

The queen had a soft aura about her, dark eyes twinkling, her skin creamy and pink, her hair thick and pulled up in a chignon of braids atop her head. The queen met Mara across the table and Mara shifted her eyes to her lap, embarrassed to be spoken about like she wasn't present in the room.

"My son says you have interest in joining the Solar Sect right away."

Mara's face contorted, glancing at Cas then back to King Acanthus who had interest spread across his face.

"While most newcomers aren't initiated into the Sect until wed, I think our high priest will make an exception for the prince's betrothed." The king gave her a compliant smile before picking up his spoon and slurping at his pumpkin soup.

She worried Acastus could see the stark confusion plastered on her face—she was certain the king could too.

The king put down his spoon to continue. "And to think such a small thing like yourself would be eager to bear witness to the grand absurdity of the church so soon! It's clear you and my son have quite the connection." She couldn't help but feel jilted at his use of *small*—she knew he meant more than just her size.

Mara pondered the way the king described the church as something 'absurd', and yet he seemed devout, her mind ebbing with wild thoughts about what his devotion entailed. What had the prince gotten her into? Mara's hand gripped her spoon tightly in her fingers, the detailing of the sun engravings sure to imprint on her skin.

She peered over at Evrardin, who stood watch at the doors, only to find him sneering at her like he was reveling in her discomposure.

The conversation continued to buzz around her while she politely ate her soup. Aevum leaned over, trying to get her attention. Mara glanced at the others conversing before she leaned across the table as well.

Aevum whispered in a hushed tone, "Do you like theater?"

Mara smirked and whispered back. "Of course. Don't all princesses?"

Aevum seemed to think about that for a moment. "Not sure. Haven't met many. I haven't been able to leave the castle much."

"Oh? Why is that?"

Aevum seemed bored by her inquiries, but he entertained her, nonetheless. "I've been ill." His voice a bit solemn. The young prince looked rather healthy to her.

Before she could ask more, the king spoke to her. "Have your journeys ever taken you to Solstrale before, Princess?"

"No, they haven't, Your Grace. But I've heard endless stories of the decadent lands."

"Nothing but good things, I hope," he teased.

"Everyone I've met has said how much they didn't want to return to Wrens Reach after visiting the seaside." She laced her words with a soft laugh.

"Ah, yes. Well, Wrens Reach has its beauty, too. It's been so long since I've ventured there."

"I'm sure my father would love a visit from the Sun King," Mara beamed.

The king smiled in return, his spoon upright in his hand and dripping soup onto the table. "It's always exciting to experience Sundance celebrations in the heart of the Sun Court. It gets rather... convivial this time of the season. You will be attending the events, will you not?"

Mara glanced at Cas who looked at her dully. "Yes, of course, Your Grace. I'm very much looking forward to partaking in Kairth's traditions."

The prince escorted the princess after dinner, offering her a tour of the castle. Mara tentatively hooked her arm with his, waving politely to the king and queen—immediately regretting such a subservient gesture. Acastus placed his gloved hand atop her fingers, his warmth radiating like a trail of fire.

The second they stepped into the corridor, away from the eyes of the dining hall, Evrardin close behind, he released her. "What the fuck?" he growled at Evrardin. Ev's expression didn't shift. The prince ran a leathered hand through his black hair, tousling it in irritation. "Didn't I tell you to familiarize her with her place in the Sect?"

Evrardin leaned back against the cherrywood wall, his hand lazily holding onto his sword sheathed at his hip. "No. You said, *she should probably be caught up before dinner.* Nowhere did you explicitly instruct me to do anything but escort her."

Acastus' eyes closed as he sucked in a deep breath, his nostrils flaring. "I swear to the gods, Evrardin. Sometimes I think you'd be of more use at the guillotine."

"Apologies, My Prince," Ev spoke mirthlessly, clearly mocking Acastus.

Mara's eyes felt like they were going to pop out of her head at the informality of their conversation. She blinked several times before the prince turned back to her.

"What was I supposed to come to know?" she asked him.

The prince's features softened marginally, his eyes darting between her own. Mara felt her stomach twist as he silently appraised her, feeling like he was deciding something. Ev watched from behind, his eyebrows raising. Both of them waiting to see what their unruly prince was going to do.

Acastus sucked in another breath, his eyes never leaving hers as he spoke. "Evrardin. Tell her the plan for the coming days. Or I swear to fucking—"

"I will do so promptly."

The prince's head snapped to Ev, narrowing his eyes. "And give her a tour while you're at it." He turned back to her. "Anywhere the princess cares to meander."

A scowl formed on Evrardin's face, clearly forlorn about chaperoning Mara—her company acting as his punishment. "Of course. I had nothing better to do anyways," he grunted.

"Are you going to accuse me of overworking you?" Acastus asked forwardly.

Evrardin held his gaze a moment longer before turning away, conceding.

Acastus shook his head in annoyance, then he reached out and took Mara's hand in his, placing a soft kiss on the back of it. "Princess," he muttered in departure before taking off down the hall.

Mara was so flustered and dazed she wasn't able to get her words out: to tell the prince she wanted to speak with *him*, not Evrardin. But what would she say? She simply wanted time to know what was going on. To steady her racing mind. But the prince didn't think that worthy of his time, so maybe Evrardin was her next best bet for answers.

She looked at Evrardin who was eyeing her with an unreadable expression. He shoved himself off the wall and began to stroll opposite her. "Come, *liten rev.*"

Mara obliged, scurrying after him like a field mouse. She glared at him once she matched his stride, having to take two steps for each of his. His eyes flickered down to her. "You know, you'd be a lot prettier if you didn't scowl all the time."

Her face contorted, aghast at his rude remark, though she should be familiar with it by now. She saw the way the prince and his guard just conversed. They lacked order. Respect. Hierarchy. Evrardin seemed able to speak freely without facing any repercussions.

They turned the bend of the hall before she spoke. "I suppose I could say the same thing about you."

"So, you think I'm pretty, then?" he asked teasingly, but his voice was harsh with indignation.

Mara had to refrain from letting her lips tip up into a smile. "Didn't know you knew how to tell jokes. Thought your mouth only capable of unintelligible animal communication," she muttered, then mimicked the grunting sounds he seemed to be keen on.

"My mouth is capable of far more than that, Princess." His fingers flexed by his side as he led her down the labyrinth of corridors.

Mara's face turned a humiliating shade of red, her sputtering words caught in her throat. Uncharacteristically, Evrardin seemed kind enough to quickly redirect the conversation. "The Solar Sect will be meeting in four days' time. Acastus wants you to be initiated into the Sun Court then. Binding your blood with his."

Mara looked up at him, confused. "But that usually happens after the wedding?"

"Usually, yes. But the Summer Solstice is happening so soon —he thought it would be best to do it then. Creates a stronger bond. The Solar Sect will be pleased to see that you've taken such initiative."

"But I haven't."

Evrardin's forehead scrunched in pain, his hand massaging the headache from his temple.

"I didn't know any of the other houses still practiced blood bonding." Mara pondered wistfully and Evrardin remained silent as she thought. "What did his father promise him?" she asked, her words becoming dissonant and demanding.

Evrardin's brows knitted together. "What? The king?"

Mara nodded.

"What are you asking?"

"What did the king promise Acastus? Land? Power? I don't know"—her hands gestured out in front of her as she spoke—"but it had to have been something if he's working so hard to make our... *arrangement* seem genuine."

Evrardin appraised her, halting in his steps. Mara crossed her arms over her chest. "He hasn't been in the Solar Sect's best favor as of late."

"And uniting with his wife helps him...how, exactly?"

Evrardin clenched his jaw, his muscles flexing under his cheek before beginning to walk again. Mara hustled to keep up. "He's to be the Crown Prince. The Sun Prince," Ev said to her through gritted teeth as if that answered everything.

She could tell he was forcing the words out, quite plainly not wanting to continue this conversation.

Mara knew each of the kingdoms possessed different innate abilities: Solstrale destined to the sun; Wrens Reach coupled with the travel god. Over the many years since the gods left—this era deemed *After the Gods*—each court's powers had been draining. All but the fae—whom didn't channel their magick from any divine force—and The Shadowed Isles—which summoned their abilities directly from the Veil, not their god. However, the Glass and Sun Court were the last of the other courts to dwindle. Perhaps Acastus was trying to strengthen his prowess, and she guessed Acastus' conjurations would somehow strengthen if he bonded his blood with hers. Or perhaps he needed her blood to match the sun's and not the travel god's. Maybe it wasn't his father who had promised him anything after all, but he was still pursuing something covert, nonetheless.

Mara stomped her feet, pouting as she followed the beast. She was being used; a pawn in the royal game. Not that she ever thought her position would be any different, but it still wasn't nice to hear.

Mara crashed into Ev's back, stumbling against him for the second time that evening. He grunted in annoyance, making her want to laugh at the resurfaced animal sounds. Mara peered at him as she slithered to be by his side. "Why'd we stop?"

Without looking at her, Evrardin gestured his head forward. Mara followed his line of sight to gawk at two heavy doors languidly swung open. They must have been twice as tall as Evrardin. Beyond the archway, Mara could see ever-growing rows of books moving in a coil around the room, some fading off into the shadows like a maze.

"Is this the library?" she asked, a dumbfounded look plastered across her face.

"And what else might you call a room stockpiled with dusty old books?"

Mara's eyes lit up, her smile growing, having no regard for Evrardin's stilted attitude. She strolled into the room, the ceiling as high as a cathedral's. The books never stopped; they climbed the wall to the top, multiple levels with gilded iron fences lining the upper shelves. Before her, a labyrinth of bookcases filled to the brim with books of all different bindings painted the room. She imagined she could get lost here if she wandered too far. Whether that referred to the unsolvable maze before her, or the way she'd get transported to new realms diving into all the books, it was hard to say.

It was incredible. She had never seen anything quite like it. She had only ever known Venmore's poor excuse of a library with so many missing volumes to sets. The shelves were crumbling like dust, books having to be stacked on the floor.

But *this*, this was out of a fairy tale.

Mara paused, facing Evrardin who was no more than a foot behind her. Her eyes sparkled in the evening light that poured in through a glass point in the middle of the ceiling. "Why did you take me here?"

"Is Kairth's library not to your liking, *liten rev*?"

Mara shook her head, her lips tightening. "No. I just meant... I didn't ask you to show me the library."

"No? And yet I took you here anyway." There was a beat of silence between them. "Was there another area of the castle you were clamoring to see?"

Mara pursed her lips, deciding not to pry any further lest he drag her back to her room and lock her in for the night. He likely knew bringing her here would quiet her questions for a while, giving Evrardin some peace as he slid into a green upholstered chair. He watched her as she twirled between the bookshelves like the motes that glittered amongst the beams of light streaking in from the stained windows.

Mara skimmed through the books, little appreciative sounds escaping between her lips whenever she stumbled upon a particularly special or sought-after tome. She spun down the aisles, marveling, before halting as she noticed the unnatural way a farther hall down one of the library's corridors seemed rotted. It was shadowed even though the candles on the sconces were lit. Stones seemed to crack and bend, its darkness sickly. She quickly went the opposite way, startled by the unnatural sight.

"Is there a forbidden section?" She rocked back and forth on her feet as she turned to Evrardin.

Ev quirked up a brow, looking surprised by her sudden appearance in front of him. "Now, if it was forbidden, why would I show you?"

"I didn't ask you to *show* me." She crossed her arms across her chest. Evrardin's dark, almost black, eyes scanned her face like he was slipping into her thoughts and shifting through her mind. She sighed. "I mean, I *was* going to ask you to show me. But I'm strictly curious if such a section exists." She knew it did—a library of this size would likely have lots of stowed-away books filled with faraway secrets.

Evrardin shook his head but pointed a finger up to the second level. Down in the corner, a golden cage reflected the light, a wall of tenebrous books trapped beneath it.

Mara smiled in amazement, her body rumbling with uncontrollable excitement. Ev looked like he didn't know how she could be feeling elated gratification from books alone. "How do I get up there?"

"Ah." He gave her a stern look, pushing himself up off the chair he was splayed in uncomfortably. "That, you can find out on your own, *liten rev*. Though I don't recommend it."

Mara tapped her foot. "Am I going to be escorted everywhere I go?" Ev nodded, stretching his arms above his head. Mara tried not to look at where his emerald tunic rose with his arms. "And none of my chaperones—?"

"I'm to be your only chaperone," he said, cutting her off.

She took in a breath through her clenched teeth. "*You're* not going to let me wander up there, are you?" Ev shook his head, his hand resting naturally on the hilt of his sword. "This is hell. I'm trapped in hell," Mara exaggerated. She turned to move toward the double doors.

"Yes, being kept in a lavish castle, servants to wait on you hand and foot, three meals a day, a bed to sleep in. Truly such a terrible purgatory. How do you manage it?" Ev followed behind her. "You should be in theater," he muttered under his breath.

"So, you understand, then," she said with a sardonic smile. "Don't worry, I'll try not to bore you with my dreadful penitence."

"Doubtful."

She gave him a narrow look over her shoulder. "And for your pleasure, I'll have you know, you're right. I happen to be a wonderful actress," she beamed, knowing his comment was a jab, but refusing to let it cut her skin.

His eyes shifted to hers, matching her intensity. Begging her to continue. That's what he wanted. So she didn't give it to him. She walked back down the hall without a sound.

Somehow, Evrardin managed to pass her, taking the lead as they walked through the endless stone halls. She supposed it was a good thing he had longer legs than her because she would rather rot away, lost in a corner of the castle, than have to tell him she had no idea where she was going.

When they made it to a spiraling staircase that seemed to infinitely travel upward, a long, drawn-out screech of metal echoed up the stairs. Evrardin tensed and Mara stood still, his foot hesitating on the step in front of her. A short man with a deep sea-green cloak wrapped around his collar came up from the lower level, moving slowly but with a spark.

She felt Ev's hand on her lower back, urging her up the stairs. She shook him off, making him clench his jaw. He was bound to give himself a headache with all the tensing he did around her, but before he could protest, forcing her to move, the small-statured man matched their level.

"Evenin', Ev," he said. His voice gravelly, like the crunching of sand in someone's fist. "Princess." He bowed at her—though he wasn't able to dip his head very low.

"Good evening," Mara said politely, taking her foot off the step and turning to fully face the man.

"Let's go," Ev grunted, both his hands on her shoulders now, attempting to turn her around and shove her up the stairs. Mara's body lit aflame where his touch lingered.

She struggled this time to shake him off, his grip overpowering hers. Mara turned her head to look at the man, ignoring the fact that Ev was trying to direct her away without brute force but failing miserably. "Where were you coming from, might I ask?" Mara inquired sweetly. Mara twisted her body, ducking beneath Evrardin's arms, and down the few steps he managed to guide her up.

"Do not pay any mind to the gravedoctor," Evrardin grumbled in frustration behind her.

"Crowrot," the old man corrected, gaining an irritated look from the captain.

"Crowrot, then," she repeated, smiling at him.

"I was jus' coming up from the crypt. Was jus' gonna go on over to the kitchens. Would the princess care t'join me?"

Mara had a strong urge to say yes. She had a slew of questions stacking up now that he said he was coming from this mysterious crypt she hadn't seen on the map she studied back in Venmore.

Evrardin gave him a deathly stare, his eyes slicing the man every which way.

Mara nodded her head, but Crowrot spoke up. "My apologies, Princess. It is unseemly to be so forward and invite such a lady to t'kitchens where t'servents eat."

"Mara," Evrardin said sternly, gaining her attention.

"Gods. You're such a goddamn bore," she growled back at him. "Why do you have to make my life miserable just because you hate your own?" She clenched her teeth, her words mumbled and directed over her shoulder. She gave Crowrot one last look. "It was lovely meeting you, Crowrot. I hope to speak again."

"Course, Princess," he said before giving a half-bow once more, smirking at her impolite remarks to Evrardin.

Mara shoved past the captain and marched up the stairs, no longer waiting for him to lead. He turned to Crowrot, telling him a thousand curses with just his eyes.

"I like her," Crowrot said.

"Don't get any fucking ideas," Evrardin grunted before storming up the staircase after Mara.

Chapter Ten

Evrardin

Evrardin's hands gleamed a slick bright crimson, the red sludge reflecting the candlelight from the sconces on the wall. The dirk in his hand slid up the torso of the corpse that sat heavily on the table before him. Evrardin grunted as he dragged the dagger, hitting bones, splitting them with his bodyweight.

The events from the night prior played on repeat in Evrardin's mind as he dug his hands inside the body's cavity. Blood pooled on the table, sloshing out from where Ev's hands assaulted the internal organs. Why had he decided not to inform Mara of Acastus' intentions before her dinner with the king? Cas had told him to tell her, but he didn't *order* it. Evrardin wasn't sure if he did it as a jab at the prince or to annoy the princess.

Maybe Evrardin didn't want to be the messenger of bad news, even if he didn't particularly like the princess. It was strange that he was thinking like that. He had become so rotten on the inside from all the misdeeds he had to do for the prince, he started to dream of the day he'd mess up and Acastus would plunge a dagger into his heart and finally put him out of his misery—metaphorically speaking, of course, the prince would never risk getting his hands dirty, he'd have one of his guards bestow the blow that would end him. Evrardin wasn't a good man. He wasn't even a decent man. Not with the blood that coated his hands and sank into his bones, shrouding him in a constant shadow built out of sorrow and anger. So his want to not be the cause of someone else's foul mood for once riddled him with vexation. And he transformed that vexation into strength as he severed arteries, yanking it from the dead men's chests.

The shuffling of boots and clanking of metal slowly played into the room. "Ev, my boy," Crowrot sang in his hollowed voice as he entered the covert catacomb.

Without responding, Ev faced Crowrot and dropped the heart into the much shorter man's hands, the thick blood that still coated the organ making a terrible plopping noise as Crowrot clutched it within the confines of his palms. Ev began messily stitching the gaping hole in the corpse back together, using thick twine and uncoordinated movements.

"Are you still upset 'bout me running into you 'n the princess—?"

"No." Evrardin's fingers tightened their grip on the twine, pulling it taut so it slithered through the corpse's skin and locked the cavity shut in one ungraceful movement.

Crowrot set the heart on the table beside him, a large red stain forming on the wood. "She's nice. I like her," Crowrot added, appraising Evrardin, looking for any indication that what he said bothered him.

"You have no idea what she's like," he muttered in response. Evrardin slung the corpse over his shoulder, grunting from the sudden weight of it.

"Yes, I do." Crowrot's voice was frenetic, his falsetto rising up and down as he spoke. "I bumped n'to her this morning." He seemed almost smug as Evrardin turned to him and narrowed his eyes.

Ev jostled the body to better get it settled on his shoulder. "What did you say to her?" he demanded, his voice thick and rough like he hadn't spoken a word in months. Which happened rather often; it wasn't until the princess became his problem that he began to speak again—more so than his usual growls of agreement, that is.

"Nothing out of t'ordinary. Simple stuff: g'morning; how do you do; did ya sleep a'right?"

Evrardin's jaw shifted back and forth as he ground his teeth together. "You better not let the prince catch you speaking to her. He would be murderous just knowing she saw you. *Twice* now."

"Mmm. Is that yer problem, then? Worried for m'safety?"

Evrardin's permanent scowl made Crowrot laugh—a jarring, crackling sound. The few teeth he had left made an appearance as his mouth widened to let out the cackle. As unnerving as the sound was, something light and tucked deep inside Evrardin fluttered at hearing the old man laugh. Being around Crowrot was the only thing keeping him going. The only thing he had left.

Ev shoved past him, the legs of the body jutting Crowrot on the shoulder. He carried the corpse deeper into the catacombs, only a faint glow from candles dispersed too far from one another to light his way. Evrardin didn't need to see anyway, he had walked these tunnels countless times; he knew every branch and turn like he had a map plastered under his eyelids.

He dropped the body off in a recess with a thud. Multiple bodies lay on the cold ground already, this corpse was just one of hundreds that Evrardin had used to line the stone walls.

Evrardin strolled back into the keep, Crowrot busy wrapping the heart in a thin cloth soaked in a dark green iridescent fluid. He placed the wrapped heart in a wooden chest along with ten others just like it. "You done for t'day?" Crowrot asked as the heavy steps of Ev ascending back into the room echoed off the walls.

Evrardin grunted an affirmative sound, yanking the soiled linen apron free from his chest and tossing it haphazardly onto one of the many benches littered with a motley array of dried plants and odd concoctions in jars. Soft moments like this reminded him of when he first befriended Crowrot. How he had been so young, training to be a guard by himself with no family, the gravedoctor noticing him walking aimlessly in the castle. Inviting him to the catacombs to watch him work, and to eventually assist him in his experiments.

"Can y'take the rats out as you go?"

A bundle of dead rats sat in a woven basket that was falling apart by the door. Their bodies were hollow, appearing like all the blood had been drunk from their veins by a vampyre. Which wasn't the case. Their blood was drained by Crowrot, not a mythical being.

Evrardin grabbed the basket and marched up the stairs and out the front door of the mausoleum. He sauntered across the graveyard, avoiding stepping on any graves before dumping the dead rats into the lake. The rats' bodies floated on the surface, but they wouldn't last long. The naiads that lived beneath these waters would snatch their snack soon enough.

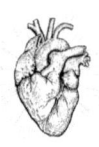

Evrardin would rather do anything than go back to Kairth, secluded in the castle, and—metaphorically speaking—forced to get on his knees for the prince. Instead, he found himself—and often at that—wandering the streets of Dalhurst, one of the districts of Solstrale on the outskirts of Kairth. The shadowed and damp cobblestone road glimmered from the candlelight burning inside the buildings he passed.

He didn't know what he intended to do, but his feet led him to his usual spot at the tavern he frequented, Sun and Sea, S&S engraved on a screeching sign that blew in the wind above the door. As he stepped inside, he was swiftly swallowed by the merriment of the townsfolks, memories of the prince's injunction to safeguard Mara playing in his mind. Although the prince hadn't divulged all the details, he had shared a considerable amount. His sole responsibility remained to adhere unquestioningly to the prince's commands, even though he often found himself challenging Acastus' authority. After all, he had little at stake—*only his life*.

The tavern was dimly lit, the cacophony of conversation flowing in and out of the insistently opening door. He strolled up to the barkeep, ordering ale from Bhedam. Ev looked down the bar, spotting many familiar faces—wanted faces; criminal faces; beaten faces. The smell of spilt rum and beef pie swirled around, and Ev's stomach rumbled.

Bhedam slid the drink in front of Ev as a hand slapped him firmly on the back. Ev's grip tightened on his drink, summoning all the patience he could manage. "Evening, Ev," the drunk man behind him said.

Ev unwillingly turned to Merrik. He was never glad to see him. If anything, seeing Merrik's face usually meant he was in for a long and painful night. Granted, Merrik wasn't to blame for Ev's sadistic pleasure in torturing himself. He could always say no—no one but the prince could force him to do anything he didn't want to.

Evrardin nodded a terse greeting as the man took a swig of his ale, some foam lingering in his mustache.

"I didn't see you on the lineup," Merrik said before raising a hand to call Bhedam over.

"That's because I didn't enter."

"No? I've never known you t'pass up coin—Another ale please, Bhedam."

Evrardin grunted. "I have orders from the prince. Gonna need my stamina in the coming days." It was a weak excuse. Evrardin was robust; if he wanted to throw punches one night and slave away all day the next, he could with ease.

"C'mon, man. I'm risking a lot of copper when I'm not able to bet on ya." It was almost a guarantee that Evrardin would win whenever he entered the ring. Merrik watched as Ev's eyes trailed a warm pie being served at one of the tables in the back. "I'll buy ya a beef pie." Merrik wiggled his overgrown brows.

Ev made a noise in his chest that sounded like disagreement, but the next time Bhedam passed the two men, he told him to bring over a slice of pie.

It was far too easy to get Ev in the ring. He cursed himself for being so pliant. He might have acted like he hadn't expected this exact situation to occur, but truthfully, fighting was the only reason he ever wandered into Dalhurst.

Maybe that's why he came. Deep down he had no other way to let his frustration out, and his body was begging for release. It seemed Evrardin was doing a lot of things lately without fully thinking it through. He didn't like to think. He liked to *do*.

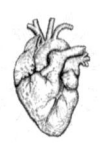

Evrardin's chest rumbled as he swung his arms around, loosening them up. He dodged a fist flying straight for his chin before dragging his hand upward and colliding with the underside of his opponent.

It was the third and final fight of the night for Evrardin. He couldn't recall the name of the poor fellow he was brawling, too engrossed in landing hits, his brain catatonic while his muscles continuously pumped with adrenaline. His body was alive, zapping with sparks, blood staining the overgrown stubble on his chin and blossoming on his wrapped knuckles, soaking the linen.

His opponent landed a rather hard blow on the underside of Evrardin's chin, making him stumble back. Ev shook his head to reorient himself, ignoring the blood that was trickling from his nose. He adjusted his stance and moved back into the center of the ring, arms up, and hands at the ready. When his opponent went to swing at him again, Evrardin ducked, sidestepped, and nailed a fist straight into the man's gut. As he hunched over, his head coming down, Evrardin raised a knee and slammed it against the man's face, a loud crunch making his ears cringe. The man collapsed to the floor, blood pooling around his face, the bell announcing the end of the match.

Evrardin had won. But that victorious sensation didn't riddle his blood with pride like it used to. Instead, Ev's shoulders slouched, his face unwavering as he was cheered on by the bloodthirsty audience. He bared his teeth in unquenchable anger. He used to relinquish throwing fists, but now he felt more rage than not when he stepped into the ring.

Outside of the ring, multiple men slapped him on the back, eager to collect their winnings, while the others, who foolishly bet against him, snarled in his direction as if Ev did it on purpose just to spite them. Multiple women gushed around him, most dressed in lewd dresses—harlots being the only type of woman who lacked enough decorum to enter the fighting halls. Ev's eyes unapologetically traced their figures as he moved, shifting from soft curves and silky skin to a belly rounded from ale and stout legs. Evrardin sighed loudly at the unseemly sight of Merrik, trying to shove faster through the crowd. "Your cut," he said before dropping a small pouch of coins in Evrardin's palm after Ev had tugged back on his shirt. Ev didn't bother counting it, he truly didn't care if he got paid or not. He pocketed the money, expecting Merrik to disperse now that he got what he wanted, but Evrardin was out of luck. Merrik seemed to have more to say—he always had too much to say.

"Heard Prince Acastus' new wife is already joinin' the Solar Sect."

Evrardin glared at Merrik, waiting for him to get to his point.

"Never seen the southern princess for myself, but I heard she's an eyesore. That true?" Merrik flipped a coin between his fingers as he spoke. Evrardin was seconds away from decking him in the face. "Heard she's a witch, just like her mother. Bet money that she'll curse the Genoivres. Acastus shoulda chosen a northern lady."

Evrardin turned and shoved Merrik, causing him to stumble back into a small alleyway, his back slamming against the exterior stone wall of the tailor's. Evrardin's forearm stretched across his throat, pinning him in place.

"Fuckin' hell, Ev. This ain't the ring!" Merrik managed to get out, his words breathless as Evrardin pressed against his windpipe, still making quips even while being suffocated.

"It's treason to speak ill of the prince," Ev grumbled, glowering at Merrik before releasing him.

Merrik took in a deep breath, his hands resting on the tops of his thighs as he hunched over before looking back up at Evrardin. "You'll have to hang the whole town in that case." He gestured around while one of his hands massaged his throat. "It's just petty gossip."

Ev ran his hand through his hair, pushing it out of his face before turning around and making his way back down the gloomy street. His body far more wound up than usual.

"Didn't know you had that much *actual* loyalty to the royal family," Merrik said, catching up to him. That was the thing about Merrik, he was like an itch on your nose when your hands were tied: irritating as fuck and never seemed to stay away. "Guess I shoulda known, you being the prince's lapdog n'all." The glare Evrardin shot Merrik should have sent a chill up his spine. He raised his hands in defeat. "Okay, shit. Thought you were more facetious than that."

Evrardin rolled his eyes. "When the hell did I ever give that impression?"

Merrik walked with a skip in his step. "Good point. Mighta made that part up—Hey! Don't look at me like that. It's hard to keep track of all my fighters. You lot of brutes are all the same."

Evrardin wasn't sure why he reacted the way he did, and he didn't care to explore it any deeper than that, afraid of what he might find. So he pushed it to the back of his mind along with all of the other baggage he didn't want to deal with.

Evrardin enjoyed the long walk back to the castle, especially at night. The stars lit the way, small flameflies igniting along the dirt path. He often took the long route, strolling the sea's edge, waiting to see if the naiads would appear. He relished his time when he wasn't being hounded by the prince. He could do whatever he wanted. Spending his time fighting dampened a lot of his pent-up frustration that he wouldn't be able to relieve otherwise.

Crowrot didn't think it was productive. He'd tell him to spend his time doing something more useful, like horticulture, which he was good at. But that was just the thing, Evrardin didn't always want to be useful. Sometimes he just wanted to exist. What was the point of living if you couldn't be useless at least a fraction of the time? Evrardin liked when he could shut his brain off and throw his fists in vile anger at other men who thought the same way.

In the distance of the dimly lit night, Evrardin could see the castle's fragmented pieces of its former self, with fallen arches, scattered stones, and a sense of shattered history. Even when the sun rose, blanketing the sandstone in a warm glow, the castle seemed to be perpetually cast in shadow, vast stretches encased in darkness, an oppressive aura lingering in every hall when it had always been swathed in light.

As he edged closer to the castle, he spotted a white figure on one of the awnings, decaying ivy climbing between the stones like a disease. That was a perfect location to overlook the sea, the spot high enough so you could gaze over the willows and juniper trees that hid the seaside. In the early mornings, you could see the fish beneath the undulating waves. On a clear night, the stars reflected brightly, making a painting of the water's surface, turning the ocean into a dark void, ready to be plunged into and pulled away to quiet oblivion.

When he got closer, he recognized the figure as the princess. Evrardin's hand tightened, wanting to shift his eyes away, unwilling to give her any more attention than he was already forced. But she stole his gaze, finding it hard to resist her. He couldn't make out the whites of her eyes from this far, but he knew she was looking at him, her head gently moving, lingering over him as he approached closer.

The moon shone brightly behind her, illuminating her figure like a celestial spirit. She wore a white nightgown, making her look like a ghost of a widow forever waiting for her husband to return home. He got a sudden burst of unjust anger knowing she was walking around the castle, not only unattended at night, but in something as unseemly as her night clothes.

A harsh wind blew through him and swept Mara's gown

behind her, sending it billowing in the wind. Her dress melted against her like water, outlining her frame in far too much detail. He could see the outline of her chest and hips, her figure lit perfectly for him. His lips hardened into a fine line before he turned his gaze back onto the ground in front of his feet.

He debated hauling her away, dragging her back to her rooms kicking and screaming. It's what Acastus would want. Yet something else was telling him to do it—something that didn't have anything to do with Acastus' demands.

His eyes flickered back up before he entered the main gate, and she was gone. Just like the ghost she mirrored, she evaporated into the night. He hoped that meant she was going back to her rooms, only to save him the trouble of having to deal with her. Or maybe his eyes had been playing tricks on him this entire time.

When he got inside the castle, his feet took up a mind of their own, leading him up to her apartments. He ignored the small voice in the back of his head telling him that checking to see if she was secure in her chambers wasn't a *command* from Acastus. And Evrardin never did anything that didn't benefit him unless he was strictly told to do so.

"Is the princess back in her room?" Ev asked the guard posted outside her door, his voice clipped.

The sentinel nodded his head. "Yes, Captain. She just went in."

"And why was she out of her rooms this late unattended? Surely a tiny princess couldn't sneak past the kingdom's best men." His eyes narrowed, ready to chide one of his men, reminding them of the consequences of such foolish mistakes.

The guard scrunched his face in slight confusion. "She wasn't unattended, Captain. Prince Acastus escorted her."

Fire formed in the pit of his stomach. Evrardin turned around without another word, his fists clenched at his side, attempting to subdue the disconcerting wave that racked his entire body. Prince Acastus had already been getting on his last sliver of sanity, but the presence of Mara seemed to be heightening his agitation.

Chapter Eleven
Mara

Mara sat on her floor, glaring at herself in the mirror. Her hair draped her face, tendrils curling and licking the corners of her cheeks as they clung to her skin. Her eyes had dark rings beneath them—sleep in Kairth proved difficult to come by.

It had been two days since she arrived and the prince had been sporadic in his sightings, only conversing with her at dinner. The queen had assured her she'd make time for tea one afternoon but had been too busy since to meet. Even the ladies of the court didn't seem interested in conversing with Mara.

The boredom washed over her, settling within her bones, making them shake with cornered angst. It thrummed through her, begging for release, her fingers restless. She had already written letters to her father and brother. She had the guards show her around, studying and admiring all of the elegant paintings. She went through and tried on all of the clothes that she found in her wardrobe. She took several baths. She perused the library as many times as she could, bringing new books back to her room every day to read. It had been too rainy for her to explore the gardens comfortably—she wanted to see the lyre flowers that Acastus had promised to be imported. As long as the soil is soddened with blood, the flowers can grow anywhere. And every time she asked a guard to take her to the oceanside, they refused, saying she was to stay inside the castle grounds—the only reprieve she had, she was being prevented from seeing.

 Mara's feet outstretched, her eyes narrowing in on herself in the mirror across the room. She still had her nightgown on, similar to the one she wore when she spotted Evrardin trekking in from the sea late last evening. The closer he got, the more she could make out. He was doused in deep red. His pants, shirt, hands, and even his hair were blood-encrusted. His shirt sat unkempt, his hair falling out around his face, loose tendrils sticking to the blood. Mara hated that she got a swirl of curiosity the second she saw him. She had so many questions. But she also didn't want to have to engage in conversation with Evrardin. With what little she knew about him, she was confident he wouldn't want to talk to her either. And even if she had wanted to, she hadn't seen him since that night.

 The moment she had mentioned Evrardin, questioning his appearance, the prince made her go back to her rooms. "Why would Evrardin be down by the beach this late at night?" she had asked, her eyes still focused on the burly man while the prince hovered somewhere behind her.

 Acastus leaned over her shoulder, spotting the armed captain walking back to the castle. The heat radiated off of Cas as he bent closer to her. He escorted her immediately back to her rooms, insisting he had other business to attend to. But Mara wasn't convinced—what business could the prince possibly have in the middle of the night? She concluded that it had something to do with Evrardin. Acastus' face had been austere when he left her, but she could see fury circling within his silver entrancing eyes.

Mara shook the memory from her mind and slid on her slippers, tugging on an appropriate dress, and left her room to head for the library, unsure of what else she should be doing. She thought she could be preparing for the Solstice, but no one was around to explain to her the events that would soon unfold in the coming days. She tried to engage the men who guarded her door and escorted her around the castle in conversation, but they would only grunt answers; they were worse than Evrardin. Company never felt so sparse.

She entered the warmly-lit library, the glow shining in from the glass cupola spreading angled beams of sun rays, capturing the dust and making them shine like stars. The guard who had been watching her during the days—so much for Evrardin being her only escort—took his usual spot against the first shelf, leaning his back on the chestnut wood, watching her as she shifted within the room.

Mara gave him a weak smile, futile in gaining any responses from him. His graying hair was cut short around his head, deep wrinkled lines cutting through his face. Mara thought he looked too old to be one of the Royal Guards, but she supposed that's why he was guarding her and not the king or prince. She wasn't worth their revered sentinels.

Mara had explored a great portion of the library by now, but there was still so much left to uncover. She strolled around, edging toward the back of the stacks. Down a far-left corridor, the light swept into shadows, the wood floorboards decaying and the sconces barely hanging onto the wall. She had a desire to slither further down the hall to explore, but with the darkness—no light from the skylight made it this far—she decided she'd finish seeking out the oddities in the main section of the library first.

After sifting through books for what felt like hours, she found herself climbing a ladder to the forbidden section Evrardin had pointed out the other day. Her heart raced as she approached closer, the bookcase encased in a golden cage. Her fingers stroked the side of the metal, gently pulling to see if there was any give. The cage didn't budge. She huffed when her fingers twisted around a lock. She knew her next mission was to find a key to open the gate. If anyone got upset, she'd blame it on the fact that she had been left alone with no one to interact with. What else was she supposed to do as she went stir-crazy?

If she sat still for too long, she'd be crushed with the reminder that she was in Solstrale, not Wrens Reach—not her home. No Jessamine or Azor. No jousting grounds or secret exits where she could escape into town and watch the fighting rings. Soon she'd be wed to a stranger, and handsome as he was, she couldn't coax down the rising disquiet, thinking about her wedding night. Of her entire future. No longer the Glass Princess. Now, under the sun goddess, she'd become the Sun Princess, a title foreign to her. Everything here was foreign to her. Even the soft sandstone walls were something she wasn't used to. And the company making her feel like an unwanted guest.

She scanned the tomes, looking for a weak spot to work one of the books out, and gazed across the title down one of the spines, *The Misuse of Moat Maintenance,* and almost audibly laughed. Why would this book be locked within the forbidden section? She assumed it must have been mixed up by one of the scribes and shoved in with the other dark and foreboding tomes.

As she worked on the gate, she noticed a tome left on one of the side study tables a few shelves down, its sides gilded in gold. Curiosity overtook her and her feet led her to the book before she knew what she was doing. Her fingertips stroked the soft leather, reading the title to herself softly. "*Forbidden Curses and Other Enormities: Speak No Evil Emendations.*" The cover had a swirling pattern engraved, little sparks jutting from its cortex, appearing like it was moving.

She flipped through several pages, finding nothing but boring historical lectures laced in the pages. She went to close the book, disappointed with a name that sounded so promising when her eyes caught hold of a word in bold: *Acquiesce and Divine Loyalty*.

She skimmed the first few paragraphs then sat herself in the chair tucked into the table, using her finger to hold her place as she read intently.

Under King Prothysis, the act of casting, brewing, or hexing any living persons to gain full submissive and unyielding control had been strictly forbidden as of 345 A.G. See also Subservient Curses
p. 468
One of the most powerful incantations, conducting an acquiesce curse, requires unmuddied blood—full connection to the gods. With the fall of the gods, full-blooded magick has dwindled drastically, intense incantations of this nature no longer accessible. However, it is said, obtaining dark magick—magick stolen directly from the Veil—can grant even the weakest magick wielder with enough prowess.

She skimmed the rest of the passage, flipping page after page. A swirl sigil indicated a new chapter, and she slowly traced her eyes over the ink. *Deities and the Threat of Sviks*.

She squinted as she trailed the passage and saw notes scribbled in the margins. She read the messy handwriting carefully.

Sviks, a deceptive creature of the Veil, live amongst the deities, but not in peace. They're known to mimic godly forms, though it's more likely they'll take the form of a lower creature, specifically a glassfairier, hoping to steal their place in the living realm. A creature trapped in the Veil but seeking nothing but escape.

A bang startled her and she slammed the book shut. Mara

reset the book so it looked like how she found it, her fingers leaving marks in the dust along the binding. She scoured back to the first floor, an uneasy, foreboding feeling weighing her down. The book was left out and Prince Acastus gave her free rein of the library, but the trepidation was relentless.

Mara tripped on her way out of the stacks, stubbing her toe against one of the dense bookshelves. "Shit," she hissed.

"Are you all right, Princess?" Sir Yven asked her as she stumbled toward him.

"Yes. Quite," she attempted to say nonchalantly.

Sir Yven walked her back to her chambers, Mara's mind spinning with her newfound information, unsure of what to do with it.

Mara attempted to repress her thoughts of treason, unsure why her mind was straying so wildly from such a simple text.

"Princess," a regal voice called out from behind her. Her heart froze.

"My Prince." Yven bowed slightly, his body shifting toward Acastus as he sauntered up beside them.

"I have it from here, Sir Yven. I'd like to speak with my betrothed." Acastus gave a derisive grin.

Mara returned a weak smile as Sir Yven was dismissed and headed in the opposite direction.

"How have you been?" the prince asked her, sticking out his arm for her to grab.

Mara obliged, resting her hand on his forearm, allowing him to lead her through the vast castle corridors. "Very well, My Prince," Mara answered, giving him the most convincing optimism she could muster. Acastus' gloved hand came up and hovered above her own before he placed it softly atop hers, sending gooseflesh up Mara's spine at the ghostly touch.

"Sleeping all right?"

They turned a corner, edging closer to Mara's chambers. "Yes," she muttered.

Cas raised a brow, appearing curious, like he knew Mara was blatantly lying about something so trivial. The dark rings around her eyes were apparent, making her hazel irises shine brighter against the dark.

As they walked arm in arm through the castle, Mara took notice of the way some corridors seemed darker than the others. Just as that one dark corner of the library where the cobblestone seemed to be rotting, places inside the castle were desolate and collapsing.

Acastus called her attention back to him. "I don't mind you spending your time in the library. If anything, I encourage it," Acastus began as she turned her head to look up at him. They stopped in front of her doors. "But I expect you to know better than to snoop around where you don't belong." His voice was low but still laced with saccharine as he spoke before the sentinel posted outside her rooms, but she knew something more cynical lay beneath, like gooey caramel that hardened once it made contact with cool air.

He fully faced her, her heart racing wildly in her chest. His arm unraveled from hers, his hand sliding up behind her neck as he leaned in close enough that only she could hear him. "Is that understood, Princess?"

Mara wasn't entirely sure what he meant, but she wasn't about to question him, suddenly out of her depth. She hadn't taken the prince for someone to threaten his betrothed.

A sharp burn etched on her skin where his hand wrapped around the back of her neck. She winced, nodding to hide her pain. Acastus gave a sly grin, clearly satisfied with her acknowledgment.

Just as fast as it arrived, the stinging was gone, soothed by the rush of cool air as Cas' hands hung by his side. He stood tall, towering a good five or six inches above her. His dark hair was pushed back apart from one rebellious curl that rested over his forehead. He truly was beautiful. But now she feared that beauty disguised something far darker inside him.

"Well," Acastus said sharply. "Go on," he gestured to her door that had been opened by her guard.

She gulped, giving him a small nod as she scurried into her room. She heard the prince chuckle as the door closed and she was left alone in her apartments again.

Mara took a deep breath, her mind spinning. Such a simple warning he gave her, and yet she could feel the fire and depth behind his words. Mara winced, reaching up to where Cas' hand had rested on her neck. She moved in front of her large mirror, shifting her hair so she could see the expanse of her skin. There, below her ear, were scratch marks puckering with blood. Mara's eyes widened as her fingers gently brushed over the skin, her fingertips staining red.

"Gods..." she said breathlessly, stunned that Acastus was able to leave such damning marks on her with what little pressure his nails applied—his hands gloved as well.

This began to feel like more than a simple marriage arrangement. The elegant walls of her room closed in on her and tears welled in her eyes, fearing she was no longer safe in Solstrale. She turned to the end of her bed where books were piled on her end chest, darting to them, ready to shuffle through and reread every passage, using the sleeve of her dress to pat the spot on her neck for blood.

Chapter Twelve
Evrardin

The eve of the Summer Solstice sprouted hushed whispers throughout the kingdom. Dark sun rays gleamed into the Sun Court, smattering the prince and his guard in a wash of warm colors. Evrardin stood before the prince who currently lounged on the throne, mindlessly picking loose threads of his sleeve.

"It's really none of my concern how the people feel about the princess being initiated in tomorrow," Acastus said languidly.

Evrardin sucked in a breath, trying to dampen his rising temper. "The people see *you* and the rest of the royal family as entertainment. This is going to start nothing but foul rumors. They're going to think she's bonding to steal our magick, to solidify the Glass Court's prowess, if she does it before being married to you." Acastus raised a brow, his eyes now meeting Ev's. "There is going to be a big crowd, Cas. I'm not even sure everyone who wants to attend will manage."

"Oh, my dear, Evrardin," Cas began as he swung his feet to

the floor and stood, "I need her to gain back her magick before the wedding. You know I don't enjoy wasting my time worrying about these nonentities and whatever balderdash about which they are gossiping."

"Well, you should."

"Yeah? And why might that be, Captain?"

Anger rose in Evrardin's throat, spreading out like prickly thorns, Cas speaking his rank in insult. Oftentimes, it was such simple things that could sprout rage within him, and it lasted longer the less he was able to relieve his stress. "She's to be your wife. Aren't you the least bit concerned about what the people will think, rushing her to be part of the sun-bearing bloodline?" Rakish thoughts crossed the features of Cas' face. "Do you really want people prying into your business? Because they certainty will once they're drawn into the promise of a scandal."

Acastus had to know Evrardin was right, of course. He couldn't have people getting suspicious and looking too closely into his life with the princess. Tomorrow was sure to be more difficult than it had to be with a large crowd watching.

"Why do you care so much?" Acastus quirked a brow.

An unsettling and troublesome pulse sparked in Ev's chest. "As your guard, it's my job to protect you—from more than just violence—"

Cas cut him off with a wave of his hand. "No. You care about the princess. It's not the same thing." Acastus' eyes narrowed on Ev, standing straighter. "Why?"

Ev's hand flexed beyond his control; the rest of his body unwavering. "Should I not? Is she not about to become intertwined with your life? If I serve you, am I not to protect her as I would all your things?"

"No. You shouldn't." Cas' words made Ev's eyes widen briefly before settling back into his brooding countenance. "It's me you serve. Not her. Not the king. *Me*. And if I want to do something that may bring my precious wife into harm's way, that is none of your concern. She and I are *not* the same. Maybe in the eyes of the Solar Sect we will be, but don't confuse yourself for a holy man, Evrardin."

Evrardin glared at Cas, unwilling to say anything that might result in punishment. Cas should be worried about gaining too much attention right now, especially from the king. Even with the extra marks from the Summer Solstice, Ev couldn't see how this was in his best interest at all.

"Don't underestimate her. She can fend for herself." Cas paced back and forth, his hands clutched behind his back. "She's a feisty one." He pondered for a moment. "I think I've grown to like her."

Ev's eyes darkened, Cas' lips tilting into a wicked smile. He always enjoyed torturing Evrardin, and now it seemed he also enjoyed ruining pretty princesses.

"So, you're just going to sit back and watch the chaos unfold around her tomorrow? Around you both?" Cas' lack of a response was answer enough. "She's not ready. No one has even informed her of what to expect." Fury laced Ev's words as much as he tried to keep it out.

"Careful, Evrardin," he remarked. "I might start to think you have feelings for *my* betrothed."

"Seven fucking hells. I don't have—This isn't about—" He shook his head in frustration. "I'm trying to protect you!"

Cas held up a hand—a demeaning gesture he did often—stopping Evrardin's growling words in their tracks. "I'm telling you now, regardless of animosity or fondness. You are to, under no circumstances, speak word to Mara about how you truly feel about her. Good *or* bad."

Ev's jaw tightened.

"Okay, good," Acastus clapped his hands. "Glad we got that sorted." Acastus looked back at Ev and rolled his own in turn.

"Fine. Tell her tonight what is to be expected of her tomorrow. I suppose she should know what's to happen anyway. Wouldn't want to cause a scene." He gave a sly smirk at Evrardin, taunting him. "She's smarter than you think, though. I'm sure she's read all about what's to come in those books of hers."

Evrardin was desperate to shift the conversation away from the princess. "And the deterioration of the castle from your intake of the Veil? What are we to do about that?"

Acastus sighed, forced to think about the subtle collapsing of the stone walls. The shadows casting around unused corridors. The crumbling of the castle's outer walls beginning to draw concern.

"I'll double the men working on the repairs."

"And the smoldering of your skin?" Ev added.

A gloveless Cas pulled his hands in front of him, appraising his blackened fingertips, almost relishing in the way the void swirled upward toward his knuckles as it began to fill the rest of his hand like smoke rising from an extinguished flame. "The gloves have been working for now. They'll have to do."

Evrardin looked at Cas' fingers with disapproval. "And when they are no longer enough?"

The ink spreading through Acastus' veins swam up his chest and the collar of his neck. They both knew it was inevitable. And rather soon at that. The darkness had picked up speed in the past week, ever since Cas captured Mara in his web. "That healer will soon be here. Less than a fortnight last I heard. Let's just hope he can help."

Cas' eyes slanted as he measured Evrardin, his old friend. However, he supposed that relationship was left in the past, along with all the other marvels that made Acastus' life worth living. For a brief moment, Evrardin could see the pride and lust dwindle to a controllable spark. Acastus' face broke its mold. "Thank you," he said softly.

Glass Hearts

Evrardin's stone eyes lightened slightly. He reached out, resting a hand on the top of Acastus' shoulder. So many things had been said already. Too many things to forget. Evrardin settled on giving Acastus a pained smile, knowing he could no longer offer him anything else out of his free will.

Chapter Thirteen
Mara

Mara clutched a chestnut-colored tome as she sat on her bedroom floor. Her silky cream dress flowed out around her, the cuffs tightening at her wrists and neck. She pushed her hair back as she dropped the large book on her wooden floorboards, prying back the cover engraved with the words *Sun Dance* and opening up to the pages that likely hadn't seen light in years.

Her finger gently traced the inked parchment as she read, her lips moving as she muttered to herself, trying to properly ingest every piece of information. Lost in thought, the creak of her door finally caught her attention. She turned to see Evrardin lingering in her entryway, shutting the door behind him.

"I knocked," he said when he spotted the surprise on Mara's face.

"Usually, people wait until they're permitted in, regardless if they've knocked." She went back to her book, trying to find where she left off. She narrowed her brows in frustration, skimming the heavily condensed paragraphs. A dirty pair of boots appeared in her periphery. She held in her huff as she looked up at Evrardin towering over her.

"About tomorrow..." he began.

"Way ahead of you." Mara used her hand as a bookmark as she closed the book to show him the title.

She felt his knees brush her back as he stood closer, leaning to read the book's cover. "Tomorrow is a... special occasion. Not sure you'll find many things of use in there."

Mara pushed herself up, leaving her book sprawled open on the floor. She spun around to face a much closer-than-expected Evrardin. She took a step backward over her tome to gain some distance between them. "Where have you been?" she demanded.

Amusement rose in Evrardin's eyes. "Been worrying about me, have you?"

Mara's jaw tightened. "Don't tell me, then. I didn't truly care, just polite conversation," she mumbled as she walked over to her bed and sat on the edge.

"Polite conversation," he muttered under his breath in mild amusement.

"Well?" she demanded. "*About tomorrow...*" she repeated Ev's own words.

He sat atop one of her dressers ignoring the multitude of other, more appropriate, options. "I should tell you how it's going to go."

"Oh, now you want to explain?! The day before!" The spite in Mara's words ricocheted off of him.

"Don't get pissy with me. I'm not the one who determines what gets told to you."

"No. Of course not." Mara fisted her skirts. "I'm supposed to just sit here and wait to do as I'm told. To stare at the wall while my insides bleed with boredom. No one to talk to."

Ev cocked his head. "Dramatic," he mumbled. "Is the prince not someone to talk to?"

"I'm lucky if he speaks to me at dinner—and lucky is a strong choice of words. He hasn't been the most talkative husband. He's proved to not be the best conversationalist."

"He's not your husband."

Mara wanted to roll her eyes—of course that was the part Evrardin chose to focus on, always correcting her. "Not yet. Just testing out how it will sound. I see it as a peek into the wonderful marital life to come."

Evrardin's lips threatened to tilt all the way into a smile.

"This is funny?" A hint of sorrow laced her fiery words.

"It is."

She waited for him to elaborate.

"You act as if this is all a surprise to you. What did you think was going to happen when you accepted the prince's hand?"

Mara bit the inside of her cheek until she tasted copper. She didn't reply to Evrardin's harsh, but true, words.

He sighed, shifting his weight. "Better than Sir Orion, no doubt."

Mara let out a breath. "Yes, well... that's quite an easy feat." Evrardin's eyes locked with Mara's. She tried to restrain the broken feelings from filling her eyes. Pain. Sadness.

"Yes, I suppose so."

Mara's eyes flickered around the room, uncomfortable holding his gaze. She knew that meant he had won whatever game they were playing, but she didn't care. It was awfully unnerving to have his full attention.

"Tomorrow morning you'll be escorted to the Old God's Cathedral, under the clergy of the Solar Sect. There is going to be a big crowd. Not only are the people excited for a wedding, but to have a royal betrothed initiated before the nuptial ceremony—a precaution never exempted."

Mara had just skimmed a passage in the tome that mentioned the ritual occurring a few days after a wedding ceremony.

"The Summer Solstice officially begins in Solstrale tonight. A far more powerful bond will be linked between you and the prince if it's done within the days of the Solstice." Evrardin seemed to have to force the words out as he spoke to her.

"And I'm to be summoned to the Veil?" Her brows wrinkled as she frowned, thinking back to that small passage she read in her book.

"Not exactly. You'll be submerged in the Hallowed Cistern, along with the prince. You'll enter a sort of harmony as your souls intertwine, bonding your blood together. It's them who will enter the Veil in your stead—your souls. Then, your life force will be forever connected with his. Your blood becoming part of the sun's." He turned away from her as he continued. "This will also connect you with the sun goddess, Trana. All royalty must find protection in the Solar Sect. It's the only way to keep the kingdom thriving under Trana's protection."

"The gods haven't been seen in centuries. Why does Acastus want my blood strengthened so much? Does the sun goddess even exist anymore?"

Evrardin ignored her inquiry.

Mara sighed and changed her course of thought. "If I'm to be the queen one day," Mara began, twiddling with a stray thread of her dress as she thought out loud, "the prince will become the Sun King. But the sun bloodline has already suffered a great decline with the loss of Trana. If he's to marry me, and I bear his children, will there even be any magick left for them to inherit? Why doesn't he just wait until I give him children—their blood would be a fusion of the two courts."

Evrardin's fist clenched, and Mara cringed at the thought of her belly round with Acastus' child. "It seems the sun's lineage is coming to an end."

"Well, why is he marrying me, then? He has a better chance

with someone else of magick heritage. A fae maybe? Wouldn't that increase the chances of—"

"I don't know. I don't have an answer for you. I don't know why he chose *you*." While she didn't know him well, she presumed he was lying. Was she to believe the prince's first in command didn't know the reasoning behind choosing Mara as a bride?

Mara stood up, her eyes no longer lingering with fire. All that was left was the melancholy that rumbled below. "Was that all?" There was no sarcasm or irritation in her voice. How fast she could shift moods. Evrardin extinguishing her fire.

"Yes," he said curtly.

Mara pulled her hair away from her face, some sprawling onto her back, turning to go back to her studies.

Evrardin went to leave before halting. He reached out and grabbed Mara's arm, spinning her toward him.

"What the *hell*—?"

"Where did you get that?" he asked, his tone tenebrous. Mara's hand instinctively reached up to her shoulder where Ev was staring. Her fingers grazed over the red marks that cut through her skin. It wasn't deep at all, but it would be a few days before the marks completely faded.

Mara was silent, her eyes flickering to watch him. Evrardin's fingers brushed the sore spot, shifting her hair to her back as he did. Mara's breath hitched as he loomed over her, touching her without her consent. His eyes finally shied away from her neck and narrowed in on hers. "Who?" he demanded.

She hadn't heard him speak so lowly before and she'd be lying if she said it didn't frighten her a little. Mara's mouth ran dry. Her heart skipped realizing how close Evrardin's chest was to hers. If she moved just a few inches closer, she would be flush against him. Evrardin's hand still gripped her other arm, holding her in place.

"Do not disobey him." His words were final, leaving no room for Mara to joke or refute. His jaw clenched as if he was connecting the dots. Like he knew Acastus did this to her. "Do whatever he commands of you."

She gave a small nod, her eyes rounded. Evrardin seemed to come back to his senses and released her. He smoothed his tunic before clearing his throat, Mara far too aware of the heat that bloomed over her arm. Without another word, he turned and left.

Chapter Fourteen
Mara

Mara woke drenched in sweat from a restless night's sleep. She peeled her dress from her body, sliding into the tub Ternia drew for her.

Mara struggled with the reality of being tethered to the prince as Evrardin had solemnly stated. Especially considering their bond was supposed to be heightened because of the Summer Solstice. She bit at her nails, Evrardin's words reverberating in the echo chamber of her mind.

The throng of onlookers would make her feel like she was some contemptuous spectacle to be mocked. She couldn't decipher why she was so perturbed by the idea that this was somehow an itinerant gala for the constituents. As a princess, Mara had done a plethora of things in front of a glut of gawking courtiers. Her father's subjects had watched her every move—they'd watch her on her chamber pot if given the chance. Yet, nothing had been as foreign to her as to what was about to happen later that morning. She was not used to the pious attention the Solar Sect was bound to grant her.

Ternia helped her dress, sliding on a light-blue silk dress, a large slit up each side of her legs so olive fragments of her thighs were exposed when she walked. The bodice was a snowy white and scooped down into a heart-shaped neckline but raised high in the back. Large flowing sleeves began at the middle of her bicep and billowed out the rest of the way down, connected to her shoulder with a thin stretch of fabric. A golden array of small sun sigils lined the hem of the dress and around her waist while a belt of golden suns hung loosely on her hips. Her bronzed hair had been swooped up into a chignon and a beaded headpiece ran down from her scalp and weaved with her bun.

She gazed in her mirror, her hair unwieldy and escaping her updo from the humidity, the curled framing tendrils frizzing outward. Freckles danced across her nose and cheeks from her recent time in the sun. A pretty gold sparkle coated her eyelids matching her dress. The golden earrings she donned featured a sun with a dagger plunging through it.

She felt exposed, more of her skin showing than she was used to. The south not quite as warm this time of year, resulting in much more conservative attire—apart from her birthday gown her father made her wear. She was almost certain the north hadn't seen snow in centuries, which she found to be a pity; Mara always loved the snow. Perhaps Acastus would let her visit Venmore during winter on the occasion.

Evrardin arrived at her door to escort her, and for once, she was thankful to see his face. While they weren't friends in any sense of the word, she knew him better than any other person in Kairth—much to both of their dismay.

He appraised her briefly. Mara expected him to compliment her, even if he didn't mean it. It was only polite to do, especially with her handmaidens and sentinels present, the spectators expecting chivalry. But he didn't.

"Shall we?" he asked, his voice monotonous as he extended his elbow for her. She surmised the prince must think her incapable of walking knowing Evrardin would only ever interlock their arms if commanded.

"Thought you were to be my only chaperone," she mumbled, filling the gap of silence. She thought back to Sir Yven, not caring as she climbed up to the forbidden section of the library after Evrardin had promised he was her sole ward.

"More important matters drew my attention," he almost snarled like he wanted to hurt her feelings, his elbow still extended for her.

She shook him off, straightening her spine, determined to show him she didn't care about his stupid remarks.

Nonetheless, she rested a hand on his forearm and began walking down the hall by his side. Only a few beats passed before Mara couldn't pretend to be insouciant any longer. "Will it hurt?"

He looked down at her, confused.

"The whole initiation affair. It didn't say anywhere in my reading what it felt like to be bonded. I just... Does it hurt?"

"No." His eyes traced hers momentarily before shifting back to his feet. "Your body remains in this realm. It's just your mind that will wander with your soul. Try to remember that. You're not physically in the Veil. Not *really*."

Mara laughed halfheartedly, fanning her fingers down her dress to keep them busy. "I don't know why I'm so nervous," she mumbled.

"It will be over quickly. The high priest usually performs such rites with impious haste. These types of ceremonies are a common occurrence—"

"Didn't you say a lot of people would be in attendance?"

He nodded.

"And is *that* a common occurrence?"

Ev paused before answering. "No."

Mara's stomach simmered and rocked back and forth. She suddenly regretted eating breakfast.

"There's nothing to worry yourself over, *liten rev*. You barely have to do anything on your part but be present. You should be used to that."

She didn't know why he was trying to comfort her—perhaps he just didn't want to have to deal with her having a meltdown, drawing attention to them. Mara finally let her curiosity get the best of her. "What does that mean?"

His dark eyes met her lighter ones, his brows furrowed in interest that made her body warm. She watched as the scar on his lips moved when he clenched his jaw. She could see the small splatter of freckles that were hidden across his dark skin and under his beard. A few peppered pieces intermingled in his facial hair along the edge of his hairline. He appeared too young to have grays, so she imagined they appeared from facing horrors rather than with age.

"*Liten rev*," she added, completely butchering the cadence, not having the captain's northern accent when he spoke what she assumed was his mother tongue.

Before he could answer, they were at the expansive doors of the Old God's Cathedral, the wood branded with suns that had sharp rays jutting out all along the crest. The Solar Sect would be just inside.

As a sentinel opened the door for them, Mara's eyes slowly widened at the sight of the crowded church. All the pews were taken and an overflow of courtiers stood in any open spot they could. "Shit," she muttered under her breath, all rationale leaving her mind.

Mara thought she felt Evrardin pull his arm closer to his

chest so her side skimmed his. Fire bloomed across her from the heat. She couldn't do this. What had she gotten herself into?

"Such a dirty mouth for someone so close to the sacred gateway of the gods," he whispered.

She barely heard him as he led her to the dais where the prince stood waiting. The room's cacophony of voices settled, all eyes following the princess. The people seemed to look at her with wonderment. They were excited for a royal wedding. The Sun Prince was uniting to carry on the bloodline, something the pious Sun Court reveled in. Their prince would be able to take the throne after his father—officially, now. And that was something they viewed worth celebrating.

Though, she felt something else in the eyes of the audience as she hesitantly made her way to the dais. The people seemed intrigued, hushed whispers floating in the open air.

The prince strolled to the steps, reaching a leather-bound hand out for Mara to take hold. His dark eyes gleamed in the light making them look paler than usual. His midnight hair had been pushed back, the ends curling slightly, a loose piece floating above his eyebrow. He was extraordinarily handsome.

"You look lovely," he said as he leaned down to match her height, his hand engulfing hers.

Mara managed a polite, "Thank you," before fixing herself at his side. The large gaping windows behind the altar let in rushes of cool air from the ocean. The cathedral sat directly on the cliff's edge; she could hear the waves crashing against the rocky shoreline below. The sun glimmered brightly off the water's surface, refracting back into the holy room, making Mara squint as she looked out onto the expanse of the sea. She decided she'd reward herself after getting through today with a long overdue perusal of the seaside. A grin stretched across her face, listening to the seagulls caw instead of the men around her.

The high priest nodded his head at the prince before turning to direct his words to the crowd which broke Mara out of her reverie, her smile fading, the sun dimming as a cloud slowly began to pass in front.

"Beloved devotees of Trana, reverent members of the Solar Sect, heed my words as we gather today, embarking the Sun Prince upon a sacred journey in honor of the sun goddess. A communion with the divine that shall illuminate our spirits and guide our paths. As the sun kisses our lands and the moon dances in the heavens, let us join hands and hearts in reverence. For in this hallowed sanctuary, under the watchful gaze of Trana, we shall partake in rites ancient and venerable." He paused as he took a moment to gaze upon the hushed congregation. "Children of the sun, followers of the light, our bloodline shall once again be strengthened with the holy binding of the Glass Princess, Maralena Faintree, with our reverent Sun Prince, Acastus Genoivre. Let us call upon Trana to weave their threads of dancing blood with purity and faith."

Mara held her breath, listening as the high priest addressed the crowd on his pulpit. He stood tall and resplendent contrary to his weeping features, clad in a dark-red robe, decorated with intricate golden embroidery, elevating his already powerful and divine status. The simple gemstones on his circlet glimmered with the colors of the celestial realms, entrancing Mara.

He outstretched a weathered hand, gesturing for Acastus to step forward into the expansive pool splayed on the dais made of ivory stone, its waters shallow, no deeper than her knee. The water shimmered in the rays that echoed through the high stained-glass windows. A gorgeous statue of Trana, a crane looking down on the gathered crowd made of the same stone as the pool, littered with wrapping vines and golden blooming flowers, separated the dichotomies of water. Acastus slid his shoes from his feet then stepped in, leaving the rest of his clothing on. His eyes shot up and met Mara's, his head gesturing to the other side. Mara straightened her back and made haste as she approached the opposite side of the pool, removing her slippers and looking hesitantly out at the crowd.

The priest seemed pleased, looking at the hefty tome he somehow held with ease in his ancient arms. "As the prince and princess succumb in our Hallowed Cistern, a mirror to the Veil, Trana will guide their souls, tethering them together for as long as they both shall live. Let the height of the Summer Solstice grant the sun bloodline its divine rite."

As if on cue, the sun gleamed dangerously bright, a beam streaking in to cast directly onto the statue of Trana in the center of the pool.

The priest glanced up expectantly, waiting for them to submerge completely in the holy water while the sun still shined at its peak. She looked at herself in the stoic water, her image distorted, but she could still see the sleepless nights in her eyes. She never thought about the reflection of water as a mirror until now.

Mara tentatively crouched in the cistern, her hands reaching out to steady herself as she sat. She didn't feel the ice-cold water, her skin still burning from all the attention, the chill welcoming rather than isolating. She took a deep breath, trying to settle some of her nerves.

Acastus smiled as he took a seat across from her. Mara's eyes intuitively flickered to Evrardin who was already intently watching her from behind the cistern, his hand on the hilt of his sword like it always was, scrutinizing her every move. She swallowed hard, her body raising with gooseflesh from the murmuring of the audience. Evrardin raised his hand discreetly and then tapped his temple once before dropping his hand. He moved so fast, she might have missed it if she wasn't paying attention. She bit her lip, trying to stop the astonished smile that pulled at her lips. Evrardin was attempting to comfort her; to remind her that this was all in her head. *She'd be fine.* All she had to do was exist.

She shouldn't have felt pacified at his one small gesture, yet her body loosened, finding comfort in the divine water. She refocused on the high priest, her ears ringing too loudly for her to hear his words. He leered over at her from his text. Acastus was staring at her too. *Shit*, he must have said something to her. "I'm sorry, what?"

The high priest didn't roll his eyes, but he might as well have. "*I said*, now you lay back in the Hallowed Cistern and let the sun goddess guide your very soul."

Acastus nodded before extending his body and sinking himself entirely in the water like a river serpent. Mara hesitated but followed suit. She could hear the high priest reciting some sort of prayer or incantation, but she couldn't make it out. All she could focus on was the fact that hundreds of people were scrutinizing her, expecting something marvelous to happen.

And what if nothing happened? Mara had never asked that. What if she screwed up and the bonding failed? What would the prince do then?

When she finally submerged herself all the way, all the murmurs were drenched by the water in her ears, and she was immediately suffocated by darkness.

Chapter Fifteen
Mara

The echoing breeze through the crown of willow trees startled Mara from the black swarm that had stolen her just moments before. She squinted, almost in pain, the wind howling and prickling when it brushed over her exposed legs.

The soft bed of moss sunk with her weight. She stared up at the dark sky through the thick tree branches, realizing she was sprawled out on her back. They created a daunting silhouette of ghostly arms. A light, milky fog haunted the woods around her, straining her eyes as she tried to focus on her surroundings. Mara's heart ramped up speed within her chest, threatening to break free from her constricting bones. All the blood in her body seemed to be rushing to her head. She turned over, putting all her weight on her hands, and heaved.

Her stomach emptied itself onto the sage green carpet. She wiped her mouth and then tried to stand. Mara attempted to rack her brain for Evrardin's words—for the words she read in the giant tome—to remember what to do.

"Okay. Okay. It's fine. You got this," she muttered to herself, her eyes widening in astonishment and fear, the indelibly dark woods around her making the air heavy on her skin. She expected the Veil to be... more luminous. Sunny, even. This felt like the opposite of where the sun goddess would reside.

She began moving, her toes wiggling in the furry moss, seeking out Acastus. He should be here somewhere, too, right? It was hard to see the forest floor with not even the light of the moon to guide her. Instead, an odd, unearthly glow in the distance created tiny specks of shadowed light.

Her toes struck something hard, and she stumbled forward. "Seven hells." She was beginning to question what she did wrong in a past life to get caught in this mess. This was not how she thought her marriage would go—albeit she knew it would be to someone she didn't love. That much she could predict.

"Acastus," she whispered. She knew he couldn't possibly hear her when she spoke so low, but she couldn't get herself to call to him any louder. The moaning of tree branches made gooseflesh rise along her arms. Mara's hand extended aimlessly in the dark, brushing against a tree's trunk, the bark rigid. How bizarre; she could feel the tree like it was right in front of her, but she knew her physical body was soaking in a pool of holy water.

Mara had never feared the dark or silly ghost stories—it used to irritate Azor that he couldn't scare her—but this was different. Mara wasn't standing in the halls she grew up in without sight, she was in a foreign forest—another realm—that looked nothing like the comforting lands she might have imagined for the gods to dwell. The gods had truly fled, not just escaping to the Veil, abandoning their people, leaving a wasteland in their tracks.

A sharp wind washed through her dress, shaking pieces of her hair loose from where it was tied on her head. A deep gurgling noise sounded from the tree and Mara stumbled backward, falling on her backside. She had grown to despise her rooms at Kairth, but she would give anything to be there right now.

The already dim light around her seemed to blacken, a chill running up her spine. She had been such a fool to confide in Evrardin. He had reassured her this was easy and nothing to worry about. She would put coin on the fact that he was back in the Old God's Cathedral with a smile on his face.

Her anger didn't have a chance to come to fruition, Acastus' form appearing before her. She almost sighed in relief. "Mara," he hummed, approaching her. There was something odd about his appearance, his eyes darkened, feathers falling from his coat.

"What do we do now?"

"Here, take my hand."

Mara bit her lip, letting Acastus' bare hand wrap around hers. Her eyebrows cinched, noticing the odd tint of Acastus' skin, realizing she had never seen his hands without gloves.

Before she could utter anything, the ground began to shake, the crumbling of sediment and stones echoing around her. She frantically turned, the ground coming to life, still clutching Acastus firmly. "What's happening?"

Mara adjusted her stance so she wouldn't topple over as the dirt beneath her rumbled. Then she saw it. She saw what was making such powerful breaks in the mud.

Shadowy hands sprouted like terrifying budding flowers, clawing and grappling with the dirt as bodies unburied themselves. Foul creatures that had shimmering skin like deep sea waters began to rise all around her. They were lanky, all bone and skin. Their fingers were sharp and pointed, unlike her blunt ones. They had hollowed faces, darkness pooling where their eyes and mouths should be, resembling a dark void trying to tempt you in.

A screech erupted from her throat as something silky gripped her ankle. She should have run when she had the chance.

She looked for Acastus, but his figure was gone—her hand holding nothing but air. She squealed, trying to kick her foot free, but when she did, another slimy hand caught her, its fingertips a dark blue. She tried to escape but more and more hands clawed at her. Their nails dug into her flesh, slicing it as easily as butter. Tears welled in her eyes, not just from the pain, but the sheer horror and shock.

The wild hands pawed at her, suffocating. She could feel them all over all at once, the slicked skin smearing against her as they grappled at her appendages, gripping her tightly.

She screamed as she tried to trudge forward, using all her strength to move her legs one step after another. The bodies became too much, and she collapsed onto her knees, feeling the life force slowly draining from her. She whimpered, the tears a steady flow as she leaned forward, the lanky hands never releasing her.

She closed her eyes, praying this would be quick and she wouldn't be left to suffer an agonizing death. Blood trickled from where their nails sliced her skin. Her breath got caught in her lungs as they pulled on her below her rib cage.

As she went to open her tear-rimmed eyes, she saw the halls of the Old God's Cathedral. She sat in the pool of water with a broken and battered choke of air, trying rapidly to catch her breath like a wounded animal. She heard the room gasp in unison. She must have sounded ravenous as she pulled air into her lungs.

"Princess," she heard from beside her, likely the high priest.

She shook as she stood on her feet, stepping out of the pool, her entire body trembling like a newborn deer. Her eyes found Acastus as he stepped out across from her. He didn't seem to be as upset as her, his clothes simply wet from the pool. Her hair now hung loosely against her shoulder blades. Her face had been tear-stained, her eyes red. Her dress was ripped and falling off her shoulders, calling into question her decency.

"Princess," the voice called again. With her mind slowly clearing, she knew it was the priest who called to her. He grabbed hold of her shoulders, speaking directly to her. "What happened?"

His grasp on her made her stomach overflow with bile. She tried to push him away but stumbled back. The prince stood and watched the chaos unfold, not aiding her. The other Sect members created a hushed whisper like a river coursing out around her. They all wanted to know what happened—as if she knew.

Overwhelmed, her eyes darted around the cathedral further, unable to focus on any one spot. She didn't know what she was looking for. Something that wasn't there. A familiar face to comfort her. Her mother's shoulder to bury her head into. Her brother. Her father.

The bodies in the room closed in on her and she never stopped trembling.

Suddenly, she was swept off the ground, a yelp escaping her. A soft fabric shrouded over her, and she immediately yanked it around her shoulders, covering her exposed skin.

Her arms locked around the neck of the grouchy man carrying her, his hair messy with curls and a scowl so ingrained in his features that she wasn't sure he would ever be able to smile without it causing pain.

Evrardin.

He marched out of the room, Mara tight in his arms. She watched as those on the dais surrounded the high priest and king, desperation on their faces as they tried to figure out why Mara came back battered and bloody.

The loud gossip of the crowd drifted away as Evrardin made

it into the hall and took heavy steps as he brought her back to her rooms. They were both silent the entire way.

The guard at her door had an incredulous expression as Evrardin approached with a very disheveled and distraught Mara in his arms. The guard opened the door for them, a nervous jilt in his movements as he watched the captain barge in and kick it closed behind him.

In unsure movements, Ev placed her down in front of her bed. She looked at him and he took a step back. The tears had dried but left messy marks down her cheeks. She clutched the fabric around her.

"What was that?" she asked, her voice raw. She wanted to be upset with him for lying, but the shock of it all was making her too astonished for anything more to say.

"Not sure," he said curtly. They looked at each other awkwardly for another beat. "I'll go get one of your handmaidens and—"

"No," she said quickly. He raised a brow. "I mean, I think I'd rather be alone right now."

He shook his head. "Princess," he began, "you'll need to be seen by the healer at least."

She swallowed hard, wincing as she did. "Will the prince..." she began. Her words failed her yet again. Was the prince going to show up to her chambers? Would he be mad? Would he question her? Would the king hound her as well? What did Mara do wrong?

She attempted to look down at her toes when his rough hand grabbed her chin, turning her head sideways. "You're bleeding," he remarked, staring at the side of her face where blood crusted with her hair. His body took up too much of her space, so close that she could feel the heat radiating from him. Mara's mouth opened but nothing came out. The spot on her chin where his fingertips lay burned with fire, a soothing feeling after the shockingly frigid air of the Veil. His thumb gently stroked her chin and her eyes fluttered shut, the gentle touch a stark contrast to the hands that had been violently prying.

Her breathing became erratic again, hyper-aware of his tight proximity and the way he intimately held her. He must have realized at the same time because he dropped his hand and stepped away.

Mara blinked at him.

"I'll send the healer in."

"Will you return?"

He cocked a brow, his face showing the most expression it had since she arrived. "Did you want me to?" His voice was quiet when he asked, confusion laced in his tone.

"No, I just—" She wanted to tell him that he had lied to her. She wanted to curse him out. To question him. To know why he carried her back to her room and covered her up when the prince seemed unfazed.

Something odd bloomed in his eyes—disappointment? "Yes. Unfortunately, I will be back." And he would. He had to escort her wherever she was to be summoned. Certainly, the king would want to have a word with her. "I can't escape you yet," he said with indignation.

When Evrardin left, Mara removed the faded fabric from around her shoulders and tossed it aside with shaky arms. She noticed the golden hardware at the head when it clinked against the hard floor. She studied it until it registered that it wasn't just some tapestry or altarpiece he grabbed to keep her modesty. It was his cloak that had been plastered to his back. Now it lay torn from where he had yanked it free, crumpled on Mara's floor.

Chapter Sixteen
Mara

Bent over, Mara slid on a pair of slippers as the door to her room opened. A familiar looming presence took a few steps in, catching his permanent grimace in her peripheral vision.

He kept good on his promise and finally returned, she'd give him that, but it was only to escort her to the council room.

Mara stood tall, turning to fully face him. Rings of worry underset her eyes, the rest of her bruising disguised by the full coverage dress she changed into.

Mara anxiously twirled the golden ring on her thumb, her hair intentionally worn down to cover the wound that now lined the side of her hairline. Her handmaidens cleaned the room around her in tense harmony, not wanting to look over at Mara. When they drew a bath for her to wash away the stinking water of the Hallowed Cistern and the sweat that doused her from the panic, she began to scream and fight against them without realizing. She knew the water that sat in her basin was not the same as the blessed and thick liquid that soaked her earlier, but her body reacted as if it was.

The tension in the room was palpable, but the captain didn't comment on it. Instead, he gestured for her to follow him as he walked back out of her chambers and led her down the many halls of Kairth.

After several beats of silence, Mara broke first. "You lied." Perhaps she was out of line for lashing out at him like this.

Evrardin refused to look at her.

"You lied," she said again but with more merit, something heavy lingering in her words.

"I didn't know," he mustered, his voice far away from her. "You act as if I ever showed you I could be trusted before this."

"Right," she mumbled under her breath. Her hand quickly wiped her face.

They walked the rest of the way in a discomfiting silence.

"Maralena, my dear!" the king practically sang as she entered the council room, his voice echoing down the vast hall.

The space was grand and tall, the ceiling rising so far above her head that she wasn't sure how they had managed to be painted in a way that told such intricate stories.

The king sat on his throne, its back carved with the sun, large slits in the chair in respect to sun rays, beams of light spiraling through the breaks from the large open windows behind him. Grand carved pillars lined the entire walk to the dais where the king was sitting, his son standing languidly beside him. A mulled-wine carpet with golden flecks shone in the abundant light that poured into the room. Up in the rafters, Mara could see almost every inch covered with a window, splayed open, and letting the cries of the birds and songs of the ocean seep into the room.

After the long trek, she curtsied before the king, bowing her head low, cringing at the soreness that traveled through her legs. The healer that came to her rooms earlier had promised to bring back a salve that would rid her of the deep-seated pain. She wondered if he had also meant the terrible visions that were continuously flashing in her mind, but she knew nothing could be that strong. Oddly, by the time he had arrived at her chambers, the visible cuts and marks had faded entirely, it was now just her joints that were sore and stiff.

"How are you, dear? Quite the scare you gave us back there." The king's voice was rich and smooth like his son's, but with an air of joviality that Acastus' lacked.

"Much better, Your Grace," she said softly, hoping the king wouldn't hear the ache in her words.

"The high priest has assured me that the bond had taken place, no need to fret on your part."

Mara almost scoffed, in awe that the king thought Mara was truly worried that the bond between her and the prince didn't succeed—a ritual the Glass Court was unfamiliar with. She couldn't wrap her head around this. Everyone seemed to be acting like what had happened earlier was completely normal now. Just a small blip.

"I'm... pleased to hear," she muttered.

The king smiled at her. "It's always hard when varying houses attempt to bond together. It had been centuries since someone of the Glass Court bonded with someone of the Sun. Apologies for your discomfort, Princess." He looked over at his son.

When Cas noticed his father's curious glare, he rushed to Mara's side, startling her. His leather-bound hands grabbed her bare ones as he looked at her longingly. "My love, how terrified I was. I am so glad you're okay."

Mara gulped at his sudden shift. His words seemed sincere on the surface, but the meat of them lacked any sort of genuineness. If he was genuinely concerned, she thought he might have followed her to her chambers after the ordeal. She couldn't help but crave that comfort in someone caring for her.

One of his hands released hers and moved to tuck a stray hair behind her ear. Mara prickled at the contact even though no skin of his touched her own. Her lips parted as he bent down close to her, his eyes taking in every inch of her face. "I suspect Hermes has taken good care of you," he said so quietly only she could hear.

Mara gave a timid nod, recalling back to the healer who had been patient with her as he examined every inch of her body. "He assured me he'll retrieve a stronger salve for the lingering aches."

Cas' eyebrow raised, the wicked thoughts brewing visibly in his eyes. "Shall you require assistance with that?"

Mara's cheeks warmed, knowing they were undoubtedly turning pink.

Cas smiled, satisfied with the reaction he got from her. He leaned forward and kissed her forehead before releasing her and ascending the steps toward his father. "Hermes is the best healer in the eight kingdoms; I have no doubt you'll be feeling well enough for tonight's summer masquerade. Ready for dances and revels." He looked down at her as he reached the top of the dais. "Maybe even more than that. It's what we all need after such an awful event."

She turned her gaze to Evrardin who stood slightly farther back. His jaw tightened, his eyes refusing to meet her own. He looked angry. Likely upset by the fact that the prince was being so kind to her, even if only an act.

"Now that my father knows you're all right, I wanted to speak with you, sweet one." Cas held out a hand, waiting as Mara climbed the stairs to place hers in his palm. He escorted her out behind the throne, slipping into a narrow hall that poured into the back gardens, the rest of the court carrying on their discussion without their presence.

The chill left her skin as the sun caressed her. Streamers and flags decorated the gardens, the golden color of Solstrale, with large suns embroidered into the cloth. The servants of the castle scattered the yard, hustling in and out of the building, preparing for the masquerade.

Mara had been excited for a chance to celebrate the events in the heart of Kairth, the city of the sun goddess. And now, she wanted nothing more than to curl up in her room—which didn't feel like her room at all—and read. The thought that she finally had a chance to get in some overdue words with the prince rattled her with buzzing adrenaline.

"Lovely, isn't it?" he asked her, his voice as soft as a cloud while he gazed at the gardens, Mara's arm hooked with his.

"It's beautiful," Mara said truthfully. Servants darted by, narrowly avoiding them as Cas began to walk her on the tanned dirt path.

"My Prince," Mara began. Acastus' eyes stayed glazed over as he admired the decor for tonight's celebrations. "I... Well, I'm not sure if..." Her throat began to close. She knew that deep down, whatever was going on with the prince, she was just a fly caught in his web. She was merely a means to an end. And she had no place to question what that end might be. Why couldn't she spew whatever she was thinking as she did with Evrardin?

Cas shifted to study her while she choked on her words. "Mara." His voice sported an air of concern.

Mara met his silver eyes, color immediately flushing her cheeks from the way he looked at her: like she mattered to him. She cursed herself at her irrational thoughts. He clearly held no true fondness for her—he made that much clear in the Old God's Cathedral.

She took a breath. "Why am I here?"

"In the gardens? I thought you privy to the abundance of blooming flora."

She shook her head, looking back at her feet as they walked, a cool breeze shifting her dress. "In Kairth, I mean. Why did you compete for my hand? Truly."

The prince sighed. "So, I take it you're not convinced your stunning beauty won me over? Made me fall to my knees in desperation." His lips tipped up with a wistful smile.

She shook her head.

"I'm sure you've noticed the dilapidated state of the castle."

Mara glanced at him.

"Affairs amongst the Sun Court and the rest of the seven kingdoms have been strained for years. Ever since the Fae King stripped us of so much, taking back gifts they had no right withdrawing." He pushed his hair back in uncertainty. "The fae who built this castle from the ground up have long forgotten to uphold their end of our treaty, letting their enchantments fade and the people of Kairth are suffering for it. My father chooses to do nothing. He thinks constant repairs will work against fae magick. Without Trana to let her powers travel through the Sun Court, I fear we will succumb to the despair of war and famine. The once fertile lands grow dry. Children are dying. Women aren't able to conceive. Solstrale is being shunned by all the northern kingdoms. They chose Faerie over us.

"Though, I can't really blame them. My father and grandfather have tricked and played the fae as fools in their reign. And now their people are reaping their consequences."

Mara desperately wanted to view Cas in a new light as he talked about the mistreatment of his people—but she found it difficult.

"And where do I come in?"

"You, my dear princess"—Cas pulled her closer to him in an act of endearment—"are what allowed me to be named Crown

Prince. My father is no longer fit to rule, but he refused to name me his heir without a wife."

She wasn't sure why she felt a pang of hurt at his words "But why *me*? Out of all the ladies you could have chosen. Wouldn't someone from the Faelands have been a better choice? Tying your kingdoms together."

"An itch for politics?" he teased, not ridiculing her for her naive thought about marriage, but earnestly jesting like one would do with a friend. "Why, I needed a glassfairer. If I'm to restore Trana's connection with our court, I'll need someone who can go between the realms."

Mara tripped on nothing, stumbling forward, the only thing keeping her upright was Cas' grip on her.

"B-But I-I can't glassfaire. There hasn't been someone with that ability in the Glass Court in ages," Mara stuttered, a mirthless laugh escaping at the end of her sentence in disbelief.

Cas' eyes remained soft as he smirked at her. "I know that's how your mother died, Princess. Your father may have hidden the truth from everyone else, but I am not so easily fooled. And I'd appreciate it if we skipped this"—he gestured a hand between their bodies—"back-and-forth. Do not lie to me. The art may have dwindled in your muddy bloodline, but with you bonded to the sun, your magick should blossom, unlocking any deep-rooted prowess you might possess."

Mara's face went hot, tears pricking the back of her eyes. She hadn't been forced to talk about her mother's death since it happened. She wanted to push the memories down, but images of her mother doused in blood, lying lifelessly on her chamber floor, flashed before her.

The rippling scream she had let out that day ghosted around her, making her reach up and place a hand on the front of her neck. She tried to control her breathing and shut out the image of a tiny Maralena running into her mother's chambers, calling out for her, excited to show Mother something as silly as how she had braided her hair herself that day. Her mother knew better than to glassfaire with the ability so subdued within the Glass Court.

"I... I don't know how. I—I never tried."

Cas stopped before a bush of newly planted camellias and reached a hand to delicately brush the deep petals. "I have no doubt Khonsu runs through your veins. I'm certain you'll learn how, given the chance to practice. It's in your blood, Princess."

Mara's throat closed in. She shut her eyes and took a steady breath. None of the gods had been seen for centuries. Konshu's gift of travel had dwindled just as all the other courts across the kingdoms' proficiencies had.

When she opened her eyes, Cas faced her and extended the flower. Mara tentatively took it from him, their fingers brushing, the coolness of his leather glove sending a chill through her arm.

"Practice?"

He hummed, his hands clasping behind his back as he began to walk again, Mara hurrying to follow in pursuit.

"I've been told you frequent Kairth's library."

Mara nodded, though Cas didn't look at her to see it.

"There are plenty of texts in there involving magick from all the kingdoms, including yours."

Yours. Acastus still referred to Wrens Reach as her home. Not Solstrale.

"And you want me to...to try and..."

Cas made a noise in his throat as if getting irritated with her passive demeanor. "To figure out how to glassfaire. Yes. I suspect you'll figure it out by our nuptials."

"But that's only a fortnight from now!" Mara's words burst out of her before she could stop and think.

Cas smiled like he enjoyed it when something lit inside her. However, she knew this game all too well—he wouldn't like it if that spark grew to a raging flame. "I believe in you," he said toward her as they rounded back to the entrance.

Mara could feel the threat laced in his speech. The way his eyes narrowed in on her as if challenging her to talk back. The switch between genuine compassion to bitterness had given her whiplash.

"And those hands in the Veil," she began.

"You've heard the stories of the lost Glass People," he said flatly. She nodded. "You lingered too long on their soil, within the Veil. And they wanted you out."

She hadn't thought it was true, that the stories her mother would tell her about glassfairers lost in the Veil turning to evil entities were just that, *stories.*

Acastus spun to face her, his guards behind him, waiting. "I'll see you at the masquerade tonight." He took her hand in his and placed a kiss on the back of it. "That is, if you can uncover me," he said with a cheeky smirk.

The blood had drained from Mara's face, unable to appease the guards by acting with modest propriety. She let them lead her back to her room where a pot of the salve Hermes had promised sat on her nightstand.

Chapter Seventeen
Mara

The stronger salve had worked wonders.

Mara lay stretched out on her bed in nothing but an underdress, dreading putting on her outfit for the masquerade.

Before coming to Kairth, the idea of a masquerade would have invigorated her. A fun night to dance and join in the revels with all the people of the court. But tonight, she wanted to lay in her bed and sulk. To ponder why this was all happening to her. Maybe it was karma for the boy she tripped when she was ten. Or maybe it was as penance for her father's sins. Or perhaps, even for never partaking much in politics, pretending outside struggles didn't pertain to her. As odd as it sounded, she knew she had to attend the masquerade, or she'd be just another spoiled noble who disregarded the intricate political workings that went into these affairs.

When Mara finally shifted through her wardrobe, she chose an outfit that represented how she felt inside. She had let her handmaidens fix her hair and dress her wounds, letting them assist slipping the dress on and tightening the bodice.

She settled on a black gown. It lacked underlayers so it sat more flush against her body, molding to her. It had long sleeves decorated in deep burgundy embroidery. The waist cinched with a red sun emblem. The skirt of the dress fell to a red gradient, the very tips of it glimmering like charring coals as she moved. She wore a golden circlet on her head with a red gem in the center and a circlet around her neck that resembled a winding vine, the gilded leaves giving off the faintest orange hue. She knew other guests would be wearing the brighter colors of summer, shorter and more breathable gowns and tunics.

She stared at herself in the mirror. She still felt she was paying homage to the sun goddess, her dress dark but intertwined with red, gold, and orange. She was the fire at the heart of the sun rather than the golden sun rays that cast light on these lands.

Her fingers stroked the mirror, and she subtly put more pressure on the reflective glass stupidly thinking about her fingers slipping through. The thought of her mother getting caught in a slice of mirrors had her lightheaded. Even if she figured out how to glassfaire, there was no guarantee her humors would be strong enough to let her travel safely. And how was she to do that without anyone experienced in the craft to help? Of course, she had books, but they could only teach so much. And why did Acastus want her gift?

She twirled the golden ring on her index finger in nerves as one of her handmaidens finished tightening her dress. While the pain had seriously subsided thanks to Hermes, she still wore the memories from the ceremony like a tattered veil.

She clutched her eyes shut in a moment of terror, remembering the sliminess of the hands that gripped her. The way their overgrown nails dug into her soft skin.

Her eyes sprung open when something brushed against her

face. Her handmaiden was tying her mask on. It was a deep burgundy, appearing black, and flickered off in points like a cat's eye. "Still no letters?" Mara asked.

Ternia's eyes fell, her hands dropping to her side and away from Mara's face. "Afraid not, Princess."

Mara sucked in a rapid breath.

"I'm sure your family means to write. Just preoccupied with some overextended political affairs."

Mara nodded, telling herself Ternia was right. She quickly wiped the tears that dared to tread down her cheeks. The absence of her father—her brother, her friend—threatened to consume her. Her hands began to shake. Mara grabbed her hand, holding it tight against her dress to still it, smiling at Ternia. "You're probably right."

When Ternia stepped around her to open the door, Mara turned to face her mirror, her fingers clenching her dress.

"Are you ready, Princess?" the guard had asked from behind her.

Tonight was all about fun. It was a ceremony of new beginnings, lust, and fertility in honor of the sun goddess. The true essence and beginning of summer. All she had to do was attend and pretend to be enjoying herself. To eat a bit, have some wine. Dance. Then she could excuse herself saying she was tired, surely they would understand given the day she had.

She pushed the thoughts of Wrens Reach out of her mind and gave a meek nod, taking a deep breath and following behind the guard.

She half expected Evrardin to be the one to escort her, but it seemed the prince required his service tonight. He had more important business than supervising her.

When Mara entered the gardens, they were even more extravagantly decorated than she had seen earlier. The bushes seemed to glow with tiny suns, and as she grew closer, she could spot the tiny flickering flameflies that twinkled amongst the leaves. The streamers that billowed across the open air reflected the golden light from the setting sun. The stone path she tentatively walked down was lined with fences of gold flora, vines creeping up and covering the white wood almost entirely. Commotion stirred in the distance; a red tent propped for festivities. The courtiers around her all donned outrageous masks, their outfits reflecting some sense of a summer scene, the marvelous hues blinding her as she scanned the crowd.

She spotted the prince beyond the dancing center. He was easy to pick out, his outfit more opulent than anyone else's. He had on a white and gold dress shirt—a jarring sight when she had only ever seen him in black—his crown gilded and darting outward like the sharp points of the sun. Jewelry hung from one of his ears, glimmering in the lights from the hundreds of melted candles illuminating the gardens. The darkness of his hair was a sharp contrast to the yellow shimmer of his mask. He looked breathtaking.

She slowly entered the revel, watching as the prince threw his head back in laughter, making the women he was entertaining blush wildly under their masks.

She was surprised when she spotted Lord Alfson hovering off behind the prince not even bothering to dress for the occasion, adorned in his usual burlap robe. He seemed anxious as he watched the prince down a goblet of dark wine.

The prince leaned forward, whispering something in a redheaded girl's ear, her face turning the color to match her unruly hair. Mara didn't know why, but something akin to envy bubbled in her stomach.

She finally tore her eyes away from her future husband and rounded a delphinium bush, taking in the flower's scent as she passed. She bumped into a stranger, her eyes coming up to take in the figure of a man in an all-orange outfit, a tulle of yellow cascading off his shoulders.

"Apologies, Princess," the man spoke.

Mara squinted. It was difficult to make out who was who when everyone had these ridiculous masks on.

When the man noticed her staring, he answered her thoughts. "Lord Cofsi," he reminded.

"My apologies, Lord Cofsi. It seems my mind struggles to recognize you. Nor did I know you were in Kairth."

"I suppose it's rather difficult to recognize anyone under these conditions." He gave her a tight smile, ignoring her latter statement. "I have come for the solstice as well as a few personal matters that need straightening. How are you liking it—in Solstrale?"

Mara cleared her throat. "It's lovely," she forced out. She technically wasn't lying. Everything about Solstrale had been beautiful—apart from the decrepit scars of the city. The only thing stopping her from attempting to enjoy herself was being alone, under constant watch.

As if Lord Cofsi could sense her hesitation, he gave a small chuckle. "Been rather tense in the Red Court these last few years. I can't imagine how it must feel to be a foreigner swept into the king's mess."

The use of the epithet *Red* Court made her pick at her nails uncomfortably. When the War of Lyres happened so many centuries ago, it left Kairth's beaches painted red, a stained symbol of their treachery. Only those opposed to Solstrale referred to the Sun Court in such an insulting manner. Mara prayed no one was eavesdropping as he spoke the treasonous words in the heart of the court.

The lord shifted from his two feet, adjusting his mask. "I've always wondered how women did it. Got swept off by some man they didn't know to a land they've never seen, and somehow managed to keep the facade of happiness."

Mara's eyes widened. The breath was stolen straight from her throat. Lord Cofsi spoke the truth, but she had never heard it offered from a man so easily. A sudden wave of easiness coursed through her knowing he understood—at least, he logically did.

"The prince and king have been so kind to me, welcoming me into their home. And Solstrale is quite beautiful—"

"You don't have to be coy with me, Princess. I'm not asking you to take a political stance, just that *if* that is how you feel, know that the Dusk Court has always been a loyal friend to the king in Wrens Reach. And that extends to you, of course."

Mara gave him a meek nod, the neckline of her dress suddenly becoming uncomfortably itchy. "You honor me."

He got closer to her and spoke in a hushed tone. "If you do not wish to go forward with your betrothal to Prince Acastus, do let me know. I'd be more than willing to work something out for you."

She was stunned by what to say next. How does one respond to something so brazen? And he didn't seem to care if people around him heard, but she supposed the guests were already inebriated and the cacophony of voices made it difficult to hear your own conversation, let alone someone else's.

"B-But, why?"

"Why would I help you?" he asked.

Mara nodded.

Lord Cofsi went to open his mouth when Lord Alfson appeared at his side like a shadow.

"Good evening, Princess." He turned and scowled. "Lord Cofsi."

"Yes, always a good evening when you make an appearance, Eldric."

Mara tried to stifle her smile at the sarcasm that dripped off Lord Cofsi's tongue.

Lord Cofsi looked back at Mara, scooping her hand into his, and placed a soft kiss on the back of it. "Princess. 'Til next time," he mumbled quietly. Mara gawked at him as he disappeared into the bustling crowd of sunflowers and roses.

"I hope he wasn't causing a disturbance. Cofsi is known to be... difficult to converse with," Lord Alfson spoke beside her.

She jumped, having already forgotten he was by her side. On the contrary, she found his company alluring, wishing to hear more of his bold words. "No. No, he was just welcoming me to Solstrale."

Lord Alfson gave a hesitant nod.

Before he could say more, Mara excused herself and shuffled over to the large buffet table. Even though she wasn't hungry, she grabbed a large puff of sweet bread and shoved it in her mouth, her mind wandering to the previous conversation. Why would Lord Cofsi offer to help her? He barely knew her.

She knew he was fond of her father, the entirety of The Shadowed Isles respected him after he gave his support when he was first crowned king, sending off half of Wrens Reach's military to fight by their side as creatures from the Veil threatened to break the bridge between our worlds. The Shadowed Isles, of course, having stronger connections to the Veil due to their location in Junefell. They tended to act as the shepherds between realms as they reigned dark magick from the Veil.

Maybe he also knew about Mara's possible ability to glass-faire. If the prince knew, it was certainly an idea to be entertained that other kingdoms knew as well.

Mara grimaced as she slowly chewed her bread, her eyes scanning the feverish crowd, their bodies loose as they spun and swayed to the music.

Her eyes landed on Prince Acastus once again, hard to look anywhere else, his outfit otherworldly as an aura in every sense of the word glowed off his person. He looked like true royalty. Like he belonged to the Sun Court. Like he ruled it.

Mara watched as a pretty woman—not the redhead from earlier—stood between his outstretched legs while he leaned back against a pillar. Her mask did nothing to hide her flirty glances, her eyelashes batting as she looked at him and giggled. Prince Acastus modeled a matching grin, his cheeks pinking from all the wine he had already consumed so early into the night.

Mara's hands gripped the bread tightly in her palms as the woman got on the tips of her toes and whispered in the prince's ear. The prince caught her by the throat as she pulled away, stopping her, a wicked smile on his lips. He leaned forward and whispered something back.

Mara turned away with a fierce blush across her cheeks.

She knew this wasn't a marriage of love. It wasn't even a marriage of *like*. But she didn't think the prince would embarrass her like this. He was unabashedly letting women flirt with him, the woman's body pressed up against his own. And he seemed to like it.

Without thinking, her feet stormed out of the grand garden, down the corridor of bushes, and into an alcove hidden against the castle. The bread in her hand had crumbled between her fingers and scattered a trail on the ground. She could hear giggling up ahead as a couple tripped over one another leading out into the courtyard.

A teardrop blurred her vision before sliding from her face and into her lap as she sat on a stone bench and removed her mask. She had no idea when she had begun crying. She quickly wiped her tears, cursing herself for being so gentle-minded.

So many other women went through this—Lord Cofsi was right. It was a lady's duty to marry. So many have done it before her and so many will do it after. She needed to get a handle on her emotions. She needed to stop every small thing from exacerbating the wound.

She felt a fool.

"All reveled out?" a familiar voice said from beside her.

Mara blinked away her tears as quickly as she could before she frowned at the overtly tall and brooding man. His eyes widened in momentary disbelief, likely trying to make sense of her weeping face.

"The festivities not entertaining enough for you, Princess? Rather be reading your dusty old books alone in your rooms?"

Evrardin's hair had been pulled back, the underneath circling against his neck, a few strands cascading against the side of his face. He didn't wear a mask nor an elegant summer outfit. Though she didn't expect him to, being the captain of the guard didn't seem to require him to partake in such rituals.

"The festivities suit me just fine." She would have been glad for anybody else's company, even the wretched lady smothered in Cas' lap.

"Then why am I finding you sulking out here? Seems you have developed a pattern of wandering off during merriments."

Mara felt her face turn red in frustration. "Honestly, Evrardin, it does not matter. Can't you just let me wallow in peace?" The anger in her voice was palpable. "Don't try and pretend like you're enjoying yourself. You'd rather be somewhere else, too."

"Always such a pleasure to be around," he said mockingly. He turned to leave her.

"And you know that's what I so desperately crave!" She

clapped her hands together in irritation. "I wish nothing more than to be pliant and easy company for you."

He faced her again, taking a few steps into her space. "Always so bloody sorry for yourself."

"What is that supposed to mean?" she asked, standing to get more level with him, though he still loomed a good head above her.

"Is this what you want?" he asked, the fury she felt lacking in his tone. "To call you a spoiled princess? Tell you how I'm surprised you're not tired from being such a pain in the ass all the time? To call you miserable to be around?"

She scoffed. "Oh, because you're much more engaging company. My mistake."

He almost laughed, shaking his head. He opened his mouth after stealing a breath, like this was tiring for him. "I'm the Captain of the Royal Guard—I'm not supposed to be entertaining." He raised his brows at her to continue.

Mara chuckled mirthlessly, the sound more of a scoff than anything. "And I'm assuming then you mean it's my place to be the pretty princess who just sits in the corner and does what she's told? To be a fun doll for others to play with? Is that my duty, Evrardin? Just a silly form of entertainment for you *men*."

Her eyes darkened in rage like she never felt before—the promises from her father, the kind words from Acastus, the face of her brother and closest friend as she left, all came rushing into her at such force. Her chest constricted in breathlessness. Her world had completely flipped in a matter of days. Everything she once knew had shifted.

And now, some godforsaken something-like-that of a knight lectured her on why she had to pretend like she wasn't fuming beneath the surface. That she couldn't weep when she felt sorrow. That she couldn't let anyone know her struggles to accept her life because then that made her ungrateful. It made her oblivious to the suffering of others. It made her shallow. Vain. It made her cold-hearted to show her naive desire for a different life. Even if she failed to accept her future—one all women seemed destined to—she had to pretend she was strong; brave enough to push through this like all the Glass Princesses before her.

And she certainly was failing. Even the simplest thing she couldn't do right, like hold her future husband's interest. Any other princess could have been enough entertainment for him, at least for more than a few measly days. He would rather have random men and women all over him than to even try and pretend to be faithful to her. Maybe she truly was that dreadful to be around.

Evrardin eyed her curiously, not mirroring the same anger she felt. "I fear that is not what is truly bothering you."

Mara's brows scrunched together, her teeth grinding. Against all efforts, tears began rolling down her cheeks. And once they began, they didn't show signs of stopping. She quickly whirled away from Evrardin, trying her best to break the flow. "How many times must we exhaust this feud?" she said softly.

"As many times as it takes."

Mara cleared her vision before glancing over her shoulder at him, confused.

Evrardin shifted his stance. "If this is how you get your anger out, fine. Let it be under the guise of naivety and privilege."

A little pang of warmth began to fill her chest. She wiped away the remaining salt from her face, hesitating to make eye contact with him. "It's so stupid. Gods, I'm so stupid." She shook her head harder this time.

"Then what?" he asked.

"The prince, he..." She laughed, finally looking into his dark brown eyes. "I know this arrangement between us has nothing to do with love. And I don't expect him to act as if it does. But at least… I mean, I thought he'd at least do me the kindness of pretending to honor our betrothal."

And maybe it wasn't all about Acastus' readiness to accept the ogling women. Maybe it was about the loneliness creeping around her. Maybe she was envious the prince was so well-liked, always in the company of others. Never alone.

He always seemed to have people fawning all over him. Even now, engaged, he didn't let that stop him from having the company of beautiful men and women. Evrardin's fist clenched, his nails digging into the pommel of his sword.

The air felt sorely awkward around them.

She immediately regretted her confession, her vulnerability shown brighter than ever today. Perhaps she should have continued to argue about how spoiled she was, something neither of them seemed to have the energy to really care about any longer.

"Dance with me?" he asked abruptly.

Mara laughed loudly, her eyes turning upward. "What?"

"Acastus has never had anything he wanted taken away from him. Without fail, he's made a servant of everyone around him. So fucking willingly too." His last words were spoken with such disgust that Mara could almost taste the repugnance. He took a breath, his eyes shifting away from her briefly as if holding eye contact was too much. "So, I'll dance with you. He'll notice."

"How do you know he'd care? He hasn't even sought me out yet tonight."

He attempted to straighten his spine. "He will," he insisted again. She figured he might be right—he did know Acastus far better than her.

Mara gulped at his seriousness, wondering if he had ever smiled in his life. She knew he must have, realistically, and a weird burst of butterflies filled her chest when she imagined a small Evrardin, running around and laughing with the other children.

She nodded, looking at him through wet eyelashes. She pulled on her mask to disguise the tears that marked her face, but before they moved from the alcove, he reached out and took the mask. "Don't hide behind it."

"But isn't that the whole point of a masquerade?" she challenged.

"Do you see me wearing one?"

"That's only because you prefer being uptight."

He hesitantly offered her his elbow, ignoring her comments. She hesitated, but accepted defeat and interlocked their arms, letting him drag her back out into the open gardens, slipping her mask into one of the hidden pockets amidst the ruffles of her dress. It felt odd, and yet, natural—like this wasn't the first time he had taken a woman onto the dance floor.

"Tell me, did you make me forsake my mask so the guests could see the tears staining my face?"

He didn't look at her as he spoke, leading her into the throng of moving bodies. "Such a cynical view you have of me." A beat of silence. "I wanted to see your reaction when I swept you off your feet."

Mara stifled a laugh. "Do you even know how to dance?"

He glared at her.

When he dropped her arm, he just as quickly gathered one of her hands in his and rested the other on her hip. Mara felt a jolt shoot through her from the warmth of his hand—especially the one radiating intensely on her side.

He immediately began to spin her around on the cobblestones surrounded by sparkling spireas, Mara's mouth hanging open in incredulous surprise.

Her feet hurried to keep up as he swayed her, and she looked down to try and find her footing. When she resolved to glaring at him, she could've sworn she saw a hint of a smile cross Evrardin's face.

"This is...rather unexpected," she mustered. The shock had snuffed all the snarky remarks from her.

He looked blatantly happy with himself for making her state the obvious. "Contrary to your omniscient thoughts, there's a lot you don't know about me, Princess."

She rolled her eyes, giving him the sour face of a petulant child.

"There she is," he muttered under his breath.

Mara's face went feverish, her spit threatening to choke her. They twirled in silence for a few moments as they fell into a simple pattern until Mara spoke. "This is so idiotic. What a dimwitted plan. I don't even want him to be jealous."

"No?"

"No. I"—she shook her head, her curls softly bouncing across her shoulders and down her back—"I think I just felt..."

"Betrayed?" He spoke like he understood that feeling.

She glanced at him, her eyes soft as she scanned his face. It felt uncanny to cooperate so effortlessly with Evrardin. Almost like they were friends. "You know, you're not so insufferable when you're not talking to me like I'm the most dreadful companion in all the eight kingdoms."

"Companions now, are we?"

"Well, what would you call two people forced to spend far too much time with one another if not that?"

"Adversarial correspondents, perhaps. Hostages. Prisoner and warden."

"See, you're even cracking jokes. *Not so insufferable,*" she reiterated with a mischievous grin.

His hand shifted on her hip without thought as he adjusted his grip and Mara's heart skipped. It was only then she truly began to take in how close in proximity they were to one another.

Her front was pressed flush against his own, one of their hands interlocked and his other far too low on her waist. If she focused, surely she could count the beats to his heart. As she scanned his face, she noticed scars under his beard, one that disappeared into his hairline, and one that bisected his upper lip.

Moving couples danced around them, all shadowed by their masks, unidentifiable as they waltzed in a blur. It almost felt freeing for her and Evrardin to be the only two without something to cover their faces. Like no one else here was real, just a minor snippet in her fairy tale, Mara and Evrardin stealing the title of the story.

"S'much easier to be pleasant when you're not getting pissed at every little trifle."

"You take me for someone just being inconvenienced? I didn't ask for this. Any of it," she huffed. "I didn't want to be taken away from my home. To come here and be left to sit languidly in my room. To be ridiculed by the Red Court," she spat, "and an awfully irritating captain. To be used for some long-forgotten ability of my house.

Before he had room to ask, she began to ramble, subconsciously trying to distract from her previous comment. "It's painful, you know? I suppose it's never crossed your mind, and you likely think it trivial, but I'm now destined for a life without love. That isn't exactly the most comforting prophecy. My scripture doesn't include another person. Not really."

His eyes danced between her own, his footsteps coming to a halt as he listened to her. His voice was soft as he spoke, and it sent a chill down her spine. "That doesn't have to be your augury."

"And I suppose that means you know what my future holds?"

"Maybe you were destined to be my downfall. My ruination." She sucked in a breath at
    his words. "You sure act like it."

An alluring shiver coursed through her as they stood unmoving amid dancers swarming around them. His eyes were locked with hers, his cruel words sounding so holy as if they were words of comfort. He gazed at her like she was enthralling him, forcing his thoughts to tumble out of his mouth without any say of his own.

"You could still fall in love with the prince," he added.

Mara's mouth went dry. She swallowed with much difficulty before speaking. "And you think it likely he would fall back?" Evrardin gave her a blank stare. "You think that's better than never loving at all? To love someone who can never return those feelings?"

He shook his head. "I don't know."

Mara's eyebrows narrowed as they stood stoic, their hands still clasped together, Evrardin's hand resting idly on her waist.

"You don't know what?" she asked quietly.

"I don't know which is better."

She let a sigh escape her. Evrardin looked at her for a moment longer before dropping his hands. On their journey to settle at his side, something seemed to possess him, his fingers floating gently to the necklace that hung around Mara's neck. His fingertips brushed it so gently that if Mara wasn't so overtly focused on every sense she was experiencing, she wouldn't have even known his skin made contact.

He touched the bleeding-heart jewel, and she thought back to the day Acastus proffered it to her in Wrens Reach.

She belonged to Acastus.

Mara watched him with steady eyes, appraising the roughness of his face and the way his rugged features only made him more handsome. Her breath caught in her throat when she accepted her attraction toward him. Evrardin's eyes flickered up her chest and to her own in response. She could see the terror that pierced through him as he realized what he was doing and to whom.

"Might I steal my soon-to-be wife?" a slightly slurred voice said from behind them.

Mara and Evrardin startled, pulling away from one another simultaneously like a naughty child might do when caught red-handed. She struggled to tear her eyes away from Evrardin and look at the handsome prince, clearly drunk off wine.

"Your mask," he muttered, his finger coming up to trace around her eyes.

"Oh, I must have forgotten to put it back on." Mara's voice came out a mere squeak, embarrassed to be given the prince's full attention.

"Hm," he tsked, looking over at the captain. He narrowed his eyes at him before looking back at Mara. "Let us revel in the Summer Solstice!" he said in mock joy, gaining cheers from those around him.

Mara nodded and took his outstretched leather-clad hand. As the prince went to lead her away, Evrardin leaned in, speaking in a hushed tone so only she could hear. "Told you it would work."

She turned her head and stared at him as she was swept away. She wasn't sure why, but neither of them seemed happy about his plan working.

For Mara, maybe she didn't actually want to spend time with the forlorn prince. And for Evrardin, maybe he didn't like the way Acastus' hands were where his had just rested.

After letting the prince spin her in sloppy circles, she looked back to where Evrardin had stood and spotted nothing but the reminiscent feeling of his presence. In fact, she didn't see him for the rest of the night.

Chapter Eighteen
Evrardin

The damp clicks of boots on wet stone echoed in Evrardin's ear. He glanced up at the door, briefly stealing his attention from his work.

"It's late m'boy," Crowrot stated as he entered the room. He removed his gloves covered in congealing blood and placed them on the wooden counter.

"I'm aware," Ev grunted out, looking back down at the body he was dissecting.

"Thought that revel was t'night. The prince not makin' you follow him 'round like a damn work mule for once?"

Evrardin squeezed his eyes shut. "Did you just come here to hound me?"

Crowrot raised a brow, his shaggy hair slipping out from beneath his hat. His wrinkled hands rested on the surgery table across from Evrardin. "I'know you've always been a grumpy sonofabitch, but what has gotten into ya as of late?"

Evrardin threw his macabre instruments down on the table.

One of the small knives he was using as a scalpel bounced and fell to the ground.

"Don't you give a shit that we're trapped here? That we can't leave even if we wanted to?!" he shouted.

"Ev..."

"No, don't try and make it seem like I'm losing my fucking mind." His hands came up in exasperation. "This place is a living hell. A soul-sucking prison. And I'm forced to kiss the ground the prince walks on, making sure not to miss a single footstep—I have to act like everything's fine? That I'm not fucking furious every waking moment of my day? Am I supposed to just let that shit go, Rot?"

Crowrot gave him a sympathetic look. He knew that Evrardin was constantly on edge—spiteful, even—because of his less-than-fortunate circumstances. Crowrot came to terms with his place at Kairth, but Evrardin never did.

"I know. I know how shit this all is." Crowrot's voice was rocky as he spoke, his throat scarred from all the shouting and cries of pain it had endured. "But I know you, boy. There's somethin' more. What aren't ya tellin' me?"

Evrardin's eyes darted away from Crowrot and he pushed himself from the table to begin sifting through the illuminated vials behind him, the motley glasses clinking together.

"Are ya not able t'tell me?" Crowrot had a bit more sympathy wrapped in his question.

Ev sighed, gripping the edge of the counter, and stared up above him like he might be praying to a god for patience. "It's not just me anymore. Not just us."

"What'd ya mean?"

Crowrot began scooping the organs and chunks of flesh that had fallen onto the ground from Ev's hasty work and dropped them into slop buckets, the sound vulgar and rancid.

"His plans don't involve just me anymore. I'm not the only one pinned under Cas' blade."

Crowrot hummed a sound in acknowledgment. "The princess," he muttered, groaning as he stood up.

Ev didn't respond, grabbing an already stained rag to wipe off the tables.

"Well, I'll be damned." Crowrot took a whiff of the bucket now filled with entrails. "It turns out you do have a heart. I was startin' t'think yous was like one of these hallowed souls," he said, gesturing to the dead, heartless body on the table.

Evrardin scoffed to hide his smirk. "Go to hell."

Crowrot's crunching laugh echoed in the small chamber. "We established we're already there, boy."

Evrardin grumbled something unintelligible as he hooked his hands around the gutted body before him. He dragged it off the table, its feet slamming against the cobblestone floor, and pulled him back through one of the dark halls leading into the crypt.

With little effort, he slung the body upon a small cart, letting out a breath as he stepped back once and scrutinized his work. A sinking feeling pooled in his stomach.

It's not my fault, he tried to tell himself. But that rationale proved futile. Evrardin's hands were the culprits of the slaughter of hundreds of innocent men. His eyes hesitantly looked down at the pile of bodies that sat heavily on the wheeled cart in front of him, their hearts all missing, their skin leathering from time.

An apology sat uncomfortably on the tip of his tongue. But *they* wouldn't hear it, so what did it matter? And even if they could, it would never be enough for unjustly taking their life.

He thought back to Mara, how she stared at him as he left her with Cas. She already thought him a monster, he couldn't imagine her reaction if she found out just exactly what it was he did for the prince.

When Evrardin made it back into the main room of the crypt,

he found the gravedoctor sitting at one of the stained tables, two plates of food before him. He looked up at Ev, his visage bearing the marks of time, making him seem much older than his years. He nodded down at the second plate.

Ev approached him, crashing onto the stool in a huff. His plate was filled with scraps from the kitchens, likely extras or mistakes from the masquerade. He picked up a burnt roll and ripped it apart in his hand, resting an elbow on the table. Blood and guts sat just inches from them, strewed in all the nooks and crannies of the room, but it didn't seem to disturb their appetite.

They ate in irritated silence until Crowrot spoke.

"Still fightin' in those rings?" He looked at Ev from behind the slab of meat dripping in his knobbed fingers.

Crowrot knew he was, this wasn't his real question.

Evrardin nodded, shoveling potatoes into his mouth. "It doesn't matter."

"What'd ya mean, *it doesn't matter*? You know what the prince'll do if he finds out."

"I don't keep my winnings," he mumbled.

"Won't make no difference to him."

"I'm not the one here we should be worried about falling into the prince's bad graces." Ev's jaw clenched, trying to hold back the anger beginning to escape.

Crowrot sighed, placing his spoon on his cracked plate. "N'when Cas beheads ya for bein' disloyal, whose gonna protect the princess, then?"

Evrardin closed his eyes momentarily, trying to retain his composure. "That has nothing to do with me, Rot."

Crowrot raised a brow. "No? Right, my mistake."

Ev's hand clenched his fork, the nerve in his jaw twitching. As if he felt the need to defend himself, he scowled. "The prince is preventing me from doing anything that benefits her, regardless. He said it doesn't matter if she becomes his wife, he comes first. She shouldn't be—*and isn't*—any of my concern."

Crowrot gave him a sideways glance.

"What?! There's nothing I can do now even if I wanted to! You heard what I just said. The prince specifically forbade it."

The old man pushed himself up, wobbling as he walked away, picking up papers scattered along one of the work benches. "Y'seem tired. Should go to bed, boy."

"Oh, so that's it? You're... what? Disappointed in me for something I can't control?"

Without glancing back, Crowrot disappeared down the corridor.

Frustrated beyond all else, Evrardin finished his meal before making his way back up to the main floors of the castle, the entire time cursing out the old man under his breath.

The sun would be rising soon, the darkness of the night still twinkling in through the windows. Evrardin could hear the faint tune of strings playing, a few scattered voices echoing down the hall.

As he turned the corner to pass by the gardens, a hand reached out and stopped him. Ev spun around to face a disheveled prince, his mask long gone, his makeup melting down his face.

"Evrardin," he slurred slightly, leaning against the wall to keep his balance.

Evrardin examined Cas' inebriated state.

"Have you seen m'wife?"

"You don't have a wife."

"Ha! That, you're right!" He slapped Evrardin on the shoulder, the heady scent of wine overpowering in their close quarters. "Find her at sunrise. Take her to the library."

Evrardin quirked a brow. "Back to warding her?"

Acastus wrote him off with a hand flick. "You'll be happy to learn that I've grown fond of my little betrothed. Maybe picking her wasn't the worst thing in the world."

Wasn't the worst thing in the world. Evrardin could picture Mara's annoyed face at hearing the prince's romantic endearments.

"She's quite beautiful, is she not, Evrardin?"

Clenching his teeth together, he gave a nod to satisfy the drunken prince.

"She's mine, you know."

Evrardin gave a curt nod again. "Well aware."

"I won't have you messing this up, you and that soft heart of yours."

Soft heart? Leave it to the prince to accuse Evrardin of possessing such an out-of-character asset. How many times did he have his wine cup refilled?

"Do not mess this up, Evrardin," Cas' words suddenly articulate. "I lack the patience. I need her skills to glassfaire, so make sure she figures it out. I don't care how."

Before Evrardin could say another word, let alone protest, Acastus had turned and danced back into the gardens, joining gorgeous members of the court, ones who would feed his narcissistic addiction.

With a tight fist, Evrardin took a breath before turning to head back to his room. After all this, everything Evrardin had done, the prince still accused him of potentially defaming his path.

Irate, Evrardin punched a candelabra he passed down one of the corridors, sending the candles spiraling on the floor, the clatter echoing off the walls.

This was Evrardin's life. This is all it ever would amount to. He was nothing more than a dog the prince could kick around, and there was nothing Evrardin could do about it. He left the mess behind him—it blended in with the rest of the decrepit castle anyway.

When he marched into his chambers, he ran his hands through his hair, pulling out the string that tied his hair back, and ripped his armor off plate by plate, shoving them in the corner of his room, the attire restricting. He went to tear off his cloak before remembering he no longer had it.

The pain in Mara's eyes as she accused him of lying ricocheted inside his head. The way she looked at him while he spun her on the dance floor. What had he been thinking?

He had to push her to the back of his thoughts. He wasn't going to mess this up. He was going to do what the prince wanted. Everything and anything he wanted. Then he was going to get the fuck out of Kairth.

Yet, his feet betrayed him. He cracked his neck before he set off toward *her* rooms.

Chapter Nineteen
Mara

Draped in her burning ember dress, Mara held one of the prince's hands, her hip in his other. He pulled her close to his chest as they twirled, his silver eyes searing through her.

He guided her through the motions the same as Evrardin had, but this felt oddly dissimilar. Her hand gripped the solid ice of his, his leathered hand crushing her own. She could see the words on the tip of his tongue, everything he wanted to say to her.

She had to restrain herself from letting her eyes flicker about the gardens for a fifth time, seeking out the brooding guard, wondering where he went off to. She hated how much she wished he was still here, watching as Acastus swept her about the celebration, waiting for her to finally return back to his side, both of them annoyed, bickering aimlessly into the night instead of having to mingle with courtiers she didn't give a shit about.

Acastus narrowed his eyes, a sinister smile plastered across his thin lips. His silvery eyes swallowed whole by his dark makeup and mask, making him more predatory than usual.

"He'll take you to the library tomorrow," he said in a deep tone.

"Who?" Mara inquired.

His eyebrows narrowed. "The captain."

Mara timidly nodded. There was something raw and angry in the prince's voice.

As if he could sense her thoughts, his hand rose from her hip and wrapped around the back of her neck in a threat buried beneath her hair. "You will learn how to glassfaire." Mara nodded again before he jerked her to look straight at him. "This isn't a request, Maralena. It's a command."

A flicker of fire rose in her chest.

He smiled. "Better keep those thoughts to yourself, Princess."

"I—I wasn't—"

He tsked, his hand squeezing harder. "You will be in the library day and night until you figure it out. Evrardin will assist in anything you might need."

She had desperately wanted to curl up in the library and read her days away, trying to forget all of this madness, but now... now she felt a murmur of terror pull at her thinking about being locked in there.

"Okay," she mumbled. She winced in his grip.

His eyes flickered between hers, his hand sliding around the the front of her neck, resting on her throat. She swallowed and Acastus smiled with the bob of her throat. "Were you jealous?" he beckoned.

Her lips parted but she did not respond.

"Did you see me with the noble women tonight? Did you wish it was you I had my hand wrapped around? Did you wish it was you I gripped by the throat?" He looked at her lips and her fingers vibrated in nerves. He pulled her closer, his fingers tightening. "Do you enjoy it now?"

Mara tried to hold back her emotions, keeping them from her face, and Cas made an odd sound in the back of his throat.

"Do you wish I would defile you in the same way I do them?"

Mara's brows knitted. She almost went to nod, perhaps giving him what he wanted, but just before she did, Cas' eyes sparkled, and he slowly released her neck.

"I don't mean to frighten you, Princess," he crooned. She hated how swiftly he was able to switch between personalities; foolish enough to want to believe his gentler words—his sensual praises. "It's imperative to the kingdom that you learn to glassfaire."

A blush of anger still laid bare on her cheeks.

"I cannot tell you why, but you must trust me even though I've given you no good reason to." His hand found hers. "Your ability will help me save Solstrale in its descent from grace as the fae turn on us. It's bigger than just me or you."

She felt voiceless, like if she spoke now, his eyes might glean gold.

"You're now aware of Solstrale's animosity with the Faelands?"

She nodded.

He let a harsh breath out through his nose. "It seems all the kingdoms are keenly aware of my father's incompetence to keep the fae on our side." He shook his head, his eyes refocusing on her. "No matter, I'll need you to help keep the fae at bay. To keep them from rebelling, though, my war council isn't as convinced."

"But, how do you know I'll be able to glassfaire?"

Cas swirled her around, his hand warm on her waist. "Your mother could. It's very likely you can, then, as well."

Mara bit her lip. "How'd you know my mother could...?" The words escaped her, trying her best to restrain those bloody memories from filling her mind.

"Some secrets are not so easily kept. Like I said, all the kingdoms stick their noses in each other's business. Each kingdom with their own spymaster." He smiled at her and her lips itched to mirror him.

Mara marveled at him as he spoke so earnestly, his features relaxed. "I'll try my best, My Prince."

"Good." He gave her a kind smile. "I want us to be friends, Maralena."

She swallowed. "I'd like that," she said, though she wasn't sure she would.

He spun her around again before taking a moment to admire her. "You look lovely, by the way."

She gave him a coy grin. "Thank you. You look lovely as well."

He laughed. "Don't let my dress maids hear you say that. I tried to tell them how outrageous this attire was, but they insisted the Sun Prince wear garb bright enough to woo the sun goddess." He rolled his eyes and Mara let her lips rise with a genuine smile.

They danced in silence for several beats as she forced her mind go empty.

"Have you not yet visited the coastal gardens? They're far more enthralling than these." He gestured to the gardens they currently swayed through, a soft violin harmonizing in the air.

Her palms warmed, the prince's eyes flickering to gold. She shook her head. She had wanted to visit the sea so desperately, but it seemed rather difficult to get someone to escort her outside the main walls. She had resigned to looking at it from the high windows.

"Hm," he hummed. "You'll have to pursue them, then. I know how much you love the wild flora." He twirled her about in a soft circle. "I recommend going early in the morning."

She let her face go alight with mirth, tilting her head sideways, about to implore more on his meaning, but the prince's eyes flashed to steel as he gained sight of his father approaching on their flank. He looked down at Mara for a final intake of her features she tried to soften, something tenderhearted cascading through his eyes for the briefest moment—so fast, she may have missed it if she wasn't watching him so intently.

"That will be all," he concluded soundly.

He kissed her cheek, sending a flush through her body before dropping her hands and disappearing behind her.

Mara instinctively reached up to her face to touch where the prince just had his lips. Aware of the audience around her, she turned and looked for some salvation, some reprieve from this tortuous event.

She lost sight of Evrardin and now the prince had slipped into the shadows. Maybe she could bother Lord Cofsi again, though she thought better of it. Instead, she awkwardly made her way to the long oak table filled with luxurious desserts before stealing a few. She hovered about the masquerade for a good while longer, mingling with courtiers and desperate to go back to her bed.

It wasn't until the sun got close to rising that she finally was set free from boring conversations and could set off toward her rooms. She reached a hand up under her curls as she scurried down the halls, her neck irritated. The spot where her nape met her hairline tingled with soreness. The exact place the prince's hand had lingered.

Mara wandered the halls, still unsure exactly where her rooms were located. Her hand now trailed a windowsill, its open glass skimming out over the ocean. She let out a sigh of solitude.

She had wanted to explore more of the castle, but when she began edging down corridor after corridor, her feet wouldn't let her continue. The halls appeared so dim—so treacherous—some of them looking like they led into the blackened night. The castle certainly needed some renovation. The lingering depths haunted her, telling her to go back. The cobblestones and wood were shrouded in shadow, desolate, and crying out. Cobwebs stitching together cragged stone.

She thought herself lucky when she happened down the wing where she resided, her heart swelling with solace. No guard stood stationed outside her door, all of them back at the masquerade. *Good*, she thought, she could still have her peace.

As if the gods were taunting her, her tranquility shattered at the sound of shuffling footsteps and a strangled male grunt rippling in her ear, framing her in place. It sounded like it was coming from within the walls of her chambers.

She gently pushed the door to her room open, gasping when she saw the blood pooled on the ground near her bed. The viscous liquid trickled between the floorboards, soaking the wood into a sore shade of mahogany.

Evrardin glanced up at her intrusion, his face unwavering even as he held a man dead beneath his palms. He straddled the body, his tunic covered in blood, some in his hair, but most drenching his hands. Her mirror stood tall behind them, the back of Evrardin's boot grazing it. Its glass had been splattered in blood and Mara's heart sank.

She darted toward him, stumbling like a newborn deer, and his eyes briefly flashed, like he couldn't decipher what she was doing.

He shook his head, recentering his attention on the dead body. With a chafed tone, he drawled, "I'll be out of your chambers in just a moment, *Princess*—" His adjuration fell short, his voice raising an octave like he was asking a question, her small hands tentatively turning his head toward her.

"Are you hurt?"

Evrardin looked like he wanted to roar a laugh, but he was too astonished to do so. His fingers released the corpse, letting it sag limply to her floor. "No," he said tersely. Confused. Unsure.

Her eyes welled with disquiet and Evrardin gave her a

hateful grimace. She glanced at his torso, his pale linen shirt now a deep crimson. "You're covered in blood," she stuttered, her words clipped and broken at the end.

He knitted his eyebrows when she sucked in a sharp fleet of air, like recognition dawned on him. "It's not mine—" Her hands shook by her side, Ev's eyes tracing them. "Mara," he breathed, standing up to his full height.

Her chest rose and fell in hectic movements, the air moving, but none seemed to take purchase long enough in her lungs to work. She froze in terror at the man desecrated on her floors, his eyes still open in shock. Evrardin's voice rang in her ear but she couldn't make him out. Images of her mother flashed in her head, stealing all the air from her every time she drew a breath in.

"Mara," he said more sternly, finally gaining her regard when he grabbed her hands forcefully and placed them against his chest.

She looked up at him like a timid rabbit, tears in the distance, her thoughts somewhere else.

"I'm fine," he all but snarled.

She nodded, biting her lip to hold the tears at bay. She cursed herself for having a meltdown over the idea of Evrardin dying like her mother had, his body torn as he got caught between the realms, blood... *everywhere.*

"Breathe," he coaxed, his voice cracking like it wasn't used to talking this delicately.

Her jaw clenched, her fingers tightening in his shirt before she truly looked at the captain—not through him. To stare at him for what he was, not the memory of her mother. "I just..." Her words lodged in her throat. "My mother... I—"

He shook his head. His grip tightened against her skin and heat waves ebbed inside her veins. "Not my blood," he said.

Was the ill-famed captain trying to soothe her?

When she seemed to steady, he gave her a long stare before

dropping her hands and spinning away from her. He effortlessly heaved the man's corpse into his arms and over his shoulder, the blood leaking from an unseen wound.

Mara might have been able to tuck away her past, but she still looked at him in shock and confusion. Something held him there a moment longer. "Someone from the Icewoods." He cleared his throat, Mara's gaze blank as she stood silently. "Was comin' for revenge on Cas. Guess that cunt meant somethin' to them."

The way he referred to Sir Orion, not even mentioning his name, made her lips twitch.

When he moved again, she called his name quietly. He stopped but didn't turn toward her. "Would he have killed me if I was in my rooms?"

Ev adjusted the man's weight on his shoulder. "I don't doubt he'd have tried."

As he left her room, she realized she should have asked why he was in the vicinity of her chambers in the first place.

Chapter Twenty
Mara

It was early the following morning, just as she imagined, when a knocking sounded at her door. Dressed in a simple beige dress, her arms decadent in sheer gossamer, the neckline shaped like a heart, and spiraling with wispy embroidery, she called for the individual to enter.

Her heart raced when Evrardin made himself present in her doorway. Biting the inside of her cheek, she turned to him. "Here to finally take me to my cell?" she dryly asked.

Evrardin gave her an unamused expression. His eyes trailed behind her, noting the slight stain on her floor, but the scene of last night otherwise vacant. She barely slept last night.

Mara huffed in response. "Well, this will be fun." The first light of the early morning melted over the hardwood floor, and she languidly appraised him. Then she narrowed her eyes. "You look like shit," she said before she could think otherwise.

"You know how much I live for your compliments. Careful, *liten rev*, I might start to think you like me."

Mara repressed her scoff, but she didn't manage to hold back her smile. "I only meant—"

"Yes, I know what you meant. And I know I look like all hells."

They turned to walk down the hall, Mara's steps a few traces behind Evrardin's faster pace. "Did you not sleep?"

Evrardin let out a groan. "No, it appears I didn't. Always so observant, Princess," he mocked, but Mara ignored his cadence. She wondered if it had to do with the assassin from the night prior. If had been up all night for the same reason she had.

A few beats passed before Evrardin cleared his throat. "Did you sleep all right?"

She tentatively gazed sidelong at him. She debated lying, but she didn't see the point in that. "Not particularly." She bit her lips. "I thought you might come back." Her cheeks went hot, her eyes refusing to look over at him, hating to admit she had hoped he would have come back to her after he took away the body. To be with her. To protect her. Evrardin's hand tightened on the hilt of his sword out of her peripheral vision.

He shook his head. "I stood guard outside your door."

She stumbled in her steps. "You..." She blinked several times, making sense of his words. "All night?"

He nodded.

"Why?"

He remained silent and she let that consume her. Mara pulled on her sleeve, the sharp end to their conversation overwhelming. She stopped in her tracks abruptly. "Oh! Wait," she called.

Evrardin turned to look back at her, spinning on his feet and raising a brow in question.

"I forgot to give you back your cloak. I, uh, washed it for you." Her cheeks blazed with heat. "You know, so it's not covered in my horrendous smell," she tried to joke, but her words were strained.

She pushed her hair out of her face and rolled anxiously on the balls of her feet. "I forgot to thank you for that. For, you know…"

Ambivalence welled in Evrardin's eyes as he studied her anxious state, making Mara's cheeks shine a bright crimson.

"Ah, forgot you took that since you only wanted to berate me the other day." His eyes averted her own. "One of your maidens can return it."

She spoke through clenched teeth, hating how pathetic she sounded. "Perfect."

Evrardin had stood in place for what felt like hours, watching over Mara as she tore through the library, trying to find anything to work with. She found things on her family's house, but very little about glassfairing. It was mentioned only by name in a tome about the gods, but it didn't give her anything of use.

She grew frustrated, a headache beginning to brew in the front of her skull. The library was stuffy, the summer sun boiling in through the stained windows. She stood, exasperated, and went looking for another book. She could feel Ev's eyes on her every time she moved, it was driving her mad.

"Do you watch the prince as attentively as this?" Silence. "He was the one with the assassin on his tail, not me."

"He's not as fun to watch."

She gritted her teeth. "Oh, watching me read in the library is fun now? You might need to get out more."

His lip ticked slightly in the corner. "Watching you fluster under my watch is fun."

Her face went warm, and he mirthlessly chuckled at how

easy she was to embarrass. "It's not hard to guess why you have no friends."

"Do you take me as someone who longs for friendships, *liten rev?*"

She circled a desk, her eyes on the books sprawled upon the tabletop. "The company of a crazy old alchemist hidden away in the dungeons is enough for you, then?"

His jaw clenched at the mention of Crowrot. She hadn't meant it as a jab, she liked Crowrot. A lot. She just couldn't stop the way she lusted to crawl under the captain's skin.

"I get all the company I need. Trust me."

Her heart raced. She moved in silence, his eyes still on her.

When she sat back down, she pulled her hair up, tying it with a spare ribbon she carried in her dress pocket, trying to cool down in the oppressive library.

"What is that?"

Mara jumped, Evrardin's harsh voice crashing through the still room like thunder. "What is what?" She hesitated before flickering her eyes over to him as he approached.

"On the back of your neck."

Instinctively, Mara reached her hand and placed it on top of where Cas had gripped her at the masquerade. She had forgotten how irritated her skin felt after Acastus had pressed his fingers a bit too harshly against her, almost like he had claws poking through his gloves. Everytime he touched her, he seemed to leave marks in possession.

In a panic, she quickly let her hair back down, ready to suffer from a sweaty neck in the hopes Evrardin would leave it alone.

"I don't know."

Her eyes widened in shock as he stood before her and shoved her hair aside, his knuckles grazing her skin in the process.

Frozen in place, she looked up at him, his gaze startling her.

"Did you walk in on something you shouldn't have?"

Mara scrunched her face. "What the hell are you talking about, Evrardin?" Her chest began to beat erratically.

He grunted before taking a step back, letting her hair cascade down her back in rushing rivulets of chestnut. "You're not making this easy."

"Making what easy?"

He went silent again, she knew he wasn't going to entertain this conversation any further.

"Is he... Is something wrong with the prince?" she asked boldly, but her voice quiet. When she got the courage to look back at Evrardin, he was giving her a quizzical look. "An affliction of some sort?"

She scrunched her nose when he didn't say anything. It was impossible to talk him into a proper conversation. It frustrated her to no end.

"Heed my words for once, and do not go snooping around. If I find marks on your neck one more time—"

"You'll what?" she challenged.

"I'll have to force you to listen." There was something harsh laced in his words—they ran up her spine and sent a trail of gooseflesh in their wake. Her usual quip slipped out of her grasp.

Mara turned back to her tomes and flipped through the texts. When she realized Evrardin wasn't moving back to his previous placehold, she decided to press him more, honestly quite tired from shifting through materials in hopes of finding any semblance of glassfairing in the texts. If he wasn't going to answer her first question, and she refused to tell him what happened to her neck, she'd shift the conversation.

"What do you do when you leave the castle at night?"

He lifted a brow. "What do you mean?"

She cleared her throat, nervously scanning the book in front of her to keep her eyes busy while not digesting any of the words.

"That night I saw you coming back from the inlet. You were covered in blood and grime."

Evrardin looked like he was thinking back to that moment. "That's really none of your business, *liten rev*."

Mara groaned at the man towering above her. "Stop calling me that!"

The smallest hint of a smirk corrupted Ev's face, her eyes drawn to the scar dissecting his lips. "Why? Does it bother you?"

She scowled at him before shoving her chair back and gathering the books in her arms to put back on the shelves. "Just tell me what it means." She went down the rows before finding the spots where she took the brown forgotten books and placed them gently back into their slot.

Evrardin followed behind her absentmindedly. "It's nothing obscene."

Wonderful. And she had to just take his word for that? She doubted it meant anything far beyond *bitch* or *insufferable-spoiled-brat*.

Putting the last book on the shelf, she spun to face him. She gasped at his proximity. "I don't believe you," she said through clenched teeth.

His deep brown eyes held hers in competition. His usual stony face appeared incensed. She swore she could feel the exuberance radiating from him in a buzz. She imagined he wanted nothing more than to pick her up and toss her out the highest window in the castle. And she was starting to think she'd let him.

After far too many beats of silence, their eyes never pulling apart, his voice cut through the tense air. "It means *little vixen*."

Surprised and for some odd reason, believing him, Mara struggled to find her words. Her hands grabbed at her dress, anxiously squeezing it in between her fingers. "Why do you call me that?" she asked breathlessly.

"Because you're feisty and elusive... and I can't seem to figure you out."

She inched closer to him, her eyes narrowing in on his. "I'm rather simple, Evrardin,"—he took in a breath, and she swallowed before continuing— "you say it all the time yourself. I'm just a spoiled princess who doesn't know how to think for herself. Can't get much easier to decipher than that."

His eyes danced between hers and then much to her surprise, they flickered momentarily down to her lips. "I'm starting to think I might have been wrong."

She swallowed. "Well, sorry to disappoint. You know how much it upsets me," she said mockingly, though she was strangely out of breath.

Evrardin took a small step, closing the space between them so her chest stood a mere inch from his own. "There you go, putting words in my mouth again." Mara swallowed, tracing his lips with her eyes as he spoke down at her. "I never said that disappointed me."

Mara's lips parted in nerves. "No?" she asked.

"No."

She found it hard to keep his stare, a fit of blazing heat covering her head to toe.

His fingers lit her on fire as they landed beneath her chin, tilting her face back up toward his forbearing one.

His name escaped her lips in a breathless whisper; both of their faces being pulled together by an unseen force. She could almost feel his lips grazing hers as he slouched over to better reach her. She was suddenly filled with the urge to run her fingers through his messy hair, to feel his overgrown stubble on her face as he kissed her, to be squished in his arms wrapped tightly around her as he pushed her against the bookshelf behind them.

His hooked fingers pulled her face dangerously close to his

own. And what was worse than that: she let him. Out of vulgar desperation nestled between them in this dark corner of the library.

Before their lips could meet, Mara whispered, "I don't think..."

Evrardin's eyes slid up from the pink swell of her lips and kept her shocked gaze for a moment, his rugged face disjointedly gentle and full of indistinct emotions.

And then, without warning, he pulled away, the heat from his body replaced by the air of the room that she thought too warm only minutes earlier but now left her freezing. His hands were back by his side, the one that was on her chin now gripping the hilt of his sword through strained fingers.

He looked at her for a moment longer before turning and walking back toward the entryway of the library. "Let me know when you're ready to leave."

Mara's hand flew to her chest, heaving in big gulps of air to try and steady herself.

She didn't want to go back to the desk she had her books sprawled upon just to fall flat under Evrardin's presence. Instead, she got comfortable on the floor in one of the many winding rows of shelves and flipped through the tomes.

Mara sighed as she propped open another large book on her lap, scanning the table of contents for anything that might be of use.

What if she simply refused to do what the prince requested? The bruise on her neck tingled as if it had ears of its own and was reminding her of how little she truly knew about him. Would she want to risk upsetting him? He wouldn't actually hurt her, would he? Evrardin's immediate recognition of the bruise being Cas' doing said otherwise.

Her finger glided along the table of contents until she stopped on the words *Khonsu: Mirror Demons*.

She quickly flipped to that page, hoping she finally found something. Anything. She was getting desperate.

She skipped the first few paragraphs, scanning for things of note, then came to a halt.

The God of Travel had been irate with the people of the south, more importantly, the Glass King, King Glaer. Khonsu and the Glass People had left this world, taking the asinine trip to the Veil, along with several other gods: Trana the Goddess of the Sun, Mölr the God of Night, Vetr the God of Winter, Dýr the Goddess of all Creatures, and Nið Goddess of the Moon.

Unlikely to make an appearance while the Glass King still reigned, reporting sightings of Glass People in their reflections began to make rounds. The king had ordered all mirrors destroyed or covered in fear of what Khonsu might do from the Veil where his powers could be properly channeled.

It wasn't until the king stumbled into a long-forgotten hall of the castle that a floor-length mirror stood at the ready. Whether it had been forgotten about and not destroyed with the others, or left unveiled on purpose, isn't known. The king faced himself in the reflection, too late to escape. Nothing happened right away, and the king laughed, thinking himself silly for being so worried. The god of travel might be able to wisp away to far reaches, but to travel through mirrors? Laughable.

The king stared at himself until he noticed his eyes going dark and his head moving as he stood still. Decaying lanky hands reached out and grabbed him, taking him through the mirror and into the Veil where everything went dark.

The king returned in pure horror, screaming down the halls. Having to be kept away in his rooms, he never recovered, muttering nonsense about reflections being but a trick of the eye. A demon waited on the other side of the mirror, waiting for its victim, mimicking them until it tore them across realms.

The king appeared too horror-stricken to recite what had occurred to him beyond our Veil, screaming in terror whenever Master Skrá tried to elicit details of his travels. The Glass King never returned to how he once was.

Khonsu is still said to be waiting just beyond our Veil for victims, stealing all he can from the Glass Court, desolate of powers. As long as mirrors are obscured, the ability of Khonsu or any of the Glass People to glassfaire lay improbable.

She carefully closed the history tome, putting it aside on the floor, not bothering to find its home on the shelf, and made her way to the library's entrance, her mind falling solemn.

Evrardin followed her hesitantly back to her rooms where she entered before closing the door, not speaking another word to him.

Chapter Twenty-One
Evrardin

Evrardin stared at the ornate details engraved on the princess' door after she promptly slammed it in his face.

He shouldn't have allowed himself to get that close to her, to have almost kissed her. What the fuck was he thinking? She belonged to Acastus. Regardless, he would never be able to express his feelings to her—unsure of what his feelings toward her even were.

Maybe he didn't hate her as much as he first thought. And he'd be blind to say she wasn't pretty. But he couldn't just use her for a quick tryst—she was a princess. And betrothed to his prince, no less. She wasn't some commoner he could use to forget about his pathetic existence for one night.

He told himself he could handle that. Knowing that he couldn't have her the way he desired, using her solely to satisfy his lust.

The way he desired, fuck. He ran his hand through his hair in frustration. Did he want the princess? There was no way he'd ever desire someone as insolent as her. Maybe it was the way she spoke to him so plainly and honestly, that brattiness—something he didn't realize he wanted if only because he was envious he couldn't act like that himself.

He stood outside her door a few moments longer, his fingers itching to knock and see her face again.

He cursed himself out before storming off. He was royally screwed.

Evrardin tried to avoid presenting the prince with bad news —it was in his best interest. Presently, he had no choice but to stride into the prince's quarters with nothing but a tainted piece of rolled parchment.

"My Prince," he revered, his formidable presence doing nothing to unsettle Cas like it once used to.

"Is it done, then?" Acastus asked without looking up. He sat across from one of his contemporaries, engaged in a game of river stones.

Evrardin remained silent, patiently waiting for Cas to finally glance at him out of sheer annoyance. He scoffed before flicking his wrist, signaling the man sitting across from him to leave.

When the man scurried away, leaving the two alone, Cas stood and languidly circled the river stones table that had been enchanted to have a cerulean stream coursing over the tabletop, cascading down to the floor. "Care to explain yourself?" he asked Evrardin, the venom rolling off his tongue with indolence.

Ev simply held out the parchment for Cas to take. As Cas opened the scroll with curious eyes, Evrardin spoke. "The Fae King no longer wishes to work amicably to restore alliances between our two kingdoms. He is insisting on war."

Acastus' eyes lazily scanned the letter. "Bloody hell." Cas' voice had a boyish rise to it that lingered between his sharp teeth. "I'm assuming this is going to hinder our efforts to get the Fae King's heart, then?"

Our. The word left a sour taste in Ev's mouth. There was no participation from the prince apart from the orders he dealt. This excursion fell solely on Evrardin.

"How predictable," Acastus spat, his fearsome tone now heightened in a tantrum. "The Fae King retreats from yet another covenant between our kingdoms. And he thinks it will be quite the effortless triumph, no doubt." Acastus threw the parchment into the fireplace on the far side of the room before waltzing back to Evrardin. "I mean, when was the last time Solstrale won a war?"

"I don't pretend to be suitable counsel for tactical war campaigns." Evrardin shifted in his worn boots, dragging his foot on the floor in concentration to keep from lashing out. This all could have been prevented. But Evrardin suspected Acastus planned to go to war this entire time, regardless of the fresh news from the Fae King.

Solstrale had been known for its vigorous army until King Acanthus' reign. The military had dwindled, so many of the Sun People growing sickly from the lack of viable vegetation as Acanthus broke allegiances with the fae. The fae were the one thing keeping Solstrale together, fae magick having constructed all its provinces. Now, with Acanthus refusing to aid the fae, they've finally severed ties in their entirety. The darkness that was still growing across the land had more to do than with just Acastus, the lack of fae magick was hastening the shift to a shambled city.

"Hmm," Cas hummed. "I'm sure they'll be at the ready now, don't you think?"

Evrardin nodded. "Not sure I'd make it out of there with them preparing for battle."

He was sure Acastus didn't care about his safe return, but rather, he needed the heart of a king and wouldn't do much to get it himself. For that reason, he still needed the captain alive.

Evrardin was a little relieved that he no longer had to spy his way into Faerie, but his relief was hindered knowing that stealing the Fae King's heart was no longer a viable solution to end this war in the hopes that the next fae ruler would be more amicable toward Solstrale. Evrardin wasn't convinced it would've even unfolded that way, but the chances were screwed down to an abysmal zero, so it didn't matter in the end.

And now this meant he'd just have to steal another monarch's heart for Acastus' ruinous plan.

Acastus' hands clasped behind his back, his hands sheathed in dark leather, a stark contrast to his loose cream shirt. Evrardin swore he could see an inky trail edging up the back of his neck as he paced, the curse only spreading as the days ticked by.

"My father, then."

Evrardin blinked before tilting his head like a dog. "Your... King *Acanthus*?"

"Yes, that is who my father is," Acastus said tersely.

"What about him?" Evrardin managed through clenched teeth.

"We'll take his heart. If we can't take the Fae King's, we'll take my father's. We don't have enough time to change plans and scout out another kingdom."

Evrardin may have been a man of little emotions, but he still didn't expect to be as stunned as he presently was. His eyebrows cinched together as he watched the prince settle into his new idea.

"Cas, I don't think—"

"I don't want your counsel, Evrardin," he spat. "We are running out of time and options!" Acastus' words screeched, his eyes going black, the smoke Evrardin thought he saw around his collar now spiraling to tickle the prince's cheeks in full bloom.

Evrardin's stance relaxed but his jaw tightened as he tracked Acastus' movements. Cas slumped back into his settee, running a hand through his midnight hair, the ink on his skin subsiding slowly. "I still expect you to be the one to do it."

Ev nodded.

"*A heart of a monarch and the thrum of new love,*" Acastus crooned, reciting the words he heard from Trana. "*An army of warriors, from the ground, to above.*"

Evrardin still remembered the craze in Acastus' eyes all those weeks ago as he told captain the Solar Sect was planning on helping him travel to the Veil.

Evrardin watched as the dark magick coursed through Acastus, his soul ripped apart as he teetered between realms. He had claimed to have spoken to Trana, a deity—the deity—of the Sun Court that had been slipping dangerously close to being forgotten. "It's rather simple," Acastus told him through bated breaths in the vast cathedral. "She insisted she'll help regrow the Sun Court to its former glory, sick of rotting in the shadows of the other gods. She'll invite an army of Sun Warriors to bid at my will. All she needs is for my blood to be reignited with magick." Acastus smiled wildly at Evrardin. "A heart of a monarch and the thrum of new love. An army of warriors, from the ground, to above," he sung like he was caught in a dream.

"What does that entail, exactly?" Lord Alfson asked timidly. The other Solar Sect members glanced at one another.

"I'll need to marry. Someone of another noble house so her magick can bind to mine. I'll need as much power as possible to bring this prophecy to light." Lord Alfson opened his mouth to speak, but Cas cut him off—Ev snickered. "First, I'll need the hearts for our warriors. And as you just heard, the heart of a monarch."

"That's a lot of power to summon, My Prince," the high priest spoke, stepping into the circle they were unconsciously forming around the marbled sun sigil on the floor.

"Yes, well, I'll need a lot of power to raise an army worthy of Solstrale, wouldn't you say?"

The Sect looked concerned.

Evrardin shook his head in disbelief as the Sect acted like this wasn't part of their great plan to save the kingdom. "Cas, I don't think this is the best way to—

"Do not speak unless spoken to," Acastus commanded, not bothering to look in his direction. Evrardin's lips instantly sealed. "Blood is the strongest magick we have."

The high priest's head turned to the side as he studied the prince. "And where would you like to begin?"

His words reminded Evrardin of the stakes. This deal he made was becoming more and more personal. The Sun King was now to be slaughtered at Evrardin's hand and...

"A shame so much blood will be shed on my wedding day. They say that's bad luck, do they not? But it's not a proper wedding without a little violence," Cas said flippantly, pouring himself a glass of wine.

An unrestrained thought raged and warred through the crevices in Evrardin's mind. "You're not to kill the princess," Evrardin stated as more of a question. "You just had to be bonded to her for the ritual to work. You only needed her glassfairing ability, not her heart."

Cas' face filled with an evil smirk. "Trana wants hearts, Evrardin. In no scenario will anyone I require outlive this. You know that." Cas gave him an almost pitiful look as he explained. "Mara is simply a means to an end. The final piece to true, unbesmirched restoration."

Chapter Twenty-Two
Mara

Mara sat in her dark room, a flickering candle by the cracked window and the moon her only source of light. She stared at her blurry reflection in the mirror, a tome laid out before her, flipped open to a page on glassfairing.

Mara knew very little about glassfairing, its custom banned from even being taught in lectures throughout the kingdom. She had already read through every book in her library at Venmore and she had never come across anything relating to the travel god, Khonsu. Those books had been locked away years before she could properly read.

But what she didn't expect to discover was how evil glassfairing was portrayed. She read through the newfound tome, gulping at the intensity of the words. She learned that it was believed that when traveling through the realms, a mirrored image of yourself takes your place in your absence—a demonic version. There was something dark and macabre about one's own reflection. It wasn't you—not really—that you saw staring back in the mirror. And sometimes a *svik*, or false self, might steal your reflection's form, edging itself into the living realm to pilfer your place.

Mara scanned the page again, though she couldn't truly read it in this dim lighting. She memorized the short passage by heart by now. It was just a blip of information, a short few paragraphs denoted to glassfairing. That was all she could find.

One must find a root to hold onto in this realm, or you risk being unable to return. Your demonic reflection would take your place forever. And one must truly want to slip into the Veil. If the desire isn't there, the deed will not succeed.

Mara tried to remind herself that Khonsu ran through her veins, no matter how little was left for the Glass People to inherit. The ability to glassfaire was nestled somewhere deep inside her. She tried to tell herself this was what she truly wanted as her fingers tentatively reached out to her floor-length mirror.

She wanted this. She wanted this. She wanted this.

Her fingers were stopped by the glass. She closed her eyes in frustration, keeping her fingertips in place.

No, she didn't want this. She didn't want to glassfaire. She didn't want to help the prince in whatever scheme he had brewing.

What she *did* want was to return home. Home to Wrens Reach. To see her father again. To hug her brother. To hear Jessamine's voice. She wanted this nightmare to be over. She wanted to get as far away from Kairth as humanly possible.

Mara squeezed her eyes even tighter as her fingers began to swim with warmth. She opened them as the sensation grew stronger, her fingers now knuckle-deep in the reflection.

Her eyes widened to giant moons, horrified and amazed at

the same time. She wiggled her fingers, trying to push deeper into the mirror.

She tried to summon her desires again; maybe her burn to return home was enough for her to glassfaire.

She wanted to leave. She wanted to get as far away from Prince Acastus as she could. She didn't want to marry him. She didn't want to ever have to touch him again. She wanted to glassfaire if it meant escaping him. And Evrardin. She never wanted to hear his gruff voice again—

A lick of flames burnt the tips of her fingers, and she yelped, yanking her hand back. She cradled her hand close to her body, her fingertips streaked with a pale red slash. She burnt herself.

She quickly touched the mirror again, but her fingers simply collided with the glass.

"Shit," she breathed. She sank back, her face falling. She had done it. Slightly, but still, she managed to edge her fingers through the layer of mirrored glass before her.

Her solemn reflection taunted her. She tossed the book across her room and stood up, marching over to her bed and collapsing into her billowing blankets.

The image of Acastus telling her she had to learn to glassfaire was seared in her mind. A flicker of fear tickled her spine. The feeling of his hand on her throat made her scream into her mattress.

She tilted her head to look at the tawny parchment splayed on her bed filled with scratchy ink. Azor had sent her a letter. A letter that made her worry no matter how insistent he was in his writing that he had things under control. But Azor couldn't avoid being truthful, something she both appreciated and hated. He spoke about the north edge of Wrens Reach where darkness began to fall on the woods. The road became so heavily coated in shadow that it was advised not to travel that way for the time being.

Azor made it sound trivial, like a minor inconvenience that would soon right itself. But in that same sentence, he told her he wouldn't be able to make the wedding. No one in Wrens Reach would. He promised to visit her as soon as he could, but that didn't stop the tears from staining the letter she held.

Azor wrote that the hovels on the northern farmlands were starting to wither as if they weren't made for the weather. But winter had left and summer had begun. There was no reason for the stones to be creaking and collapsing.

Mara knew there was more to all of this, something deeper.

Chapter Twenty-Three
Mara

A GUST of hot air swam up Mara's skirts as she scaled the halls of the castle, attempting to hide amongst the never-ending shadows to avoid Kairth's guards. Mara had discovered she could slip out on guard rotation without being seen. However, that meant she was roaming the castle at far too early an hour, yawning on cue.

Slipping around a corner, she heard a rumbling, similar to the sound she heard in the Sandwoods. Fear closed in around her heart, freezing her in place, but she didn't hear the sound again, chalking it up to her imagination because if she didn't create it in her head, that meant something big—something dangerous—lingered in the halls of Kairth. Perhaps it was a bad idea to roam alone before dawn.

She waltzed onto the gallery walkway, not fully assured she knew how to make her way back and stopped at one of the windowless arches. She rested her arms on the edge and looked out at the expansive sea. She sighed, laying her head atop her arms, watching as the blue waters sparkled with hints of orange from the barely rising sun. The shores danced with a blush of pink, the sun refracting off the translucent red flowers that lined a small section of the beach, secluding it.

She hadn't been able to go down to the ocean yet, busy with everything Acastus was having her do. And none of her guards would take her. They'd say it was out of their authority. She could explore the castle, but that's where the extent of her freedom lay. She would have asked Acastus and pleaded with him to escort her to the ebbing waters, but she found herself shy, unwilling to disturb him. And ever since he left that mark on her neck, she had begun to fear him.

Instead, she slipped off to the cobblestone staircase on the adverse side of the gallery, leading her down to the rocky shore. When her feet touched the soft grass, coming off the stairs, she turned back to make sure no one was watching her. The castle was so quiet early in the morning that all she could truly hear was the crashing orchestra of the ocean. She smiled, hiked her skirts up, and started her trail down to the sandy shore.

She had to dance around bends in the faint path, passing bushes of beautiful flowers and random overgrown benches angled for the guest to be able to look out onto the horizon. Her hand trailed the stone fence that appeared to be guarding a small garden. She was so close to the shore that her chest was growing giddy with pure, unadulterated excitement. She went to descend the last chunk of sandy steps when she spotted something moving in the gardens. She paused momentarily, focusing her eyes past the tall flora, lush vines, and multiple tiny birds that chirped as they hopped along the garden's verdant floor.

Her breath lodged itself in her throat when she got on the tips of her toes to try and see what was swaying the bushes. She was hoping it was a wild rabbit, but instead, she saw a familiar rusted tunic. Evrardin. It was easy to tell it was him, even from behind as he knelt on the ground and clipped away, pruning the flower bushes before him.

It took Mara a moment to process what she was watching: Evrardin tending to the gardens. Her first instinct was to assume this was a directive, a duty he was to maintain, but why would anyone here instruct the Captain of the Royal Guard to dally around the gardens before the crack of dawn?

She went to open her mouth, to make a jest, to embarrass him, but then she quickly sealed her lips. If Evrardin saw her, he'd surely drag her back inside to the safe confines of the castle. Instead, she resolved to silently watching him for a few moments longer, pushing her luck. Evrardin grunted as he heaved himself off the ground and Mara had to bite her lip from making a joke about how ancient he was.

A small bird tapped on the front of his boot and Evrardin glanced down. She half-expected him to punt the thing, but he reached for it and let the bird hop onto his finger, lifting it to his shoulder. This must have been something he'd done before because Evrardin read the bird correctly, the tiny bundle of feathers seemingly satisfied as it sat happily on his shoulder.

Ev slid his shears into his belt and grabbed his shovel from the ground, strolling off into the depths of the gardens. She could have sworn she heard him mumbling something to the bird if only the damn ocean wasn't so loud. It was jarring to watch him in the cool light of early morning. He was jagged and rough around the edges, surrounded by billowing floral shrubs and fragile petals, his calloused hands softly working the stems as he plucked away dead leaves. It was all so difficult to digest.

She was tempted to ogle more, but she thought better of it and hurried down to the sandy beach.

The second her feet touched the sand, she pried her slippers off and let her feet sink, the grainy dirt squishing between her toes. She took her time and approached the water, almost afraid of the vastness. The sheer size of the sea made her shiver.

Still, she made her way closer, but she paused when her feet touched damp sand. In a few beats, the ocean ebbed up the beach and crashed gently around her ankles. She grinned, the cool water tickling the back of her leg as it fled back to the sea. She hiked her skirts up as high as she could without exposing herself, sighing as the cold water melted around her thighs. It cooled her off from the summer heat, the air stifling even with the sun barely rising.

She stood frozen like this for several minutes. She kept telling herself she'd leave to go back before she was caught, but she couldn't get herself to move. Her feet had sunk into the wet sand below and she smiled at the lulling rhythm of the moving water.

Mara gasped when she saw a fin flap above the surface out in the distance. It happened so fast, she was sure she imagined it. She should have gone back, but it only made her that much more curious. She debated tossing her dress on the shore and swimming out in her undergarments, but that would be foolish, she hadn't the faintest idea how to swim.

She realized the ocean water wasn't frightening her like her tub did after the bonding ceremony. Maybe she was finally recovering.

"Go in too far and the nereids will drag you under."

Mara jumped at the voice carrying across the rippling water. She didn't have to turn around to know it was Evrardin standing on the shore, watching her.

"Good. Maybe I'll marry a water nymph. That sounds far superior to my current arrangement," she said over her shoulder. She was tempted to berate him for his earlier deeds, but the thought made her blush without proper reason. So instead, she kept his gardening and discussion with a tiny birdie to herself.

"Yeah? You do know princesses can't breathe underwater, right? Even self-assured ones like yourself."

Mara shook her head. "I'd learn how to, of course. They'd teach me after finding out what marvelous company I am." She gave him a devious grin before looking back at the horizon.

"If you expect your shining personality to save you from these beasts, you are poorly mistaken."

"Are you this cynical with everyone, Captain, or just me?"

"Can't say I've been known for my charms. Not a trait partial to my designation."

She turned and began to stride out, her thighs having to strain to move in the deep water. "Oh, that's truly disappointing. And here I was, thinking I was special."

When she made it back to the shore, she dropped her skirt, the fabric clinging to her salty legs, and she grinned at Evrardin.

He scowled back at her, and she giggled, which only proved to irritate him more.

"Your sour attitude will not ruin my day today, Captain. I just got to touch the ocean. I was standing in the actual sea!"

Evrardin ran a hand through his loose hair. "If you liked it so much, why are you standing with me up on the shore?"

Mara's eyebrows scrunched together, forgoing her movements to reach down and grab her slippers. "Aren't you going to escort me back inside?"

"Do you want me to?" he asked with a raised brow.

Mara's head tilted to the side slightly. "I... I mean, I would rather stay here and wander the tides a little longer." Her voice was soft, the roaring ocean wind carrying it the small distance to Evrardin's ears.

He gestured his head toward the water with a grunt. "Before I change my mind," he chided.

Mara blinked several times. She was about to hound him, ask him why he would let her spend more time in the ocean where she hadn't been allowed, but she didn't want him to drag her back in. She gave a timid smile and turned, walking back into the water, dropping her skirt and letting it billow behind her in the waves. "Won't the nereids eat me?" she joked.

"No. Unfortunately for me, they only seem to enjoy drowning men."

Mara wasn't sure if his comment implied he was upset he couldn't go into the water or because Mara wouldn't be devoured by a mythical divinity.

She laughed either way, the sound carrying across the water's surface.

He watched her in silence until the sun began to rise in its entirety. He didn't have to tell her, she made her way back to him on her own when she noticed the time and let him escort her back to her rooms. He didn't seem concerned about her soaked dress being a tell-tale sign she was out by the ocean. It wasn't like it was outwardly forbidden, she just couldn't get anyone to take her. Evrardin was the captain, no one would question him. If she was safe in anyone's company, it would be his, much to both of their dismay.

Mara began toward the library—a place she was steadily growing to hate—alone this time, after dark to fool her wardens that she was safe inside her room. To scour the shelves, pulling anything that might be of use and hauling it back to her rooms to stare at for hours. All to please the prince.

The prince didn't have to threaten her for her to feel fear. His candor and eyes were enough to warn her from defying him. And

Mara lacked cowardice. She felt like her spine had been taken from her. She wasn't like all the brave maidens from her fairy tales.

Evrardin would surely agree that she lacked courage—he'd probably say she lacked any substance at all.

As if taunting her, her mind recalled the previous day when he got a little too close in the stacks of the library. Her heart had been ready to burst out of her chest. She tried to suppress that feeling. The body reacts to stimuli, and a man being so close made her nervous. She had every inclination to get weary when an armed guard invaded her personal space in the dark, secluded corner of the library. It was nothing beyond being frightened of him.

And this morning, when he allowed her to frolic in the waves a bit longer...

Mara's mouth went dry trying to shake Evrardin from her thoughts. He was starting to complicate things, and that annoyed her.

With nothing but a piece of bread in her pocket, Mara clung to the cobblestone wall at the faint echo of footsteps. It wouldn't be the end of the world if she was caught—Acastus instructed her to be in the library day in and day out after all—but she didn't want some annoying man—especially her familiar brooding one—hovering as she tried, and failed, to make sense of glassfairing.

She poked her head beyond the corner, spying the grand gilded doors to the library as a wisp of dark gray slipped down the corridor. She inched further out to try and get a better look.

She recognized that small stature, the way the person hobbled. Crowrot.

What was he doing in the library? Not that it should be odd to find anyone exiting a library, but she thought it interesting for him to be departing so late in the evening when she was just arriving, the wall sconces waning in the shadowed night.

Inside the dusty room that smelt of parchment and melting tallow wax, she scoured to see if any books had been mislaid, or if there was a gap in one of the shelves she knew were filled to the brim. Skating around the stacks, a small puff of dreary smoke drifted from a candle on a desk in the corner where she had sat one of the previous times she was here.

The table had nothing on it but one, single book. She squinted, the room dark with the sun tucked away and the candles not all lit.

"*The Misuse of Moat Maintenance: A Treatise on the Practicalities of Castle Infrastructure,*" she read aloud. Curiously, Mara recalled this title, boring as it was, but from where? Mara drifted into the seat and flipped through the text, convinced this was the book Crowrot had just been scanning.

Shock struck her, remembering this title from the forbidden section. Last she remembered, the tome was locked behind gilded bars, assuming it accidentally got shoved in with the wrong lot—how could something about infrastructure be forbidden?

When she began reading the text, it was exactly as the cover made it appear: dull and technical, almost unreadable without interest in the finer points of castle infrastructure. She sighed, a bit disappointed, and kept lazily flipping through the pages until the content suddenly shifted. Mara steadied her hands and sat up straighter. The book had an ornate page with the words *Phantom Atonements: The How's and Why's of Dark Magick* written in deep blue ink.

Mara arched a brow, suddenly enthralled. The pages that followed were vastly different from the first half of the book. Her fingers traced over various spells and histories of archaic summonings. There were drawings of diagrams and sigils that marked the parchment. Her heart raced; she felt like she shouldn't be reading this at all.

Then she paused over a peculiar line of wording written in gilded ink. *Phantom Curses and Other Casualties.*

A phantom incantation can often be used to replicate something otherwise impossible. Archmage Delair was the first to discover such a spell—later coined as a curse. Such a powerful incantation has only been successfully completed by blood relatives of superior houses; the god humors that run through their veins seemingly necessary for such evil. However, it's been theorized by archmages that consuming draugr flora—the only flora in our realm that stems directly from the Veil—can grant a person enough dark magick to perform such spells. *Refer to section 9.4 for Risks of Flora Consumption.

When a member of House Blackwing, in the present-day province of the Realm of Lost Men, summoned a replica of his sister's brain in an attempt to save her, only atrocious things followed. Marquess Blackwing had created a phantom forgery of his sister's brain days following her death—a lygi limb; lygi stemming from the old-world word "to lie." When the lygi brain was placed in a freshly deceased corpse, his sister did, in fact, come back to life. Though, she was described as a monster, demons clogging her thoughts. She couldn't do a thing without the assistance of her handmaidens. And when she did respond to stimuli, it was with screeches and growls.

He was forced to cut down his sister, watching her die for a second time.

Since Marquess Blackwing, the curse has been banned in all of Junefell. But of course, this excludes the Ghost and Dusk Court. Texts documenting the detailed ritual to produce a lygi incantation have long since either been destroyed or locked away with unbreakable curses by talented sorcerers.

Mara sat dumbfounded before the text, trying to digest all she had just discovered. She watched as the inky words on the page began to fade and swirl into new sentences. Her eyes struggled to keep up, the writing transforming to an excerpt about the consequences of insufficient depths for castle moats. She quickly skimmed through the following pages, watching as the words drifted away and were replaced by useless nonsense.

"Wait, wait, wait!" she whined. When she realized all the pages had switched to match the cover of the tome, she closed the book with a hostile sound. She wondered how many more tomes in this library appeared mundane and simple on the outside but were filled with forbidden knowledge and erased history.

Chapter Twenty-Four
Mara

Mara sat languidly on an ivy-infested stone bench that overlooked the cliffside and down onto the sea's fatal waters. She hoped to see a nereid again and perked up from her book every so often. She leaned on the bench completely so her back was flat and held the book up in front of her, mumbling some of the words unintelligibly as she read. She was so exhausted from everything that had been happening that she prayed Acastus didn't find her relaxing on this bench, forcing her back to the library to study more on glassfairing.

"What'cha doing?" a tiny voice came from behind her.

A salty breeze blew Mara's hair to the side, fluttering the pages against her fingers that held her place. She turned to see a sideways Prince Aevum. He rocked back and forth, his hands clasped behind his back.

"I am reading, little prince."

"Anything interesting?"

Mara smirked, sitting up and swinging her feet back around.

She folded one of the pages down and closed the book. "Nothing of note."

Aevum walked around the bench and gazed out of the opposite arched bay window, beyond the castle's deteriorating roof, and over the pastures of the city. Mara strolled up behind him, resting against the stone pillar like Azor might have done, crossing her arms. "Craving the bustle of the city?"

Aevum sighed, leaning his chubby cheek on his palm, looking wistfully into the distance. "I'm not allowed."

"What do you mean you're not allowed?" Mara stood straighter. "I would think out of anyone here, the prince would be able to explore the streets of Kairth as he so pleased."

Aevum shook his head, his eyes tilting down.

Mara bit her lip, feigning a startled gasp. "Are you a wanted man?"

The sides of Aevum's lips ticked up playfully. "Possibly."

Mara's hand moved to her chest like a damsel. "What did you do? Am I unsafe in your company, Prince?"

Aevum giggled, the sorrow in his eyes flickering, then he finally turned to face the princess. His eyes sank, his smile slipping. "I'm... unwell."

Mara's eyebrows knitted in concern. "You're sick?"

"Cas and Father say I'm not well enough to travel anymore. And that includes the short ride into the city."

Mara bit her lip, wanting to ask what sort of ailment he had, but she managed to maintain her gentility and didn't prod.

"It's the plays I miss the most," he sang. He fell back dramatically onto the bench, his fist against his chest, imitating a melodramatic suicide scene.

"Oh, I can see you have kin for the arts, little prince."

He smiled. "And do you?" he asked her.

"I like to think myself a well-versed actress—my brother and father always said so. I have been told I can be quite theatric," she joked and gave him a cheeky smile, thinking back to the time Evrardin told her how histrionic her character tended to be. Aevum giggled. "But either way, I do love to read them. To get lost in their stories and fairy tales."

"Would you recite one for me?" His eyes pleaded, his face suddenly lit from within.

Mara's cheeks rose with heat, she had never acted in front of anyone before—unless her lies truly counted as theater. "You'd want that? I can't promise you I'll be any good."

Aevum clapped his hands before grabbing one of hers, nodding his head. He began to drag her away and Mara made a mental note to come back and grab the book she left on the stone bench later.

Aevum pulled her through the castle and into a beautiful sitting room. The fireplace crackled with a low fire, the summer warmth not quite heating a room so deep within the cool cobblestoned walls. There were upholstered settees the color of pale daylilies. The carpet was soft and intricate with weaving patterns and golden tassels. Large bookshelves lined the walls, stacked high with books, packed even more than the ones in the library. She strolled along the edge of the dark oak shelves, her fingers trailing the vinyl of the books' spines. She realized they were all adventure stories, fairy tales, or extravagant playwrights. She smiled at Aevum who followed close behind her.

"And whose room are we in?" she asked him. She picked up a tome filled with dark tales of ancient lands and mystical beings, flipping through it before replacing it.

"Cas used to like to study in here."

Mara glanced at him, and he averted his eyes. She tried to imagine Acastus pouring over tomes with great interest late into the night, a dying candle his only light source as his finger traced the pages.

"Though, not so much anymore. I tend to it now."

"A whole study to yourself?"

Aevum grinned, pulling on the collar of his tunic, then nodded.

Mara continued to waltz past the bookshelves, taking in all the patterns.

"Do you have a favorite?" Aevum asked her.

"Hm," she thought. "I've always enjoyed the masques performed at feasts in Venmore. Though, my favorite academic drama might have to be *The Tragedy of the Sun and Wolf*." She half-expected Aevum to look put off at her choice: a tragic love story. But he grinned at her. Mara wondered if he was truly that starved of entertainment and friendship that he would have been glad for any play she mentioned.

"Would you do that one for me?"

A mirthless chuckle escaped her. "Are you trying to make a fool of me?"

Aevum straddled his legs as he took large steps, focusing on the rug's pattern beneath his boots. "Why would I do that?"

Mara's eyes crinkled, Aevum's innocence a fresh breeze on her clammy skin.

"Or you can just recite it, if you'd prefer," he said more demurely, his eyes flickering around the room like he was nervous she was going to abandon him if he didn't settle his excitement.

Mara had never properly acted, but she didn't see how doing this for Aevum would hurt. In truth, she thought it might be fun to be extraordinarily dramatic. To live out the drama she had read countless times. To play a character that was not her, hopelessly in love, even if it did end tragically. As a princess, she would never be allowed to perform in a show. While nobles used theater as entertainment, the actors were always lowborns.

She made her way to the bookshelf and began looking for a copy even though she knew it by heart. It was a rather prevalent tragedy, so she'd be surprised if it wasn't here—*Oh*, she found it and tugged the leather into her palm.

She spun to Aevum who had made himself comfortable on the rug, leaning back against one of the sofas. She moved with a tiny jump in her step. "Shall we?"

She began by reading the exposition, using a silly voice for the narrator, gaining an amused chuckle from Aevum, then switched to her own lilt when it was time to recite as Trana, the sun goddess.

She imitated how she imagined a beautiful crane would walk and talk, taking a moment to look at the gorgeous illustrations that mirrored the words on the pages. "But, Sister, time is rising on us. There is no realm where we can stay together forever. While I wish to be by your side, always, we cannot become our own within the confines of sisterhood."

Mara moved sideways to depict her shift in character, ready to become Trana's sister and give her retort. "Alone? Do you know how the world treats lonely girls, Trana?"

She shifted again, taking on Trana's more lengthened stance, using her free arm to flail before her in plea. "Máni, please, you must consider—" Mara's words were lost in her throat when her eyes flashed at the door. There, leaning against the frame, stood Evrardin.

Aevum rose to his knees to peek behind the backrest at what Mara had been lost to and waved him over. "Ev! Come watch. Mara is performing a tragedy!"

Evrardin's countenance didn't change, but his lip wavered with great subtlety. "That so?"

Mara's face turned red, her hand falling to her side, the book resting against her skirts. "How long have you been watching?"

Ev made his way to Aevum and sat on the cushions behind him, shifting his sword as he found an agreeable position. "Might have missed the beginning, but I've seen quite enough to know you're just as good an actress as I imagined."

Mara pursed her lips. She knew his outward compliment sounded polite, but it was a quip in disguise. She sucked in a breath, letting the playfulness of today wash over her. She decided she did not care if Evrardin was to watch—even if he would tease her later for it. She was doing this for Aevum. And to be completely honest with herself, she felt like she was reveling in the merrymaking more than she had at the masquerade.

Evrardin ruffled Aevum's hair before leaning back against the sofa, his arm extending over the back, looking mischievously relaxed.

"Quite comfortable?" she implored, a bit of snark in her tone.

Aevum grinned and gestured for her to keep going. Mara continued the sequence, switching between the two divine sisters, arguing with herself about separating. In the end, Máni would be right. Separating to follow their path would only weaken them, leaving the sisters open and exposed.

Then Sköll, the mythical wolf that chased the sun, and Hati, the brother who chased the moon, arrived, taking stage left. They had been sent by Fenrir, their monstrous father, to retrieve his debt from Trana and Máni's sire. With their father dead, the two wolves assumed the debt the sisters owed for their sire's wrongdoings.

Trana and Máni attempted to outrun the wolves, symbolizing the passage of time as the sun and moon moved throughout the day cycle. When the moon or sun fell to an eclipse, it's said that Sköll and Hati were catching up to the two girls.

But then, Sköll did something not in the divination: he fell in love with the sun. Trana had transformed over time into something he couldn't live without. Her warmth seemed to fuel him. But his wolfish side isn't something the gods would let him repress.

Mara paused in her reading. "This might get tricky playing both lovers," she mused, wondering if Aevum would settle for her to just dramatically read the script aloud instead of acting.

But instead, Aevum turned to Evrardin lounging behind him and nudged his leg. "Ev, go play Sköll!"

"And why can't I play Sköll?" she asked with feigned hurt. "You sure he wouldn't be better off playing Trana?"

"Hm," Aevum pretended to contemplate her words. "You're right. Trana's elegance does line up far more accurately with Evrardin."

"Are you saying I'm not elegant?" she asked aghast, her hand rising to her chest, her feet stumbling over a rung in the rug.

"That's exactly what I'm saying," Aevum giggled.

Mara's jaw hung open briefly at his dry words then burst out laughing. It felt so good to laugh. And not just at someone's stupidity, or a pretend, courteous laugh. But to really feel the joy ebb through her.

She swore she saw Ev smirking in the periphery of her vision, though the tears in her eyes made it hard to tell.

When the two finally stopped giggling, Aevum looked over expectantly at Evrardin.

Evrardin scoffed at the small prince. "Aevum, I do not act. I am Captain of the—"

"Yes, yes. I know. You're far too important for such frivolities." Aevum sighed and sank back.

Mara scowled at Evrardin, irritated he had upset Aevum who was starving for company. "Captain!" Mara scolded. "You really want Aevum to die of boredom?!" Mara flashed her eyes at Aevum and he smiled in covert communication, understanding her crazed expressions. The prince collapsed sideways, sliding against the sofa, his head thumping as it hit the rug, pretending to be dead, an odd gurgling sound rumbling in his throat.

Evrardin shook his head at their dramatics. "Maybe theater is the path for *both* of you. Not prince and princesshood."

She crossed her arms and gestured to the spot on the carpet beside her. Evrardin huffed an annoyed breath and stood. He used Aevum's head to help him stand which resulted in a titter from the prince.

When he got to Mara's side, he seemed somewhat discomfited. Gratification swelled through her seeing him out of his element. And to think, all it took was playing pretend for the prince. She tried to hold back her amusement to not deter Evrardin and handed him the leather-bound play.

"Don't you need to read from it?"

"I have the dialogue memorized already."

Evrardin shook his head as he held the book in his large hands and skimmed the following few pages. "Course you do."

Mara rolled her eyes then began to recite her lines. "The stars are not easily moved. They will not allow us to be together," she cried dramatically.

Evrardin cleared his throat, reading in a monotone voice. "My summer sun, my darling Trana, for I could forsake my father in hopes of following in your shadow. The stars no longer pertain to my will. I fear I cannot carry on without you. And that holds a much deeper terror than the gods could ever instill."

Mara looked away from Evrardin and spoke to the bookshelves. "Look at yourself, my sweet wolf. For the monster you might become, you were always meant to mold to. A fate we cannot escape. You are to hunt me down, and Hati, my moonlit sister. The stars have spoken, I cannot be with you."

Evrardin closed his eyes, but not before glaring in disapproval at the stage directions. He fell to his knees, shaking his head like this was all so fatuous. And yet, he read his lines. "The only monster I'll enrapture is in a world without you."

Mara spun to face the captain. "You have lived many

centuries without me, my wolf. And you will live many more. Fate brings us together, 'tis true. But only for destruction." Mara tried to summon tears, one stray droplet sliding down her cheek. Evrardin almost looked impressed as he peered up at her, his head coming to her waist.

"You do not mean that."

Mara shook her head and fell to her knees to match Evrardin, who made tentative movements in recoil. The script instructed him to embrace Trana and he looked as though he was debating following through—maybe he'd skip to the next line.

"Come on, Ev," Aevum encouraged over the lull.

Ev glared at Mara as she waited patiently for her counterpart. He shook his head and huffed. *And he wanted to call her dramatic?*

"You wound me," Evrardin began, reaching for Mara.

He seemed to hesitate, so Mara made the move for him. She waddled on her knees and into his arms, her hand fanning her forehead in faux distress. "I feel my heart shattering, my love. I cannot bear this if you continue to torture me so."

Evrardin held the book out and used his other hand to execute his mandated actions. His hand slid to her cheek, forcing her to face him. She moved into his grip, allowing his control, peering at him, reminding her of the sacred paintings she often studied in the halls.

"Can you trust me?" he whispered.

Her heart quickened even though she knew this was acting, suddenly thrown off. Mara's hand clutched Evrardin's wrist and Aevum made a little noise of distress, whispering, "Don't do it," on the sideline.

"Forever."

Evrardin pried his eyes from Mara's face in his hand and skimmed for a follow-up line. He scrunched his brows. "What? This is moronic," he said in a mock aside.

"Just do as it says," Mara chided.

Evrardin shook his head in distaste but continued, back in his Sköll persona—which sounded eerily similar to his own lilt. "Then forgive me for what I have to do." His hand slid to her neck, gently resting his fingers along the expanse of her skin.

Mara pretended to be suffocated by his embrace. Evrardin remained stoic and she flashed her eyes at him. He looked back at the text and read with a huff. "For as you break, my sweet sun, my heart goes with you."

Mara went limp and Evrardin seemed startled, catching her in his arms and lowering her to the floor. "Is this part of it?" he asked her in a hushed tone.

She held back a grin and nodded her head. Then her hand moved to hold his cheek in a loving embrace and his back straightened. "It's okay," she cooed. Trana had known all along Sköll would be the death of her. Time was not on her side. She could only outrun the wolf for so long. And his blooming and vigorous love had only played her—both of them—for a fool.

Even after all the heartbreak and blood, Trana still loved him. How foolish was that?

"Forgive me," he said with a strangled noise. He was trying to appear sullen. When his eyes drifted back to the text, they rounded.

"You don't have to actually do that," she whispered, her cheeks heating, knowing what he read.

The next stage direction called for a lover's final kiss, both Trana and Sköll embracing, the life slowly depleting from her as Sköll kissed her delicate lips one last time. And shortly after she faded into nothing but a shadow, he would go with her. For she truly had become his heart even if he couldn't escape their fatal fate.

They were already so close that Evrardin only had to lower his head slightly toward Mara's. She swallowed and Evrardin's eyes darkened, her throat bobbing beneath his palm. She thought he might kiss her then, amazed he'd follow through so thoroughly with a play they were amateurly performing for the young prince.

She could feel his breath against her nose, her eyes fluttering as she looked at him. With a fleeting, graceless movement, Evrardin placed an almost undetectable kiss on her forehead.

Mara was thankful this was her character's death scene as she got to close her eyes, afraid of how she might have looked if she had to keep eye contact with him any longer. Ev gingerly let her slide to the rug so she laid prone.

She cracked an eye open as he stood. "Go on, give us your closing monologue."

He cursed under his breath, but Mara could see he wasn't as irritated as he put on. He might have even been enjoying himself.

"For as the sun lets the shadow approach and get too close, the darkness swallows it whole. Even the dark pulse of my heart cannot bear the actions that led to my sweet sun's death, my heart tied with hers, collapsing in on itself as I mourn her corpse beneath my feet. I pray thee who hear the tragedy of how the sun lost its shine, learn that what is written in the stars cannot be evaded. It cannot be fought. For with this dagger, I plunge into the depths of my despair, my heart no longer beating now that my light has left my life."

"*Exeunt omnes!*" Mara called.

Aevum clapped joyously. Mara was convinced he would have been happy no matter the narrative of the tale, he just wanted company and some rudimentary entertainment. She understood that loneliness all too well.

Evrardin outstretched a hand and Mara hesitantly took it, letting him haul her to her feet. She stumbled from the sheer strength of him, tumbling into his chest.

"That was wonderful, Mara! Would you put on another?"

Mara laughed, reaching out to take the book from Evrardin's

hand. Her fingers grazed his and their eyes met momentarily. "Oh. Maybe another time, tiny prince. I think I'm all acted out."

Aevum nodded, plopping himself down on the sofa's cushions. "Yes, very well. But I shall hold you to that promise." His fingers played with the hilt of Ev's sword that he left sheathed and leaning against the sofa.

"I made no such promise! I said *maybe*," she playfully argued.

"Says who? Evrardin, didn't she just promise she would act out another play for me tomorrow?"

Mara scoffed, widening her eyes at Aevum in a mock reproach.

Evrardin watched the engagement unfold between the two, his lips pulled into a taut line. "Enough, Aevum."

Mara scowled over at the captain. But the playfulness seemed to die in the room as Evrardin's eyes narrowed in on Aveum.

"The Crown Prince wanted me to inform you he expects you to join his company this evening."

Mara's heart constricted at the swift tonal change in Evrardin's words. He had seemed almost insouciant just moments ago—well, to those familiar with the brooding man—and now he spoke his words with grave malignancy.

Mara's hands found her hips in irritation. "Do you do everything the prince demands of you?"

Evrardin turned to her in a swift gesture, making Mara jump back in alarm. "Do not mistake this"—he gestured between the two of them—"for friendship, Princess." She went to open her mouth and his eyes narrowed. "Do. Not. Argue. With. Me," he growled through gritted teeth.

Mara blinked several times, trying to digest his vicious remarks. She looked down at Aevum, who she expected to be jovial, convincing her that this was just Evrardin being a bore and not something more. But instead, the prince looked between them in dread.

"I... wasn't trying to..." Her words got lost as Ev leered at her.

His fingers twitched, begging to reach out and strangle her no doubt. She imagined what they might feel like around her neck, suffocating her just as Sköll did to Trana. He stood straight, entering her space, looming over her like a deadly curse. She swallowed hard, willing her legs to move back. The back of her knees collided with the sofa and she fell to a seat. "Go to Acastus and your father at nightfall," he growled at Aveum before grabbing his sword and storming out of the room without a second glance.

Aevum walked over to Mara, putting his hand on top of hers. "I hate when he gets like that."

"Like what?" Mara asked, hoping her voice didn't sound as broken as she felt.

"He'll be fine one moment, then the next, he's angry beyond belief. It's not his fault, though."

"Then whose fault is it?"

The little prince sighed wistfully, sinking into the feathered cushion beside her and leaning on her shoulder.

CHAPTER TWENTY-FIVE
MARA

THE SUN still sat below the horizon when the captain knocked on the princess' door.

She opened it with sleep-laden eyes, rubbing at them. She trailed up the captain's figure. "Is there a reason you're bothering me before the sun has even risen?"

"Put some clothes on and come with me."

She scoffed, her body coming to life at his rude demeanor. "What? Why would I do that?" She retained her yawn. A small piece of her wondered if the captain was still in his foul mood from yesterday, misleading her, wanting to drag her away in the early morning to rid him of her presence once and for all.

"I'm going to train you."

Her brows creased together, her hand gripping her door tightly. "You're going to... What?"

His jaw ticked like he was angry. He was always angry. "Come with me now, *liten rev*."

She wanted to argue with him. To tell him off for being so

cold to her yesterday when she thought they were finally getting along, but something else inside her was too curious to fight. She pursed her lips, studying him as he waited. She finally grunted before shutting her door and throwing off her chemise.

"Wear pants," he spoke through the heavy wood.

She swore under her breath, tugging on a pair of trousers. She slid the olive-green pants over her hips, the soft satin blouse billowing over her arms, then topped it with an olive dress to disguise her clothes. She appeared back in the doorway moments later, letting Evrardin guide her out to the gardens.

Gooseflesh pilled on Mara's arms as the soft howl of the dark morning wind rushed through the open windows.

It was silent between the two as he led her down the corridors. She wondered what he had crossing in the depths of his mind, tracing his dark features with her eyes. "Quit staring at me," he mumbled.

Mara felt a flush rise to her cheeks. "I don't understand what we're doing."

Evrardin opened his mouth, but no words came out.

It was only another moment until they reached the gardens in the courtyard. "Out here?" Mara asked as the warm summer air blew the skirts of her dresses around her feet.

"Not quite. We're goin' out by the honey trees. Can't be spotted there from the castle. It's too far."

"The prince won't be looking for you?"

Evrardin grunted in response.

"Evrardin," she hissed.

He didn't stop.

"Evrardin!" she shouted, halting.

He finally turned, clearly agitated, to face her.

"Where are you taking me?"

"The gardens. I told you—"

"But *why*? I don't see why you're dragging me from my chambers so early in the morning. To what? Train me? And I'm supposed to just be compliant, why? You've given me no reason to trust you."

He sucked in a breath, glancing down the hall to make sure they were alone. "You should learn how to protect yourself."

She shook her head. "I don't understand—"

"Unfortunately, I'm not someone you can trust." She didn't know why, but these words hurt. "But I am someone who can help you. Let me train you in self-defense."

Mara's eyes softened, swallowing hard at Evrardin's intense stare. She wanted to ask more, but the solid way the captain pleaded made her want to trust him, even with his previous statement. "Okay," she said gently, unsure of what she was agreeing to.

The captain nodded, turning around to lead her out into the gardens.

The moon cast a faint glow over the foliage, the flowers and shrubbery shining like they were shrouded with a silver blanket.

Evrardin peered down at the princess as they walked side by side. "Nervous?" he mocked.

Mara glared at him. He was goading her. "So, what if I am?"

"I don't know. I guess I always thought of you as a bit defiant. Thought you'd be used to this"—he gestured his head forward—"kind of thing."

Mara's fingertips brushed across the petals of a mourning flower as they strolled past. "And do you spend your time thinking of me often?"

"Never good things."

"Course," she agreed. "And never on your own will, I presume?"

"Nothing is ever on my free will when it comes to you."

She imagined he would be scowling. His face giving away something to insinuate that the idea of her disgusted him—that thinking of her when she wasn't around made him sick. Yet, when she glanced at him, he seemed more... guilty.

"You usually talk a lot when you're nervous," he stated flatly.

Mara sighed as they crossed the bridge over the small, silver pond. Its banisters an icy blue, almost transparent. "If you must know," she began, dragging out her syllables, "I'm not keen on the idea of falling into bad graces with the prince."

Evrardin's teeth clenched, grinding the ivory of them against one another. "You won't." Two simple words the princess couldn't fully trust.

"Good. Because if I do, this is your fault. Let the record show that I tried to argue this."

"And I suppose you'll make it clear to the prince that it was all my doing—that the captain forced his tiny betrothed into unseemly circumstances?"

Mara pursed her lips. "Are you implying he wouldn't believe me?"

"No. I'm implying I know already that you care not about throwing me to the wolves."

She huffed in annoyance, following a few beats behind his gait.

They approached a small nestle of honey trees, their bark golden, the honey oozing from their pores, glistening in the moonlight. Mara immediately swiped a finger through the nectar and brought it to her mouth. Her eyes closed as she savored the flavor.

"Honey is rare in the south," she said. "They don't take well to the cold, and there's so little to exist that it's never imported."

Evrardin watched her for another moment as she examined the trees, marveling at their amber leaves.

"Shall we get started?"

Mara refocused on Evrardin as he unsheathed a knife from his belt. She nodded and began to undo the laces of her dress.

Evrardin's eyebrows immediately shot to his hairline. "Princess, what're you—?"

He was almost mesmerized—entranced, even—by Mara as she slid the sleeves of her dress off her shoulder and shimmied out of it. Mara carefully folded her dress and placed it behind her and the captain cleared his throat. "You told me to wear trousers," she blushed. "I didn't think it'd be appropriate if I was caught in this," she explained, her hands gesturing down her body to her newfound clothes.

"Right. Smart," Evrardin added. He handed Mara the knife he held, tearing off the sheath as she accepted the weapon. "Keep this on you at all times," he demanded.

Mara flipped the dagger over in her hand. The hilt was simple: a faded silver, a blue gem in the center. The blade smokey and well-kept, its beauty soft and quiescent. Artisanal.

"A gift?" she jested.

"It may not be the kind of adornment you're used to, but it will do the job."

She rolled her eyes. "I didn't even say anything."

"But you were thinking it."

"Why do you always assume you know what I'm thinking? Like you know me so well?" There was a pause as they glared at one another. "If you had cared to ask, I was admiring it. I think it's rather pretty."

Evrardin's eyes narrowed as he stalked toward her. For a moment, a flutter of fear crossed Mara's heart. "S'not supposed to be pretty. It's a weapon." Evrardin's hands moved, wrapping the sheath around her waist. His fingers quickly secured the belt, pulling it tight enough to make her gasp.

"Just because something is designed for malice, doesn't mean it can't be marveled at. Plenty of things destined for bloodshed are disguised in beauty." Her eyes met his. "You're to tell me you don't revere the swords you spend hours polishing?"

"I'll tell you, I don't waste my time honoring the apparency of such ordinances when their only purpose is to be sharp enough to end a life."

"Maybe that's your problem, then. You lack the couth to appreciate the subtleties of malevolence. The tiny intricacies that artisans take in these things you brutes deem weapons."

"Is that so? When I gut innocent men because my prince commands me to, is that beautiful?"

She scrunched her face. "Is a sword not a symbol of strength and protection? Is an ax not a savior against injustices? A warhammer that of virtue, or spears of comradery?" She sighed. "The sword is not at fault for being wrongly used."

"Is there a reason you're eager to lecture me?"

"You say I lack worldliness, yet you are nothing more than a savage who acts on impulses instead of rational thought." She crossed her arms in a huff.

The corner of Evrardin's mouth ticked. "Ready?"

Mara nodded, her waist still feeling the aftershock of Evrardin's hands grazing her.

"Now, assuming you won't get into any real skirmishes, I'm just going to teach you how to escape an assault. And how to retaliate."

Mara had the nerve to want to chastise him for thinking she wouldn't see any real battle, but he was right.

"Okay."

"I'm serious when I say keep that on you." He gestured his head toward the belt. "Even if you do it solely because it matches your outfit."

Mara glared at him and chose to ignore his quip. "It's a bit conspicuous, don't you think? Not sure the prince will approve of me walking around like this."

"Good thing we're not askin' him. Keep it under your skirts."

The conversation of what was beneath Mara's skirts on

Evrardin's lips made her blush. She nodded, mirroring him, and took out the new weapon.

Evrardin raised his hand, looking like he was readying to pounce. "All right, try and attack me."

Mara looked at him dumbfounded. "But you're unarmed."

Evrardin laughed. "You think I need a weapon to defend myself against *you*?"

Mara's neck pinked, and she averted her eyes to tuck away her embarrassment. "I…" she stuttered. "I don't know how."

Evrardin's dark eyes softened slightly, but the rage was still there beneath the surface. "And I'll show you how. But first, I just need to get a feel for how you move."

The pink on Mara's neck climbed farther up to her cheeks. Still, she nodded like she felt confident, attempting to imagine it was her brother she was sparring with. She had sparred many times with Azor, but never truly learned anything of use—she just wanted to be able to hit him with a wooden stick.

Mara took a step toward Evrardin, jutting her dagger out. In one fell swoop, Evrardin dodged her arm, using the momentum of her step to get behind her, bringing her hand with him, and holding it behind her back.

He held her for a moment before letting go and she stumbled forward. "Good. Next time, don't show your attacker where you're going to strike by extending your arm before you even move your feet."

Mara blinked rapidly, still a little dazed by Evrardin's swift movements. "Right," she mumbled.

"Again," he commanded.

Mara repositioned herself and this time, she leaned into him but brought her hand up on his side. Evrardin was quicker though, and he caught her hand in time to stop her from hitting his armor. He clutched her wrist between his fingers, her dagger falling to the ground. "Now get out of my hold."

Mara wiggled her arm, trying to pull it back.

"No. You have to move closer in order to get further away."

"That doesn't make any sense," she said exasperated.

"Push into me, then twist yourself so you go under my arm, and I'll be forced to release my grip."

Mara sucked in an aggravated breath before doing what he instructed. She twirled and contorted her body.

"Use what you have," he growled irritated.

"I'm not armed," she spat back through bated breaths as Ev held her, her dagger mocking her in the grass.

"Your nails. Make me let go, Mara."

Her fingers scratched at his arms, digging her nails into his skin. She might have protested hurting him, but for once, she had no problem doing as he instructed. Her foot slipped behind him so Evrardin had no choice but to let go.

They did this for what felt like hours before Mara was huffing for air. She leaned back against an ivy-covered stone wall, her hands on her knees as she struggled for air.

"Ready to go again?" he teased.

She scowled up at him, her heart rate slowly resetting back to its normal rhythm.

Evrardin flipped Mara's dagger in his hand as he waited for her. She slowly pushed herself back up and stalled, not wanting to practice any longer. Maybe this wasn't such a good idea, no matter how practical.

But if she was to voice this, she'd never hear the end of how spoiled she was. How she can't be uncomfortable for ten minutes even if it meant saving her life. So she refrained.

Instead, she strolled over to a bushel of blackwood flowers, marveling at the depth of their color, the sky slowly beginning to glow as the sun inched upward. It was rare to find ones quite this dark. It made her eyes feel a little woozy as she stared at the black petals—they seemed to steal all the light from around them.

"Wow," she muttered, leaning in closer to see if she could make out any of the flower's texture. "The gardener here is truly something else," she praised, standing back up to her full height.

Evrardin laughed. Mara shot him a look. "What's so funny? Are you truly so corrupt, you can't admire pretty flowers either?"

He shook his head. "Quite the opposite, *liten rev*." Evrardin crossed his arms over his chest, his lip quirking at the side. "You just might think differently if you knew who *he* was."

"Oh, pray tell," she mused. She strutted back over to him and met his eyes, her hands behind her as she awaited his response with a coy smile on her lips.

Evrardin returned her stare, not speaking. He caught the dagger on its blade and extended the hilt for her to take between her fingers.

"You are the gardener," she spoke softly.

"Don't sound so admirable, Princess."

She shook her head, the tendrils of her hair sticking to the sweat on her face, taking the dagger from his extended hand. "This is more than a hobby?" she asked. She looked around at the beautiful flora. "You grew these?"

"No. Not all. But this area is mostly my doing, yes."

"You've yet to surprise me so."

"And what is it about my pastime that surprises you, *liten rev*?"

Mara bit her lip, dragging her foot in the grass. "It's just... they're all so... pretty." *And Evrardin was so... not pretty.*

He took a step closer to her. "You think me only capable of ruining things?"

"I didn't say that."

He smirked. "But you were thinking it.".

Then his hands were on her, grabbing her waist and spinning her around. Mara gasped as he clutched her tightly in his arms, her heart racing, dropping her dagger in the chaos. He engulfed her against his broad chest, his grasp tightening. "Now, escape," he instructed darkly.

"That's not fair! You didn't let me prepare!"

"And you think your attacker will give you time to get yourself situated?"

Mara hated the way her heart skipped. "I don't know, in the right attire I can be pretty convincing."

He scoffed, but it almost sounded like he had a smile plastered on his face.

She struggled at first, wiggling against him. He grunted as she shook her shoulders back and forth, trying to slip out of his grip, but it was no use. "Quit squirmin'," he said, strained. "And slide your leg behind mine. Then put all your weight on the back of my knee."

She narrowed her eyes, trying to focus. She was blind as she pushed her foot back, trying to wrap it around Evrardin's leg. He was so much taller than her, it made it nearly impossible. Mara arched her back into him, her leg extending, her backside flush with his front. She whined as she finally hooked her leg over his and placed her weight into him.

Evrardin released her and she stumbled forward, catching herself on her knees and palms. She stood up, a small smile on her face. "So, did I do it right?" she asked. That felt exhilarating. She didn't want to admit the rush she got when she realized she could escape his lethal hold.

Evrardin's face didn't return the same joviality. "Think that's enough for today." His voice had gone irritatingly hoarse.

Mara blinked rapidly a few times as Evrardin picked her dagger off the ground and flipped it in his hand, handing her the hilt.

"But I thought we were just getting started." Mara reluctantly took the dagger from him.

"Put your dress back on," he demanded. He spun around,

walking over to the bridge to wait for her. Her eyes trailed his hand as it landed on the hilt of his sword, shifting his belt as he moved, awkwardly adjusting his trousers.

Now Mara was positive her face turned bright red. She struggled to pull her dress back on, her hands a bit shaky as she tried to push down the rising warmth inside her.

Chapter Twenty-Six
Mara

"And he expects me to have already learned how to glassfaire?"

Mara's palms began to sweat at the sheer intensity of Evrardin's gaze. She wanted to curse out his ruggedly handsome face and his body's reaction to her this morning for making her suddenly wracked with nerves in his presence. Not that he was handsome to *her*, but she recently realized, after getting so close to him in the library, and earlier in the sitting room with Aevum, that there was something that *others* might find attractive in his grunginess. And that startled her.

His dark hair always had curly strands cascading onto his forehead and on the nape of his neck; the bits by his ears were peppered ever so slightly. He had overgrown stubble that somehow managed to consistently look like he had shaved a week ago. His deep brown eyes captivated her when she saw them in the light, his irises having the slightest hint of green. His features were sharp, but in a jagged semblance where he reminisced a nascent marbled statue that had yet to be polished. His eyes were always heavy when he glanced at her, his dark circles reflecting Mara's. He stood tall, like no one else could command him even though he was devastatingly loyal to the crown and did anything Acastus said.

She stared at the scar that bisected his lips, about how long-since-healed it appeared. How the lightness of it stood in such stark contrast to the depth of his dark skin. She wondered what he had done to earn that, and if the other man looked worse. And the faint scar she saw on his collar when his tunic was unbuttoned wide enough, thinking of how it trailed beneath the cotton of his shirt, and she wondered how many women ever had the pleasure of seeing how far it went, tracing it with soft fingers, raising gooseflesh on his skin. To hear his husky voice as he told them the story behind it, maybe clutching the women so close to his body as he spoke that they could feel the rumble from his chest, his eyes growing lustful as he appraised their feminine curves.

Mara almost choked when she caught her reverie, scolding herself for thinking about Evrardin in such an amorous light. She need to remember that he lied to her—but she was beginning to question why she should care to hold that grudge. *And* she was to marry the prince.

So many reasons to dislike him, she thought. And yet, there were also so many reason to like him. Perhaps even more so than the former.

Evrardin stole her from her inner torment. "He expects more than that, Princess."

She sighed, kicking her feet like a child as he escorted her down the many decrepit halls of Kairth, trying to channel that lingering desire out through her feet. She strolled around a shattered windowpane, glass scattered on the ground, a cool breeze casting in and shifting the cobwebs and moth-eaten drapes.

"And if I can't give him what he wants?"

Evrardin didn't look at her, instead, he kept his eyes forward, his hands clenched at his side, silent.

A large wooden door saved her from several tortuous minutes in silence beside the captain, its hinges propped open, letting the sound of the prince echo into the hall. When she stepped through the threshold, she couldn't help but marvel. The room was rather formidable, the expanse of every wall covered with mirrors. They were all different sizes, some ordained in ornate frames. Some were rusted with splotches of smog that blurred the glass. Some touched the floor and stretched up far beyond Mara's reach. They fit together like a motley assortment of puzzle pieces taken from all different places, not a single pair from the same home.

"What is all this?" she asked absentmindedly, slowly spinning, witnessing her reflection dance between mirrors like she was trying to catch it. Sconces sat awkwardly between mirrors, a flicker of golden light beaming from one end of the room to the other. The beauty of it was almost harrowing.

"It's all for you, my love," the prince hummed.

Mara halted and looked over at him.

This wasn't for her; she didn't want to glassfaire. She had seen nothing but misfortune befall those who passed into the Veil, including herself. And the prince knew it wasn't really for her either. But it was unspoken that the semantics of it didn't matter. The prince needed her to do this for him, and she needed to do this if she wanted to live. It was that simple.

His hands were held tightly behind his back and his face was tilted down at her with an aggravating sense of arrogance, but she could see his muscles beneath his tunic spread taut. He was on edge.

Lord Alfson stood far too regally behind Cas, his face pointed like it always was when she saw him. "I expect you're quite ready to glassfaire," he said with haughty disposition. She'd give anything to release the quips that lined her tongue.

The prince impatiently rolled on the balls of his feet and waved her over. "Come."

She slowly approached and he grabbed her shoulders, ruffling her silken dress, turning her so she was facing a lengthy mirror. She stared at both of their reflections and held back a wince.

She remembered the excerpt she had read earlier, thinking back to the words. She was surprised to learn about the first glassfairer—he had been lost to what was happening, disoriented in a land where he forgot all sense. He had spent too long a time exploring a realm he was not welcome to. Her mother always told her that those who mirror traveled had to act with great haste. If one was to prolong their lingering in the realm of the gods, you'd be met with a terrible, inconceivable fate.

Though, they never perfectly fit into this realm, your reflection the opposite of who you truly are. Then she wondered, if someone already existed here as evil, would that mean their demonic-self would be benevolent? Would Acastus' reflection be good and kind-hearted, then? Maybe she'd like to meet this version of him.

"It's rather straightforward," Lord Alfson began, though he had no room to talk when she was the one conducting the task. "Simply break through the mirror and step into the Veil. Not even your full body. The prince would be satiated with a hand or leg for the time being."

"How generous," she dully smiled. She had a feeling no amount of effort would truly satiate the prince.

The prince grinned. He wore a cravat today that enveloped most of his neck. He appeared more covered every time she saw him. She thought it odd summer attire, but she kept that thought lodged in her throat.

"So, Princess," the prince crooned. His voice was mellow and even, like a practiced singer. If she didn't know any better, she might have been captivated. "Show us what you have been working on with the use of the magick blood that now courses through your veins." He nudged her closer to the wall of mirrors.

Mara turned and grimaced. "I...It will take time." Mara recalled all the information she had read. "I have to root myself in this realm before I cross to the Veil." She had to keep her footing here to not let her reflection steal her place.

The prince nodded but she could see the frustration brewing on his features, his eyebrow twitching marginally. "Go on, then."

Mara gave him one last glance before she approached one of the grander mirrors. She tried to think about everything that would root her in this realm. Her brother. Her father. Jessamine. The chance of returning home. And without her consent, Evrardin willed his way into her thoughts.

She shook her head, putting him at the very bottom of the list. She took a breath before going through the list again: seeing her brother's face. Getting the chance to curse her father out then falling into his arms as he held her, stroking her hair like he would when she was a child. Jessamine's warm scent of milkweed and sugared plums, her mouth curved up absentmindedly as she rambled on about some fantastical notion she had for her future.

Grounding herself was something she could do, but the part she struggled with the most: she had to want this. She had to *want* to travel through the mirror. If she could manage that, her heritage would do the rest.

Mara tentatively placed her palm against the reflection, swallowing gulps of air, trying to keep her chest from rising too rapidly. She *did* want to glassfaire if it meant making Acastus more amicable. She didn't want to cause a disturbance. If this is why Acastus wanted her as his bride, then she'd give it to him.

Mara hadn't felt her hand sinking precariously into the mirror's surface, but she knew it was happening when her fingers weren't stopped by the glass. She could sense Cas inching closer, his eyes sparkling in her mind as he witnessed her magick. Mara squeezed her eyes tighter, willing all the strength to keep her thoughts flowing in the direction she wanted them to. *She wanted this.*

The path she walked began to waver as her heart pounded, her thoughts flashing with her mother. The way she died getting caught between realms.

She didn't want to do this. This couldn't be lower on her list of activities she wanted to do, right under prying her toenails off one by one.

Her eyes squeezed so hard together she was beginning to get a headache. *No*, she told herself. She wanted to do this. For her family. To keep Cas wanting to marry her.

She fell into war with her mind.

Abruptly, the connection fell when she thought back to how betrayed she felt the day her father gave her hand away to Acastus. She *didn't* want this. What she *did* want was to go home. Though, even now, she imagined home wouldn't feel quite right. She wanted to see her father's face, but at the same time, it made her nauseous to think about him. Tears welled in her eyes when she couldn't place her home in any tangible location.

Mara's hand felt like it was being licked by flames, then it quickly shifted and she thought her whole hand was stuck under a pile of burning embers. Her eyes shot open and she stumbled back, tripping and falling to the floor. She screamed, her arm singed with all-consuming heat.

Acastus looked at her dumbfounded, unmoving, regarding her as she began to weep, her body molten. She cradled her hand to her chest, her vision blurring and inking at the edges.

She could hear the men talking, but it sounded like her ears were swollen with water, their words indistinguishable. The heat from her arm began swimming a steady stream into the rest of her body. She bared her teeth in pain. She didn't know how she could survive this severity for much longer, her mind going numb.

A voice managed to break free from the rumbling. "Princess!" Evrardin squatted on his haunches before her. He reached out to grab her shoulders, to shake her to his attention, but she yelped at the contact. "What is it? What hurts?" he asked frantically.

The tears sizzled as they streaked her cheeks. He was all she could see when she willed her eyes to him. Everything else was going black. "Hot," she cried, her voice breaking. "I feel like I'm on fire." She ended her sentence with a whine, unable to speak further, afraid steam was coming out her throat.

Evrardin took a moment to think, then moved like he wasn't thinking at all. He swept Mara into his arms against her mumbled protests.

Cas was in his ear. "Where are you taking her?"

Evrardin ignored him as he shifted into a sprint before the prince could order him to stop, Mara cradled to his chest. The few bits of armor he donned were a cooling relief, but that too turned warm from her lasting contact. Mara's vision moved out of focus as she let Evrardin carry her. She rocked up and down as he ran, his steps unsteady. He looked down, her eyes fluttering, her mouth open as she panted. "Hang on," he promised.

"Make it stop," she murmured. She swore her body was going to be covered in burn scars by the time this was over. She had never felt such pure agony before.

"I'm trying, *liten rev*," he said in soft distress. He didn't look back at her as he descended two flights of stairs and hurried out past the gardened courtyard.

All time seemed to slip away from Mara as she laid helplessly in his arms. She wished he would just put her down already, she couldn't stand his contact for much longer. His arms were just suppressing the heat against her body.

Her eyes opened, not sure how long she had them closed for, as she heard the splashing of water. Evrardin's gate slowed, but he still moved hot-footed, forcing his legs to slosh through the sea. A few more steps and he was waist-deep, plunging them both into the cerulean ocean as he toppled forward.

Mara gasped for air as she sank with him, her whole body melting in the waters. He held her close as he waded deeper until he was standing on his feet and only his head and shoulders poked out of the tide.

He clutched Mara against his chest, allowing her hair to get wet to cool her face off as well as her flaming body. Mara was breathing so rapidly that she thought she might be choking.

She flailed and grabbed onto his shoulders, clinging around him. Evrardin hesitated before his hands found the low of her back and pressed her firmly against him. The immediate fear of being forced into the cistern filled her. She was back there again, drowning in hands that clawed and pulled at her. She didn't want to go back.

She hadn't realized she was mumbling *no* over and over again until Evrardin cooed in her ear. "You're safe. I'm here. You're just in the sea. M'not gonna let anything hurt you."

His hand came up to stroke her hair and she loosened in his arms, sinking against him, her body's tension slowly ebbing away with the push and pull of the icy water.

"You can't promise me that." Her voice was hoarse, her face still buried in the crook of his neck, her arms strangling him as she tried to catch her breath. The heat still thrummed in her veins, but the cold water was matching it, making her sigh in clamorous relief.

"And yet, I'm going to anyway."

Mara's legs wrapped around Evrardin as she clung to him, her body settling into his hold, allowing the cold water to surround her. His hands stayed firmly on her back as he listened to her panting, waiting for her breathing to steady. The waves were gentle at this hour, rocking their bodies back and forth. Several minutes passed until Mara became conscious and timidly pulled away from him, her arms on his shoulders, her face meeting his.

They were in the water farther than Mara had waded earlier; so deep, that Evrardin almost couldn't touch the bottom when waves rocked through them.

"I don't know how to swim," she said in distress like he might let her go now that she seemed to be springing back to her normal self.

"I won't let you drown," he said, his voice far lighter than his shouting words from earlier.

"Good," she breathed. "Because I'd never forgive you for that."

"Naturally." He smiled as if relieved to hear her attitude, and Mara's breath caught at the unfamiliar sight. His eyes seemed to sparkle in his grin, Mara's mouth becoming dry.

The corners of her mouth began to tilt up to mirror him, but they halted when she realized her legs were tightly wrapped around his waist. "Oh. Uh," she stuttered, her legs falling away so she was floating solely by holding onto his shoulders. "Sorry, I…"

Evrardin's arms went lower, going under the backs of her thighs and heaving her so she had no choice but to let her legs tangle around him again. She made an odd noise as he forced her to hold on to him. His arms brushed her bare thighs as her dress floated upward. She would have tried to suppress the blush rising to her face, but she knew she was already beet-red from the fever.

"The only reason the nereids haven't stolen me yet is because I'm holding on to you," he said, reasoning why he wanted to keep her so close. Evrardin's words sent a chill through her. He made it sound like *she* was doing *him* a favor.

He stood there with her in his arms until she began to get gooseflesh, her body spiraling with ice. Her teeth were about to start chattering when Evrardin began to exit the waves. She hadn't even thought about how cold he must have been as he stood there with her. His fingers had gone blue, but somehow, she knew he would have stayed in that frozen ocean for as long as it took.

Mara didn't fight him as he carried her. Her eyes widened, a nereid staring back at her in the distance over Evrardin's shoulder, her hair a deep green that glimmered bluer when she moved. She could have sworn she saw the creature smile before diving back under the waves.

When they reached the sandy beach, he slowly dropped her legs so she could stand on her own. She adjusted her dress, his hands lingering on her waist a moment too long.

When she looked up at him on unstable legs, she realized he was staring at her body. A bit confused, she glanced down to see her dress clinging to her every curve, her nipples pebbled and her breasts visible from the sopping caress of the fabric. Her hands went to cover herself in embarrassment and Evrardin's eyes shot to hers.

She thought he was about to mouth an apology, but instead, he said, "Your slippers."

Mara raised a brow and flashed her eyes downward. Her slippers must have fallen off in the water because now her bare toes were sinking into the sand. Before she could utter any sort of response, Evrardin swept her up into his arms again.

"Ev!" she shrieked. He began walking. Of course he wasn't willing to entertain the idea of her making her way back over the grounds and through the rocky terrain of the castle without something on her feet.

She huffed in annoyance and the edge of Evrardin's lip curved. She unwillingly clung to him, the breeze sending cold shudders up her spine now that she was soaking wet. She gave a mirthless laugh, imagining how odd they must have seemed to any onlookers: Evrardin carrying the princess in a mad dash to the shore; them both coming back, her still in his arms, but now they were drenched; sand falling from her hair that was plastered to her back.

She buried her face against his chest, hiding from the people she knew they were passing. She could feel their eyes burning holes in the back of her head. "Are they all laughing?" she asked him quietly, her words muffled against the leather of his tunic.

Evrardin's fingers pressed into her flesh tighter, almost like he was itching to physically shield her from the onlookers. "If any of you value your well-being, I suggest you go about your day and quit fucking gawking at your princess."

The few lords and ladies quickly settled back into whatever pulled their focus before the captain and princess entered their vision. They were smart not to cross the captain.

"Thank you," she murmured, tilting her chin so she could look at him.

She watched as he bit the inside of his lip. "Yeah, well, I'm sick of them treating others' sorrows as some wicked form of entertainment."

Mara didn't know why, but her heart skipped a beat.

Another guard met them at the gates, his face disguised by his helm. "Prince Acastus is requesting your presence in his chambers, Captain."

Evrardin nodded. When they were out of earshot, he grunted in annoyance.

"Are you in trouble?"

Evrardin made an odd sound in his chest. "Probably."

She pondered with that for a moment. "And me?"

"What about you?"

"How mad do you think he'll be?"

"Mara..."

"I know he's going to be mad. Don't lie to me."

"I wasn't going to," he retorted, shifting Mara in his arms to get a better hold, his hand brushing just below her breast.

"I failed. I know he's going to be livid. This is all he wanted me for, and I can't even give him that." She willed the tears away, afraid of appearing even more pathetic.

Evrardin's gaze hardened, and Mara balked when he didn't respond.

He brought her to her rooms, carrying her to her bed and setting her down gently. He appraised the arm that had been lodged in the mirror, her skin charred and turning red the further it spread. The ocean's chilled waters had done a good job of numbing the pain, but it still brewed beneath the surface.

He quickly looked away and hauled the large bunch of blankets at the foot of her bed around her to warm her even though she had stopped shivering now that her body temperature was evening out.

He pulled the blanket around her neck and paused, gaping at her. Her cat-like eyes were wide as she waited for his countenance to give something away. She thought he might say something, but if he was debating it, he decided not to.

He let her blanket go and Mara's hands replaced where his had been. Without a second glance, he left her, her handmaidens rushing to her side before she could call out to him.

Chapter Twenty-Seven
Mara

The fever that burned through Mara remained steady. Her body never reached parity with the blazing heat she felt in that mirror room, but it still suffocated her. Despite it all, her body shook with chills.

Hermes had been in and out of her room the past few days, monitoring her to ensure she didn't become worse. However, she wasn't certain what he would do if she did manage to fall more ill. Was there a procedure for people who got injured getting caught between the Veil, a magick that has been forbidden for the past century?

By the fourth day, Mara's fever had subdued enough that she felt like she could breathe again. She played with the fraying edges of her blanket as she soaked the bed sheets with her sweat, bored beyond belief, wanting to get out of her stuffy rooms more than anything.

"Princess, the prince is here to see you."

Mara looked up and willed herself not to make a sour face.

Acastus had visited her every day since the incident, which only mildly surprised her. What shocked her the most—much to her regret—was that she hadn't seen or heard anything from the captain. She worried Cas truly had punished him for saving her.

She had grown to like Evrardin. He was the closest thing to a friend she had since arriving in Kairth aside from Aevum. She had gone from dreading seeing his face, to only being moderately irritated, to even sometimes wishing he would stand closer to her, would touch her, press his body against her, pin her against—

The prince strolled to her bedside. At one point she would have been inflamed to have the Sun Prince see her a sweaty, sickly mess, but she lost her will to care at all what the insufferable prick thought about her uncomely appearance. Oh stars, she was becoming as foul-mouthed as Evrardin.

"How are you today, Princess?" he asked like he did every time he came to her chambers. His gaze lingered on her burnt arm, stained a dusty-red shade like she had truly been scarred by flames.

"Better."

That first day Acastus came to visit her in her chambers after the incident, he apologized. She warned herself that he was keen on lying, putting up a well-played front, but deep inside, she wanted to believe he was being genuine. It *felt* like he was being genuine when he said it.

"Good, good," he muttered, slowly making his way around her bed, picking up a few of her books with feigned interest as he went. He donned a long black frock, contrary to the summer heat, a high-necked shirt, and dark gloves embroidered with silver threads. His hair had been slicked back, the ends curling slightly. He seemed more sallow than usual, a ghost pretending to be a prince.

"I've come to discuss the wedding," he said casually as if that was the most normal conversation topic in the world to be having at this time. He clasped his hands behind his back as he stood at the foot of her oversized bed. Mara locked eyes with him, listening. "The date has been set for a week from today, rather than a fortnight. I'm assuming that will still give you enough time."

Mara's heart sank to her gut. This was really happening. He still wanted to marry her. "Enough time for what, exactly?"

Cas' raven shoes clacked softly on the rug as he rounded her bed. He stopped before her and sat gracefully on her mattress. Mara couldn't control the way her body jerked back.

His hand gently patted her leg through her emerald throw gilded in the afternoon sun. "For you to master glassfairing." Mara's eyes widened. "Well, maybe not *master*. But for you to have learned the basics, at least."

"Acastus, I can't... I don't know if I can..." she sputtered. "You still want me to figure out how to glassfaire?" She couldn't hide the horror from her voice.

"Of course. Why wouldn't I?"

She was dumbfounded to have to spell it out for him. "I mean, I almost just died attempting it. I thought that maybe..."

"That I wouldn't require it of you any longer?" His voice had a jest of arrogance.

Mara nodded timidly.

"Oh, my love," he cooed, reaching for her hands and holding them atop her covers. "Glassfairing is the only thing you're good for. And I sacrificed a lot to get you. I can't have a useless woman for a wife, now, can I?"

Mara's stomach churned from the disturbing nature of the words he spoke so delicately.

"Can I?" he asked again.

Mara shook her head, wanting to be compliant. To give him what he wanted.

"Good." Cas smiled, but it never reached his eyes. His fingers gently stroked the side of her hand, her eyes tracing them before glancing back at him, and her lips parted. His eyes, usually silver and dark, were gilded. She swore she had seen them that yellow shade before, but it was always such a quick flash, she thought it a trick of the light.

"I'm sorry," he muttered, tilting his chin down. "I...can't stop it."

Mara paused, holding her breath. "Stop what?"

His lips slanted, holding her hazel eyes with his, and a swarth of regret pooled within them. She didn't know why, but she was tempted to reach out and rest a hand on his cheek. The way he fixated on her, his face contorted to self-loathing, reminded her of Azor the day of her birthday when he said he had tried talking to her father.

"Cas," she whispered.

"I never wanted it to go this far. You have to believe me." His words pleading. The temptation to pull him into her arms vibrated her limbs, but she remained frozen.

As quickly as the gold had arrived, it fled. The silver ice returned to his iris, standing, he flattened his clothes before strolling to the door. "I'll have your maidens brought up to speed. Many preparations to come. I want this wedding to be everything you've ever dreamed of."

A sick chill ran down Mara's spine and she shivered. Cas turned to go but Mara spoke up, halting him in his spot. "Did something happen to the captain?"

"Why would anything have happened to him?" he asked over his shoulder. "Do you know something I don't?"

"I just haven't seen him. I thought he might have been—"

The prince laughed. "Oh, isn't this perfect? You care for him. And you thought him capable of the same." He clicked his tongue like one would scold a child. "I'm afraid the captain has been performing his duties as usual. If he wanted to visit, I'm sure he would have." A beat passed and she thought he might exit. "He can't save you, Mara." He spoke with both a broken sense of remorse and a fiery tinge of malice as if he was at war within himself.

The princess' chest tightened, shrinking further into her bed as Cas walked out the door. She had hoped that after Evrardin had saved her, they might have come to some semblance of a truce. A neutrality. Knowing now that he wasn't being prevented from seeing her, and yet he never visited, made her heart beat a little bit slower.

It was late when Mara finally had enough of rolling back and forth in her bed. She swung her feet off the side of her mattress and put on her robe. She had no idea what time it was but she figured it must have been past midnight. The windows were black, the light from her candle reflecting off the glass in a wash of ivory.

She grabbed the tallow candle on her bedside and slid out of her chambers. Sentinels were no longer stationed outside her room, but they still lined some of the halls and roamed the gardens. She wasn't sure when exactly there stopped being a guard rotation for her door, but it sent a wave of unease through her.

As she approached the library, another idea surfaced. The turn of the hallway beyond the library where she remembered seeing Crowrot rise up the spiral staircase from what had been referred to as the crypt called out to her.

Mara hesitated as she looked at the big wooden door of the library, teetering back and forth on her toes, quickly making her way down the hall before she could change her mind. She had spoken to Crowrot once one early morning, but it was simple pleasantries. She recalled how the old man had told her to give Evrardin a wider allowance, that he wasn't the easiest man to be acquainted, but he had his reasons. Mara admired how much Crowrot seemed to care for the captain.

She found the staircase that Evrardin had previously walked her up and she now looked down it instead. It was dark, but there was a faint glow of a candle around the corner.

She carefully descended the cobblestone steps, her hand dragging against the wall to keep her balance. The lower she got, the slicker the stones seemed. She pulled her hand back in disgust momentarily but quickly placed it back to guide her when she wobbled in her step.

At the last step, she faced a dark antechamber with a heavy wrought-iron door that had been left slightly ajar, a chink of light speckling the soggy stone tiles with little stars.

She set her candle down on a hole in the stonewall where a brick clearly used to live. She leaned against the door and peered in but couldn't get much view of anything through the small sliver. She gently opened it further and the sound of iron dragging on stone echoed off the walls. She cringed, squinting her eyes and baring her teeth.

"Come in," a raspy voice spoke.

Mara took in a breath, admitting she was caught before she pushed the rest of the way into the room. She strolled into a large chamber littered with cobwebs and tallow candles that had long since molded to the wooden table in the center. There were shelves crammed with bottles of all sizes and colors. A litter of chairs in various states, most of them covered in books and discarded pieces of tattered clothes. Her eyes scanned the room, but she tried to be polite and keep her face from making any insulting expressions.

She spotted Crowrot in the back as he heaved a stack of books onto the table, hunching over it. She watched as he did it again with a grunt. The desk beside him had clear vials bubbling from an unknown heat source, the smoke rising and winding in a series of tubes. A faint clattering sound of coins being jostled together created a soothing ambiance.

She hurried over to him, her slippers getting damp as she made her way across the room. "Can I help you?" she asked him.

"Oh, thankie, dear," he said. He pointed to the books on the table and asked her to dig through them. He told her he was looking for *Arcane Musings of Decaying Ailments*. "Don't got t'most efficient of systems. Could do with a bookshelf or two, but t'floor works fine all t'same."

Mara smiled as she made neat stacks, going through each book he laid on the table. A rusty smell made her look over her shoulder as she gingerly shifted the stack. She thought it might be rude to ask him what that sour smell was, so she tried to ignore it.

Her hands hesitated as she picked up a faded emerald book, its cloth engraved with gilded letters that looked like they had once been vibrant years ago.

The name is what caught her attention. It reminded her of the tome she found in the library after she saw Crowrot exiting in a hurry.

"What's this?" she asked him.

He paused and stood, groaning as he straightened his back and peered over to what Mara held in her hand. *Shorthand for Alchemists*.

"Tryin' to get better. Ev says he can never read my handwriting."

Something about Crowrot's reasoning had Mara raising a brow. He grinned at her and turned around. When she looked back at the book, the text had shifted. *Realm of the Deities*.

Crowrot began to hum as he continued to tidy his space,

searching for the odd book he mentioned earlier. Mara set the book on the table with what little room she had and flipped it open. She skimmed several pages before halting on a chapter on demonology and the shifting nature of curses.

Her fingers traced over the parchment, lingering on the shifting words. She leaned in closer to the text, trying to digest what she was reading. She thought back to the tome she suspected Crowrot of leaving in the library, not digesting any of the current words she scanned.

Mara winced, the subservient curse ringing in her head. Something clicked. Something about the prince. Something about Crowrot caring so much for Evrardin—

"Find somethin' interestin'?" Crowrot asked, nudging her side and looking down with her.

"I just..." Her finger scanned the page, a realization surmising in her mind. "Is...?"

Crowrot looked at her. "Go on," he encouraged.

Mara turned to the side. The wrinkles around Crowrot's eyes made him appear weathered, but they were still bright and full of color. "Do you think the prince would ever do such a thing?" she asked, pointing to the heading titled "Curses and Bargains."

"I'm afraid I don't know t'prince well enough t'make assumptions of that nature." His words were telling her he had no idea, but the cadence of his voice was hidden with something different. He didn't break eye contact and gazed at her like he was waiting for her to say something more. Something he knew but couldn't say.

Mara's eyes danced between Crowrot's. "Did you leave the *Phantom Atonements* tome for me to find?" Her cheeks warmed when she realized how self-centered her idea of Crowrot leaving something out for her to find sounded.

He hummed. "Why would I have done that?"

"Because... Is Evrardin...?" She closed her eyes, trying to find her words. "Is the captain cursed?"

He clicked his tongue and turned around, digging through his pile of haphazardly thrown tools and trinkets. When he faced her again, he extended a small vial with dried petals of a warm blush.

She took it into her palm and admired the beauty of the flora trapped in time within the glass.

"The captain's got a pastime."

The small petals almost glowed. She recognized them as blight flowers, a very complicated flora to grow and harvest. He'd have to be a skilled horticulturist to cultivate something like this, especially with how vibrant the aura the petals emitted was. Before she could speak, her lips parting, Crowrot urged her back. "Now, you'll want to be gettin' back to your studies, Princess. You'll do no good bein' caught with the likes of me down here." She held up the book in want and he nodded. "Yes, take it with ya."

As she stumbled to leave the dark quarters, her eyes snagged on a wooden bucket in the far corner. She adjusted her vision, her steps slowing incongruously realizing it was filled to the brim with hearts. Her lips parted but she managed to restrain her gasp.

She turned to Crowrot over her shoulder, and he paused his movements, knowing exactly what Mara took inventory of. He shook his head, halting the question on the tip of her tongue.

The contents emitted a soft green glow, but even with the peculiarly unnatural color, she could tell they were organs usually kept locked in one's chest cavity. The question of what species the hearts belonged to made her skin crawl with gooseflesh.

She swallowed hard and muttered her thanks as he shooed her out, shutting the metal door behind her. She swallowed hard, shoving the vial into her skirt pocket, and began rushing to get back to her room, her heart racing, forgoing the candle she left outside his door. Her stomach rumbled with unease. Acastus was the only thought that was entrapping her mind. Maybe the hearts should have been on her list of growing issues, but it seemed rather moot in the grand scheme of things. It was a dank dungeon, Mara was sure it was just animal hearts used for an assortment of odd reasons, probably an ingredient mixed with the hodgepodge of vials on the shelves to create bizarre concoctions and experiments.

Chapter Twenty-Eight
Evrardin

The fiery prince glared wickedly at the healer by his feet. "You mean to tell me," Acastus growled out, "that you traveled all this way, just to reiterate how useless you truly are?"

The healer refused to recoil from Cas' darkening words. "As I stated when I arrived, I do not pretend to be sufficient in cursed ailments."

"You're the most prominent magick healer this side of the Gilded River. Your fucking title deems you a bloody oracle of restoration for fuck's sake."

"I can understand your frustration, My Prince. But no one in the east deals with dark magick to any degree. It's been a forbidden act for centuries. You won't find any healer here who will offer their assistance."

Acastus half-grinned, his eyes sharpening and flickering silver.

"My Prince, perhaps the oracle need only time to rest after his long journey. Surely—"

Acastus cut off the arbiter, standing swiftly from his seat. "I'm to believe no archmage in the east breaks the law? Is that what you're suggesting?"

The oracle shifted on the balls of his feet, the only indication he was unnerved. "Of course there are. But no one in their right senses would ostentate a rogue archmage if they valued their life. Not even for the prince of Solstrale."

The air thickened in the room, Acastus' council members silent, lost for words to placate their leader. Acastus let out a stifled laugh before his gloves made a ripping sound. It took Acastus two steps to reach the oracle, claws outstretched from the holes in his leather gloves, navy feathers sprouting out of his skin where the sleeve of his tunic rode up. His inhuman digits wrapped tightly around the healer's neck, the air whooshing out of his mouth in a single breath.

Evrardin rolled his eyes in annoyance, his fingers pinching the bridge of his nose.

"Charlatans. The lot of you." Acastus' voice was drenched in muck and silt, his regal lilt abandoned, his irises corroding entirely slate-gray.

Evrardin glanced over to Acastus' council, waiting for one of them to step in and alleviate their prince. When no one moved, Evrardin mirthlessly smiled. "Cowards." Evrardin may have been prohibited from interfering, but the royal arbiter, high priest, master of coin, and warmonger were not cursed to the prince like the captain was. Their lack of measure stemmed purely from sheer cowardice.

Blood began to pool out between the gaps of Acastus' fingers, the oracle sputtering as the liquid filled his throat and cascaded out of his mouth. Acastus' lip ticked and a crack sounded from the oracle's neck. He immediately went slack in Acastus' unnaturally strong grip before he threw him back, his body slumping over like a wet rag. Red now stained the navy feathers on Cas' arm, his hand shaking violently. Acastus stumbled back, clutching his weaponized hand to his chest as if it had lost all sensation.

He groaned, the feathers slowly falling away and returning to his normal—albeit ashened—arm. However, without notice, one tattered feather floated silently to the floor, fluttering in a whirl before getting stuck under one of the table's legs.

Evrardin took an exhaustive breath before stalking over to the deceased healer and scooping his corpse into his embrace. The rest of his council watched on in apprehension, glancing at one another.

Lord Alfson approached the prince, offering his aid, and Acastus shoved him off, standing back to his full height. As Evrardin escorted the healer's body out, a blood trail marking behind him, Acastus' shouting grew fainter. "This was your doing, Alfson."

"My Prince, he is most reputable. I had no inkling he wouldn't be sufficient—"

Evrardin carried the body down the corridor, shaking his head at Acastus' refusal to be guided. To heed anyone's advice, warning him he was using too much dark magick. He wouldn't be able to stop the change if he kept exhausting his body like that.

Lord Cofsi came around the bend and halted when he spotted Evrardin. "Do I even want to know?" he asked, referring to the bloody corpse Evrardin carried.

Evrardin couldn't tell him even if he asked. "No."

Lord Cofsi seemed hesitant, like he might inquire further, but the prince's shrieking rang down the hall. Cofsi nodded his head in understanding. "Is the high priest in?" Cofsi asked, gesturing his head back the way Evrardin came.

"Yes."

The prince's voice cursing out his council echoed off the walls.

"Though I'm sure he wished he wasn't," Evrardin added.

Lord Cofsi gave him a tight smile.

"If you go now," Ev began, "you might walk in on something you shouldn't."

Lord Cofsi almost smirked, something secret passing between the men. "Understood."

Evrardin began walking again and Lord Cofsi continued his trek toward the vestry.

Chapter Twenty-Nine
Mara

Mara peered out the bottom half of her windows that weren't stained, looking out beyond the castle walls. She could just make out the crashing waves of the ocean where Evrardin had carried her a week ago and a blush rose to her cheeks. She half expected to see him walking up the hill, covered in soot and bruises, just as he was the first time she caught him strolling back to the castle at night. But he never appeared.

She tried to suppress the feeling of disappointment—which was easy to do because it was rapidly replaced with vexation. She hated herself for hoping this had meant he cared for her—even though it simply made him a decent person for making sure she didn't burn from the inside out, but it had felt like more than that. He had disobeyed Cas' directive. He had tried to comfort her when he brought her to the Hallowed Cistern, and then again, offering pacifying words when he led her to the king and queen.

Still, Evrardin eluded her, not showing up to visit once. She had no idea where he was off to. He was often plastered to the prince's hip like a sore that wouldn't go away, but he was nowhere to be seen. And Acastus was never much help.

You care for him. And you thought him capable of the same.

She ground her teeth together, straining her jaw, remembering the shrill and threat laced in Acastus' speech. Maybe she did come to care for Evrardin—she had no choice, he was the face she saw the most trapped in this castle. She had no one else. But even with that excuse, her body sank at the idea that he didn't feel the slightest bit of fondness for her in return.

Mara's face scrunched into a frown, her eyes underlined with purple circles, her hair falling flat against her head.

She was dressed in a simple gown, its cream skirt embroidered with white and gold threads that created ornate patterns up onto her bodice. The sleeves were soft gossamer, making her look like a specter as she roamed the halls—emphasized by her blanched appearance. She was on her way to the study Aevum had shown her, hoping to find the tiny prince to talk to. But at the very least, she'd be able to shove her head in the books and pretend like nothing in her life was going south, so to speak.

A guard she didn't know the name of but had seen before strolled by her side, his face permanently stained in a scowl. His beard was thin and patchy, covering the pock marks along his cheeks. When she glanced away from him, she noticed an influx of people treading the halls, all headed in the same direction.

"What's happening?" Mara said aloud, not directed at anyone in particular.

Her guard spoke without looking her way. "There is to be a public execution in decree of the Solar Sect."

Mara's made a face of distaste. The chaos and entertainment an execution brought wasn't just a threat to the farmers and peasants, it was a spectacle for the nobles. She watched in astonishment as highborns raced through the castle, bits of laughter and gossip echoing the halls. They seemed more excitable than usual.

"Who?" she asked.

She froze when she heard a group of girls skim past her. "It's the first killing ordinance of the prince!"

"How kingly of him," the girl giggled.

"That means he'll be there. He'll want to watch his decree!" one of them said with an air of hope.

The girls giggled and squealed, yearning for a glimpse of the Sun Prince. Mara looked at them with disgust, though she couldn't blame them for how they acted. They were raised to know no different. Even she might have felt like this if it had been happening in Venmore. A thrill to break up the boring days she tended. She winced at the thought.

"The prince ordered this?"

The guard didn't respond. Mara huffed in annoyance then hurried on, following the crowd to the Old God's Cathedral.

When she arrived, the seats were all but overflowing, newcomers having to stand, but they didn't seem to mind. Holding such a rally in the Old God's Cathedral was a charade meant just for the Sun Court. People talked amongst themselves with excitement. And somehow, pretending like this was some holy act of their goddess, it set right their sins for celebrating the death of another person.

No one noticed her as she waded through the bodies, trying to get a better view of the dais. Her guard begrudgingly shoved people out of the way to follow close behind her.

Then she saw him. For the first time in days.

Evrardin.

He was standing tall beside the prince, his armor polished gold, reflecting the light in soft rose and poppy hues. His hair was neater than usual, but only slightly, and pulled away from his face. He looked off blankly into the crowd, almost like his body was set in stone, his soul somewhere else entirely.

As Mara got closer, she thought she saw glassiness coating his eyes. A sudden feeling of immense dread and doom sank in her chest.

She went to step toward the dais, to go up to the prince, but the guard grabbed her shoulder and pulled her back. Evrardin's eyes darted to Mara in an instant, then quickly settled back on an arbitrary spot in the distance.

"The prince is requesting you stay put," the guard said flatly.

Mara looked at him and then back at the dais. She tucked herself off into the corner, not wanting to gawk, but knowing she had to watch. The prince stepped out from the gathering of his court to approach the scaffold, a smile on his face, the audience falling quiet.

"Conspiring to kill the prince is an act of treason, if not an act of war." Acastus spoke to the crowd with a bravado that displayed how righteous he thought himself. "And of course, punishable by death!" The crowd erupted into murmurs of praise and excitement, a few people even clapping. His voice sounded so oddly unlike himself.

Cas glanced behind him and gestured forward, silently commanding his guards to carry the victim out, condemned to an inescapable fate. An older man made it into her sight and all time seemed to freeze.

Mara's jaw fell slack. Her knees weakening, her eyes expanding to moons. Crowrot. This was the execution of Crowrot.

Her hands clenched into fists and her eyes darted around the room, this had to be a mistake. Crowrot conspiring to overthrow the prince? That sounded as unlikely as it was for her to joyfully wake before noon.

Crowrot let the two guards drag him forward without struggle, his outfit the same as the one she saw him in last night. His face calm like the sedentary water at the bottom of a fountain, his eyes crinkling as he smiled at Evrardin.

"No!" Mara called, but it was snuffed out by the rambunctious crowd. The guard behind her tightened his hold on her shoulder, making sure she didn't try and run forward. The guards kicked the back of Crowrot's legs, forcing him to bend and collapse to the floor. His hands were tied behind his back, not even allowed the dignity to at least face his death as a free man.

Tears obscured Mara's view, everyone becoming a blurry mess before her. "No, no, no," she mumbled to herself like a chant, shaking her head. She felt nauseous as the crowd shouted profanities at Crowrot, bespeaking to see his head chopped from his shoulders. How could they be so heartless?

Mara wanted to do something, to be a hero from one of her fairy tales, but what could she do as a tiny princess? The prince had a wild look in his eyes—he wanted this to be a show. He was out for blood. He was giving the court what they wanted, uncaring if the punishment was just. There would be no stopping this. Mara prayed that the ceiling would cave in, giving Crowrot a chance to run for his life.

"I've been too lenient with you. My father should have killed you all those years ago." He scowled at the old man. "Any final words, Gravedoctor?" the prince asked, bending over slightly to be at eye level.

Crowrot gave him a warm smile, one that he had reserved for Mara the day before. She hadn't a clue how he could act so calm in the face of death. Crowrot's mouth moved, but she couldn't make out what he was saying.

The prince bared his teeth, but something wavered behind

his eyes. He shook his head before looking over to the right at Evrardin. "Evrardin, if you will."

Mara noticed there was no vocational executioner. No towering figure in a black cloak, his eyes shielded from view.

Evrardin's head snapped toward Acastus. "You can't be serious," he said astonished, panic rising in his throat.

"Do I honestly look like I'm in a jesting mood?"

Evrardin's hand tightened on the hilt of his sword. His eyes danced over the crowd, watching helplessly at the way they applauded the prince, egging on Crowrot's inevitable demise. Then his eyes unwillingly, but inevitably, found her. Darkness shrouded his features. Her tears never stopped rolling, her face surely stained and her eyes red. He looked at her like he was begging her for something, but she didn't know what.

"I can't."

"I'm *ordering* you to execute this traitor."

Evrardin's throat bobbed as he looked back at Crowrot. He slowly approached him. Crowrot looked up at Evrardin with a bit of reverence and kinship in his eyes. Mara suspected the captain and gravedoctor had been closer than she once assumed.

Mara could only read their lips now, her ears ringing. "It's okay, m'boy."

Evrardin took in a deep breath, Crowrot's approval doing nothing to comfort him. He unsheathed his sword, the iron glistening in the air. "Do it," Crowrot demanded, his features becoming stern. "Do it!"

Evrardin stood up taller before mumbling "I'm sorry."

As the piercing slice of his sword hit the chopping block, Mara shut her eyes, an uncontrollable sob retching in her throat. Her tears slowed, the clamorous crowd numbing her senses as she stumbled backward, caught by the guard—but not *her* guard.

Chapter Thirty
Mara

When morning came the following day, Mara slumped out of her bed, momentarily forgetting the events of the day prior until she shifted the drape from her mirror and saw her haunting reflection.

She shoved that memory back down, her eyes bloodshot, and she looked ready to blow over with one gust of wind. Her two arms appeared from two different people, one her normal olive tone, the other encrusted a faded red, her fingertips dusted with ash. The darkness marring her skin may have alarmed her at any other moment, but with the grief that lingered in her chest, nothing seemed to matter. Her fingers danced over the red marks on her throat that Acastus left the prior night, after he visited her rooms shortly after the execution, his words haunting her into the morning light. "You'll get more of your friends killed if you decide to stray to other texts again." His hand locked around her neck as he spoke. She didn't panic like she thought she would have, the suffocation a numbing sensation to the loss of Crowrot.

She slid on a new dress reluctantly, its black fabric mimicking how she felt inside. It wasn't customary to wear black in mourning for the executed, but Crowrot didn't deserve to be treated as a traitor to the crown. She pulled her hair back in a braid, her handmaidens absent ever since she screamed at them to leave her alone as she stared at her reflection in hatred.

She had written Azor multiple letters, but she was worried they weren't getting to him. She hadn't heard anything from her family since her brother's first missive telling her about the darkness spreading on the northern front. She felt so alone without any communication beyond the walls of Kairth.

She was tempted to reach out and shatter the mirror, and she hadn't even realized she followed through with her daydreams until the shards were scattered amongst her feet and dress skirt.

She stared at the silver daggers, not hearing the footsteps till it was too late.

"I've been waiting."

A bit startled, she turned to face the voice, Evrardin looming in her room's entrance, his appearance not any better than her own. His jaw clenched so tight, she was surprised he managed to get any words out at all. Evrardin appraised her, then flickered to the scattered glass on the floor behind her silhouette.

"I don't want to go," she said like a stubborn child. She knew he was here to escort her to the libraries, likely on Acastus' orders. No, she *knew* it was on Acastus' orders, otherwise the captain wouldn't have succumbed himself to such trivial affairs. She assumed Acastus needed someone as loyal as Evrardin to ward over her, not trusting her to stay on task any longer.

Evrardin's face loured and contorted into animosity. "You don't really have a choice, though, do you?"

She wanted to ask him if he was talking about her, or himself.

Mara's jaw tensed and a pang of pain slid through her burnt arm, taking a step back, her bare feet slicing on the exposed sharp edge of her broken mirror, blood seeping onto the floorboards and between the glass.

Evrardin's eyes went dark. "Is this what you've been doing? Wallowing in self-pity?"

Mara scoffed. "You're right. I'm throwing a tantrum because I didn't get my way. That my day was ruined because some servant had to go and grab the attention of the prince." She hadn't realized she began to shout. Evrardin looked at her with a hardened gaze. She shook her head and turned to begin picking up the pieces of her mirror.

"*You* killed him. And here you stand, acting like a child," he spat.

Mara whipped around so fast she thought she might snap her neck, her damning thoughts brought to life by the captain. "Fuck you," she shouted. Everything within her was reaching its boiling point, ready to bubble over.

Evrardin took a step farther into the room, ignoring her profanity, and Mara swallowed on instinct, the shadow he was creating around her haunting. "I know he was killed because of some forbidden tome he showed you. Did you go seeking him out for help?"

Mara furrowed her brows remembering her visit to the crypt to speak with Crowrot. The magick tome he let her have. The tome he had left misplaced in the library.

"You did," he said, answering himself in realization. "Fuckin' hell," he cursed, his hands squeezing into fists. "There's no way he'd turn you down if you asked something of him. *You got him fucking killed*," he said again, this time with far more distress.

"I—" she stuttered. "I didn't kill him." She wanted to scream, but her voice came out in small spurts. "I didn't know—I didn't mean..." she trailed off. It wasn't just her own self-reproach; Crowrot would still be alive if it wasn't for her.

Mara buried her face in her hands. She let out a sob, her tears barely rolling out, most dried up from the night prior, before running her hands through her hair and pulling it taut. "I killed him..." she whispered. Her eyes looked through Evrardin, the events of yesterday flashing in her mind again. Her heart ached.

Evrardin's scowl grew, his features turning darker as he watched her spiral. He acted like he came for a fight. Like he wanted her to fight him on this. He *needed* her to fight him on this.

"And now you wish for me to console you. To help you bear the burden you created."

Her tears turned angry as she glared at him, her fingers tensing like she had claws. "This is not something I wished to happen," she growled. Evrardin's glower matched hers. "And I will not let you convince me to fight with you."

He shook his head, and she saw the anger flow all the way to his fingertips.

"I'm sorry. I'm sorry he made you swing the sword."

Evrardin seemed shocked momentarily by her words. He stepped into her space and Mara clenched the shard of glass she forgot she was holding, blood seeping through her fingers. "Any other man would have killed you for this."

Mara blinked rapidly several times, digesting his threatening words.

"Any other man would kill whoever it was that took his family away. And that's what you did, Mara."

Mara tried to keep face, her eyes narrowing, but she could feel herself slipping. "So why don't you?" she goaded.

"Trust me, my hands are itching to tighten around your neck."

"As are mine," she challenged, his body so close that when she moved her hand forward, the sharp tip of the glass she held poked into Evrardin's chest. She quickly moved her hand up, holding the glass dagger to Evrardin's throat, her eyes wild and full of both remorse and anger. She held the dagger just as he had shown her in the gardens. She was done letting everyone walk all over her. She was *done*.

He inched closer, forcing the glass into his skin, enough to draw blood. Mara's eyes briefly flashed with horror.

He glanced at the blood swirling down Mara's arm from her palm. "You've done nothing but torture me since you've arrived here." He grabbed her hand without her realizing, their eyes locked on one another, both snarling. "What I wouldn't give to shed you from the role you seem so eager to take in my life."

"And what role is that?" Her words came out sharp, but she was wavering inside, the full weight of his awful admission hitting her in a potent shove.

"My ruination." His hand clasped hers tighter and she thought he might rip her sideways, slit her throat with her own weapon. "I've dreamt of ending you." Much to her surprise, his fingers loosened hers so she was forced to drop the glass, not allowing it to dig any further into either of their skin. His words a whisper. "Though, those tend to be the nights I sleep the least."

She didn't know if the tears in her eyes were from anger or pain. She felt the full weight of his culpability and she wanted to shed the feeling like a serpent would its skin.

Mara's gaze finally met him again and his balance wavered, sparked with fire. "But you never came!" she spat.

Evrardin's hand retracted, resting on the hilt of his sword. He gave her a puzzled look.

"You didn't come! You didn't fucking come!" She was a tolling bell as she repeated herself. "You've become the only person I have here." *And he left her.* He didn't visit her during the entirety of her time bedridden after he hauled her to the sea; holding her so delicately in his arms, afraid she would wither away before his eyes. And now he despised her, lambasting her for something she hadn't meant to cause. "I have no one else. *You* have no one else." She didn't say it as a jab, but rather an audit of his own sanity. Her hands shook. "I've been alone."

"Loneliness isn't the worst thing a person can face," he said harshly, the loss of the gravedoctor lingering on his tongue.

"No. It's something you're quite used to. And now you wish it on everyone else." She choked on her final words, her stability crumbling. She was alone. She had no one to help her. No one to take her hand and lead her through this mess. No one to fall back on when she soaked her hands with Crowrot's blood. No one to hold her face and remind her to breathe as she sobbed. She didn't think Evrardin could be that anchor for her, yet she yearned for it every day that had passed without him.

"I couldn't," he grumbled. Mara tried to steady her breathing and glared at him. "I had to follow Acastus' orders."

"To do what?"

"I can't tell you."

Mara wiped her tears, disregarding Evrardin's eyes as they traced her movements. She knew the reason his mouth was sewn shut, but she asked anyway. "Why?"

"Mara," he warned darkly.

"No. Tell me why!" she insisted. "Tell me why you do everything the prince asks of you. Tell me why you obey his every fucking whim." She shoved his chest forward with her hands, but he did not budge. "Tell me why you let him command you to kill your friend!" She hadn't realized the tears were still falling until she felt the warmth trickling down her neck.

Evrardin clenched his teeth, resentment coating his eyes. "I can't," he managed to get out.

"I know," she said more gently. "I know he has you under an incantation." The shock was evident on Evrardin's face, and she gave a mirthless laugh. "I figured it out." She gestured her hands around nervously. "You know, from all those dusty old books I've been reading."

Evrardin pursed his lips. He went to open his mouth, but nothing came out.

Instead, he edged into her space and brushed a stream of tears away like he lost his self-control. "You didn't get him killed," he breathed, barely able to get the words out. Anger at her still lingered in his eyes and chest. He glared at her like he was debating slipping his hands around her neck to let out the madness. She gazed at him with such painful longing as his thumb caressed her skin that it physically hurt. "I shouldn't have accused you of that. I'm just..." his words trailed off. "I'm furious that it was *my hands* that ripped away his life. Acastus gave the orders, but it was my sword that separated his head from his body. And that old man is too bloody stubborn for his own good. If he wanted to help you, there was nothing either of us could have done to stop it."

Mara nodded, her hands gingerly reaching out across the short distance between them, clinging to his belt to steady herself as her mind reeled. She understood the need to blame anyone else. If he couldn't take it out on the prince, the real culprit of their misery, then she was the next best target.

He shook his head, his fingers tracing the necklace gifted to her by Acastus as he had done at the masquerade. Gooseflesh rose on her arms at his nonchalant affection as he aimlessly touched her. They stood in each other's embrace, blood trailing Evrardin's shirt and wetting Mara's hand, tears staining her sunken face, Evrardin's eyes dark and heavy with loss. The two of them lost in a painting.

His hand skimmed her collarbone, then gently caressed her neck. "What happened?" he asked, his breath shortening as he assessed the bruising forming on her throat.

Mara reached up on instinct, her fingers brushing his, before stepping backward to put distance between them. Her feet crushed more glass as she moved, wincing in pain.

Evrardin was quick to pick her up, effortlessly carrying her to her bed and placing her down so she sat on the edge. He squatted before her, his hand roughly grabbing her ankle like he still wished to punish her, and pulled her leg up enough so he could see the bottom of her foot. He wiped the glass from the sole then quickly did the same with the other. He was swift and terse with his movements, not caring when she whimpered in pain. But still, he kneeled before her and did what she could have done herself. Before he stood, he grabbed her hand and turned her palm up. Her fingers closed, blocking the already scabbing wound from his vision.

Mara's entire chest must have turned red from the intimate touch—she hadn't realized he could be that temperate. She wondered if Evrardin was savoring the feeling of how revenge would taste on his tongue as he studied her.

"Let me help you," she finally said. Mara felt paralyzed; frustrated beyond words at how trapped Acastus made them both feel. She at least wanted to help Evrardin break free from his chains. Free him of Acastus just as she yearned to be.

"You can't," he said flatly.

"You don't know that," she argued, though she knew he was right.

"*Liten rev*, you can't help me. And *I* don't want *you* to help me. If you get yourself into any more trouble with Acastus... I don't know what he'll do." Evrardin gave her a despairing plea to at least allow him to prevent her from facing Acastus' wrath if he couldn't avoid it himself.

His use of her pet name put a blush on her cheeks. She hadn't realized she missed him calling her that until she heard it in his deep baritone—soft words that were meant just for her, even if he did speak it with malice.

"Evrardin, please," she began to implore, knowing she had no idea what she could possibly do. Her begs felt like they were more intended for the gods, not Evrardin. She was lost as to how to even dive into the concept of saving Evrardin from his curse, but she wanted to do what she couldn't for herself.

"You can't help me." His next words congealed in his throat, viscous pleas she never thought him capable. "Please, *liten rev*. Don't try to do anything to figure this out. I won't be able to protect you from Acastus if he were to discover your treason."

"I can handle his—"

"No. You can't," he said sternly, a hint of drear in his words. "I'm not worried he's going to reprimand you, Princess. Acastus' is..." His words were choked in the vise that became his throat. "Acastus will punish you beyond your imagination if he finds you interfering."

"Interfering..." she repeated. "With what, exactly?"

Evrardin sighed, his eyes shifting about the room. "Don't do this. I'm fucking begging you." A chill ran up her spine at Evrardin's vehement beseech. She had never known him to beg for what he wanted.

Mara stood from the bed, ignoring any pain she felt on the soles of her feet, their faces as close as they were in the corner of the library all of a week ago. "Okay," she whispered. Defeated. She knew she'd never be able to resolve his words down to the truth while he still lingered under this curse.

His dark eyes studied her, but she couldn't decipher his thoughts. Mara bit her lip and Evrardin's pupils seemed to double in size. He cleared his throat before speaking again. "Let me train you.".

"What?"

His hand gently touched her neck, his thumb stroking over the bruising. Mara swallowed hard. Fire flickered in Evrardin's gaze. Could he ever truly protect her?

"I can't always be there for you. And I don't trust Acastus to not put his hands on you again. Let us focus back on your training."

Mara pondered for a moment, her thoughts lost as Evrardin rested his hand on her exposed flesh. Her hackles rose from his feather-light touch. She recalled the last time they trained, how close they had gotten. How his body had responded...

She nodded, afraid her voice would betray her. As she gazed at him, she could still see the hint of resentment behind the shadow of his eyes. He may have taken back his words, but something egregious still blossomed in his chest as he breathed her in. He hated her for everything she was making him feel.

She wished she could absolve him of his pain. She'd gladly take it in his stead if it meant he'd stop punishing himself for what he couldn't control. Her eyes fluttered downward, a bit embarrassed as he embraced her softly, and she chided herself for falling so easily for his charms, begging to be his light source, to take away his sorrows.

She nodded. Evrardin's hand danced under her chin, his fingers needing to touch her olive skin, and turned her face to look at him once more. He tore his hand from her gravity and cleared his throat, shaking himself from whatever spell Mara seemed capable of enthralling.

"Tomorrow night, then."

A pang throbbed in her chest as Evrardin guided her down the hall to the libraries. She was going to figure out how to break the spell Acastus cast on Evrardin under the guise of researching glassfairing.

As she tirelessly tossed through tome after tome, she pretended not to feel the heat of Evrardin's eyes following her dutifully as she moved through the library, likely warring with himself on whether to hate her for all of eternity or kiss her against the shelves.

Chapter Thirty-One
Lord Cofsi

Lord Cofsi made haste as he darted down the halls, a feather weighing heavily in his pocket. He knew he had to move fast, he was beginning to worry Acastus might declare that the Dusk Lord was overstaying his welcome.

Cofsi was determined to seek out the princess and warn her of Acastus' state. He knew Evrardin would take issue with warning Mara about anything that Cofsi thought important enough. He'd have to do this without his permission.

Cofsi slid into the confines of the stuffy library, spying a languid Evrardin as he stretched backward on one of the chairs, his lack of armor a sign of rebellion, a loose piece of parchment on the desk before him.

"Captain," Cofsi greeted.

Evrardin returned his stare, not bothering to adjust his sitting position to be more respectful, but he did grab the parchment and fold it into his pocket. "Cofsi," he mumbled, his hand scratching his short beard.

"Didn't know you could read," he implored, his hands locking behind his back.

Evrardin scoffed. "You don't see me with a book, do you?"

Cofsi suppressed the grin willing its way to his lips. "Is the princess here?"

"And why might you be seeking her whereabouts?"

Cofsi would have considered scowling if he wasn't all too familiar with Evrardin's brooding demeanor and uncanny ability to dodge questions. "I must speak with her."

Evrardin gave him a blank glare, kicking his foot back.

Cofsi gritted his teeth in annoyance. "It's rather urgent."

The captain seemed keen to remain silent, he only took orders from the prince, he had no obligation to tell the Dusk Lord where the Crown Prince's betrothed was lurking. But Mara stumbled, dropping a book somewhere deep in the stacks, her curses trailing out to Cofsi's ear.

Lord Cofsi gave Evrardin a darkening look of vexation before tracing the sound of Mara's voice like a warm pie on a windowsill, mumbling back at the captain over his shoulder. "I don't know why I asked. You wouldn't be in here if it wasn't for her."

When he found the princess, she looked away from the book she was reaching for. "Lord Cofsi," she spoke through a genuine grin.

"Princess." He stretched his arm easily and swiped the tome she had wanted and placed it in her hands.

She nodded her thanks before folding it in her arms. "What can I do for you?" she asked.

He shifted on his feet, leaning against the bookshelf, one of the skylights refracting the gold streaks in his hair. "I was hoping to bring something to your attention." He paused. "If you have a moment."

"Oh. Yes. I..." Mara's words got lost in her throat.

"I realize this might be an awkward timing, as I'm sure you're quite busy." He glanced at the tomes in her hands, black ink staining her skin. He knew she was doing this for the prince. "But I'm afraid this must be discussed sooner rather than later. And I needed to talk when I knew you'd be alone."

Mara rubbed her lips together, her throat bobbing, nerves clearly visible on her face at Cofsi's low-spoken speech.

Cofsi turned to glance down the stack, reassuring himself they were alone in the maze of books, Evrardin still sitting back by the entrance, no lone librarian hovering about. His eyes traced hers, the lightness of them constructing a weightlessness. He shoved his hands into his pockets. "I do not wish to place you in any more danger than you are already, but I must tell you that I'm well aware something dark is brewing within the prince." He leaned his face closer to Mara as he delved into more details about his visit. "As you know, I came for the solstice celebrations. I'm worried my time here might be coming to an end. I plan to attend your wedding, Mara, but I make no promises."

Mara furrowed her brows in confusion, her lips parting to pose a question, then shutting again.

"The balance of the kingdoms is falling," he said flatly.

"What do you mean?"

Cofsi took in a sharp breath, pushing her down the aisle and around the corner. When he let her go, he gestured to one of the enamored stained-glass windows of the library, arched and glittering in the last rays of the setting sun. The art depicted all the deities, all sized the same apart from Trana, who posed closer to the viewer. "The balance of the kingdoms, Mara. The unity of the courts. The distribution of divine powers. It's what keeps everything from sinking into the Veil. The Sun Court's power surmounts while the others slip. The balance is shifting and becoming off-kilter."

Mara turned to face Lord Cofsi. "Is that why my mother got

caught between the Veil? I knew the gods had left us, but I didn't realize…"

"I can't know for certain what happened to your mother, but I do know it's becoming the cause of all sorts of travesties across Junefell."

Mara shook her head. "Why are you telling me this?"

"Because, I think you're the only one who can stop it."

She scoffed. "Me?"

He could see the disbelief on her face. She truly thought he was pulling her leg. "Princess," he said earnestly, Mara's smile faltering. Cofsi grabbed her hand and her lips parted. "The Shadowed Isles are known for our heightened senses, same as Wrens Reach being littered with glassfairers. I can sense the imbalance. And it has led me here. To Kairth. To Prince Acastus."

Mara's brows unfurrowed as she thought. Cofsi narrowed, sensing her revelation. "I believe the prince is the cause of the disturbance."

She shook her head, halting him from speaking any further. "But how does this have anything to do with me?"

"I do not yet know your role in the prince's schemes, but he must be needing your glassfairing ability for his own malicious intentions if he wants to marry you. You're the key to whatever terrible mess he's befalling upon the kingdoms. Just look around" —he gestured to the decaying walls of the library— "Kairth is cascading to pieces, shrouded in dark shadows. And this is beginning to extend beyond the castle's stone walls—the darkness unbalanced. If Acastus keeps at this, the dark will outweigh the light." He swallowed a breath. "The kingdoms must always be left in balance," he stressed.

"I… I can't be of help. I don't know what I could possibly do. Why can't you ask someone like the captain? Surely he—"

"I do not tell you these things to guilt you into biding my dirty work. But you must know, the prince is up to something malicious. It's not just a trick of your mind. And you are one of his closest, unsuspected confidants." Her breath caught in her throat. "Evrardin isn't to be trusted."

Mara's eyes mooned and Cofsi bent his brows in pain. "Maybe once, long ago. And sometimes even now I trust the captain far more than I should. But to you, Princess, you cannot put your faith in that man. He wouldn't want it either."

"But you can?"

He shook his head. "That is not the point. I have known Evrardin all his life. Even when he was still a lonesome bastard of the king in the Wastelands. Do not mistake my distrust for mal intents. I hope to trust him again one day, and I just might be forced to soon, but you need to be wary. No one here is your friend. You are in dangerous territory, Princess. Trekking on threatening waters."

Mara's face contorted to bewilderment, her mouth opening and closing like a fish out of water.

Cofsi sighed. "I came to Kairth because Evrardin asked it of me. And now I see just how sideways the kingdom has sunk. You must be diligent if you're to live through this. I do not wish to frighten you," he added after seeing the shift in her countenance at his looming threat. "I only wish to save my people."

"What am I to do?"

"Glassfairing isn't the only magick you can channel."

Mara raised her brows at him.

"Perhaps it would have been, but after bonding with the prince, the power that runs through your veins is far loftier. He must have informed you of that, no?"

Mara nodded.

"Good. Well, you are able to do more than just your house's magick, Mara. And I suspect it would do you good to learn more than just how to glassfaire."

"Like what? What should I be studying?"

Cofsi sighed. "I wish I could tell you, but to be outright, I'm not entirely sure." He stood back and glanced at the stained-glass to ponder. "I don't know what I'm doing," he mumbled to himself, his fingers touching his forehead in frustration. He shifted back to look at her. "Had you spoken with the gravedoctor before his untimely death?"

"Crowrot?" Mara asked a bit dumbfounded. "But what would he—?"

Cofsi hushed her, footsteps beginning to rapidly approach the two converted in the dark corner of the library. Cofsi searched her eyes before grabbing her hands again, something soft tickling his palm, her cheeks heating at his forthright touch. "Be safe," he whispered before darting off, winding down the stacks and out of sight.

Chapter Thirty-Two
Mara

Mara blinked several times before looking down at the soft feather Cofsi had placed in her hands. Its navy color immediately flooded her mind with images of the creature that lurked in the depths of the Sandwoods.

Her brows furrowed... Were her fingers turning black? She flipped her hand over, holding the feather tight, noticing how the redness from being burned by the mirror had darkened, the tips of it turning to coal and slowly smoking up her hand.

Evrardin strolled into her space, and she quickly shoved the feather and her hand into the skirt of her dress.

"What did the Dusk Lord want?" he asked in spite.

"He was just making sure I was comfortable here."

Evrardin scoffed, following Mara as she shoved past him and out to one of the desks in

the open hall. "Then why are your cheeks so red?"

Mara shied away from him, pretending to analyze the stack of books she set down. "It's warm in here, is all."

Anger flashed in the captain's eyes. "Being alone with a man in the dark shadows of the library isn't very proper," he grumbled.

"Oh, but it's okay when it happens with you?" Mara's skin prickled at the memory. At the way the captain had almost kissed her in these very shadows.

"I'm your ward."

"It's really none of your concern what Lord Cofsi wanted with me. If he wished for you to know, he would have told you." The warning to not trust Evrardin repeated inside her several times.

"Everything you do is my concern," he growled.

Mara swallowed hard. She knew he only meant he was her warden because the prince commanded it, but his words still made her shiver.

"I wish to go back to my chambers," she said in a frail lilt.

Evrardin scoffed as if he was still angry at her for more than just the present conversation. "Of course. Whatever the princess commands."

She gritted the ivory of her teeth together, pausing, her back to Evrardin. "I hate when you do that, you know." He was silent as she looked over her shoulder. "I do not wish to command you, Evrardin."

He brought her to her rooms in barbed silence, and she hoped his attitude wouldn't be so foul when she was to meet him later that night for training.

Chapter Thirty-Three
Mara

It was cold the following night when Evrardin insisted they begin their training again.

The chill, despite the season, made Mara's chest clench with something similar to dread. "It's too cold to go in the gardens," she whined.

Evrardin looked at her, annoyed. "It's summer," he said as if that suddenly made the dropping temperature bearable.

"And yet my limbs may fall off from frostbite."

She swore she almost saw his lips quirk up. "Coming from a lady of the south? Sacrilege."

"Well, I thought it to be warm in Kairth. I didn't bring my winter furs."

"They haven't stocked your wardrobe with enough options?"

Technically, her wardrobe was overflowing with gifted attire, plenty of them suitable for this weather. "You know," she began, her voice lilted in condescension, "as insufferable as I usually am, imagine how dreadful I'll be when I'm freezing and uncomfortable."

Evrardin glared at her for a moment before saying, "Fine."

She expected more of a fight but was satisfied just the same to be getting out of the crisp dusk air.

They arrived at a wooden door down several confusing hallways. Evrardin pushed the door open, no guards in sight.

"Where are we?"

She stepped into the room and immediately knew the answer to her question. They were in Evrardin's chambers. Something of a blush rose to her olive cheeks and she bit at her bottom lip. The room smelt of him: summer mint leaves, smoke, and a little like burnt fire whiskey.

"I take it this is your room," she said, hands behind her back as she strolled the perimeter, appraising all his things.

"How'd you figure?" he asked wryly.

Mara studied the barren walls, the few weapons he had were stacked on a birch wood desk. There was no window—which Mara thought archaic—making it feel like a prison cell. The room was messy, but not in a way that would make you assume a young boy resided here, but rather, someone who lived the same way their chaotic mind functioned.

"Hm, that's odd," she mumbled to herself as she glanced at the bed and then his various garments on the floor.

Evrardin took the bait. "What is?"

Mara hummed, then clicked her tongue before strolling back to Evrardin who had been watching her the entire time she perused his quarters. "Nothing. It's just, someone of your *bravado*," she said mockingly, "I'd have expected women's clothes to be strewn about the room. Pray tell, is it difficult picking up barmaids when your communication skills rely solely on a series of grunts and glares?"

Evrardin's jaw grew taut. "Not at all, Princess. In fact, I think they're rather fond of my grunts. I just have the mind to keep my escapades beyond the castle's walls, to not make jealous fools of the married noblewomen."

"And you spend a lot of your time beyond the castle? In town, I imagine?" she tried to add in, curious where he went off to when he left Kairth.

"Why so interested in my excursions?" He raised a brow at her, his visage more expressive whenever they went on their teasing romps. "Were you hoping to meet me there?" he jested, a sly grin forming on his lips.

Mara's eyes widened briefly before she steadied herself. "And I suppose you'd like that, Captain. To tear off the dress of a princess instead of the usual cheap harlots you pay."

Evrardin's fist clenched as he took a step closer to her, slouching over her slightly. "Maybe I would."

She averted her eyes, almost choking at his words. She tried to shift the conversation. "A bit rash to take me here, don't you think? If the prince finds out..." Her gaze met Evrardin's, her eyes more worry-ridden than earlier.

He ran a hand through his unruly hair as he created distance between them, the heavy aura that seemed to close in on her when he got so close slowly dissipated. "He won't. He doesn't come down here. Only place I could think of that I knew he'd never visit."

She nodded and took a few more awkward steps around his room before facing him several feet away, awaiting instruction.

"You going to undress?" he asked.

Mara smirked. "What a distasteful question to ask a princess."

"You seem to be keen to your title today, hm, *Princess*," he said, drawing emphasis on his last word.

"Yes, well," she shifted on her feet. "It's the last stretch I can use it before it becomes something else entirely. Suppose I'm getting my fix."

"You realize you're not to become queen after marrying the prince."

"No. Not yet. But I imagine it'll be sooner than I'd like." She studied him, waiting for his features to give way to something—anything—to tell her she was on the right track with Acastus' plans.

Evrardin's eyes dragged over her, his gaze lingering before removing his armor and setting it on a ragged table behind him. Mara watched, almost entranced by the wide expanse of his back as he stripped down to just his linen trousers and tunic.

"I," she cleared her throat, "thought it best to wear my usual attire. That's what I'm most likely to be wearing should anyone actually attack me." Mara's hands clenched, attempting to keep her burned hand—the hand turning black—closed, shielding it from Evrardin.

Mara thought of her wedding day that was rapidly approaching. About how Acastus might attack her if she didn't cooperate. Picturing Acastus forcing her, putting his hands on her, making an uncontrollable shiver of fear rake up her spine. But as she looked back at Evrardin, the image slipped away—a fleeting thought.

Evrardin readied his stance, gesturing his head at Mara to do the same. She dug her dagger out of her skirts, then, without much warning or thought, he darted at her in one swift stride. Mara squealed as his hands wrapped around her waist, his hand sliding up to her neck.

"Almost too easy," he scoffed.

Mara shimmied herself out of his grip. "You didn't tell me we were starting!"

"I told you—your attacker won't be giving you a fair warning. You expect them to send you a letter in preparation?"

Mara's lips formed a tight line and she bit her cheek. "Do you really think they might? A two-day notice would be most convenient now that you mention it." She pursed her lips, her dagger moving with her gesturing hands.

He fixed his posture, then came at her again. This time, Mara was able to swerve out of his way, but his hand still managed to hook onto her midsection. He immediately dropped his hands, not wanting to waste time—if he could get a solid grip on her, it was pretty much set in stone that he would win.

Time and time again they recounted back to their original stances before going at it again. Mara was losing her breath, but she continued, not wanting to give Evrardin any satisfaction.

Mara stumbled out of Evrardin's arms, catching herself on the oak desk in his room. "Shit," she groaned.

Evrardin gave a mirthful chuckle as he adjusted the sleeves of his tunic. Mara caught her breath, glancing at his desk as she used it to hold herself up. She perused a few random tomes. Most of them were about weaponry and she wanted to scoff—of course that's what he would be reading. But as she was about to turn back around, her sight snagged on something of interest. Hidden, stuffed into a book on the far back of the shelving, was a folded piece of paper. What caught her eye, however, was her name scribbled in scratchy ink. Just her first name—not even the full length of it, but simply *Mara*.

Her heart raced as she tried to pry her eyes away from the lettering. Her fingers itched to reach out and take the paper, unfolding it to read what was written in secrecy, but as she did, the blackness on her fingertips stopped her. The note had to have been from Azor, who else would be writing her letters? Her chest rose in fury; he intercepted a letter meant for her, her eyes growing dark in intolerance. *Evrardin wasn't to be trusted.*

When she turned around, Evrardin's sleeves rolled up to his elbows, his hair falling in tendrils around his face, curling slightly from his sweat, she lost all nerve to ask him about it. She was fine teasing and arguing with him, but to mention something with her name on it felt too personal. It would feel too real, too intimate, even if it was meant for her. She clawed in her skin, desperate to know why he would keep a letter from her, but she swallowed her words and ground her teeth together.

She forced it to fall to the back of her mind.

"Try and drop all of your weight into my hold. It will throw the attacker off—especially if they have their hands around your neck"—his eyes flashed to the marks on her throat—"and you'll be able to fall to the floor. Then slip around them and run."

"Run?"

He nodded.

"What if they chase after me?"

"Mara," he sighed, as if this conversation was agonizing for him. "No matter how much we practice, you won't be able to best a grown man. This is your first real taste of combat. It would take years to bring you to speed. Your only means of survival is to run the second you get free."

"But what if they catch me?" she whined again.

"Don't." His words were dark as he spoke. "Don't let them catch you."

Her lips parted as she tried to steady her breathing. Then she nodded.

"Right," he said, orienting himself. He waited for Mara to ready, then he took the one long step to reach her and hooked his hand around her midsection. He spun her so her back was pressed to his front, his hands wrapped around her, one gliding across her neck. She lost her breath momentarily. She stood flush against him, and she could feel his heartbeat. She prayed he couldn't feel hers.

Evrardin's voice was a warm whisper in her ear, and she

struggled to stay balanced when he spoke, raising gooseflesh along her neck. "Now, drop your weight."

She gasped silently, her hand finding the one hugging her around the waist, the other still clutching her dagger. Her eyes fluttered when he whispered her name, trying to get her to focus. "Mara, drop your weight," he said again, but his words trailed off, as if he, too, was losing his composure.

The sweat along Mara's chest made her dress cling to her and it pressed to her skin with every shallow breath she stole. She remembered how last time this position ended, abrupt and of discomfort, so she wondered why he would do it again so readily. Her chest rose in rapid repetitions.

"*Liten rev*," he grumbled.

His hold on her relaxed slightly as she spun to face him, his hand resting on the low of her waist and the back of her neck. She watched his throat as he swallowed, gazing at her, her body melded with his, his hands slowly dropping lower and gripping her dress by the waist.

She breathed his name in return and his eyes shadowed. She felt her heart race when he looked at her lips for the briefest of seconds before locking eyes with her again.

"I...uhm..." she dragged, trying to gather the will to push him away. She didn't want this. She didn't even like him. Well, that was no longer true. It might have started as a strong distaste, but she had grown used to his appearance—she might even say she grew to find comfort in his prickly presence.

She had thought back to that night in the library multiple times now, against her better judgment, and every time it made her cheeks redden. And when he had carried her to the sea, his hands carefully holding her afloat in the ebbing water, promising not to let go, something kindled between them. She had pushed it down, back where it came from, stomping it out while she cursed, refusing to acknowledge it might have been a romantic inclination that was drawing her to him.

The way Evrardin was staring at her now, something pulled her closer to him rather than away, just like in the library, all thoughts of her mistrust with him fleeting. His hand slid up her side, leaving a path of fire along her hip before resting it on her cheek. His grip was soft, a striking feeling when she was so used to his roughness. He held her face like he wasn't sure what he wanted to do: if he was to shake her violently or pull her flush against him. She waited in anticipation, throwing her thoughts to the wind to carry away. She'd put it in his hands. He would decide what would come of their embrace.

All thoughts of Acastus and the wedding and Crowrot and the mysterious letter he was concealing drifted, all she could think about was Evrardin, and it was killing her. She didn't want to be ravaged by his terribly handsome face, but she had never craved someone's touch as desperately as his. And truthfully, if he didn't kiss her now, she would feel embarrassed, ignominious, and foolish for wanting him when all he'd ever vocally expressed was animosity.

"Are you going to kiss me?" she whispered. Her face and neck crept with a blushing storm, surprising even herself.

"You want me to?" he asked in return.

Her lips parted, somehow breathless as he held her. His thumb moved down to her lips, brushing across her lower one. She didn't want to be just another notch in his belt. A prize for how weak she could be and how easily he was able to conquer her.

And still, she did what she knew she shouldn't—she nodded.

She wondered what Evrardin was thinking, if he was laughing at her in his head, but that rumination quickly slipped her mind as he lowered his face slowly, still giving her a chance to halt his movements. Impatient, Mara pushed onto the tips of her toes and connected their lips.

She had kissed boys before, but they were always her age, rushed and inexperienced. She had never truly enjoyed any of those encounters and so she didn't know what to expect when she desired to kiss Evrardin. But he didn't kiss like those boys did when she was sixteen, or eighteen, or nineteen. It was different. He was slow as he moved his mouth with hers, taking his time, as if this kiss was its own entity—not just a hasty means to an end. And his short beard tickled her, rough against her face, but somehow pleasurable as she nervously moved her lips to his rhythm.

His left hand squeezed her hip as he pulled her closer, his other hand slipping to the back of her head and weaving through her hair. She dropped the gifted dagger to his floor, her hands finding his tunic, her fingers knotting in the fabric, afraid she might collapse to her knees if she didn't cling to him.

The warmth surrounding her doubled, everything heating as he stood so close, their bodies melding with one another. She wanted to slide her hands through his hair—the scruffy mess that she always noticed first whenever she saw him. He groaned as her hands trailed his abdomen, her hands sliding up his chest to wrap around his shoulders. Mara couldn't quite reach his hair, even with Evrardin hunched over.

As if he could read her mind, he backed her up, his arms and lips never parting from hers, until they reached his bed. He turned so he could sit on the edge, wedging Mara between his thighs. With him sitting, she now matched his height, making it easy for her to lace her fingers through his tangled hair. His grip on her tightened when she raked her fingers through his hair.

The scruff along his jaw scratched her as she kissed him, the feeling igniting sparks. Evrardin's hands rested on her upper thighs while his tongue worked along the edge of her lips before meeting hers. She whined on reflex and he was quick to spin her around, pushing her back onto his bed, one of his knees between her legs, devouring the gasp she let out. Their mouths were messy and rushed.

Evrardin pawed at her skirt, hiking it up until it was balled in his hand, the apex of her thighs exposed beneath him. Their lips parted and Evrardin rested his forehead on hers, both of them panting.

Before either could speak, someone knocked on his bedroom door.

Evrardin looked at the door in annoyance then back at Mara, still sprawled beneath him, breathing heavily. His calloused hand seared an imprint where it rested on her exposed thigh and she was all too aware of what almost just happened. He cleared his throat and stood, gawking at her. Mara pushed herself up and adjusted her dress.

"M'sorry," he finally said. She wasn't sure what he was apologizing for. For taking advantage of her? For stopping?

She tried to appear calm, unfazed. She couldn't decide if this interruption was a blessing or a curse.

Evrardin went to the door, his hand jiggling the handle, before turning around and gesturing for Mara to hide. She opened her eyes in realization and quickly tucked herself away on the other side of his bed.

"Lord Cofsi," Evrardin greeted.

Mara pulled her knees to her chest as she listened.

"Evrardin," he replied, likely bowing slightly in respect. "I wanted to speak with you."

"Yes, I can see that."

The Lord gave a mirthless chuckle, he almost sounded nervous. "I was hoping to discuss matters surrounding... the *state* of Kairth." The Dusk Lord danced around his last words.

"You've caught me at a bad time."

"Right," Cofsi said as if he should have known better than to surprise the captain with a visit to his chambers. "Tomorrow, then? Say, after breakfast?"

Evrardin grumbled something Mara couldn't hear and then the door closed.

Mara popped out of her hiding spot and marched around the bed, up to Evrardin. He likely expected her to ask him what that was about—what Lord Cofsi wanted—so he appeared shocked when she asked something far more unnerving. "Do you care for me?"

Evrardin blinked stupidly a few times. "Do I...?"

"Care for me," she finished straightforwardly. Her hands were on her hips as she demanded an answer, quite a shift from the flustered state he just had her in moments ago.

Mara took his silence and one scornful laugh as answer enough.

Her face glazed over with ice, mirroring how Evrardin usually looked. "I should get back. I don't want to get caught."

She hesitated before sidestepping him and leaving his room. He knew she might get lost trying to find her way back, but he never moved his feet to follow after her, and that hurt the most.

He was a coward.

Chapter Thirty-Four
Lord Cofsi

Duskwood had grown dimmer than Lord Cofsi would consider typical. While always darker than its two sister isles, the blackening trees and haunting shadows that began to dress his home had started to raise alarm.

Lord Cofsi had an inkling where he could find his answer, but he didn't want to stir his people if he didn't have a definite cause to do so. He knew it had to do with the Veil, The Shadowed Isles wielding dark magick at its heart, making it the closest place in this realm to the Veil. If the isles were sinking in shadow, it's because the bridge between worlds was deteriorating.

In Kairth, Lord Cofsi arrived alongside other nobles and leaders of different kingdoms, allowing him to blend in with the celebratory crowd. He didn't want to stick out, especially given the animosity between practically every kingdom and Solstrale. And yet, when Prince Acastus' silver eyes spotted him, he was immediately dismissive. While Duskwood never had a great fondness for Kairth, it was odd to Cofsi that Acastus would hold such animosity. He acted like he held a personal vendetta against Cofsi.

Even without the prince's words, he dug out his answer that first night in Kairth. He took notice of the way the Sun Prince wore head-to-toe coverings even with the heat from the beginning of summer. All things pointed to him.

He knew it was the Sun Prince bringing darkness over the lands—the irony not going unnoticed. Now if he could only find out *why*, then the possibility of stopping this would become attainable. All he had to work with was a growing suspicion.

The morning following his surprise visit to Evrardin's chambers, he waited on the edges of the dining hall. "Cofsi," a deep voice said from behind. Cofsi jumped, startled by the guard's presence. "What? Couldn't sense me coming?" Evrardin poked.

"I was distracted," he responded, brushing invisible lint off his shirt.

Evrardin didn't speak, he just stared at the man.

"Shall we talk somewhere more private?"

"That'll just draw suspicion. Best we speak in the open."

Evrardin was right. No one would suspect the conversation Cofsi was about to have with Evrardin was anything but superficial if they did it during a casual morning stroll in the gardens.

Ev gestured his head, urging Cofsi to match his gait as he took off.

"I guess I should just get right to it," Cofsi started, clapping his hands together. "I know the prince is using dark magick."

Evrardin stopped in his tracks. He turned to him, his eyes rounded, before shaking off his bewilderment and continuing down the path. His fingers tightened around the hilt of his sword. "Could sense it, I suppose?"

Cofsi clicked his tongue in thought. "In a way... Yes. I could sense it. But not in the way you think."

"And what do I think?"

Cofsi shook his head. "This isn't the time to argue semantics, Evrardin. I know he's using forbidden magick. And I know he's using it on you. What for? That is the question of the hour." He looked over at him expectantly.

Evrardin took a breath and glanced at Cofsi, shaking his head.

"Can't tell me? Or won't?"

"Take your guess."

Cofsi stroked his faint stubble, considering the small things Evrardin was saying to him. He figured he might have been somehow blocked from speaking about whatever the prince wanted him to avoid. But he knew it wasn't out of loyalty. Not after that spectacle in the Old God's Cathedral. No, it was from forbidden magick.

"Right. We'll have to get more creative then—to communicate. What kind of language did he use? Maybe he slipped in his word choice, allowing space for you to weasel."

"I thought this wasn't the time for semantics."

Cofsi was tough to irritate, but Evrardin knew how to get under his skin. He lightly chuckled, tucking his hands behind his back as they continued. He was waiting for him to say more, treating Evrardin like a petulant child.

"What makes you so sure I even wish to discuss this with you?"

"Because you're clearly fucking miserable serving him." Cofsi flashed his eyes at the captain.

Evrardin grunted in annoyance. It was hard to overlook the constant agony plastered across his countenance—even if he was naturally gloomy.

"And, let me remind you, you were the one who invited me here. Were you just planning to berate me the entire time?"

The captain fell silent.

"Evrardin," Cofsi said with a quiet urgency. He paused as a

couple strolled past them. When they were out of earshot, he focused back on Ev. "I can't help the kingdoms if I can't find the root of the problem. You can water and prune a flower all you wish, but it won't grow if its roots are rotted and without nutrients."

Evrardin rolled his eyes. "Out with it already."

"The Shadowed Isles have been seized by the darkness that I see spreading over Kairth. I wish to bring this to an end before it infects all the kingdoms." He interpreted the expectant expression on Evrardin's face as indifference. "You may not think yourself responsible for all of that, but do you truly wish to sentence everyone else here to purgatory when our world is taken over by the Veil?" Cofsi gave a mirthless chuckle. "Yes, I know the darkness is spreading from that. I just don't know exactly how or why the prince would want that. I need you to help me stop him."

Evrardin continued the rest of the walk in silence. "Maybe we'd be better off," he finally mumbled like he was imagining the peace he could finally find if the darkness took his life.

"Is there truly no one you care about here? No one you'd want to save from the dark?" Cofsi tried to talk logically to Ev, who was too stubborn to want to play his part. It didn't matter that he didn't sign up for all this. It was laid at his feet, and he had a choice to make.

Evrardin veered off the path and into a small section of the gardens. He removed his sword and placed it on the grass. He wasn't wearing armor this morning as he knelt before a blossoming lyre flower.

"Gods, is that a bleeding heart?"

Evrardin nodded as he began to clip away dead petals.

"H...How?"

"With death."

Cofsi knew there wasn't a threat laced in his words, but rather, a reminder of who he was.

"So, will you help me? Help all of Solstrale and the other seven kingdoms before your prince takes things too far?"

"*Your prince*," Evrardin growled to himself. "I'll see what I can manage." Those were the last words he was willing to express to Cofsi.

Lord Cofsi nodded at him out of respect even though his back was to him, and he made his way back down the path.

Chapter Thirty-Five
Evrardin

So many things were raging in Evrardin's mind when an annoying woman slid up beside him. He looked at the bane of his existence with something akin to wistfulness.

She peered back, her head tilted and smiled. "I thought we could go into town today."

"Did you now?"

She nodded and rolled on the balls of her feet as they stood in the library.

"Since when did these escapades become a way to entertain yourself instead of training?" His voice was low as he spoke.

"I never said we wouldn't train." Mara led the way out of the library having flipped through every book she needed for the day. The sun was setting and cast a warm ray of watercolors on the floorboards through the stained-glass windows.

"It's too dangerous."

She scoffed. "I'm not a child, you know. I can handle going into town."

Evrardin sighed dramatically and Mara tried to hide her smirk. "It's not about that, Princess. If someone were to recognize you... Or one of the other guards saw us leaving..."

"You're the captain, though. Are you not?"

"They are sworn to the crown. Not me."

Mara bit her lip, trekking back to her apartments, Ev at her side. They both seemed willing to pretend that night in Evrardin's room never occurred because neither of them brought it up. Mara almost seemed too talkative in the library, describing in detail every tiny thing she was doing, as if she could cover the embarrassing fact that she let him kiss her with her ramblings. And neither addressed the hard-hitting question Mara posed aggressively to Evrardin right before she parted.

When they finally got to her rooms, Mara slipped in and urged Evrardin to follow her.

Mara dug through her wardrobe and pulled out a plain brown cloak, thin enough for a summer night. She turned to Evrardin and swung it around her neck in theatrics, then pulled up her hood. "Unrecognizable," she mused.

Evrardin shook his head.

"And don't act like you don't know a discreet way out of the castle. I saw you coming back that one night. You were nowhere near the gates." Mara blushed and Evrardin remembered how he stared up at her in her thin nightgown.

He gritted his teeth.

"Come on! How else am I supposed to learn the ways of true common living if I am forced to stay behind these walls? You complain about my brattiness, yet you do nothing to fix it."

"I could think of a few ways to fix it," he mumbled to himself. When she didn't respond, he rubbed the back of his neck. "Fine. But we're only staying for training, then we're to come right back."

Mara nodded and mock saluted him. "Yes, Captain."

This was not the best timing for Evrardin to be leaving the grounds, but he agreed with Mara, it might do her some good to see what more Solstrale had to offer other than this decrepit, soul-sucking castle.

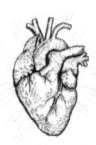

Evrardin led her to the catacombs even though it pained him to enter that room, knowing his friend wouldn't be inside waiting.

He led her down a side corridor that Evrardin used to exit the castle frequently. Mara stumbled behind him, fumbling in the dark. Evrardin had the layout memorized and could walk it in his sleep. Mara, on the other hand, was sticking her arms out like feelers trying to navigate after him. She tripped over a loose stone and stumbled forward. "Shit," she cursed. "Wait up." Urgency laced in her voice.

Evrardin took pity on her, only a few steps away. She let out a breathless gasp as he gripped her hand in his much larger, calloused one, directing her out of the castle.

When they made it under the moonlight and into the graveyard, Evrardin dropped her hand, and she wiped hers on her skirts as if just touching him was somehow tainting her. He flexed his fingers in response before looking back at Mara. "So mysterious," she teased.

"Keep running that mouth and I'll take us right back."

Mara pursed her lips. "Sorry," she mumbled.

Evrardin was a bit surprised by her submissiveness. She must really want to go into town. Someone like her had seen gaudy and beautiful places before. Dalhurst was sure to disappoint.

The captain was all too aware of the questions Mara was sure to ask him, so to avoid such annoyances, he strolled ahead of her, using his longer legs to his advantage. He could hear her stumble, trying to keep up with him as he led the way down the dirt road to Dalhurst.

"Do you go into town often?" she asked, slightly out of breath.

Evrardin grunted.

"Is that a yes?"

"I'm shocked you're not able to decipher my grunts by now."

Mara managed to match his stride, clearly walking much faster than her natural gait. "Is this place special to you or something?"

Evrardin glanced sidelong at her, raising a brow in question.

"I only mean, you seem to avoid talking about your excursions in Dalhurst. And you clearly didn't want to take me here."

"None of that means I have some sentimental reason for doing so."

"That doesn't answer my question."

"Have I been known to answer your questions?" he said with a bit more spite than he meant.

Mara huffed and began to walk slowly so she trekked behind him again.

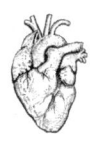

When they finally reached town, Mara smiled brightly as if she wasn't facing an impoverished town, the air mangy and filled with thieving and impecunious peasants.

She took in her surroundings animatedly, trailing the cobblestone buildings and dripping candles lit in the windows. People passed by, not taking notice of either of them as they were swept away in their own worlds.

Loud rustling and out-of-tune music pooled from a tavern door as a woman stumbled out. Mara grinned at her and tilted her head to get a look into the bar before the door closed.

"Can we go in?" she asked.

He stared at the lone woman. "No. We're not here to socialize."

"But—"

"Evrardin," the plump woman spoke as she approached the two of them.

Evrardin's jaw clenched, refusing to look at Mara. He could feel Mara glancing between the two of them as the woman came under the moon's light. She had on a simple brown dress, the corset pulled tight, her chest billowing at the top. Her curls were pulled back in a chignon, tendrils falling out in loose loops. She was rather pretty, and with the attitude she exuded just by existing, he figured Mara would agree with him.

"Gwen," Ev replied to her, his words terse.

"Oh, are you in one of those moods where you pretend like you don't want to see me?" She laughed, her finger reaching out and falling down the front of Evrardin's shirt. He stood still, not uttering a word in response. His eyes finally flickered over to Mara. "Oh. You're with another girl, then." Gwen seemed displeased as she gave Mara a once-over and turned her nose in disapproval. "Can't say I'm surprised."

"Let's go," Ev spoke flatly in Mara's direction. Evrardin grabbed Mara's hand and dragged her away from the bustling tavern entrance.

"I'll be here when you get sick of her," Gwen snickered. Mara turned to look at her as Ev pulled her along. Gwen smiled and gave Mara a little condescending wave.

Evrardin didn't let go of Mara's palm until they reached the stable, a few horses inside the hay-filled pens. The stable master nodded at Evrardin from behind his newspaper as they went inside.

"We can train here," he told her.

"Who was that?" Mara asked, ignoring Evrardin's words.

"Doesn't matter."

"Why don't you want to tell me?"

"She's a barmaid," he snarled.

Mara bit her lips before her eyes darted to Evrardin's. "*Oh*," she muttered in the realization that Evrardin and Gwen's past wasn't exactly tasteful.

Evrardin turned away from her and strolled to the back of the stables where the floor transitioned to dirt. Mara hesitantly followed close behind.

He slid off his sword. "What? Are you jealous?" he harshly teased.

Mara bit the inside of her cheek, throwing her cloak to the side and shifting to her fighting stance.

Evrardin swallowed, Mara's eyes hard to see in the faint light, but he could still tell the way they glassed over. She *was* jealous.

Evrardin's shook his head as he tried to focus back on training. This just painted another reason why nothing could ever happen between the two of them. He wasn't a good man. He would make her nothing but miserable. So instead of reassuring her he had never been intimate with Gwen, he let her believe her own conclusion. He did not owe it to her to clarify. They were nothing to one another.

Evrardin darted toward Mara, his hands going for her hips like they so often did when they practiced. If he knew one thing about Acastus, it was that he didn't know how to fight. If he was to attack Mara, he'd go for her waist or arms first.

Mara tried to sidestep him, but he was faster. He hooked an

arm around her waist and she began to hit his chest with her fists. "Let me go!"

It took him a moment, caught in a bit of incredulousness, before he dropped his hands and Mara stumbled back. She tripped over her own feet and fell to the ground.

Evrardin reached out to give her a hand, but she refused. She stood, brushing her legs off before realizing she had fallen into a pile of horse shit.

"Gods," she moaned. "Are you fucking kidding me?"

Evrardin would have found her impolite speech humorous if she didn't look like she was on the verge of real tears. "Mara," he said without any real thought of where his sentence was going.

She hid her face from him and grabbed her cloak. "Let's just go. This was a stupid idea."

Evrardin was certain she was jealous, but with the way her voice wavered, he figured something else must have been bothering her to be quite this upset. And he didn't take her for the kind of girl who would cry from dirtying her skirts.

She stormed out of the stable and onto the dimly lit street.

"Wait," Evrardin called after her. He scooped his sword up and hastily slid it around his waist before stumbling to follow her.

She stopped, much to his surprise, and he almost tumbled into her. She turned to face him, the tears he thought he had seen welling in her eyes now a vacant expression.

He scanned her face before speaking slowly. "Let's get you cleaned up before we head back." Her eyes almost seemed hopeful and Evrardin impulsively squashed it. "If you show up with horse shit on your dress, that's sure to raise the suspicion of your handmaidens."

"Right," Mara mumbled as if she had originally thought he was offering to fix this for other reasons.

She followed behind him like his shadow. They were back in

front of the tavern from earlier and he hoped they wouldn't see Gwen again. He did always find her eagerness quite irritating.

Evrardin held the door open, and Mara hesitantly stepped into the hustle of moving bodies. Drunkards laughed and sang all around her. Her eyes twinkled. But the smile didn't form on her lips.

She waited patiently, studying the room, her hands clasped in front of her as Evrardin talked to the bartender.

"Evening," a deep voice spoke beside her. Evrardin's eyes flashed over to her, grinding his teeth as he waited for Bhedam.

Her mouth parted as she turned to the stranger. He was a man, probably in his thirties, his brown hair unkempt. His clothes were dirty, from working he presumed.

The captain thought he heard him ask to buy her a drink. Ev waited irritatingly for her response.

Mara stuttered on her words. "Oh. I don't think..." Her eyes darted over to Evrardin who stared at his hands, making it seem like he wasn't listening. "Actually, yes. I would love a drink."

The man got a pint from one of the barmaids. He leaned back against the bar and handed the ale to Mara. She took it in her fingers, sipping it, then peered at him from over her rim.

"Can't say I've seen you before," the man began. "What's your name?"

Evrardin leaned against the bartop, his body slowly simmering. He had the urge to tear Mara away from that man, but he knew he had no good reason. Bhedam spoke before the captain could hear Mara's response. "Here ya are," Bhedam said, sliding Evrardin a key to a room.

"Thanks," Ev mumbled, looking back at Mara whose face was flushed a pretty shade of red.

A man behind her stumbled as he drunkenly danced, almost falling into her. But the man shamelessly flirting with her reached out and pulled her against his chest, watching as the man crashed backward, passing out on the floor.

"You all right?" he asked.

She looked up at him, flustered, and Evrardin hated the way another man's arms wrapped around her. He seemed too keen on clutching her body to his, his fingers digging into her arm and threatening to leave bruises. Mara winced.

Evrardin didn't hear what Bhedam said as he shoved through the few bodies that separated him and the princess, the stranger's arm immediately darting away from Mara's body, holding his hands in the air in defeat. Mara turned her head, Evrardin standing right behind her with a deathly regard in his eyes. "Unless you don't mind losing them, I recommend you keep your hands to yourself," he said quietly.

The man backed away. "Shit, not trying to start any trouble here."

Mara turned to Ev and he had to pry his eyes away from the challenge. His gaze softened, but only slightly.

"Come on—got us a room," he all but growled.

She swallowed in embarrassment at the implication of his words. She looked back at the rambunctious crowd wistfully before leaving her drink on the countertop and going up the stairs, following Evrardin to one of the rooms. "Did you defend my honor because Acastus commanded it of you?" she asked quietly.

"No." *Fuck.*

She wiped her hands on her skirts. "Why was that man so afraid of you?" she asked.

It took him several moments to respond. "I have a... reputation around here." he begrudgingly told her.

"What sort of reputation?"

"Mara," he warned.

"Fine. Don't tell me. I'll just go back down and ask around—"

He grunted in annoyance. "I frequent the fighting ring."

"You fight?" she scoffed. "What? For money?"

He nodded.

"And I'm assuming you often win if he was that afraid by just your presence."

Evrardin didn't answer but she seemed to infer what he meant.

"We'd make a good team," she mumbled under her breath.

He glanced at her in confusion.

"Oh, I... I liked to go into town back in Wrens Reach and bet on matches. And I got pretty good at winning."

His lips almost curved in amusement. Of course Mara snuck her way into seedy taverns to watch fights. And of course she was good at picking winners. His chest tightened at the idea of her watching him fight—of her cheering him on.

She stepped through the threshold of the room and Evrardin set the candle he was holding down. The room had a few others lit and it created a warm glow on the floorboards. The noise from downstairs could still be heard but it was far fainter.

There was a basin of water before the small bed and Evrardin nodded toward it. Mara quietly approached the steel bowl, setting her cloak on the bed before reaching to undo the straps of her dress.

Evrardin cleared his throat. "I'll be right outside."

Before he could close the door, Mara stopped him. "Wait." He turned to her and she flushed. "I...My dress." She spun so he could see the way her fingers couldn't reach the back ties. "My handmaidens usually..." Her voice trailed off.

Evrardin nodded. "Right," he said agitated, like this was just another instance of her being spoiled rotten—she couldn't even remove her dress by herself.

He strolled over to her and brushed his fingers against hers before taking over. His fingers buzzed as they worked.

He should not be stood in an inn, alone with his prince's betrothed, taking her dress off of all things, all while she was assumed to be tucked safely in her bed back at Kairth.

He quickly undid the ties for her and exited the room before she could say anything more. He leaned his back against the door of the room, itching to go downstairs and have a drink. "Bloody hell," he mumbled to himself. He had grown so used to contempt and spite, he hated these flux of new feelings Mara was stirring from him. It sat uncomfortably heavy in his chest.

He just needed to get her out of his system. But he couldn't do that. She was forbidden fruit. Maybe if he found Gwen... No. He shook his head at the idea and brushed his hand down his face in irritation. The thought of being with someone other than Mara didn't give him that spark he was continuously chasing every time he was with her.

"Fuck." He was fucked. He closed his eyes and pressed the back of his head against the door. She was becoming too much. It wasn't her fault, though. It was Evrardin's.

"Okay." He heard her faint voice from behind the wooden door after several minutes of torture.

He entered the room again and Mara stood in her dress, the back damp, but free of horse shit. She turned from him shyly, exposing her olive skin behind the untied laces. His mouth ran dry as he came up from behind and began to redo them. He tried not to notice the freckles spread across her skin, or the way her body moved like she was trying to control her breathing. And he definitely tried to avoid looking at her exposed neck, her hair pulled over her shoulder.

"Thank you," she muttered.

He hadn't known her to speak so softly around him and it made him feel guilty. Like he had done something wrong.

They stood at just the right angle so that Evrardin could see Mara's face in the full-length mirror across the small room. She had closed her eyes, her fingers squeezing together as his faintly brushed her back while he tied up the loose laces, gooseflesh pilling across her shoulders.

When he was done, he refocused on her hands and noticed a strange coloring on the tips of her fingers.

She turned to face him, and his eyes had narrowed in on her, shocking her out of her bashfulness.

"What happened to your hand?" he asked assertively.

Mara's hands quickly went behind her back. "Nothing."

Evrardin looked over her shoulder and in the mirror. Her fingers laced together but he could see the black smudged on one hand. He reached for her arm, but she pulled away. "Let me see."

She shook her head, backing up.

He trailed her, his footsteps matching each of hers. "Mara," he growled.

"It's nothing to worry about," she sputtered.

"That's for me to decide." He closed in on her and she gulped.

"Evrardin, please," she begged.

He reached out to force her hand in his, wanting to inspect it.

With wide eyes, she stumbled away as he closed the distance, falling back. She should have collided with the mirror behind her—trapping her—but instead, she fell through the silver glass.

Chapter Thirty-Six
Mara

Her eyes were as wide as two moons as she sat on soft grass, looking through an ornate frame and onto a blurred Evrardin who looked straight past her, perplexed.

Could he see her? Mara wondered.

She stood and turned. It was similar to the plane she found herself in during the bonding ceremony. But it was much lighter where she now stood. She realized she was standing in a clearing, but there were gray buildings in the distance all around her. She refocused on the oval-shaped blur she knew was Evrardin, still in the small room at the tavern. She watched in amazement as he reached out like he was going to stick his hand in through the mirror and manifest itself before her. But his fingers stopped as they met the glass.

Mara had the urge to look around her, the strange buildings in the distance emitting a faint fog, making them radiate like motes in the sun. The only sound was the whistling of the wind through the crowned trees behind her.

Even with its aberrant, dull beauty, she couldn't suppress the intense anxiety that triggered in her body. She remembered the last time she was in the Veil all too well. The hands that clawed at her, the voice that spoke her name.

She shuddered and hustled toward Evrardin, standing helplessly before his grainy image and took a deep breath. If she made it through one way, she'd be able to get back just the same. She didn't quite believe her own words as she pictured the blood spilled beneath her mother, but she stuck her hand out anyway and watched as it sliced through the glass like a puddle. "Oh," she muttered.

A familiar hand wrapped around hers, fingers settling over her wrist, and tugged her with a hard yank. Mara came tumbling out the other side of the mirror, colliding with Evrardin's chest as he fell to the floor. She landed on top of him with a grunt, his arms gripping her waist, her head resting against him. She squeezed her eyes tight; she was worried she'd never be able to pry them open again.

She must have been shaking because Evrardin whispered soft words in her ear. "You're okay," he told her quietly, his hands getting a little too comfortable as they splayed over her back, keeping her close.

She finally let her eyes flutter open and she tilted her head to look at the captain currently clutching her in his arms.

She hadn't noticed she had been crying until his thumbs swept under her eyes to clear away the tears. "What just happened?" she asked, glancing behind her, trying to see if she left a trail of blood.

"I was about to ask you the same thing."

Realizing she was sprawled on top of him, she hastily pushed herself away and caught herself against the bedpost.

Evrardin sat up and marveled at her. "You really went through," he said in disbelief, sitting back on his hands.

She looked at her palms, making sure she was in one piece. "I... I did."

Her lips wanted to tip into a smile, but she was quickly reminded that this was exactly what Acastus wanted. She could finally do the thing he needed her for.

It was like he could read her mind because his eyes shifted in dread.

"You can't tell him!"

Evrardin got to his feet and rested his palm on the hilt of his sword. "I wish I couldn't."

Mara's face bunched up and she began to breathe rapidly. "No. No, you can't. Please, Evrardin. You can't tell him."

"You know I can't lie to him if he asks."

"But... asking isn't commanding."

"I'll try to skirt around the topic. But, *liten rev*, if he demands me to recount anything important happening, I'm afraid I'll..." He couldn't finish his words.

The tears welled truthfully now. "Don't call me that," she said through a broken lilt.

"Princess," he coaxed.

She took a deep breath before composing herself and opened the door. "We should get back."

Evrardin hesitated before following her out.

Chapter Thirty-Seven
Lord Cofsi

Two armed guards stormed into Lord Cofsi's guest chamber, startling him. Cofsi sprung upright, eyes still laden with sleep. "What is the meaning of this?" he demanded.

Ignoring Cofsi's request, one of the guards grabbed his arm rather tightly, hooking it behind his back and dragging him from his bed. Cofsi stumbled, trying to shake out of the guard's grip. He took in the appearance of the two martial men: they were about his height and only armed with a longsword strapped against their hips. Cofsi might have been able to fight one, but not two.

Cofsi grunted as he struggled against his confines.

"You've been accused of conspiring against the prince."

Cofsi's brows furrowed as he resisted every jostle. "W-What? That can't be—" Cofsi's thoughts were cut short with one simple name. *Evrardin.*

Evrardin must have told the prince of Cofsi's bargain to provide him with information about Acastus' inner political workings. He always knew Evrardin was a sadistic bastard, but he never thought him nefarious enough to betray innocent people. Did he truly hold that much loyalty to the prince that he would risk the life of the kingdom he was sworn to protect?

Cofsi knew the prince would be anything but aware of his meeting with Evrardin, something so below his caliber of importance. Cofsi concluded that Acastus likely didn't demand any conspiratorial intel out of Evrardin. No, Evrardin had told him on his own violation.

Cofsi seethed all the way to the dungeons, grateful at least that it was the middle of the night and no nobles were lingering about the halls to gawk at him. Though, he supposed it didn't matter much. Word would break loose first thing in the morning. Everyone in Kairth would be aware of Lord Cofsi's arrest. Now he just hoped what little evidence Acastus might present wouldn't be enough to convict Cofsi of treason.

Cofsi was shucked into a damp cell, the small torches creating a burning glow over the wet stone. The iron gate dragged along the ground, making Cofsi wince.

"Do I at least get to know how long I'm intended to be held?"

"Until the prince wishes to bring you to testify. But with the weddin', I wouldn't expect anythin' soon."

Cofsi grumbled curses to himself, the guard's heavy footfalls echoing through the corridor. He didn't know Evrardin as well as he used to, but he couldn't imagine him truly wanting to see Acastus succeed—whatever that may entail. Cofsi paced back and forth; why would Evrardin do this? Cofsi groaned when his foot sloshed in a puddle, soaking the shoes he had haphazardly pulled on in the mad dash to the dungeons.

Cofsi approached the bars of his enclosure, his hands tightening on their warped surface. He began to regret his insistence on trekking to the Summer Solstice alone, wanting to protect his people if things had gone askew. Well, they had gone wrong, and now Cofsi was in Kairth without an ally.

He rested his head against the cold metal and sighed. But then something odd struck him, his heightened senses tingling within his blood. When Cofsi took a breath in, instead of smelling the wet mold of the stone dungeon, he smelt blood and decay. Decay strong enough to mean hundreds of dead bodies.

He looked up in confusion, expecting to see a pile of corpses rotting in front of him, but it was just more cells. He breathed in again and could tell the bodies were tucked away. They were certainly in the dungeons, but they smelt faint, like the dungeons went beyond just these confinements and instead had a labyrinth of hidden alcoves and halls.

They seemed relatively fresh too, with how potent the scent was. Recognition bloomed in Cofsi and he held his head higher. He began laughing to himself. First quietly, then loud enough to echo down the halls and gain a scolding from one of the sentinels.

"Fucking Evrardin," he muttered to himself in reverence. Cofsi knew Evrardin was under some dark spell that forced his loyalty to the prince. He was likely sworn not to share any sensitive details he heard from Acastus. There was no way for him to tell Cofsi of Acastus' plans. But he could show him. "That sly bastard." Cofsi had a grin on his face that began to sink. He knew Acastus was doing something with hundreds of corpses, likely intertwined with dark, forbidden magick. But now Cofsi was trapped in the dungeons. He couldn't do anything locked down here.

His fingers tightened on the bars. He'd have to find a way out.

Chapter Thirty-Eight
Evrardin

Evrardin watched her from the doorway. Mara had locked herself in the library with her dusty tomes for the past day and night after she and the captain returned from Dalhurst. She fell asleep at one of the desks, her face squished against sprawled-out books.

She knocked her chair over when she stood, darting out of the library with a tome tucked under her arm. When she made it to the library's exit, she crashed into the one person she apparently dreaded seeing. "What are you doing here?" she hissed at Evrardin who had been leaning against the archway, arms crossed over his broad chest.

He furrowed his brows, taking notice of the tome she clutched tightly, and he wondered if she thought he might rip it from her hands.

"Never mind," she added before he could respond.

She took off down the halls, heading back to her rooms. Evrardin followed, calling out to her.

She ignored him, and he huffed his annoyance as he trailed her. He knew in the halls, out in the open, wasn't the best place to talk anyway. He'd wait till they could be more secluded.

She went to shut her door, but Evrardin kicked his foot in the archway, stopping it before it could close fully.

She groaned, backing away and throwing her book on her desk in defeat. Evrardin crept in after her and shut the door.

"What do you want?"

"Feisty, today, aren't we?" he taunted.

She pursed her lips and spun to face him. "Did you tell him?"

Evrardin's face remained stoic knowing she'd ask him this, but it still left a sour taste in his mouth. "I didn't."

She let out a shallow breath. "Good."

"But," he began. Mara's head snapped back to attention. "He asked me to fetch you. He wants to see your progress, you know, with the wedding tomorrow. I'm afraid he'll—"

"The wedding is tomorrow?" she asked aghast.

Evrardin tilted his head. "Yes," he said hesitantly, unsure if she was truly asking him or being sarcastic.

Her eyes moved around her room and tears began to well. Evrardin entered her space and tilted her head up toward him. His thumb wiped her tears—something he had no business doing—and she choked out a laugh. "Who would have guessed the prince's lethal captain could be so benevolent."

Evrardin's jaw tightened. "If you're worried about glass-fairing again—"

She cut him off, shaking her head meekly. "I don't want to marry him," she sobbed. She closed her eyes. Evrardin half-expected to mock her and tell her she was being puerile again; worrying about being wedded to a handsome prince and not the actual thing that could kill her—though, maybe they were one and the same. But instead, his hand fell from her cheek.

She opened her eyes to look at him and his gaze had averted

to her side window, like something out there was far more entertaining than the crying princess in here.

"I'm sorry," he started.

"For what?"

He wanted to tell her. He wanted to express how he felt. To tell her something real—*anything*. To let her know he didn't hate her or that he didn't want to hurt her. He wanted to save her from all this. He wanted to tell her how much royalty contradicted everything he stood for, how she had been nothing but a spoiled brat in his eyes since the beginning, but as he grew fond of her, he no longer felt that hatred for something she couldn't control. He'd give anything to let her remain an untouched princess. But his lips were permanently sealed.

His mouth opened but nothing came out, shutting it again.

She smiled, the tears stopping, but their streaks still marring her face. "You can't tell me," she surmised.

He gave her a wistful look.

Her eyes lit up in realization in return. Mara strolled around Evrardin and pushed the drape off her floor-length mirror. Evrardin watched her silently as her fingers splayed along the surface. She gestured her head to call the captain over. With uncertain steps, he stood tall beside her, both of them peering at their reflection in the mirror. Her dress a soft blush, flowing freely around her skin, the weather exceptionally warm today. Him in his typical gear, though he lacked any armor, his sword always on his hip. Both of their faces tired, their eyes trying desperately not to scan over one another's bodies.

Mara pondered for a moment before beginning her line of questioning. "Are you sorry for something you've already done?"

Evrardin looked away from their reflection and down at the princess, his brows knitted together. "Mara—?"

She cut him off, shaking her head slightly. "Look in the

mirror," she said softly. "Cofsi believed I could perform more magick than just glassfairing."

He opened his mouth to argue, hesitating, but he followed through with her commands.

His hackles rose as she rested her hand on the surface, the mirror becoming gel under her fingertips. He thought it might be so easy for her to push her hand inside, to glassfaire, but rather, she studied Evrardin's reflection. He was about to speak, to ask her what the hell they were doing when Mara gasped.

"What?" he asked impatiently, his eyes flickering to her hand, wondering if she was being harmed by the mirror again.

"You answered," she whispered, not able to remove her eyes from Evrardin's reflection.

"What the fuck are you talking about, Princess?"

She closed her eyes in annoyance before tilting her head to speak directly at him. "Have you ever heard of the stories they'd tell of the Glass People? How they reside on the other side of mirrors, a haunting reflection of the person in the living realm."

Evrardin didn't respond, confused as to where she was going.

Mara huffed. "I share the Glass King's blood, just as Acastus shares the Sun King's. I'm able to connect to the Veil and see your true reflection; the reflection your counterpart mimics back"—a beat passed—"at least, I think that's why I'm able to do this." She watched him in the mirror attempt to process her words. "He's the opposite of you."

His nose scrunched in irritation before marveling at her. "So, you can see...?"

"I can see your true answers. Your reflection isn't bound to the prince like you are."

His eyes narrowed in disbelief like he wasn't trusting a word she said.

She looked back at the mirror. "Are you sorry for something

you wish you could do, but can't?" she asked, referring to his apologetic statement moments ago.

Evrardin tentatively faced the mirror, his mouth and head stoic.

Mara grinned. "The answer is yes."

He figured she could have guessed that, but he didn't have an explanation for why she would lie. So he found himself believing in her ability to connect to the Veil.

"And do you know whatever cynical plan Acastus is plotting?"

Evrardin's eyes shied away for a moment.

"Yes, thought as much," she spoke. "And tomorrow is more than just a wedding, isn't it?"

He saw no movement, but Mara did. But he didn't need to, he knew his reflection had nodded. Her leg began bouncing uncomfortably. "Am I in danger?" When her eyes locked on Evrardin's in the mirror, she winced. *He* nodded. "Are you in danger?" She paused to look at him in the flesh as she asked, then turned back to the mirror, her fingers itching.

His counterpart surely nodded.

"Hells," she cursed. "Okay. Am I in danger..."—she hesitated with her next words—"from you?"

The captain's eyes snapped to hers.

She swallowed hard. "You didn't move. I'm assuming you don't know." She glanced at him, both of them locked in one another's corporeal gaze. "Against your will, I hope." Her words were shrinking as she whispered them.

She regretfully glanced at the mirror to see his counterpart nod again.

"And..." she halted. Nerves had bubbled up in her throat. She looked more afraid of this next answer than she was asking if she was at risk of harm's way. Her fingers tapped along the glass' surface, swallowing her reserves. "Do I still irritate you or have you grown to enjoy my terrible company?" She let out a mirthless laugh, unable to meet his eyes. "Tell me, Captain, have your inclinations for me changed since our first encounter? Am I still destined to be your ruination?" She gave him a sideways smile to soften the weight her feelings had on those words. She gritted her teeth like she was in agony. Was Evrardin in that same agony?

A passion he knew he should ignore forced his hands to move, grabbing her chin, and compelling her to look at him instead of his reflection, her lips parting in surprise from the contact. He didn't want this imposter to answer for him. Even though he couldn't verbally answer her, he could show her. Evrardin closed the distance between them and crashed his lips to hers in an abrupt, fluid movement. She yelped in surprise but immediately fell against him.

He stole the breath from her entirely, her hands shaking. He kissed her like he had been dreaming of doing this since their time in his bedroom. Like this had consumed his every thought and he was trying to memorize the way her lips felt against his, worried this was the last he'd know of them. He backed her up so her knees hit her bed and she was forced to sit. His hands rested on either side of her thighs, moving his mouth against hers more roughly now, his beard tickling her cheeks. Every single thread inside him ignited. One of his hands moved behind her, holding her bottom with a ghostly touch, his fingers playing with the fabric of her skirt.

He spoke between kisses, her hands snaking up to rest on either side of his shoulders, sighing in relief as his body overflowed with nerves. "We should"—*kiss*—"go find"—*kiss*—"Cas before he—"

"Don't you dare cut this short again," she said, drawing away.

He let out a low chuckle and Mara's cheeks bloomed a faint

pink like she wasn't used to the rich baritone of Evrardin's real laugh.

"If I remember correctly, last time was not my fault."

She rolled her eyes. "Fine. We can go find Cas if that's what you'd rather—"

He slammed his lips to hers, pushing her back onto her soft mattress, cutting off her snarky words. He fiddled with his belt and threw it, along with his sword, to the floor. "That is *not* what I'd rather be doing," he mumbled aggressively against her mouth.

"Show me," she challenged. "Show me what you'd rather be doing." She pulled him closer to her and a swirl of lust at her fiery words made him growl low in his chest.

Evrardin's hands tentatively stroked up the side of her body, his mind reeling with everything that could go wrong. She wasn't his to have. He could never have her, not fully. He tried to block out the way he knew this would hurt her, let alone himself. He'd never even be able to tell her how he truly felt. He should stop.

His self-doubt was cut short when Mara's fingers toyed nervously with the hem of his shirt, pulling it from where it was tucked into his trousers.

Part of him wondered if Mara was just using him as a distraction—something to keep her mind off glassfairing again and forced into a loveless marriage tomorrow. If he was a better man, he'd stop what he was doing. But he never claimed to be a good man.

Evrardin sat back slightly, breaking their kiss, and pulled his shirt over his head. Mara bit her lip, her breath catching in her throat as the light seeped in from her window, cascading over his chest, making it glow with evening gold. Pale and long-since-healed scars cut through his chest, marring him all over, a constant reminder of all the terrible things he'd endured. He wanted to tell her about them, but somehow, even with all that was currently unfolding in the small of her room, that felt too intimate.

He was gentle as he nestled himself between her legs, her dress hiked up, exposing the softness of her thighs just above her stockings. His calloused hands palmed the flesh before tentatively shoving her skirt until the apex of her thighs was exposed to him. She flushed pink, just like the lyre flowers Evrardin tended to.

He admired her figure, the gentleness of her. The way her hips curved, and her chest rose in rapid breaths. The soft beauty of her stunned him. Her legs squeezed together on instinct but were blocked by his waist. He wanted to tell her how beautiful she was, but the words were lodged in his throat. Instead, he came down to place kisses along her thigh, leaving a trail as he went higher and higher *and—*

"Evrardin," she whispered.

"Yes, Princess?" He looked up at her, his mouth mere inches from where he wanted it most.

Her fingers twiddled anxiously across her chest, her face flushed and lips swollen. "You're not doing this as some cruel trick, are you? Or because Acastus is twisting your arm for some godforsaken reason?" The cadence of her voice was unstable, a rope bridge hanging on by single threads. She avoided his eyes, the vulnerability something she never appeared keen on. All her doubts laced into that question.

The exhilaration filling his chest abruptly, and against his will, shifted to an emotion unbeknownst to him. Well, not that he didn't recognize the feeling of self-loathing and vitriol revulsion, but rather, it wasn't familiar that he was feeling those notions toward *himself* because of *someone else's* perception of him.

"Princess, I—" He couldn't form the words. He desperately yearned to tell Mara that his animosity had permeated into the adulation of an admirer. "No. I am not doing this as a guile or some perverse directive from Cas." His hand clenched her skirt. He could still see the unease behind her countenance, and it made him nauseated. There was nothing he could say, so he resolved to drowning his words in her pleasure.

He slid his hands beneath her thighs like a serpent, clutching her as he dragged her closer to him. A tiny yelp escaped her as Evrardin kissed her center. She gasped, her skirts rising to her stomach as her fingers released the fabric, her arms flying back on the mattress. All Mara had worn beneath her frock was a simple chemise and stockings, the weather too warm for anything else.

"I want this," he murmured against her. Her hands slithered into his hair, her fingers parting his dark brown locks. *I want you,* was on the tip of his tongue.

She choked, trying to restrain whimpers. Her hand cupped her mouth as Evrardin kissed her intimately, her soft thighs trapping his head. She sank back onto her pillow, her noises blocked by her palm.

Evrardin pulled back slightly. "If you keep dampening those pretty lil' sounds, I'm going to make you scream so loud, Acastus and the rest of the castle will know exactly what I'm doin' to you."

Mara's eyes rounded and she swallowed hard, her hand falling to her side.

"Good girl," he murmured before attaching his lips to her once again. He liked it when she listened almost as much as when she didn't.

She squirmed on the bed, her fingers wiggling with the need to rise to her mouth, but she refrained. Finally, the motion of Evrardin's tongue and the way his mustache tickled overwhelmed her, the whimpers and moans cascading out of her mouth unrestrained.

Evrardin faintly rumbled against her as he groaned in satisfaction. His hands pressed on her stomach to keep her from arching off the bed, a sly smirk on the edge of his lips at how vulnerable and messy he had the Glass Princess.

Would she be thinking about how many women he had to have been with to know how to please her this well? She moaned his name, desperate for more than his tongue.

Evrardin's head shot up. "Fuckin' hell," he said breathlessly, his lips glistening and his hair disheveled. "Didn't think I'd ever like the sound of my name." He thought of all the times Acastus had called his name then recited out orders he was bound to follow. But the way Mara whispered his name in the secrecy of her room had unclenched something deep inside his chest.

Mara blushed, her cheeks a permanent pink.

He moved atop her, grabbing the hem of her skirts and yanking them up until she sat upward and began pulling at the laces on the back of her dress. Evrardin's hands wrapped around her, his fingers replacing Mara's. He undid the ties, his eyes challenging hers in battle as he studied the landscape of her face.

"Beautiful," he mumbled.

When he got to the final lace, her dress sleeves hung loosely over her shoulders and exposed her collarbones. He licked his lips unconsciously. Mara shyly slid the dress from her body until Evrardin impatiently tore it from her.

She gasped at the cold of the room as it wisped over her bare chest. She was entirely without clothes except for the stockings that were now bunching down her thighs.

Evrardin settled on top of her better and she was forced to lay prone, staring helplessly and wistfully up at him. If he had imagined this moment a month ago, he'd think he'd have her bent over a desk, taking her without remorse, not caring what came afterward. He never thought he'd feel something this strongly for a spoiled princess. He didn't want to flip her around and make things quick, searching for his own release that wouldn't ever provide him with the relief he sought. He wanted to take his time.

To go slow. To soak her in. He almost moaned looking down at her; the way she was sprawled back to his mercy, not fighting him for once, her hair in loose waves decorating her pillow. Her lips red and swollen. Her cheeks a lustful pink. Her body exposed for him and *him only*.

His hands halted all movement when his eyes trailed along the chain of her necklace, down to the red rubies poised as blood that hung just above the swell of her breasts. She was Acastus'. Evrardin was about to betray all he stood for, destroy his vows, and besmirch the Crown Prince's betrothed. The man he was sworn to protect. He fisted her hair, his eyes darkening as he stared at the charm. Mara's lips parted, a quiet breath escaping.

"Tell me to stop," he pleaded softly. His eyes flickered to hers and the light waned behind them, taking her in. He asked her like it was painful for him to do so. That if she didn't, he was going to break, shredded at the seams.

"Why? It's not like my words can stop you. Not like *his* can."

"You know," he began, his thumb brushing her cheek, "I still listen to other people on occasion, even if I'm not forced to carry out their will."

She hesitated. "Do you want to...? Stop, I mean." Her face contorted with trepidation, almost afraid to ask the question.

"No," he gave a mirthless laugh, and Mara's cheeks warmed. "I think it might kill me if I do. But, Princess, I don't want you to—"

"Since when does it matter what I want?" she said, *almost* playfully. Evrardin didn't take her jest in the same lighthearted way she spoke them. As much as he yearned to shed light on her privileged standing, he didn't want to see her shifting into self-loathing.

His eyes narrowed, his thumb no longer stroking her cheek delicately. "*Liten rev*, I—"

She cut off his sorrowful words. "Please," she begged. "Make me forget."

"You sure?" he asked. He spoke the words to Mara, but he couldn't help but wonder if he was also asking himself. He was leading himself straight into a masochist affliction riddled with untouched emotions that would rise to the surface and drown him in an ocean of madness. He wanted to chastise himself for being so altiloquent, but his feelings that started slow were now vehement and ruthless. She was dragging him in every direction, shaking his core—which had long since been buried—loose, and she was as good as blind to it.

She nodded, her hair staticky as it rubbed against her silken pillow.

His hand caressed the edge of her face and Mara leaned into the touch. He couldn't remember the last time he had been so gentle with another person. He had become so used to the weapon Acastus made him out to be that he forgot contact between two people could be anything but violent and brimming with savage lust.

His other hand twisted down between her legs, and she gasped. Evrardin's eyes darkened.-"A soul destined to ruin," he whispered his prophecy, his lips just barely brushing across her own. "And my ruination you have become."

He remembered his words at the masquerade when he bitterly told her she was destined to ruin him. To be his downfall. How he had spoken those words like a curse, but now he recited them like this was the only thing he had ever wanted in life.

Gooseflesh rose along Mara's neck and trailed down to her arms. He left a ghost of a kiss on her cheek before he loomed over her again. His fingers left her to fumble with his trousers, pushing them off, surprised he had the patience to slide them down and not shred them straight from his waist.

He gripped himself in his fist and lined himself up with her.

He hesitated when he caught sight of the worry in her eyes. Evrardin was much taller and broader than Mara. It only made sense that he'd be larger in *all* aspects. "I'll go slow," he told her.

She nodded. Her fingers dug into his biceps, waiting anxiously for what was to come.

Evrardin notched himself between her thighs and his hand moved to rest beside her face on the mattress. His fingers slid into her hair, squeezing, as he edged himself inside slowly. His dark eyes found hers, searching her face for any regret or remorse. When he found none, relief coursed through him.

He almost wanted to ask her if she had done this before, but he figured it would be best not to. If she said yes, he knew he'd surge with unjustified jealousy. And if she said no... Well, it didn't really matter—he was going to take his time with her regardless.

Mara's eyes fluttered as he sank in further. "I hurtin' you?" he asked through bated breaths.

Mara shook her head. "No. Keep going. Please."

Evrardin obliged, analyzing her face each time he surged forward, ready to stop the moment she showed signs of discomfort.

Then he sank inside her to the hilt. "Fuck," he growled. He looked between their bodies and a chill pebbled across Mara's skin when he groaned in his throat. "So fuckin' tight," he mumbled absentmindedly.

Bolts of fire filled his stomach. Mara bucked her hips upward and Evrardin's eyes snapped back to hers.

"Careful, Princess," he tsked. "I'm barely holdin' back as it is." His northern accent heavier with his deep and breathless words.

"Then don't," she baited sweetly.

Evrardin's eyes softened, his fingers mixing with her hair. "You don't know how badly I wanna. But not this time." He wanted to take her how he pleased, but not right now. Not for their first time together—he wanted to be slow and easy for her just as desperately.

She didn't comment on the fact that his words implied there would be a next time and he was glad for it. Before she could think much more of it, Evrardin began to pull out of her, gently. Her nails dug into his back as he pumped into her. He was slow in his movements, pulling out a little farther with each jerk of his hips. "God. The amount of times I've imagined this," he cursed under his breath when Mara spasmed around him.

Her legs wrapped tightly over his hips, helping to pull him against her each time he bottomed out. "Tell me how it feels," he all but growled. Desperate to know if she withered in pain or pleasure.

"S'good," she slurred, her breath catching.

He smirked then started a steady rhythm, the faint echo of their bodies coming together filling the room. Her cheeks turned red, and he hoped no one was outside her door to hear—he hadn't locked it.

Mara rolled her head to the side in obscene ecstasy. Evrardin's calloused hand slid over her chest and palmed at her breast. He wanted to tell her how fucking good she felt. Better than anything he had felt before. But those were words forbidden by his prince. And the way she felt now, Evrardin was worried this desire was destined to be insatiable.

The twinkle of blood-red glistened as the light poured into the room at the perfect angle to hit the rubies of Mara's necklace. Evrardin's brows furrowed in anger, irate that Mara could never be his.

Shit. *Did he want her to be his?*

Yes.

Yes. He very much wanted that.

His movements became harsher, trying to drown out the raging, unfurrowing emotions happening inside him.

Mara yelped as he became more forceful, her arms clutching around him, holding on for dear life. Her jaw hung slack, unable to form coherent words as Evrardin got lost inside his mind.

Mara's soft, thoughtless murmurs pulled him back to the present, his hand finding her cheek and turning her head back in line with his so they could lock eyes. This was far more intimate than anything he had ever done with another woman before, and he let out a shuddering breath he hoped Mara didn't notice.

He kept his hand locked lightly around her neck, his fingers splaying up over her jaw like vines, determined to keep her from shying away. He wanted to see in her eyes what he was doing to her. And knowing he couldn't speak it, he wanted Mara to see what she was doing to him just the same.

Mara gasped when Evrardin adjusted angles slightly, her eyes fluttering, wanting to close as she focused on the pleasure.

"Mara," Evrardin said in a harsh tone.

Her eyes fluttered open again.

"Keep your eyes on me." He never spoke this much during sex, never felt the need.

She opened her mouth, the snarky protest forming behind her eyes, but Evrardin thrusted in rather powerfully at the same time and a moan escaped her lips instead, her nails digging into him.

"I want to watch as you come undone."

Maybe she would have said something along the lines of *What makes you so sure you have the skillset to undo me?* But with the sounds he was emitting from her, there was no way to hide the fact that she was losing herself. Deep whimpers and sharp yelps muffled behind Mara's teeth with each of his animalistic thrusts. She nodded.

He felt her growing close, her muscles clenching, Evrardin

groaning in response to her body. He wanted to have her every which way, but he was lacking the ability to control himself; to come to a stop long enough to throw her into a new position. This was it, both of them nearing the edge so fast, and he didn't care.

"Will you kiss me?" she whispered to him. Her cheeks immediately went crimson, shocked she muttered those words at all. She looked like she wanted to correct herself—apologize even—when Evrardin's mouth slanted over hers.

His fist tightened in her hair as he moved his lips against hers in heady need. Mara tilted her chin up higher, letting his tongue slip into her mouth. She groaned in the back of her throat unabashedly. His other hand slid up her chest, surely leaving marks as he roughly pawed at her.

"M'not gonna last"—*grunt*—"much longer," he managed through clenched teeth. "I won't finish inside, *liten rev*," he tried to reassure her. He was determined to have enough control to at least do that much.

She shook her head, her ankles locking behind his back. "Don't leave me," she hissed.

His pupils blew, his eyebrows narrowing as he tried to restrain the sheer pleasure he got from those words. "Fuckin' hell," he cursed, his fist clenching her hair tighter, his lips meeting hers again. "That mouth," he scolded, knowing she ruined him for anyone else.

"I never want anyone else's mouth on mine again but yours," she said faintly, her voice rising in octave as he moved.

He lost it. His brows knitted as he watched her flush across her entire chest. How she went embarrassed at her confession even as he was ravaging her. "I want to watch you come for me, Princess," he coaxed softly.

He felt her clench tightly in response. And with several more thrusts, his hand slipping between their bodies, his finger circling her, that was finally her undoing.

She clenched wildly around him. He couldn't stop thinking of her ramblings. If she truly meant them, or if she spoke them in the spur of the moment, lost to the warmth.

His scruff tickled her as he pulled back, his lips still ghosting hers, breathing heavily as he made feral noises, following close behind her, unable to hold back even if he wanted to with how fiercely she tightened. How wildly she spasmed around him.

"Seven fuckin' hells," he groaned deeply enough that his words were almost unintelligible. She pulsed so fervently around him he thought he might black out. His hand fisted her bed sheets, trying to control himself as he rutted several more times, giving her everything he had.

He might have stopped to wonder why his other escapades never felt like this, but his mind was preoccupied solely with the princess squashed beneath him.

She gasped for air, her hands on either side of his cheeks, sharing the same breath as he steadied himself.

His half-lidded eyes danced between hers before he fully collapsed on top of her. He buried his head in her neck, his hair tickling her face. He kissed the spot where her shoulder hugged her nape, muttering something against her skin too quietly for her to make out.

He rolled off of her to the side, regretfully leaving her warmth, making her sigh with a high-pitched breath, letting them both find control in their racing hearts. He looked over at her and his breath got locked in his throat. She was breathtaking. Her brows were lined with sweat, her legs still languidly separated for his viewing pleasure, her chest rising and sinking rapidly. His eyes glazed over as he took in her ransacked appearance—messy, and all his doing.

Her beauty infuriated him. The way he had never seen a more heavenly sight than that of Mara overspent, her hand aimlessly clutching his without realizing as she tried to collect herself. He didn't deserve her or the bliss that just ensued between them. He had never thought something like this could be more than just carnal desires, but the way his heart raced and his fingers twitched in her small grasp told him otherwise.

His eyes moved downward, tracing over the shiny metallic surface of the necklace she wore symbolizing Cas' ownership over her. Over them both. Evrardin sat up with a grunt.

She was not his to have.

Chapter Thirty-Nine
Acastus

Acastus rolled his shoulders, running his fingers through his hair, before swaggering into his father's chambers, the dark magick tingling his tainted hands. He cleared his throat, gaining the king's attention as he lingered in the doorway. As someone who didn't seem to fear his father any longer, his heart was racing awfully fast.

"Lord Cofsi," his father boomed as he spun to face his firstborn son.

"What about him?"

The king chuckled knowingly. "Enough with the pretenses, Cas." The anger was beginning to rise in the usually stoic ruler. "You had him tossed in the dungeons like a common thief. Under what ruling do you think this justifiable?"

Acastus strolled to the pile of fruit on the king's breakfast table. Unease swelled in his chest but he made sure to keep his exterior even. "We do not throw *common* thieves in the *royal* dungeons."

The king slammed his fist against the wooden dresser beside him. Cas glanced up at him before placing a grape into his mouth.

"I should unname you my heir," he grumbled, his voice dark and sickly, exactly how Cas remembered him talking to the Fae King as a child.

"For doing what is my right?" Acastus snarled. "And who might you name in my place? Your wife? Aevum, who is but eight years of age?" Acastus mocked the idea. He was the king's only child of age. He had nobody else to name.

"You have been nothing but a languid prince, no real missive in life. And now, you've been conspiring behind my back. Do not think I don't take notice," the king boomed when he watched Cas' face contort in faux confusion. "I've let this go on for too long."

"And what are you going to do, Your Grace?"

The king's lip quirked at Acastus' disbelief that he could be treated as anything but a crowned heir. That none of this had even the slightest possibility of being taken away from him.

"Out," he demanded, sick of looking upon his son's likeness.

Acastus shook his head and removed his gloves. His father gawked at the inky trail that spiraled up his son's arms and deep within the sleeves of his jacket.

"Cas," he gasped. "What have you done?"

Darkness stained Acastus' golden eyes. "They always say I'm lazy"—he made wide gestures with his hands—"that I don't do anything myself." He reached for the dagger at his hip, unsheathing it. "But they never talk about *your* hindrance. *Your* lack of ambition." His father didn't move, unconvinced his son would ever do him any harm. He thought him too petulant to become an assassin. Too arrogant. Too unwilling to get blood on his hands. But his hands were already stained, what was a little more color?

The prince approached the king before stumbling slightly. Cas reached for his own throat. A shout begged to escape—tried to pry his mouth open. His voice betraying him. *Stop!* it screamed.

Cas shut his eyes, balancing himself, pushing his conscience down, down, *down...*

He wanted to laugh at how trusting his father was in his belief his son was too weak to harm him. And he did, chuckling slightly, when the dagger slid across the king's throat, blood spraying out and covering Cas in crimson.

Chapter Forty
Mara

Mara and Evrardin hastily retied and pulled on their clothes, slipping out of her room. A sigh of relief escaped her realizing there were no sentinels posted at her door. Mara had been knotted with worry that one of the guards might have overheard their pants and soft mutterings as they entangled on her bedsheets. She was relieved to know no one had the chance of eavesdropping on her rendezvous, running to tell the prince.

Evrardin remained silent as he led her through the halls she was only now beginning to feel a familiarity with. She swallowed hard, hoping he wasn't regretting his decision to lie with her. She tried to dampen that welling spark before it blossomed into something she'd rather not deal with.

Her fingers twisted with the sleeve of her dress, lost for words to share with the captain—which she imagined he'd be grateful for.

"Relax." His deep voice broke through her reverie.

She glanced at him. "I am."

"The prince is going to sense something if you keep looking like that."

Mara arched a brow. "Looking like what, exactly?"

"Like you just had a secret love affair with your betrothed's most loyal friend the day before your wedding," he whispered, leaning close enough to sting.

Mara sputtered. "You are not his friend."

"It's called an analogy."

She shook her head. "If everything is accurate save for one small detail, it's more of a confession than an analogy."

He repressed his annoyed growl. "Is that not exactly what an analogy is?"

She grimaced. "No. It's a metaphor with commitment issues."

"Right. My apologies, Princess. I forgot how well-read you are."

She swallowed hard before speaking again. "This doesn't make us friends."

Evrardin's hand tightened on the pommel of his sword. "Well aware."

She wasn't sure why she said it. Maybe it was the fact that he was already teasing her about the events that just unraveled in her chambers and she didn't want him to think she was more attached than she truly was. She told herself she wasn't attached. He certainly wasn't. He had years of experience; this was just another notch in his belt. She didn't mean anything beyond that to him.

She hated that he was doing this to her mind. Her chest tightened at his nonchalance. She swore this was pure lustful desire, nothing more. And yet, the mere thought that Evrardin didn't want her for more than pleasure crushed her. Made her want to weep on her knees and curse the gods out for torturing her like this.

Even if he had wanted her for more than that, it wouldn't—*couldn't*—happen. She was to marry the prince.

"Why haven't you left yet?"

It took Mara a moment to register Evrardin's words. She glanced sidelong at him as they moved. "What?"

"After Crowrot's execution. Why haven't you tried to escape this hellhole?"

"You think me petty enough to leave because things are getting hard?" Maybe she could have tried to escape and leave Kairth. But then what? Was she to leave the kingdom as it fell apart, risking the semblance of an influence she might possess to change things? Leaving hadn't even crossed her mind.

She went to say more but he cut her off, his words low, rumbling in her ear. "You have *nothing*. What is keeping you here?" His words hit her with malice, like he wanted to hurt her.

She straightened her spine, not noticing Ev's eyes still on her as she willed herself to face her betrothed.

Mara escorted herself into Acastus' chambers, Evrardin turning to wait outside the closing doors.

"Princess," Acastus sang, his voice slippery like that of a serpent.

"My Prince." Mara curtsied awkwardly.

He reached for her hand and placed a delicate kiss on the back. Mara's cheeks warmed in aversion as he subtly pulled her closer to him before dropping her hand.

"I'm afraid I have terrible news."

Mara's expression contorted into something of concern. The prince's words seemed remorseful, but a falsehood was laced in between.

"My father is dead."

Mara paled. She was shocked, alarmed, unconvinced, sorrowful. All at once. And still, a brief lilt of brightness fluttered over her features, imagining the wedding being postponed. Or better yet, canceled altogether now that Acastus didn't have a father to please.

The guilt immediately infiltrated her chest.

"I'm incredibly sorry, My Prince. How did it happen? He seemed perfectly well yesterday."

Acastus sat on his settee, crossing his legs and gazing at her. She flushed under his watch, trying to appear nonchalant—easy.

"They say it was an unfortunate case of summer fever."

He said *they* like he was unconvinced of the medics' credentials to accurately decide the cause of death.

"And the queen? How is she managing?" Mara wondered if she should visit her, or if she might rather be with family.

"Gone, too, I'm afraid."

Mara coughed, choking on her words. "The queen is also dead?"

Acastus shook his head. "Poor choice of words," he corrected. "She's been missing since the death of my father early this morning. I'm entirely convinced she had something to do with it."

Mara shifted on the balls of her feet, the room growing heavier.

Acastus outstretched one of his hands and Mara tentatively closed the distance between them, allowing him to take hold of hers. "I hope this news won't ruin tomorrow."

Mara raised her brow. "What do you mean?"

"The wedding, of course. Can't possibly be good luck to lose a father the day prior."

"We're still going through with it?" she blurted.

Acastus' grip tightened on her hand and she held back a wince. "Of course we are, foolish girl. My father may be dead, but that holds no bearing on this union. If anything, my father would want us to continue in his honor."

Mara highly doubted that but she simply nodded. She was used to Acastus' volatile emotions with her by now.

"The people will need something positive to distract from this... affair."

"Of course. I meant no offense. Just...I thought you might want time to grieve."

Cas' eyes glazed over her skeptically. "And what better way than to have a wife to console me at my side?"

Mara gave him a half-hearted smile.

Acastus took a deep breath in, his eyes narrowing. He stood from his seat, reminding her just how much taller than her he was. She prayed he couldn't smell Evrardin on her. That would be ridiculous... As good as Evrardin had smelt, she shook off the idea that his faint scent of burning wood and mint lingered on her clothes.

"And once we are unionized tomorrow, you are to glassfaire. You will make us the most powerful kingdom in the realm, Princess."

She swallowed her breath. "How...?"

He dropped her hand, snaking it between their bodies, the soft leather of his glove gliding against her cheek as he tucked a tendril of chestnut hair behind her ear. "Now, don't you worry your pretty little head, my love. You'll follow my instructions, and if you do well, maybe I'll keep you around as my queen after all."

His eyes stared lovingly into her own. The further she looked, the more darkness she could see swirling behind the shadows.

"Now, go. I want you well-rested for tomorrow's festivities." His final words poured out around his sharpened teeth like a threat.

Mara curtsied before darting out of the room, Acastus' chuckle haunting her down the hall.

"Mara," she finally heard.

She slowed her steps and spun to face Evrardin who was staring at her like she had two heads.

"What happened—?"

"I think he plans to kill me," she said through a vicious whisper. She met Evrardin's eyes, pained to find his expression neutral. A deep surge of nausea coursed through her making her knees buckle. "Which you already knew," she said slowly, pronouncing each word with lingering hurt. Her vision went hazy, her eyes roaming his body. She noticed a bit of blood encrusted on the bottom of his tunic. Blood she hadn't noticed until now. She almost stumbled back in horror. "You killed the king?"

"No."

"But you assisted in his death in some way?!"

"Mara..." he pleaded.

She blinked rapidly, finding herself falling into a stupor. "I never should have trusted you." She intended for her words to slice through the air, but they came out more a whimper. She should have taken what Lord Cofsi said more to heart.

She turned on her heels.

"*Liten rev*, please, just listen to me," he called.

She stopped, turning just her head to look over her shoulder. "Do. Not. Call. Me. That," she spat through gritted teeth. She jerked her arm back as he reached for her. "And tell me what?!" she almost shouted. "You couldn't tell me even if you wanted to, right?"

Evrardin didn't respond. She hated that she was right. Hated that she still yearned for his touch.

She rushed back to her room, her heart pounding too loudly to hear if Evrardin trailed her or not.

She knew he was under Acastus' curse. That he had to do anything he said. But the way his face didn't even twitch when she said Cas was going to kill her made her shiver. She had let him get so close to her. She let him...

She cursed under her breath. He carried this knowledge, and he still caressed her tenderly. Kissed her lips with such urgency that she thought she may never get a proper breath in again. His hands explored her, knowing she was promised to someone else. Knowing that someone else planned to take her life. Knowing he had helped kill the king just that morning.

Maybe she truly hated him after all.

***

Mara sweltered in her rooms as she poured over one of her ancient tomes. She was brewing with a tortuous amount of stupid and reckless ideas, ones she should keep locked inside her, as she searched for anything else she could that might be of use.

Tomorrow, she married Acastus, and, for good reason, she suspected a terrible fate awaited her at his hands. He was going to kill her. Evrardin made that much clear. But when? She had no idea if it would happen tomorrow or one of the many long days glued to his side ahead of her.

As she studied her bookmarked incantations, something pulling her back to the phantom spell. A tome Crowrot left purposefully open for her to find. He was killed for his treason, so it must be worth something.

She stared at the spell time and time again. Even though she had officially been bonded within the Sun Court, it stated clearly in the text that the Sun Court hadn't been potent enough in centuries to possess enough dark magick to perform a *lygi* invocation.

Her eyes scanned an open tome to her left, flipping through information about herbs and flora of all different species. Her eyes grew heavy, and the ink began to blur together. She stopped flipping when a drawing of a draugr flower appeared on the page before her. A spark ignited as she read over the description. When used properly, one could summon dark magick from the Veil, letting their veins flow with that of a deity. Maybe if she used the flower...

She shook her head; she didn't know where she'd obtain a flower that rare. They had been outlawed. And did she really want to possess that kind of dangerous, dark power?

Though, she couldn't help but wonder what would happen if she had created a *lygi* form of herself. Could one perform the incantation deeply enough to construct an entire body out of dark magick alone—not just a brain like Marquess Blackwing?

Chapter Forty-One
Evrardin

Evrardin eventually mustered the energy to push open Mara's door.

"Cold feet?" he teased but instantly regretted his coarse words.

The hour was far too late to be summoning him to her room, but he came regardless. The last thing he wanted was for Cas to be alerted.

"Shut the door," she commanded before focusing back on her books. He was used to finding her with books spread before her, but this was something else. She looked like a madwoman. There were countless tomes propped open, Mara sat in the middle of them, shifting around on the floor to jump between pages. Her hair was a wreck, pulled back out of her face, wired up so late into the night. A pang of concern bloomed in his chest.

"Care to explain why you've called upon me so late?"

She smirked. "And not why I think I have the authority to call upon you at all?" She glanced at him before darting back to her pages.

Was she not going to acknowledge what happened in the halls earlier?

Apparently not.

"Do you know where I can get a draugr flower?"

"Sorry?"

She looked at him. "You have to know where. You're a florist after all."

"I resent that title."

She sighed, irritated. "Evrardin, please."

He hesitated, her plea tightening his muscles. "What could you possibly need with a draugr flower?"

"I... I can't tell you."

"Then I can't answer your question."

She let out an aggravated huff. "I can't tell you because you report to Acastus. I need you to trust me on this. Please," she begged. She seemed to not care how stupid she sounded, begging on her knees to a man who proved to have little respect for her.

He thought for a moment too long, leaving room for it to click inside Mara's head.

"You've grown some, haven't you?"

Evrardin shifted his stance. He hated that she managed to get him to squirm from lack of trust rather than anything else.

Her tongue rolled across the front of her teeth, studying him for only a moment longer. "That will be all."

Evrardin scoffed. "You're dismissing me?"

She didn't bother looking up from her book. "I got what I needed from you. And you're clearly in no position to offer any further assistance. I'd like you to leave my chambers."

He paused, lost for what to say. And anything he wanted to say, he couldn't.

"Yes, Princess," he managed through bared teeth. "I seem to have gotten what I needed from you as well."

Only ten minutes later did Mara crack open her door. She gasped, her hand gripping the door handle tightly, Evrardin looming over her in the doorway. He traced the tear marks that painted her eyes red, and he flourished with guilt—with hatred. How tough she acted, but he knew he hurt her deep down. She let him get under her skin, and now she was worse off for it.

"What are you still doing here?"

She donned a dark cloak and boots. He knew she was about to sneak out to the gardens, hunting the draugr flower she knew he grew. But she wouldn't find it there.

"Do not say another word," he said aggressively. His fingers squeezed his sword, itching to grab her hand and drag her along. Instead, he used his words. "Stay close."

He didn't wait for her to respond, especially considering her response was likely to be a rebuttal and trailed down the hall.

They walked in uncomfortable silence to the catacombs, and he almost smiled when he heard her soft footsteps begin to follow him. He expected Mara to rattle off a thousand questions as he brought her into the dank room, but she remained quiet. He wondered if she could feel Crowrot's presence like he did.

He walked over to the wall littered with various tubes and vials, some spilling with glowing liquid. He heard her gasp as she took it all in. "They're so pretty," she muttered. How she found such a mundane apothecary pretty was beyond him.

He pulled down a jar on the top shelf with black petals inside. He turned, expecting to find her back at the table set in the middle of the room, but she was right behind him, and he collided with her. His free hand steadied her shoulders, her body flush against his chest for a brief moment before they pulled apart. Her cheeks pinked and he swallowed, his mouth dry.

He held up the vial to distract from their awkwardness. It had taken him years to grow and harvest this much dried draugr flower, so he caught even himself off guard when he handed her the entire thing without a word.

"Will I need this much?" she asked aghast.

"You tell me."

She crossed her arms. "Right. I think it's enough."

He held in his laugh knowing she had no idea what she was talking about. Then his eyes narrowed. "This is dangerous stuff, Mara. You have to be careful."

She surveyed the jar like it was the most magnificent thing she had ever seen. She nodded.

Evrardin moved closer, his hand grasping the side of her neck and letting his fingers lock in her hair, affection he had no right confusing her with. She yelped in surprise at his touch, not expecting the harsh way he forced her attention. He tilted her face to look at him. "Promise me you'll be careful."

"What does it matter? I'll be dead soon anyway."

His eyes darkened in the torchlight. "I won't let that happen."

She laughed boisterously. "You can't promise me that."

He knew he couldn't, but it didn't hurt any less when she said it. He opened his mouth, his lips curling, but nothing came out. He cleared his throat. "I wish I could promise you so much."

"Don't," she whispered.

She leaned marginally into his hold before realization made her stiffen.

His eyes danced between hers before begrudgingly letting his hand fall from her curls. "Mara, I didn't mean to—"

She cut him off, shaking her head. "You wanted me to learn how the real world works for myself. To see how things truly are and not just pleasantries dotted on noble ladies. Isn't that what you wanted, Evrardin? For me to see the grit and grime of the realm?"

He remained silent as she moved closer to the door, casting her in shadows. He couldn't make out her face clearly enough to read her expression in the soft candlelight. She tucked wild strands of hair behind her ear, her fist clutching the draugr flower close. "You should be glad I see you for what you are."

"And how's that, Princess?"

"Unworthy."

She wasn't the damsel getting her delicate ego wounded like he once thought.

And yet, he hoped she might argue with him—to tell her he may have been shitty before, but he wanted her, at least as a friend. That he was remorseful in any semblance. That he didn't mean the foul words he spat at her.

Her gaze traced the expanse of his throat as he swallowed. He tilted his head, speaking solemnly. "Took you long enough."

She pursed her lips and nodded. "Thank you. For this." She held up the small jar in her hand. "I should get back."

He didn't move or acknowledge her, only traced her movements as she scurried out of the catacombs and back from where they came. He almost stayed down in the dark tunnels, but he followed her up the stairs soon after, not able to resist trailing her. And he lingered behind her without her notice, making sure she made it to her rooms without running into trouble—gods knew she was a magnet for that.

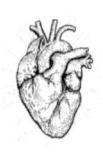

The summer sunlight poured in through the cathedral's rose and gold windows as dawn broke. Acastus was painted in an array of warm colors as he adjusted his jacket on the dais. The holy room was empty save for the prince, and now Evrardin as he made his way farther into the space.

Acastus' eyes met Evrardin's and he swore he spotted a tinge of remorse in them before splitting back to their usual vengeful darkness.

"This is it," Acastus boasted as Evrardin ascended the short staircase of the dais.

Evrardin hoped Acastus would rant about his final moments as a bachelor, but he was always sorely disappointed. Instead, Cas said the words he had been fearing most.

"Such a shame I'll have to kill my poor wife so soon after marrying her. Quite the unexpected wedding gift, I suppose."

Fury laced all of Evrardin's muscles in a burning rope of jute. "She is only to glassfaire today."

Acastus gave Evrardin a condescending smirk. "That's how it started, yes. But the late king's heart won't be sufficient." Acastus seemed peeved, like his father's death, and now his aim to murder his wife, was an inconvenience. "She failed to enlighten me that *a heart of a monarch and the thrum of new love* referred to one, singular person. Knowing that would have saved me an insurmountable amount of trouble."

"Cas, there has to be another way to do this. You don't need more blood on your hands," Evrardin pleaded. He was tied between wanting to fall to his knees and beg for Mara's life and wanting to wrap his hands tightly around Acastus' neck—neither of which he could do.

Acastus tsked, tugging his black gloves on tighter. Even with his conservative attire, the dark, smokey trellis peeked beyond the hem of his collar. His eyes washed over black. "This won't be on *my* hands."

Evrardin shuddered to think he once considered the prince his friend.

"It will be on *yours*." Acastus' words ripped through the warm air of the cathedral, reaching Evrardin's ears like a curse.

Chapter Forty-Two
Mara

Mara thought she would cry seeing herself in a long, regal gown. But the tears never came.

Her wedding dress was a long cream color with only one layer of underskirts to keep the cloth closer to her skin. The bodice was embroidered with threads a powdery green, reminiscent of the soft turning juniper leaves, the pattern resembling the roots of a tree. Her sleeves were fitted to her elbow, then danced out in long tufts of muslin. The edges were gilded in unnatural silver, the seams of her dress looking like she had a pool of melted stardust shadowing her. Her eyes were painted with a silver glimmer, and she wore a sparkling circlet to match with an emerald jewel in the center.

She scowled at herself in the mirror while her handmaidens yanked and pulled her dress taut. The wedding was to be a small affair and something about that bothered Mara. Maybe she was worried there wouldn't be enough people to witness Acastus' cruelty.

Mara had clutched the one solo letter Avor had sent her and her eyes traced across every word. He wasn't going to make it to her wedding. She knew that now. She knew the darkness preventing his travel through the Sandwoods had to do with the prince setting the kingdoms out of balance. Her brother wasn't going to swoop in and save her. She had to save herself.

Mara gave herself one last pitiful appraisal in her mirror, wanting to shatter it to pieces as her reflection taunted her. Why did she have to be cursed with this terrible ability? She wished she never felt the power at her fingertips.

But if she couldn't glassfaire for the prince, she was sure he would have simply found someone else from the Glass Court.

"From the prince," a woman's voice spoke, breaking Mara free from her thoughts.

Mara turned to the handmaiden, outstretching a bouquet of bleeding-heart flowers. Mara laughed loudly, taking the bushel from her. The other women looked at her with unease as the princess broke down in a fit of giggles.

Mara wiped the tears from her eyes and walked to her door. "Let us get this over with."

"Don't sound so eager, Princess. One might think you've truly fallen for the prince."

The familiar voice startled her as her door swung open to reveal Evrardin. He was donned in fine armor that she had seen the other guards wearing, but Evrardin seemed himself above. The silver plates matched Mara's starlight gown. Her eyes traced Evrardin's body, neither of them smiling at his jest.

"I didn't expect to see you," she said finally.

"No? And where might I have been instead?"

Oh, she hated how nonchalant he was acting. As if her world wasn't crashing down on her. As if he didn't know or care about her fate.

"Gathering innocent hearts for the prince, I presume," she

said sweetly. Evrardin tensed, clearly not expecting her to outwardly state Evrardin's missive for the prince when others were around. She grinned, knowing that it irritated him. It was a shot in the dark after seeing that bucket filled with hearts in the catacombs, but with the way Evrardin stiffened, she knew it to be true.

A bead of sweat rolled down Evrardin's face, getting lost in his beard. "You can play later." Evrardin gestured down the hall. Mara raised a brow, studying the tension that spun behind his inner workings. It was like he had been pulled so tight that with one sudden movement, he'd tear apart.

As they started toward the cathedral, warm light glistened over Mara's dress and weaved in through her chiffon veil that hung off her chignon. She twiddled her fingers around the flower's stems. It was only her, Evrardin, and two other guards who shadowed them in the halls. She looked up at him, but that was a mistake; he had never seen his eyebrows quite so knitted together. His fist was turning white from how hard he was holding his sword's pommel.

"The petals... I had—"

His eyes darted dangerously to hers. "Do not tell me anything," he all but growled.

She held his gaze until they reached the staircase, having to hike up her dress and watch where she was going. Evrardin offered his arm, and Mara took it without hesitation, much to her surprise.

He sighed. "I'll have to report anything you tell me to him. It's not that I don't want to know."

They turned a bend on the stairs.

"I know."

When they finally got to the cathedral's entrance, blood rushed so loudly in her ears that Mara couldn't hear the limited voices inside. She hated how complicated her relationship with the captain had become. She wondered if it would ever unwind itself, smoothing out all the kinks and wrinkles they seemed keen on leaving behind on the fabric of their fondness for one another.

She prayed to the sun goddess painted above the archway. She prayed she was right in assuming she was going to have to glassfaire almost immediately after bonding with Acastus, her throat still lingering with the foul taste of the draugr flower. And she prayed she'd have the strength and wit to do whatever it was she needed.

"Some words of encouragement would be nice," she said quietly, not realizing she said it out loud.

Evrardin shook his head, letting her arm fall back to her side. "Unfortunately, I have none."

Chapter Forty-Three
Mara

An expansive mirror leaned against the back wall on the dais, glimmering from the sun rays bleeding in from the red stained-glass windows. Mara held her breath as she stepped through the threshold, taking in the several heads that turned, the murmuring falling to silence.

Lord Alfson sat at the front of the small affair, his gray robe washing out his usually dark skin, now a pallid sheen. Several other men sat in the pews, but none she recognized beyond knowing they were members of the Sun Court. She assumed they were from the king's council... which would now be the prince's council if she was correct on the hierarchy. Or maybe they remained loyal to the king and would only support Acastus when he was married and sworn in.

Acastus' eyes locked on her as she strolled down the aisle, her back stiff from her corset, and her mind reeling with all the possibilities. If she didn't already know how cynical his stare actually was—the intentions behind his eyes—she might have fallen to her knees. He looked at her almost like he craved her—longed for her. The large statues of previous kings loomed as she passed under the pillars carved from stone. She pulled at the sleeve of her dress, the breathable material now suffocating.

She glanced at the Hallowed Cistern as she went up the steps to meet Acastus' hand, blocking out her previous memories in this room. Looking over her shoulder, she realized Evrardin had left, nowhere to be seen. She thought he would have been behind her. She hated how isolated she suddenly felt.

Acastus stole her hand, pulling her into his space, his gloved fingers finding her chest, right above her heart. A silent gasp slipped past her lips. Acastus held his place on her heart as if he were counting the beats. It must have seemed so intimate to the audience.

Before she could process the words to speak, he dropped his hands and removed his gloves, shoving them into his pocket. Mara's eyes rounded. Acastus' hands were stained black, the skin appearing rotted and smokey like he had shoved his fists into a pile of ash.

"Your hands," Mara noted foolishly.

"After today, the state of my skin will be no concern." He gave her a saccharine smile. He let her study his appearance a moment longer before gesturing to the high priest. "Come. Let our houses unite."

The time had finally arrived for her to take Acastus' hand in holy matrimony—the symbolism of his tainted hand not lost on her. She was to be his wife. To become the Sun Queen one day soon. Though she had a strong inkling she might not make it that long.

Her throat itched and she swallowed to try and soothe it. The petals had gone down easily, but her body was beginning to reject them. She wasn't sure what was to happen, but her books led her to believe ingesting a draugr flower would fill her with dark magick, at least momentarily. And she needed that sort of power if she was to cast a phantom spell. She shouldn't have had the confidence in being able to cast a dark incantation, enthralling her body to morph, without any real previous training. But she had to try.

The ceremony was quick, straight to the point, blurring as it unfolded like she had tears in her eyes. She was almost grateful her brother and father couldn't make the trip, her body feeling dirty as she bound herself yet again to the Sun Prince.

They held hands, a cloth soaked from the Hallowed Cistern wrapped around them by the high priest, his mutterings binding them together. She felt a rush of energy infiltrate her fingertips, then the feeling dulled.

"Forever bonded, here and now," they muttered at the same time before Acastus leaned in. His mouth slanted over hers, a blush ebbing across her face. A sense of coldness surprised her when his free hand rested against her cheek.

He almost looked remorseful as he pulled back, their eyes meeting one another in a flash of gold that quickly fluttered into a foggy cloud of silver mist. But that compunction slipped away like a fleeting dream.

"At last, your heart is all mine," he said faintly. He slipped the cloth from their hands and her heart raced, a rushing river pumping in her ears.

Focused too intently on Cas, scuffling feet and brazen chat made her turn to the cathedral's entrance. If Mara had thought she had been aghast before, she would have been sorely wrong.

Several guards lugged a wheeled cart into the room, heavy with something glistening a glowing green. She covered her mouth with a yelp as the cart grew nearer and she could make out the more minute details. It was filled with hearts. Human hearts. Hearts that were covered in a green sludge.

They were piled high, still stained with blood, but notably kept clean and orderly. Mara thought she might forget how to breathe, the sight so horrifying. She stumbled back, only smelling copper when she finally managed to steal a breath.

Acastus leaned closer to her ear. "Quite odd seeing them green, I know. It's only to preserve them. Some gathered so long ago." Acastus begrudgingly stole Mara's attention as he spoke. "I'm going to need you to slip through this mirror, darling wife."

Mara blinked rapidly several times, the dragging of more carts into the room stacked high with fleshy organs pulled for her attention. "N-Now?"

Acastus' snapped his fingers and two guards on the dais immediately moved to the lengthy mirror and rested it against the stage at a slight angle. Cas grabbed Mara's hand rather roughly and pulled her with him as he rounded on the mirror, shoving her forward.

"Go through," he demanded. "Then reach out your hand and pull me in."

"Pull you in? But you can't bring—"

He shook his head, peeved. "You share my blood now, Princess. Your magick is connected with mine. You'll be able to guide me through as easily as you can move between realms yourself."

She closed her eyes and spun toward the mirror, her throat burning. She had practiced this, it wasn't going to end up like that first time. She managed to cross over before.

Desperation coated her body in sweat, wishing for Evrardin's brooding presence behind her, anchoring her. But he wasn't here. It was just her. She had to be her own anchor.

"Mara," Acastus growled impatiently.

She sucked in a staggered breath, summoning all her willpower, and stepped in toward the mirror. She didn't open her eyes until she had taken several steps without crashing into the glass surface. The Veil looked different than she remembered—the mirror acting as a gate depending on its location. She wiped her sweaty hands on her dress before shoving her arm through the back of the mirror. Acastus' cold one immediately interlaced with hers and she pulled him in, just as Evrardin had done when he pulled her out.

She marveled at the way he bullied his way into the Veil, an unnatural gleam highlighting his entire figure as he broke the barrier. He appeared to be made of sea glass as his form entered before it dissipated back to being corporeal flesh made of blood and bones.

"Enthralling," he muttered in tepid disbelief. Acastus continued to gleam like he was lined in silver. It reminded her of her dress, the way the seams made her seem otherworldly.

Mara stood back slightly to watch as Acastus took in his surroundings, turning back to the illuminated anthesis of the mirror.

"Hm," he hummed in what sounded similar to disapproval. Was the Veil not to his liking?

The prince—*her husband*—stepped back through the mirror, and Mara stared at the blurred portal perplexed.

She was about to follow when movement stirred the silvery ripple, Acastus stepping through again. But now he held a barrel of hearts.

Mara held back her startled gasp and stared helplessly as Acastus leaned back and forth between this realm and the cathedral, hauling barrel after barrel of gory hearts in the space on the gray grass before her feet.

"What are you doing?" she pleaded. She tried to squeeze past him, to run out into the cathedral and beg the high priest to stop whatever it was they were planning. To beg the Solar Sect to think rationally, to not disrupt the land of the gods.

But Cas blocked her, shoving her back. "Do not get in the way," he growled, his voice sounding wholly unlike his own.

She helplessly gazed at the hearts that thudded onto the slick grass. Human hearts. This was what Crowrot had been doing in the dungeons, in the depths of Kairth. Collecting human hearts. And Evrardin had helped—more than helped; no doubt he was the one stealing these hearts... She didn't want to think about that, about how he obtained so many. About the torture of having to kill on Acastus' orders, unable to refuse.

After heaving several more times, Cas paused and glanced at her. If only she were strong enough to fight Acastus, to be able to stop him in his tracks. He dropped the last of the hearts with a wet thud, flexing his hands and wincing as if his muscles were causing him pain. His eyes were black when they met hers and gooseflesh rose along her spine in a sickly trail.

"My offering to Trana."

She tilted her head like a confused hound.

"My father has been too lenient on the other kingdoms. Letting them disregard centuries of peace. But *I* plan to restore Solstrale's honor. *I* am bringing back the gods." The cynical smile on Cas' face corrupted him.

Trana's name rang repeatedly in her head. The gods had been gone for centuries. But it seemed Acastus wanted to bring her back. Mara didn't think it possible, and for a moment, she thought he had completely lost his mind, functioning on pure insanity this entire time.

"And you, my dear wife, are the key to it all."

Mara twisted her hands behind her back, the venom rising in her throat like tar.

"Don't look so surprised. You knew I needed you beyond just taking a wife. I need a noble heart, a sun heart, a heart beating with new love, to bring Trana back."

"I'm not—

Acastus' face filled with rage, the harsh lines contorting to anger. "We've been bonded. You're part of the Sun Court now. You carry my blood within you. And while you weren't my first choice, my father's heart proved to be a disappointment. Trana's confounding verselet wasn't exactly writ to be forthright."

Mara sucked in a breath, the chill air suffocating her already constricted throat. She felt the licks of magick in her stomach, the darkness of it gently cradling her. She'd have to do the *lygi* invocation now before it consumed her entirely.

Just as glassfairing, one didn't recite speech to conduct a dark incantation such as a *lygi* spell. It was all through thoughts and innate power. She tried to tune out Acastus' many words, focusing solely on the idea of casting an alternate version of herself. Of her heart. Of her mind.

She was shaken from her thoughts when Cas grabbed her arm and hauled her back into the cathedral, the step through the mirror making her lightheaded, shoving her to her knees. She tried to stand but he pressed harshly on her shoulder.

Cas' mouth moved, his teeth peeking out as he snarled at her, but it landed on deaf ears. Confused, Mara tilted her head, her vision vibrating. She felt her stomach twist and turn as she blinked several times, correcting her sight—she felt like she might keel over. Snippets of clarity allowed her to realize she was gazing back in the vast expanse of the Veil.

Back in the mirror realm... Her head pounded as she tried to think, fragments of Acastus' voice digging into her skull. She tried to remember Lord Cofsi's words. Could she be back in the Veil even though the prince dragged her to the living realm? Her ability to glassfaire mixed with draugr magick allowing her to perform such an intricate spell? Could her true soul linger, her *lygi* form glassfairing with Acastus' pull?

Her stomach tugged at her, twisting in knots, a headache brewing in the front of her skull. She looked out onto the foggy tree line within the Veil, but her body felt like she was still kneeling in the cathedral. How odd. Her vision blurred and she closed her eyes, focusing on Acastus' rumblings until his voice was crystal clear in her ears, hearing his every word. "Evrardin. Do it."

Mara was able to look out through her deceiving body, seeing Ev in a haze as he strode up the steps to Cas with much trepidation. She had never seen such fear laced in his eyes—she wasn't sure she had ever seen fear laced in his eyes at all.

He unsheathed his dagger, his hand shaking as if he was fighting against an invisible specter attempting to hold him back. He blinked several times, trying to orient himself, and looked to Cas beside her. "Please," he begged his prince.

Mara's heart fell at the pleading in Evrardin's voice. He sounded broken. Not like his usual brazen self.

"Don't make me do this. Tell me to do anything else, Cas. Please."

She swore there were tears in his lilt, the words watery and serpentine as they slid into her ear.

"Get it over with, Evrardin! I'm sick of your insolence," Acastus almost shrieked.

"I'm begging." The end of his words were muffled by a loud intake of breath, his chest moving rapidly up and down.

Mara focused on Evrardin, the background blurred, as he took more aggressive steps toward her. She could feel the lick of grass on her ankles now, her body back in the Veil while she stared out of false eyes onto the captain. He sat down on his haunches and then she could really see him. His eyes brimming with tears. He tried to hold back blinking, but it was futile. The droplets slid down his face, his eyebrows narrowed in anger. He looked like he wanted to avert his gaze in shame, but he couldn't.

Mara reached her hand out and slid her thumb over his cascading tears. She knew she made contact, but she couldn't feel it, couldn't feel his skin under her fingertips. She could hear Cas muttering something in the distance, but her only focus was on Evrardin.

"I'm sorry, Princess. I don't—" His words broke. "I don't know how to stop this." He slid his dagger up her chest, the metal gliding against her dress and making her wince. "I can't control my hands." The roughness of his voice sent shivers rippling along Mara's skin, both in the Veil and the living realm. His eyes cast a dark shadow, his limbs shaking as he tried to halt their movement. "I should have cut them off when I had the chance."

"It's okay," she cooed softly. *This would be okay.* If this truly was her *lygi* body, then no matter what Evrardin was forced to do to it, it would dissipate once the spell wore off and she would turn full again where her mind sat in the Veil.

"Trust me," Mara murmured.

Evrardin tried his godforsaken hardest to hold back his hand as he held her, his whole body shaking, but his hands were compelled to betray. He couldn't fight it. There was no way he could fight it. And for the next several agonizing beats, he was going to think he really killed her. She hadn't the strength or time to properly explain.

She wished she had thrown caution to the wind and told him her plan earlier. Maybe some of this could have been avoided. Although, it could have been disastrous just the same if Evrardin had been forced to tell Acastus.

"Do it," she insisted.

Evrardin's brows knit together, tilting his head in confusion.

Mara sat upward, reaching for his lips, his dagger plunging into her chest as she kissed him. She felt the whisper of the dagger, then no pain at all. She knew her lips had touched Ev's, the warmth and slight tickle of his beard a ghostly feeling on her face and fingertips. But when she opened her eyes, she was alone in the Veil. Evrardin nowhere in sight.

She leaned over and emptied her stomach as the full force of her soul centering her true form in the Veil hit her. She stood and straightened her dress. When she looked down as her hands smoothed the fabric, water droplets sliced through the air.

She didn't bother wiping away her tears as she lifted her skirts and busted into a mad dash.

Chapter Forty-Four
Mara

The decaying reed tickled Mara's legs when she hiked her wedding dress up, her feet sinking into the mud. She swallowed heavy breaths as she ran through the wetlands—no end in sight.

She slowly came to a stop, spinning around, her eyes searching the hazy land. Aerosols sparkled through the air like a dream. *Where would the break into the Dusk Court be if I were it?* she thought. She chided herself; she was not fit for this. She shouldn't be the one to save the kingdoms. She wasn't clever enough. She wasn't brave enough. She surprised herself at how fast she was able to lock back her tears, the horizon glowing faintly, calling to her like pages that had yet to be written.

Words from Lord Cofsi rang in her ear about the balance of the kingdoms and the way that reflected into the Veil. The Shadowed Isles were on the other side of Junefell, its islands all bordered by water. If Mara slipped into the sea, using its surface as a mirror, would it take her to the other side of Junefell instead? Would it land her in The Shadowed Isles? She gritted her teeth in anticipation, wondering if this idea was marvelously clever of her or exceptionally dimwitted.

Mara shifted on her feet and darted to the horizon where she could see the edge of the sea. The waves crashed in the distance, echoing no sound. Before she could reach the beach, a faint rumbling made her halt.

The rumbling vibrated through her again, only this time, it was accompanied by hands outstretching from the dirt. Mara immediately filled with the same terror that coursed through her when she was bonded with Acastus in the Hallowed Cistern. She feared the hands would claw at her again and she bared her teeth, about to sprint to the ocean, when she realized they weren't coming for her. No, the hands were pulling themselves free from the dirt, heaving the bodies attached to them out onto the surface. Dark knights, absent of any distinctive features, all swirling with faded smoke, rumbled the ground as they woke.

The forgotten Glass People.

"Shit," she gasped. One of the creatures snapped its head toward her at her words and Mara spun on her heels, darting for the waves.

The wind rustled her hair, her feet sinking into the dark sandy beach. She approached the water's edge hesitantly, checking over her shoulder to make sure the creatures weren't following. She edged into the water, the chill licking her ankles. She stared at the surface of the ocean, trying to focus past the foam and shifting tide. Then, it came into view. She could just barely see the faint image of a castle's room. It was faded and blurred, the same way Acastus and Evrardin had looked as she stared at them through the mirror.

She took a deep breath in, hoping this would work, and squatted, pushing her hand under the tide. To her shock, her hand didn't feel wet, but rather, light, as she wiggled her fingers. Her hand was touching air. She closed her eyes and dove into the water, half expecting to collide with the sand in the shallow tide, but instead, she collapsed onto cobblestoned ground.

She brushed off her skirt as she stood tall, spinning around the room. She wondered how much of her travel had been through sheer physics and manifestation.

The windows along the wall established it was dark outside, the pale glow of candlelight illuminating her vision, the room eerie in a comforting way. Elegant bookshelves made from dark wood lined the back wall, beautiful tapestries in between them, embroidered with what looked like moths. A circular rug splayed out on the floor—multiple, actually—all symbolizing the shifting phases of the moon. A tree towered in the corner, its bark dark and thick, branches sprawling out along the ceiling like it was part of the structure holding it up. Tomes laid open on the oakwood table, various quills and intricate tools splayed beside them.

"Who are you?" a shrill voice asked. She spun to face a woman in a deep-colored robe, too dark for her to tell what shade it belonged to, an iridescent yellow underskirt peeking through, making her look like she was lit up from within. Like she got her light from the reflection of the sun, just as the moon did each night.

Mara hadn't realized she was marveling at the woman instead of responding. "Guards!" the woman shouted. Immediately, the clanking of metal filled the room, two Dusk Guards storming in and heading straight for Mara.

"Wait!" Mara cried.

The guards wrapped their armored hands around her biceps, almost hauling her completely off the ground.

"Lord Cofsi sent me!" she pleaded.

The guards began to move her away when the woman held out a hand. They paused as she slowly approached Mara.

"Lord Cofsi isn't presently in Luna. He's traveled to Solstrale for the Sun Prince's wedding."

"Yes. That's where I've come from."

She appraised her, giving her a skeptical once over. "By your lonesome?"

Mara nodded.

"You expect me to believe you made it to The Shadowed Isles alone, dressed like that? And I'm supposed to trust your words because you referenced Lord Cofsi by name?"

Mara heaved in an unsteady breath, wiggling against the bruising grip the men had on her arms. "No. I mean yes. I... I came here by glassfairing."

The woman tilted her head, her eyes flashing with recognition. "You're the Sun Prince's bride."

Mara nodded. "Maralena. And I've come to beseech your assistance."

The woman's brows knitted together, and then she motioned for the guards to drop her. Once they moved out of the room, the woman encouraged Mara to sit.

"Why would my nephew send you here?"

Mara tried not to ponder about family trees at this moment, brushing off her comment about their relations. "I believe he went to Solstrale because he knew the Sun Prince was up to something... dark. He confided in me. Told me about the magick the Dusk Court carries. I..." She hesitated. Should she trust this woman she didn't know? She really had no other choice. "The prince is threatening all the kingdoms."

The woman peered at her skeptically, her hands weaving together in front of her. "And how might he be doing that?"

"Dark magick," Mara whispered.

The woman hummed. "And what is it you need from me?"

"Lord Cofsi mentioned something about the prince shifting the kingdoms out of balance. Solstrale possesses too much power.

I think..." Mara bit her lip. "I think he's made a deal with the sun goddess."

The woman paced across the room, eyeing Mara occasionally when she spoke.

"But I don't know how he plans to do it."

"And what has he given the sun goddess?"

Mara pondered a moment, remembering all those fleshy hearts. "Hearts."

The woman sighed, shaking her head.

"What?" Mara asked.

"Hearts are often exchanged for soldiers. For bodies. The prince could very likely be garnering an army of creatures of the Veil."

Mara's eyes widened. "Creatures of the Veil?"

"Yes. There are many lost souls in the Veil—so compliant to any divine force. Take the hearts of dead men, give them to the sun goddess, and she lets her creatures slither into the corpses on our side of the Veil. And they can't help but leave slivers in the break between realms—bringing darkness with them."

Shit. "I'm never going to be able to stop him," Mara panicked. What was she supposed to do against divine warriors? "I have to get back to Evrardin."

"Ah." The woman clicked her tongue. "The prince's lap dog."

Mara's face contorted. "Don't call him that. He doesn't have a choice!"

"No? And why's that, child?"

Perhaps if Mara told this woman, she'd be able to help. Mara trusted Lord Cofsi, and if she was amongst his court, she'd trust her too. "He's under a subservient curse."

"Something only done with draugr magick," the woman thought aloud. "Something only the Dusk and Ghost Court possess."

Mara nodded, looking at a tiny green flame that floated in a lantern on one of the tables. "Please. The prince... he's..." Mara's eyes lingered on the mossy light before slowly shifting her gaze back to the woman. "If you know how to break it... Please—" Her words got lodged in her throat.

The woman sighed, shaking her head at Mara. "Tell my nephew to warn me next time he sends runaway brides to my chambers."

Mara gulped.

"That kind of dark magick uses blood. I'm going to have to assume the prince used blood magick to bind this person to him. So the only way to break it is by using his blood in return."

"How am I supposed to obtain his blood?"

She tsked. "That is not my problem to solve, child."

"Please, my lady," she begged. "I don't know what I'm doing."

"Willow," she corrected.

"Please, Willow," Mara tried again, her hands clasped together on the table in front of her in plea.

Willow said nothing before turning around and strolling up to the bookshelves behind her, her finger gently brushing against them as she read the spines, searching for the right one.

When she found what she was looking for, she yanked it from the shelf, not worried about the books that began to tip over and splayed it on the table before her. Willow fingered through the pages silently. After several beats, she spun the book and shoved it across the table toward Mara.

"Here. Read up."

Mara studied the text, her eyes hesitant as they looked down from Willow. She mouthed the words as she read, her eyebrows squinting.

"It's that easy?"

Willow scoffed. "Easy? You think finding draugr flora is easy? You think digesting just the right amount so you don't succumb to the dark is easy? Even skilled sorcerers fear this incantation." She scoffed. "I'm not surprised the prince has fallen to the dark. Those not of our courts are not meant for dark magick." She seemed to want to roll her eyes, peeved by the idea of someone in the Sun Court—of all courts—using dark magick.

Mara grimaced. "But if I was to find the flower, how would I break the curse? I don't have the prince's blood."

Willow shook her head, irate by the young princess. "Lord Cofsi likes you?" she asked rhetorically. "He always did like a weird lot." The woman appraised Mara, making her shift uncomfortably. "If you can somehow manage to find a draugr flower, all you'd need to perform blood magick is for it to bind with your blood and to will the curse to break. But since you're breaking someone else's subservient curse, you'll need their blood instead."

"What do I do with the blood once I get it?"

"Didn't you just read the passage?"

Mara gritted her teeth. "It wasn't exactly written with lucid instructions."

Willow chuckled. "Yes, well. Sorcerers tend to not be straight forward. You'd have to ingest both items. Then summon the will. But only once the two have bonded."

"And..." Mara began again, gaining an eye roll from Willow, "if I was to do two incantations with draugr, would I need double the amount?"

She hummed. "Not necessarily. As long as your blood is coated for the time being in the dark flora, it will allow you to cast dark spells. But take too much, and you will never return to your previous state. And even if you do everything perfectly correct, a piece of you will always be bound to darkness."

Mara winced, trying to digest her words and not let them frighten her. "Would my blood work?"

"Were you the one to place the curse?"

"No, but..." She tried not to look as stupid as she felt. "I've bonded with the prince—with the Sun Court. Would that mean my blood is his?"

Willow began to shift through her belongings on various tables in the room, tidying as if Mara was not present. "No. You might be bonded, but it's not authentic enough. And if he placed the curse before you were bonded, you'd have no connection at all."

Mara let out a frustrated breath. She shouldn't have taken on something this complicated. She was no sorcerer. She wouldn't be able to help Evrardin, just as he had told her.

"However," Willow began, standing up straight and turning to Mara, "I don't see why actual blood relation wouldn't work."

Light fluttered across Mara's eyes. "Like a sibling."

Willow pursed her lips in thought. "Yes, like a sibling."

Aevum.

Chapter Forty-Five
Evrardin

Evrardin stared at the princess' corpse, limp in his hands like she had fallen into a fitful slumber. He expected his chest to feel deathly, drained completely by Acastus, like sludge clogging the cavity, but what brewed inside him was fire. Uncontainable rage surged up his feet, his spine, and pumped his heart. His hands would have been shaking if he wasn't clutching so tightly to the princess.

"Her heart, Evrardin," Acastus said languidly, like this was an inconvenience for him.

Evrardin's jaw clenched. His dagger slid against Mara's chest, then he pushed down, cutting into her clothes, and more importantly, into her flesh. He sawed away like he did all the corpses he was presented with, but tears welled in his eyes this time, and his lips parted in a silent gasp. This felt like retribution for all the heinous and reprehensible atrocities he'd laid out at the prince's feet. Like it was destined to happen.

He wondered if Acastus were to demand he stop feeling sorry for himself, if then the pain would subside.

"Always set to be my ruination," he repeated to himself. Mara's blood soaked his hands, the color an unnatural crimson. "I was never meant to be yours." His words floated away into the room, lost to the chaos.

When the heart—Mara's heart—was cradled in the palm of his hand, he cursed at his dagger. The dagger gifted by Cas meant for executing his misdeeds, never for hurting the princess.

"Finally," Cas huffed, snatching the heart from the captain's hands. He swore he saw it beat faintly. Acastus took the tome from Lord Alfson, scanning over the words, then handed it back before closing his eyes. The hearts had already been carted into the Veil, all but Mara's. Draugr magick was muttered between the prince's blanched lips silently. With his gloves shed, the darkness that swirled around them stood in sharp contrast to the glowing red that dripped through his fingers and down his arm into the sleeves of his jacket.

Evrardin carefully studied Cas' movements. When Evrardin stood, a desecrated Mara at his feet, his own heart had felt like it had been carved from his chest cavity. He was the monster he always knew he'd become.

Acastus shrieked and Ev's eyes darted to him. Alfson stumbled closer. "What's happening, my prince?!" he all but shouted.

The high priest grabbed the book that Cas dropped at his feet and scanned the pages. "He did everything perfectly."

Evrardin saw the mirror, forgotten at the back of the dais, move. When he focused on it, a large crane stepped out and into the world of the living. Its figure was lanky and tall, its face surprisingly humanoid. The feathers on its belly were ombre red at the edges, the rest of its chest a creamy white that appeared dirty, like it had rolled in ashes. Navy feathers sprouted along the perimeter of its body.

"Trana?" Evrardin muttered.

The high priest's gaze flickered to where Evrardin stood hunched and followed his line of sight, the prince's cries muffled as his body contorted beyond possible lengths. "My goddess," the priest cried, falling to his knees, ditching the tome, and reaching forward in prayer to the sun goddess.

The bird tilted its head and edged closer, moving slowly, like it wasn't attached to its own body. "Do not bow," it cackled. "You pathetic humans. So shadowed by your greed, your slimy eyes can't even tell a *svik* from your own deity."

Cas' body began to feather, blood pooling around him as wild feathers burst from his skin, each one echoing a scream from his lungs.

A *svik*... A false entity of the Veil. A creature that would imitate even that of a sun goddess to free itself. Evrardin clenched his jaw.

Alfson looked around like he was lost. Evrardin shook his head, charging at him. He grabbed his arm tightly and Alfson yelped. "Going somewhere?"

Alfson's eyes glazed over in hatred, thinking the captain so far beneath him that it was an insult to even be close enough to touch. "Unhand me."

Before Evrardin could decide if he was to slit his throat or not, Cas' screeches died, the silence making the room all focus on him. His body had contorted into the mirror image of the crane beside him... Then the crane also began to shift, turning human.

"What in the gods and stars—" Lord Alfson said, dumbfounded by the circus before him.

"It was a *svik*," the high priest spat. "The prince couldn't tell Trana apart from a godforsaken *svik*!"

"Yes, use your goddess' name in vain," the former crane cooed in a scratchy voice. "She will not welcome you."

The high priest stumbled, physically taken aback as though

condemned. His whole life spent worshiping the sun goddess, only to be told she would not accept him.

The *svik* resembled the prince, a mop of greasy hair on his head, his cheeks sunken in, his clothes nowhere to be found, but clearly still the body of Acastus. A fucking *svik*. Acastus was misled by a fucking *svik*! A foul creature of deception, able to disguise itself as anything, even a deity. Impersonating the sun goddess, a crane, the entire time. It explains why Cas had been choked with feathers, why he had begun to change if he used too much power from the Veil, like when his body shifted that time in the Sandwoods. Evrardin had thought it was from using his power to subdue the Glass King, to get him to change the way Mara chose a suitor, his body shifting not long after into the form of Trana. But he had reverted after a bit of forced rest. This entire time, it had been the *svik* trying to break into our realm whenever Acastus channeled magick from the Veil to do his bidding.

"Pardon my indecency," he spoke, gesturing to his naked form. "I have been locked away in the Veil for centuries now. Surprisingly, there are no tailors." His joke did not land except to himself as he cackled, the sound painful, like a howling kettle.

Cas' clothes had fallen to the floor, his body no longer needing them as he stood lean and tall as a crane. The *svik* began to grab the prince's discarded attire and slip them on.

"Evrardin," Cas grunted. "Find the Sun Warriors." He sputtered up sludge. "Lead them before *he* gets control of them."

"Cas—"

"NOW!" he boomed.

Evrardin had no choice but to turn from the commotion, away from Mara's body, and stride out of the cathedral. The *svik* had convinced the Sun Prince to set him free in the guise of summoning a warrior army in the name of Trana. And Cas still thought he stood a chance.

The castle began to shake, loose stones crumbling around

Lore Olesya

Evrardin as he hustled through the many halls. The fae magick that lingered in Kairth's castle would be pushed out as dark magick filled its place.

Chapter Forty-Six
Mara

Mara stared at the dark sea outside of the castle, a guard beside her. She had crossed through the Veil via water twice now, what was one more time? A small ripple of remembrance at the first time in the Hallowed Cistern coursed through her. She tried to shake the abhorrent memory.

The guard watched her curiously, likely never to have seen glassfairing before and wondering if she could even do it.

She took a breath and crashed into the waters. When she opened her eyes, she was not wet or surrounded by suffocating ocean water. Instead, she rose on the other side of Junefell, but now with the knowledge of how to break Evrardin's curse.

She sat on the edge of the sea back in Kairth, the sky darkening despite the time. Her heart rushed with ebbing waves of sickly apprehension. She stood and darted to the grand castle, far more decrepit than the last time she laid her eyes upon it from outside the walls. Shadows loomed in each nook, behind each bend, threatening to engulf the castle in darkness forever. When she got to the gates, no sentries were standing watch, but there were people—courtiers—crossing every which way in a panic.

"Trana has returned," one man said as he passed.

"The prince is going to curse us all."

"They're coming through the mirrors!"

Mara needed to find Evrardin. She wondered if he'd still be in the cathedral, but she couldn't risk showing her face, alive and well.

She descended the steps two at a time, thinking about approaching the dungeons, when she remembered Evrardin's room was in this general wing. She wasn't sure he'd be there, but maybe she could arm herself. She hadn't any other idea on where to find a weapon besides the dagger she had dropped in Evrardin's rooms when he had kissed her. She pressed down the rising warmth at the thought. If she was to encounter the prince, or Alfson, or even Evrardin, she wasn't sure she'd be safe; she needed to get her dagger back. It was gifted to her after all.

It took her several tries to remember the way, but she finally found his secluded door, sucking in rapid breaths. She didn't risk knocking and drawing attention to herself, sliding into Evrardin's room without notice. It was dim, a candle left burning by his bedside. A wave of morning rain and mint leaves filled her senses. It smelt like him. She tried to assuage the ruddiness that rose to her cheeks as she turned, spotting the dagger nowhere. She was thankful he didn't have a mirror, no warriors able to enter and drag her under.

"Shit. Where could it be?" she muttered to herself.

She had to find it and break this curse before Evrardin did something that couldn't be undone. She had to let him know she was alive, to help him stop Acastus. She turned to leave but stopped when the sparkle from the dagger resting under his pillow shone. She bit her lip, quickly shifting through her ideas, and settled on her worst one.

She took the dagger, its metal far heavier than she remembered, and strapped it back on her hip. She tried to ignore the way her fingers tingled as they brushed the soft fabric of his bed.

She clutched the pommel of the dagger as she witnessed the captain do countless times, ready to depart. On the nightstand beneath where a sword had been mounted, the piece of scratch parchment she glimpsed when she was in his room last stood stark in her vision—the one with her name on it.

She didn't have time to go snooping, but that didn't stop her. She rested her hip against the wood of his dresser and her arms moved against her will, snatching the paper that peaked out from the book it was shoved hastily into. She ground her teeth together, fluttering the paper in her hand, unsure if she should read it. Anger feathered her chest, remembering how Evrardin couldn't be trusted. And here he had stolen a letter addressed to her.

Maybe 'Mara' could be referring to another woman, the writing possibly from his hand. Maybe she shared the name with someone in town. The thought sent an unjust rage of jealousy through her and she threw caution to the wind, unfolding the note. She began to leave his room, deciding to read while she moved.

Her eyes mooned as she read, her face turning bright red.

I do not claim to be a poet. And this is not a line of poetry, but a ballad of betrayal. For everything I stand for, for all I have sworn, all the rites I've chanted. And it was you, liten rev, who ruined me. I think I knew when I first met you that you'd become something more to me. And you have. But nothing good. You're a weakness— a light I cannot reach. Your being taunts me every time I close my eyes. So many unholy thoughts come to mind. Things I have no right to think about. I dream of how you scowl at me with disdain, and all the lies come so naturally: the way you bother me to no end, irk me, irritate me, make my life so much more tedious than it has to be, how you're only a means to an end. But those are not the words I wish to say. They're not the words I truly feel any longer.

Princess, I fear I have grown rather fond of you. It pains me to say how much your snarky attitude has won me over. And I hate that I want to tell you how pretty you look or how humorous you can be, for you could never be mine, even if you foolishly mirrored my feelings in return. I hate that you've made me keen on your wit and theatrics. I hate it more than you will ever know. Not because I think these feelings beneath me, but because I'm not destined to be anything more than a chapter in your story. I can do nothing but cause you pain and suffering. And for all the pain I cause you, you throw it back at me tenfold. You're to be his. I want you to be his. I want you to marry him, my ties to the prince finally torn so I can get as far away from here as possible. I've never craved leaving more than I do right now. You've led me to nothing but destruction. You've taken everything from me, and you don't even know it. You've fucking ruined me, Princess, and I will never forgive you for that.

The letter ended abruptly, an ink stain on his final words as if he had thrown it to the side in haste or frustration.

Mara wasn't sure what to think. Was he planning on giving this to her? Was it fair for her to base his feelings on words he likely never intended for her to read? Regardless of the ethics, her heart swam with a rage of rapid emotions. When had this note been written? But she couldn't dwell on that right now. She had to find him and figure out how to get Cas' blood, sure she'd never find Aevum in time. Maybe Ev would know of a way to get his blood... The plan didn't seem the most foolproof.

She picked up speed, heading toward the dungeons, still

grazing on Evrardin's words, when she stumbled over someone hiding amongst the shadows, catching herself on the cobbled wall. "Ah, shit," she cursed.

When she turned around, she was faced with a tiny prince.

"Aevum? What are you doing down here?"

The small boy grinned at her, but it quickly faded. He was scared. She could see it in his eyes. "I came to hide."

"To hide?" Mara asked. "From what?" She shoved the letter into one of her skirt's hidden pockets.

Aevum shifted his weight between his feet, his face pallor and sickly. "Shouts were coming from the cathedral. At least that's what Lord Davenport was saying when my lessons were interrupted. I tried to find Mother. She's missing, you know? I didn't know where else to go. Everyone is running mad in the castle."

"And you came to Evrardin's room for refuge?"

He nodded. She couldn't help but warm slightly at how Aevum trusted Evrardin enough to seek him out as recourse. Then Mara noticed black swirls curling from the collar of Aevum's shirt and she tried to disguise the panic.

"Let's get you there, then." She reached for his hand and held it in hers. It was cold. "I'll get you all tucked away, snug as a bug. Then I'll go find your mother and bring her to you. Does that sound good?"

Aevum nodded, smiling at her despite the pain he seemed to be in.

She led him back to Evrardin's room and slipped him under the covers. His eyes sparkled just like Acastus' as he gazed at her, trusting her without question.

She didn't want to have to ask this of a child, but she had to try.

"I know you're not feeling well," she cooed, her hand holding his above the blankets. "But I was hoping to gain a favor from you."

"Anything," he said. She wanted to sob at how giving he always was.

She pulled out the small vial from her skirt pocket and popped off the cork. She shook out the dried red flowers that Crowrot had said came from Evrardin. She hadn't thought too much about why she had grown wonted to carrying it around with her. Perhaps because it acted as her last physical connection to the Gravedoctor. Or maybe because it was cultivated from Evrardin's hands.

Chapter Forty-Seven
Evrardin

Evrardin strolled deeper into the heart of Kairth, steadily approaching the dungeons. When he made it to that familiar door, dread consumed him knowing Crowrot wouldn't be inside. He had entered the dungeons since Crowrot's death, but the guilt hit harder each time.

He fisted his hands, his knuckles turning white as he entered. He had killed Crowrot, his truest friend, and now Mara, the woman he had grown to love. Only destruction cultivated from his hands no matter how much he tried to stop it. Perhaps he should just stop trying altogether. He wasn't sure how he kept moving, how he hadn't fallen over from despair yet. Perhaps his curse was forcing him to stay alive, to not allow himself to collapse to the floor in pain at what he had done.

Rumbling noises echoed down the catacombs and he gritted his teeth. He felt like he was walking in a nightmare—and not just today, but ever since Acastus bound him, every day was torturous.

The iron from the door dragged along the cobblestones behind him and Evrardin turned, surprised when a woman tumbled into the room. Her eyes were ablaze as she looked around, searching. Then she landed on him and her face went white.

"Gods," Mara cursed at herself, her voice stuck in her throat, raspy and worn.

Mara.

Evrardin didn't move, caught in a trance. He couldn't process what unfolded before him—was his mind playing tricks?

Mara swallowed before whispering his name, both of them gawking at one another. He wobbled sideways, catching himself on the workbench, all the air knocked out of him. Her hair was disheveled, her dress dirty and torn. Tears welled in her eyes, and she seemed to be breathing rapidly, unable to truly catch her breath.

He could not make sense of her presence. The silence ricocheted between them, the thrum of his heart loud in his ears.

Finally, he spoke. "Princess..." The last thing he remembered was her lying sprawled beneath him, bleeding out on the cathedral floor, all *his* doing. *His* knife the culprit. *His* hands marred in her blood. And he left her there, too.

She sucked in a sharp breath, a whimper forming in the back of her throat and she took several steps toward him. She kept moving, kept getting closer. Evrardin was waiting for the moment his eyes would adjust, and he'd realize this was all a hallucination, but the closer she got, the more she looked like herself. She stood in front of him silently. Then her lip pursed and tears began to fall down her cheeks in a rushing rivulet. She hiccuped, sobbing with her whole being. It took Evrardin several seconds before he reached for her, before he placed his hands on either side of her face. Knew she was real beneath his fingertips.

She admired him through red eyes, an emotion he didn't

deserve from her. His thumb inefficiently wiped away her abundance of tears. She opened her mouth, her breathing unsteady, and spoke in a broken lilt. "Do not let your mind convince you this is all a trick. I'm really here, Captain."

His lips curled to speak, but nothing came out, his eyes blinking rapidly to try and clear his vision. She sounded like Mara. Looked like Mara. "How?"

"I fear we don't have the time for me to explain."

He shook his head. Mara's tears slowed, solemnly smiling, Evrardin's hands caging her as he studied the expanse of her face. He stared at her like he hadn't heard a word she spoke. "Princess, how the fuck are you standing here? Have I gone mad?"

One of her hands reached out to grip his tunic, her fingers twisting the fabric roughly. "No. I'm here. I used the tome Crowrot gave to me. Conducted a *lygi* invocation." She gave him a little shrug.

His eyes danced between hers, his heart beating so hard in his chest that he thought it might bruise his ribs. His hands pawed at her, sliding up and down her arms in choppy movements. Then his knees couldn't stand it any longer. He collapsed to the ground before her, making her gasp.

His arms wrapped around her waist, pulling her body into him so his head was buried in her skirts. His chest heaved, his vision growing dark. One of her hands stroked through his hair, letting him hold her tighter, his grip sure to leave bruising marks. He could hear her crying continue, her body shaking as she held him against her. *Fuck*, she was truly here... alive.

"Evrardin..." Mara muttered, her voice laced with mild astonishment.

He breathed her in—her lavender scent—his fingers grasping at the softness of her dress, leaving a trail of bloody handprints. He pulled back and tilted his head to look at her, resting his chin on her stomach, all inhibition lost to him. He couldn't remember the last time he let his emotions command his body on their own accord.

Mara cried and yet her smile was so wonderfully bright, her fingers halting their movements through his hair, tentative to his reaction. "Never thought I'd see the day you'd get on your knees for me," she said timidly.

He chuckled a warm, broken sound. Then he smiled back. Truly smiled. A foreign feeling—a reason to grin from ear to ear. He couldn't remember the last time he felt so relieved and grateful. "I'd do anything you ask of me."

Mara's eyebrows knitted together.

He stood in one swift movement, his arms trailing her back. Mara opened her mouth to say something, but the sound was muffled by Evrardin slanting his lips over hers, tasting the saltiness of her tears. No other thoughts mattered to him at this moment. Not the fact that the princess was officially wed to the prince. Or how the undead warriors were rising through the mirrors of Kairth. Even the impending doom from Acastus' fallacy shrouding the castle was lost to his mind. The only thing consuming him was Mara and the relief that she was alive.

Evrardin moved hastily over her lips like she might slip through his fingers again at any moment. His hands held her lower waist against his hips, moving to hold her face between them, allowing him to deepen the kiss. He made a noise in the back of his throat as Mara went onto the tips of her toes to push against him harder. He moved against her so roughly she was forced back against the wall, a small mewl escaping her as she collided with the stone. His lifeless heart began to beat again.

His hand slid to her neck, his fingers hooking around that godforsaken necklace she still wore, and he gave one sharp tug. The chain broke and he threw the cursed jewel to the floor. She gasped and he unwillingly tore his mouth from hers, both of them clawing for air, his head only a fraction of an inch away from hers, his breath fanning over her lips. "I've wanted to do that for so long," he admitted.

Mara looked at him through her lashes before dropping her face, his hands falling down but still trailing along her skin as if he was afraid to fully let go.

"I'm sorry for leaving you," she told him. "For not telling you my plan."

"Mara, I told you not to tell me any details. It's my fault." She turned her attention back to his face. "Either way, it's my fault. I'm the one who drove a—" His words slipped, unable to speak of what he did in the Old God's Cathedral.

She shushed him. "No more blaming. We are not at fault."

His hand clutched one of hers while she dug through her pocket and pulled out a vile of darkened blood, holding it between them. "What is this?" he asked, tentatively taking it from her grip.

"Aevum's blood."

His eyes darted to hers in disbelief.

"I know how to break your curse, Evrardin." She smiled, her teeth peeking out between her lips. He had the urge to push her against the wall and attack her mouth again, but he refrained. Now was not quite the time. And he prayed to the gods he didn't believe in that there would be a time—that he'd have so much more time with her.

"With Aevum's blood?" His tone icy like it usually was when he mocked her.

Her eyes danced around the room. "Well... not exactly. But yes."

"Mara, what is happening?"

"It's too long a story to tell, but I know now that I need Acastus' blood to break your binding to him. And I thought that might be a little tricky given the situation"—she gestured around her in mirth—"so, I thought Aevum's might work in his stead. Same blood." She bit her lip and shrugged again.

"*Liten rev*, I don't want you to—"

"You don't need to fight me on this." She gave him a stern look before yanking the vile out of his hands, popping off the cork, and downing it in one thick gulp.

Evrardin's eyes rounded. He froze as he watched her, her lips slightly red from the viscous liquid. "You downed that rather easily," he mused with a concerned expression, almost convinced she had done this before.

"Maybe I'm secretly a vampyre." He went to open his mouth, but she shook her head. "Let me concentrate." He nodded. "Okay," she said extremely gently, like coaxing a scared kitten.

She closed her eyes and Evrardin figured she was speaking to herself in her mind. She reached for his hands, holding until she finished praying, and his fingers clenched around hers. His eyes roved over her face. Over her soft pink cheeks. Over the slight pout of her lips. Over her messy hair that hung in wild ringlets. He understood how men could go feral, barbaric even, for a woman. How wars might be started over their beauty. Because now, with her back, palpable in his hands, he knew he'd burn anything that dared to threaten her. He'd fall on his sword sooner than bring a dagger to her skin again.

She fluttered her eyes open, and he expected some bright light to beam from her and onto him, but nothing of the sort happened. A dreadful feeling swarmed in his gut, worried this hadn't worked.

She took a deep breath. "Go ahead."

He paused. "What?"

"Do something he forbade." She looked at him expectantly, but he could see the nerves riddling her, worried this had all been for nothing.

He danced between thoughts in his head, shifting through all the things Cas had cursed him not to do. He could waltz up to the prince and slit his throat with ease. Or begin to walk in the opposite direction of the catacombs. Tell Mara of every ill plan the prince had lined up. Strip himself of the armor he was instructed to wear. Leave Kairth behind and walk straight out the front gates. There were plenty of options to test Mara's ability to break curses. So he surprised himself when he opened his mouth.

"I fear I've grown to love you, *liten rev*," he said softly. A sentiment so unfamiliar to him, he was surprised his lips had the ability to move in that manner, to shape those words. Words he had been forbidden to utter.

Mara's eyes lit and she sputtered. "W-What?"

"Gods be fucked, you did it." He took her into his arms and spun her once before dropping her back to her feet. She giggled and the sound would have made him succumb to her if he hadn't already.

"Evrardin," she said out of breath, "why did you...?"

He tucked a wisp of her hair behind her ear, looking at her longingly, his expression wistful. But it was gone as quickly as it appeared, the darkness shrouding him. "The prince forbade me from ever speaking my feelings for you."

"What? Why?"

He grunted. "Guess he saw me as a threat."

"When did he do that?"

Heat rose to his cheeks at how long ago Cas commanded that of him. He had only known Mara for two days and already his feelings for her seemed to be lingering on his words—at least enough to make Acastus angry.

"You love me?" she asked.

He nodded. "Afraid I do."

Before Mara could reply, they were jostled back to reality, the ground shaking beneath their feet.

"Fuck," Evrardin all but growled.

"What is that?"

"The Sun Warriors." Ev grabbed Mara's hand and began to lead her away from the catacombs, no longer having to heed Acastus' orders to stay in the dungeon. "Acastus summoned them from all the dead soldiers I... killed. They're waking up. I have to sever the tie Acastus made with the Veil."

"*We*," Mara corrected.

Evrardin looked down at her and he pulled her along. "No. I'm not risking—"

Before he could finish, Mara hiked her skirt up and pulled the long dagger from Evrardin's room she had strapped to her hip.

Evrardin marveled at it. Then his eyes focused on hers and narrowed. "Have you been in my room?"

A blush rose to her cheeks. "I went looking for you... Then I found Aevum and stuck him in there."

He nodded.

"That reminds me, I think it's time you tell me how pretty and humorous I can be," she said, quoting him. "You know, now that you can speak freely."

Mild confusion was quickly snuffed out by a mischievous smirk that teetered on anger. "Sneaky *liten rev*," he cursed, a slight grin playing on his lips, hiding his bashfulness at realizing she must have read the humiliating letter he wrote to her, solely to get relief from the flood of feelings he was developing, never intending for her to read it.

The castle shook again and Evrardin pulled Mara against his chest to steady her, stones crumbling around them.

"Something happened to Cas," Evrardin muttered into her hair as he held her.

When the building stopped moving, Mara looked up at him, waiting for him to go into more detail.

"He was tricked. This whole time he thought he was working for Trana, but it was a *svik*."

"The esteemed Sun Prince was fooled by a demon in disguise?" she asked with spite. "Does that mean his plans won't work?"

"Afraid not. A *svik* is powerful enough to connect the realms on their own—to bring about an army of warriors, at least with the hearts he was given in exchange. But he took Acastus' place, leaving Cas a feathered mess on the ground last I saw. Seems he's finally fully transformed."

"What does that mean for the *svik*? Why would he want the army?"

"I don't know. I think he just wanted to be human—Cas was his best bet. And an army on his side doesn't hurt if he wants to remain alive." Evrardin shook his head. "If we can sever the realms, the Sun Warriors won't have the energy flowing through them any longer."

"I don't think the *svik's* shift will hold. The heart he took, it wasn't my real heart. I don't know how long it will last, but it will fade eventually."

Evrardin's eyes danced between hers and he relished in her scrutiny that once filled him with vexation.

Chapter Forty-Eight
Lord Cofsi

Lord Cofsi timed the warden's rotation precisely enough to reach through the bars of his prison, slamming the warden against the metal as he yanked him toward his chest, hitting his head and falling unconscious. It was almost too easy.

Cofsi squatted and shifted on his feet, leaning enough to snag the keys strapped to the guard's belt. When he was out of the stronghold, he took in a deep breath. The corpses he once smelt no longer lingered like decay, but something sweet coated the air. Something you only smelt on living beings.

He broke into a run, using his senses to guide him down the pitch-black catacomb halls. The ground slowly turned muddy, his boots soaking in muck. But the mud didn't smell quite like dirt. It smelt of iron and blood. Cofsi took a deep breath to compose himself. He hoped whatever Acastus had done was still able to be undone.

He reached a room, a small light flickering from a tallow candle. Tables were stretched out like an operating table. Flickering light dusted the room in a haze, every surface filled with vials of bizarre and unknown entities. Blood soaked the wood of every surface and Cofsi grimaced. He had reached the end of the catacombs and yet he found no bodies.

He shook his head. "Shit."

When he found a wrought iron door in the back, he shoved it open and stomped up the circular steps. He landed in a small room he presumed to be a disguised entrance. Exiting, sunlight seeped in and slowly covered the expanse of his body from the window. He was back in the main section of the castle and he found his way to one of the many expansive studies. A mirror lay cracked on the ground, a woman cowering in fear from the wraith that towered over her. Cofsi reached for her, but before he could get close enough, the wraith attacked, killing her in one blow.

He stumbled back and quickly darted down the halls. The mirror he passed in the council room stunned him. Dark hands clawed out of it, wrapping their wicked fingers around the frame, hauling their body out into the living realm. Cofsi realized that Cas' army of Sun Warriors were made of abandoned Glass People. Creatures so corrupted by the Veil, there was no way they could be controlled.

CHAPTER FORTY-NINE

EVRARDIN

"Wait here," Evrardin said as he unsheathed his sword.

"No. I'm coming with you."

Evrardin growled in his chest. "This isn't up for debate."

Mara squeezed the dagger in her hand. "No?" She grinned. Before Ev had a chance to deter her, she took off and darted into the cathedral, Evrardin hot on her heels.

"*Liten rev*," he swore like a condemnation.

Mara gasped when she entered the large room, the Sun Sect gathered around a fallen crane which she assumed was the creature Cas had mutilated into. They appeared too busy with the commotion to notice the two of them.

"The gods abandoned humans for good reason," a dark-haired man who looked an awful lot like Acastus chimed.

Mara's attention shifted to the speaker.

"That's the *svik*," Ev told her.

"If we kill him, will that stop the connection between this realm and the Veil?"

Evrardin took a moment to think. "I don't know. Maybe. But we need to do something to cut off the Sun Warriors' power."

"Looks like we don't have any other choice, then."

Evrardin told Mara to stay back as he began to approach the human *svik*. A member of the Sun Sect, Lord Alfson, moved to halt him.

"Out of my way," Evrardin demanded.

"I don't think so, Captain."

"You do realize the reason your prince is on the ground is because of this... *thing*." Evrardin gestured his sword at the *svik*.

"That may be so, but Kairth has been restored. Power brought back to the Sun Sect from the connection this *svik* brought. We owe him a great deal."

"So, you don't care about the thousands of people the warriors will desecrate?" Evrardin asked, astonished. Everyone knew Lord Alfson was malignant, but he never would have predicted this. Not of such a holy man.

"If that's the cost, so be it."

"Don't make me cut you down, too, Eldric," Evrardin threatened.

Lord Alfson grinned, the rest of the Sun Sect coming to his aid.

Evrardin's eyes darted to Mara's frame as she attempted to move stealthily along the flank of the room, weaving between pews, edging her way toward Acastus.

Eldric followed his eyes, a sly smirk forming on his rotten face. "I don't think so, Princess," he said with disdain.

Eldric moved to approach Mara, the Sun Sect surrounding Evrardin in an attempt to arrest him.

"Do not touch her," he growled.

Lord Alfson turned back to Ev, his eyes glazed over with corruption, just the way Cas' had begun to look. "You think you can stop us now? After our lineage has become so powerful again?"

"Why don't you come over here and find out," Evrardin goaded.

Lord Alfson bellowed, mocking him.

Evrardin grunted as he swung his sword wildly, knocking back several members of the Sun Sect. Evrardin was just a mortal man, but the rage that had been welling inside him for years had finally been set free. He was able to let it out, the toxins fleeing his system. His sword clashed against another, sending the man stumbling back. He jutted forward, plunging the tip into the high priest, a shriek leaving his lips.

Lord Alfson looked astonished, bewildered by the brute force. "Captain, you're too late. There is no point in this."

Evrardin didn't acknowledge him, his sword moving from one body to the next, blood pooling on the ground in a mirror to the Hallowed Cistern. Red starbursts splayed across Evrardin's armor and skin, his eyes furious, slaughtering anyone who stepped in his way.

His mind only halted when a feminine voice finally cut through to him. "Evrardin!"

He stopped, yanking the sword from the entrails of his final victim, his eyes glaring at Lord Alfson, standing stunned. If Eldric was a smarter man, he would have run when he had the chance.

Evrardin's eyes flickered over to Maralena, her hands clutched around one of Acastus'. With his attention on Mara, Lord Alfson set to flee, the only option to dart around the austere captain. But that was his fatal mistake. Evrardin spun on his heels so fast that Eldric didn't have time to react, the blade of his sword already slicking through the sinewy threads of his neck, severing it completely from his shoulders in one swift swing.

Mara cried out in shock, her eyes watering. Evrardin bolted

to her side, collapsing on his knees, his entire demeanor shifting. He expected her to cower away from him in horror at the carnage he was the root of, but instead, she leaned into him, the blood on his armor soaking her clothes. "Are you okay?" he asked her breathlessly.

She nodded against him.

Both their attentions were pulled down to the dying crane before them as he laughed breathily. "I was right," he screeched. Acastus' eyes moved between his once friend and wedded wife, almost happy to see the way they clutched one another. "I'm sorry," Acastus said, his gaze solely on Evrardin.

Ev didn't speak. Didn't move a muscle, just stared at the feathered mess that he once called his friend—though, that was many years ago.

"I don't expect you to forgive me, Ev." Acastus began to sit up, his body groaning.

Evrardin sucked in a rapid breath when Mara reached out to make it easier for Acastus to sit up. How she could find the sympathy to help this man who uprooted her life and made it a living hell, he did not know.

"Was it worth it?" Ev whispered.

Acastus' eyes met his in shock, frozen at his words.

Loud, echoing stomps ricocheted through the cathedral, Evrardin instinctively reaching out for Mara. "It's them," he said solemnly. It was the Sun Warriors. They would soon reap whatever destruction the *svik* commanded.

Chapter Fifty

Evrardin

Evrardin made the foolish decision to trust Acastus. "Do not let harm come to her, or I will come here and gut you slowly like I've been yearning."

Acastus gave him a faint nod, perhaps offering his friend this one last kindness.

"Evrardin," Mara said as he stood to leave.

"I have to stop him."

"I know... just..." Mara paused, wild thoughts crossing her deflated expression, his heart lurching. "Just come back to me, okay?"

Evrardin wasn't used to someone depending on him, beckoning him to return. Standing as the culmination of someone else's hope. For someone to want him. Someone waiting for him to return safely. Someone who would mourn him loudly. He had believed that when he left this realm, he wouldn't have a single person to grieve him. This was an entirely new responsibility he had never realized he craved.

All his fondness and reverence resolved to a curt nod before taking off and running as fast as his feet would take him out of the cathedral.

He made it to the outside theater, spotting Cofsi, illuminated with green liquid.

"Ev," he called out, his voice elated in surprise at his presence. Evrardin turned to him. "I tried to stop as many as I could, but they all began to wake. I…"

"I know. There's no way you could have stopped them all."

Cofsi shifted his stance, exasperated. "What in the gods' names do we do?"

Screams echoed down the halls, a chilling voice lingering in the dark passageways before making it to Cofsi and Evrardin's ears.

"We kill the *svik*."

Evrardin had Cofsi hot on his heels as they darted outside and into the large archway, the *svik* looking down onto the hundreds of Sun Warriors now polluting the streets of Kairth. He appeared like he was contemplating how his newfound life would play out. *Svik's* are rather irritating creatures, always scheming and plotting. And now one had the power of the Sun Warriors, bound to the *svik* that surfaced them, Mara's heart fueling the connection between the *svik*, Acastus, and the Veil. The creature's voice scattered in the air as he demanded his warriors spread throughout the city, seizing control for himself. Becoming the new Sun King in Cas' stead.

Lord Cofsi and Evrardin shifted to make moves toward the *svik*, but their actions fell short as several Sun Warriors cut through their path. "Shit," Cofsi cursed.

Ev counted. "There's only four—we can take 'em."

Cofsi bit his lip. "Oh, yeah. Four Sun Warriors. No big deal," he mocked.

Evrardin pretended not to hear his disbelief, but Ev, too, was thinking this might not be an easy feat—if possible at all. Evrardin slid around the bend of the awning and charged at one of the ragged Sun Warriors. Though they were undead, they looked collated. Their beings were full with wispy tails trickling off their skin. Some had helms that obscured most of their faces, but through the cracks and openings, Evrardin could see the decaying flesh beneath.

The Sun Warrior spun and clashed his sword with Evrardin's, making him stumble back a short way. He hadn't thought they'd be quite so strong, the mystique of them only something he knew from the old legends. He tried not to think about how this was his own doing. Every single one of these men —if you could still call them that—were fueled by those he had slain. The hearts he collected for Acastus. If anything, he deserved to be cut down by one of them. The poetic justice of it all is what motivated Evrardin to continue fighting.

To his side, Lord Cofsi's hands smoked, a black mist dancing off of his fingers. The Shadow People were known to control shadow magick, but only those in The Shadowed Isles truly knew what that meant. They weren't ones to share such sensitive information willingly.

Lord Cofsi managed his shadowed hands on one of the Sun Warriors, their armor cracking where he touched. Ev faced his own warrior, their swords connecting time and time again. He ducked under a powerful swing, just barely avoiding decapitation. "*Stars and runes.* These bastards won't die," Ev growled as he swung his sword again.

"Maybe because they're already dead," Cofsi drolled beside him as if he wasn't in the process of fighting for his life.

Off in the distance, Evrardin could see his men attempting to stop the warriors, but their efforts were fatal. No human was a match for something powered by the Veil. Even those who hadn't pilfered a weapon were quick to tear the flesh off the humans who tried to stop them. Their grasps seared marks and nails dug holes.

Evrardin finally managed to land a good enough swing that the steel slid right between the warrior's armor, where their neck met their helm, slicing through. His sword didn't break free of the warrior's flesh, but it went deep enough to open a wound too big to survive. Green pooled where red should have been. The Sun Warrior stumbled but didn't fall. "Gods be fucked," Ev said exasperated. "They're bloody invincible."

Cofsi huffed like he rolled his eyes, sending shadowed hands to grip the shoulders of a Sun Warrior approaching Ev's flank, sending them flying backward over the railing.

The sun cast an eerie shadow, the castle slowly fading into darkness. Cofsi took a brief moment to look at the Sun Warriors heading down into the city and the loud cries of the people. "They're headed to the streets, Ev. How the fuck do we stop them?"

Ev took a breath after shoving two warriors off of himself. "I have no fucking idea." He tried to channel his energy back, shaking his body out, his arms sore from blocking such powerful blows.

"Killing Acastus won't do," Cofsi spoke his thoughts aloud. He groaned as his shadow magick slid around the waists of two Sun Warriors and sent them flying down the steps.

"No. The *svik* will still have their connection to the Veil through Mara. And how would we kill it anyway? Creatures of the Veil cannot be killed in the living realm."

"That thing is being fueled by the hearts?" Cofsi called out.

Ev dodged the swing of a warrior's sword before angling his own to slice through its flesh and severing its entire arm from its body, whooshing through a ghostly cloud. "Yeah." Ev tried to recall the prophecy Acastus had spouted. "Needed the hearts to raise the warriors."

"That all?"

"Cas needed—*ugh*." Ev was cut short as he jutted his sword into the belly of one of the undead, green leaking around his blade. "He needed the heart of a monarch, which turned out t'be the princess'."

Cofsi pushed his hair out of his face, leaving a trail of sickly green in its wake. "She's part of the Sun Court now."

Ev raised his brows in irritation.

"Ev, she's bound by blood to Cas."

The captain shook his head and shoved a warrior back with both of his hands, letting a grunt pry its way through his teeth. "Is there a point to all this?"

Cofsi stabbed two Sun Warriors with his sword, straight through the heart, and let go, both of the warriors stuck together as they tried to move it in opposite directions.

"Mara's blood was corrupted! If Cas had been using dark magick this whole time, his blood is tainted. It's why Mara came back from the bonding terrified. She had crossed over to the Veil. Mara is connected to the Veil. She can kill the *svik*!" Cofsi called it out like he was elated.

Ev shook his head, running back up the steps with Cofsi hot on his heels. "She can't kill that thing."

"She's gonna have to if we're to live to tell the tale."

Chapter Fifty-One
Mara

Mara rested, sitting back on her haunches as she flattened her bloody dress. She gazed wistfully at Acastus who sat propped against the back wall of the cathedral where large windows opened up to view down through the courtyard. Cas' crown sat in a puddle of blood by his mangled feet.

"We can't just sit here," Mara insisted without any real solution.

"Let's just hope the gods are watching," he responded in his scratched voice.

Mara could hear the screams of the people even though they were a great distance away from the city. She held back her tears.

"Why are you crying, Princess? This was no fault of your own."

She wiped her eyes, her fingers moving to pull at her skirts. "Of course it is. I'm the one who opened us up to the Veil."

"I forced you to," Cas said softly. His eyes were stark silver; the shade Mara had gazed into countless times since arriving in

Kairth. Except this time, they didn't flash back to gold. This was Acastus in all his glory, his true self. Something about the benevolence of his true self made her linger with remorse.

"And I was too much of a coward to say no."

"I would have killed you, Mara."

"And I would have saved so many people if you had taken my life," she spat. She took a moment to breathe, trying to focus her attention on things that could help, not past mistakes. "If Evrardin manages to stop the *svik*—"

"It doesn't matter if he does. The Sun Warriors are being powered through the Veil. The only way to stop them is to sever the connection altogether."

Mara grabbed at her chest, her fingers digging into her skin, her heart throbbing in pain.

"What is it?" Acastus asked her.

She squinted her eyes in a grimace. "I... I don't know. My chest... it's—" She began coughing violently, blackened blood spewing onto her hand. Her eyes widened. Mara's thoughts wandered back to what Willow had warned her about with the draugr flower.

But take too much, and you will never return to your previous state.

Had Mara consumed too much? She looked up at Cas in panic. "I..." she began. "I took draugr remnants." Her words were hard to get out, her chest throbbing.

Acastus' eyes darkened. "How much?"

She winced, her eyebrows furrowed as she pleaded.

He shook his head. "Shit."

The whites of Mara's eyes began to blacken, and she looked at Acastus in horror. His feathered hand reached for her. "The darkness is taking you," he said rashly.

"I took too much." Her heart raced in her chest, making her nauseous as more blood leaked from her lips.

"No." Cas shook his head, propping himself upright with great distress. "Dark magick already coursed through you from the bonding... I had been using draugr."

She swallowed the thick liquid that wouldn't seem to stop pooling in her mouth. "But... But I took..."

He sucked in a breath. "Yes. Taking draugr, whilst already possessing dark means, is too much for a human body. It's going to drag you under."

Mara's eyes were as large as she had ever pried them open, her irises lost to everything else. "Oh no," she whispered, the horror dragging in each quiet syllable.

"The connection has to be severed. The draugr will leave your body if it has no place to thrive."

She winced. "Yes," she groaned, frustrated, "but how?"

He reached for her hand, holding it in his. Her fingertips were turning black the same way Cas' irises blew, blackening his eyes.

And even if you do everything perfectly correct, a piece of you will always be bound to darkness.

"I'll kill him," she muttered, digging in her skirts for her dagger. She clutched it in her hand.

His fingers found hers, releasing her from her dagger as she stared at him. "It will only weaken him, Mara. I told you, we're both connecting the Veil—"

She gritted her teeth. "I know. I just... I need to know the captain is okay."

She imagined Acastus had once been so full of life and kindness. Maybe he was not perfect, but he wasn't malevolent like the monster the *svik* turned him into.

"Maybe you could forgive me," he grumbled to himself. "Only knowing me for such a short period of time. But Evrardin had been under my command for years against his will, slowly dying inside."

Evrardin came tumbling back into the cathedral, his heavy footsteps headed straight for the princess. She stood abruptly to face him, and he faltered in his step. "Princess." The word came out as a breathless whisper. His eyes narrowed at Cas who was attempting to stand up. "What did you do to her?" His voice was dark as he charged the prince disguised as a crane. Ev's hand wrapped around Cas' lanky neck and held him pinned to the stone wall, dangerously close to the open window. He seemed tempted to toss him out and let him fall on the rocks below.

"You can still save her," he managed in strained, sectioned breaths.

Evrardin tightened his grip.

"Sever" —*cough*— "the connection."

Evrardin had never looked so deadly. He shoved away from Cas, letting him collapse against the wall for support before pivoting back to Mara.

"You need to kill the *svik*. You're the only one who can." Evrardin's hand tentatively reached out and caressed her cheek, her black eyes finding his. Her hair began to darken now, the black swirls sliding along her skin just as Cas' did.

"That will break part of the connection?" she stated more as a question, her head pounding, making it hard to think. Her eyes flashed to Acastus who gave her a knowing look while his hand massaged his bruised neck. "No," she answered herself. "The Sun Warriors will still have their connection to the Veil through us." She gestured between her body and Acastus. "They'll still be invincible."

Ev shook his head in frustration and Mara began coughing again, clutching her stomach in pain. Blood trickled between her teeth and Evrardin's fist turned white by his side.

"Then I'll kill Acastus," Ev spat.

She frowned, reaching out for one of his tightened hands and held it in hers, the blood smearing on his palm.

"That won't work," Cas called from behind.

Lord Cofsi shouted from the main doors, his voice echoing into the cathedral. "I can't hold them back much longer." Mara wondered how long the lord had been standing there.

The building shook, stones crumbling, the top of the cathedral with its grand paintings, chipping and tumbling in on itself.

Cofsi locked the doors with his sword before sprinting to the dais where the party of three mirrored one another.

"Mara must do it," Cofsi said flatly.

All eyes shifted to him, but Cas was the one who spoke next. "The Dusk Lord is right. Only Mara can kill me and the *svik* both. And if she kills me—" Acastus took a weak step closer and Ev shifted his chest and blocked the princess. "If she kills me, her connection to the Sun Court will sever ties. She will no longer serve as the conductor for the Veil."

"And the Sun Warriors will cease to live... in a manner of speaking," Cofsi added.

"What about the *svik*?" Evrardin added. The platform shook, cracks splitting the floor. Evrardin grabbed Mara in his arms and held her steady.

Mara shoved him away, snatching his sword, his hand releasing it with ease from the surprise, and stormed to the side doors.

"Mara!"

She was going to kill the damn *svik* and end this shit once and for all.

Chapter Fifty-Two
Mara

Mara left a trail of blood as the three men chased her. She escaped through the side door then scurried past the high priest's vestry and out into the main courtyard. There she spotted Acastus' replica summoning dark magick far faster than Cas ever could throughout Kairth. The Sun Warriors at their disposal, they stormed the streets beyond the walls and into the city.

Mara clutched Evrardin's sword and headed straight for the *svik*. Sun Warriors cut her way, Ev and Lord Cofsi rushing to hold them off.

She'd never be able to overpower a creature of the Veil. But she had to try. What other option did she have?

She clutched her sword tightly in her palm trying not to look as terrified as she felt. The *svik* grinned as he approached her. She swallowed hard, holding her weapon up high in the air.

With one quick movement, the *svik* was on her, locking her in his grasp. Her body swam with sickly chills, the arms around her familiar, but different just the same.

She wiggled as he held a bloody knife to her throat, tempting her to move, to be able to drag the knife under her skin. She panicked. The metal of his knife began to graze the skin along her throat. Blood pulsed loudly in her ears. She closed her eyes and summoned all the courage she could, then dropped her weight.

The *svik*, caught off guard, released her, and she stumbled behind him. She thrusted her sword toward him, but she was too slow. The *svik* had already spun to face her again, dodging her blow with great ease.

"You're no match for a deity, Princess. You're not the hero of this story." It was Cas' mouth that moved, but a screeching, unhuman voice echoed out of his lips. A voice she remembered haunting her in the Veil that first time she entered it during the bonding ceremony.

"It was you. It was always you," she realized, dumbfounded.

"Humans," he condemned. "So easy to fool. So willing to see what they want."

The *svik* charged at her and Mara turned to flee. The path to the captain was blocked by Sun Warriors that now surrounded the two men, leaving Mara with no choice but to retreat inside the castle. She stumbled down the hall as the *svik* chased her, his footsteps lithe and approaching fast. She barely stumbled into the Old God's Cathedral when the *svik* locked her wrist in his clutches, taking away her chance to swing at him. Her hands shook, her eyebrows knitting as the creature in Cas' form loomed above her, giving her an inhuman grin.

It opened his mouth to speak again, but collapsed instead, catching itself on its hands and knees, begging for air. Mara stood stunned, the weapon she held still locked in the air, frozen in the pose the *svik* had just trapped her in, and she looked at between them in confusion.

Commotion stirred and she glanced over her shoulder. Cas stood behind her, his body beginning to morph back to his original form, feathers falling away from him and leaving pale skin behind. Mara gawked.

There was a dagger—her dagger, the one she pilfered from Ev's room—lodged in his chest. He limped as he edged farther off the dais.

"What did you do?" she asked exasperated.

He grinned. "Always focused on the wrong thing," Cas said through the blood welling inside him. "Kill the *svik* now that he's weakened."

Acastus collapsed, mirroring the *svik*, blood sputtering from his mouth. He was killing himself so the *svik*'s connection would falter, just enough for her to be able to kill it fully. And with the *svik* and Cas dead, the connection would be no more.

"Go!" he shouted urgently, his hands clawing at his throat as he tried to breathe.

Mara stabbed the creature without thinking, knowing she might back down if she thought too much on it, and it screeched so loudly she had to let go of the pommel and cover her ears. As it ceased to exist the second Mara sliced through it, her *lygi* heart swept back into her body. He had no fuel to be a deity on this side of the Veil any longer. He was never the real threat.

Mara glowed faintly and she felt a wave of unease spark every part of her body, her *lygi* form dissipating in the cathedral, her true form whole again.

With the *svik* dead, Mara's heart morphing back into her chest, Cas was the final connection, his blood magick letting the Veil pour into this realm.

She spun and darted a few steps to reach him. Mara's eyes traced his movements and then she let out a hollowed gasp, her face blanching, her heart sore.

She clawed at the dagger, prying it away from the prince. She had been too forgiving, for now, she wanted him to live.

"It was the only way to end this," he choked out.

Glass Hearts

Mara's eyebrows furrowed, her head scooping low to be closer to Acastus' mouth.

"I'm sorry," he muttered. "This will free him, you know."

She knew exactly who he was talking about. Mara shook her head. "I already broke the curse."

He laughed, blood coagulating in his throat, the sound sickly. "I always knew you were smarter than you put on. But I meant more than just the curse, Princess."

Her fingers stroked his cheeks, tears from the pain dribbling down his face as he sank lower.

"Protect Aevum for me," he pleaded.

Tears fell from her eyes against her will. The Sun Warriors dissipated in the wind, dying in the living realm, killing them permanently, an eerie silence casting itself over the castle. She went to respond, but the light had drained from Acastus' eyes. The gold and silver both absent.

The Sun Prince was dead.

Chapter Fifty-Three

Evrardin

Evrardin fell as those not meant for this realm dusted in the air, all at once. He heaved in breaths, glancing at Cofsi with a silent, *What the hell?*

Cofsi wiped the blood from his forehead and strolled over to give Evrardin a hand. The *svik* and the hundred Sun Warriors slain had Kairth returning to dark halls and empty streets.

Ev might be tempted to jest and say, "*All is right with the world once again,*" but his mind went straight to Mara. "I have to get to the princess," he rushed out to Lord Cofsi who nodded.

"I'll begin to... clean up," he responded dryly, wiping green sludge from his dress shirt.

Evrardin darted to the stairs, the path of bodies left strewn about the room jarring, shattered mirror-glass mixed with blood. He slipped into the cathedral, Lord Alfson's head lulled to the side, blood congealing on the ground. The Solar Sect members who didn't escape were lifeless, their bodies spread on the floor.

He traced over the gore until he spotted the weeping figure of a princess against the back wall.

He approached her, her form contorted and bent over Acastus, and he said her name softly.

She faced him, her eyes—back to hazel—widening in recognition. And her hair returned to the chestnut hue it always was. Her skin had mostly cleared, the red burn path still scarring her right arm, but no longer ashen. She sprung to her feet, clasping her arms around the captain's neck. He bent his knees for her to reach, and his arms reciprocated the embrace. When was the last time he hugged another person? He truly couldn't recall.

She pulled back, her feet a foot off the ground as he held her. "Are you okay?" she asked.

He couldn't restrain his smile—*she* was asking *him* if he was okay—then pressed his lips to hers. Her fingers slid into his hair, intertwining with the blood, both their hearts racing. His arms tightened their hold on her waist, pulling her into his chest as close as he could. She hummed against him, whimpering in joy that he was alive enough to be kissing her.

Evrardin loved her.

He reluctantly dropped her to her feet, breathing deeply. Her wedding dress was stained red, blood pooled all around her feet. Evrardin's brows raised as he followed the pool to Acastus' human form lying lifeless on the floor.

"Did you...?" he began.

Mara shook his head. "No. He... He did it himself."

Evrardin's hand was on Mara's shoulder, then it slid onto the back of her neck, holding her lightly as he studied Acastus' corpse.

"He shifted to his human self after he severed the connection," she answered his unasked question.

Evrardin nodded, his hand sliding down her back, leaving a

ghostly trail. She reached for his hand and he instinctively winced. "You're hurt," she murmured.

"It's nothing."

She rolled her eyes. "Has anyone ever fussed over you before?"

This felt an odd conversation to be had amongst the carnage, but when did they ever have a normal conversation?

"Not that I remember. But you don't—"

Her finger came up to his lips, pressing lightly to hush him. "We should get cleaned up anyway."

Evrardin grabbed her hand before she could retract it from his face. Her fingers were tinged a faint ash as if she had touched fire. Just as Cas' had started.

"It's fine," she insisted. "I don't think it will go further than this. Cas was using the draugr magick far more than me. And with the connection severed, the pain has subsided."

He appraised her, taking her word, but worry still vibrating in the back of his mind. He wasn't used to worrying about another person quite like this.

Evrardin and Mara left the cathedral, but not before Evrardin turned around to take one last look at his friend.

Chapter Fifty-Four
Mara

The darkness had almost immediately begun to rise from the depths of Kairth. The crumbling and decay remained, the Fae magick still missing, but the dark cloud Cas brought onto the city slowly lifted.

Mara hadn't the heart to tell Aevum of his brother's demise, but when they retrieved him from Evrardin's quarters, it was as if he already knew.

"He's dead, isn't he?"

Mara bit her lip and looked to Ev.

"Afraid so."

Aevum sighed. "I feel like he died long ago," he mumbled solemnly. He looked at them with teary eyes. "My pain is gone." He tried to smile.

"It is?" Evrardin asked, bewildered.

Something in the blood of the two princes were linked well enough that the affliction handicapping Acastus spread onto his brother, just as it had since Mara was bonded.

Mara and Aevum departed soon after, taking him to the east wing of the castle not littered with bodies. She was reluctant to depart from the tiny prince, but he insisted he would be okay in the care of handmaidens he trusted. "My mother..." he said slowly, just as Mara went for the door.

"I haven't seen her. Aevum, I'm not sure—"

He cut her off. "No. I know where she is."

Mara looked at him confused.

"Evrardin had told her to flee." Mara's head shook in stunned silence. "She's from the Dusk Court, you know? I think that's where she returned."

"But why would she leave you behind?"

"Ev promised to keep me safe. Knew I wasn't well enough to travel."

Mara's heart swam at the protective nature of the captain.

"Well," she began, "you might be better, but you still need your rest."

He nodded and she placed a kiss on his forehead. She smiled at the handmaidens in his room who vouched to keep watch over the little prince.

Before long, Mara sat in the bathing room alone, beginning to tear her dress from her body. When she spun around to set the dress down, she yelped. Evrardin stood in the doorway as he so often did, looming over her.

"Seven hells, Ev. You gave me a fright."

"Apologies," he teased. "How is Aevum?" he asked her as he strolled farther into the room.

"As well as one can expect," she muttered, using her arms to subtly disguise her body under her shift.

Distress crossed her face. "He'll be okay," the captain said.

She nodded, her eyes avoiding him. "I know."

"Then what is it?"

She twiddled her thumbs and Evrardin entered her space, his fingers tilting her chin so she was forced to look at him.

"What's to happen to us now?" she asked, her eyes broken.

"We can think about that later, *liten rev*. We only just escaped the day."

She nodded but she knew Evrardin could still see the worry lingering in her countenance. She grabbed his wrist and turned his hand over, examining the wound that had begun to encrust crimson. "Sit," she demanded, moving over to where there were extra linens.

"Oh, now you want to command me?" He raised a brow.

Mara scowled at him over her shoulder until he sighed and took a seat. She came to his side, taking his hand in hers, and pushed his sleeve up. She could feel his eyes burning through her as she began to clean the wound. She wrapped it slowly in the linen to seal it off, tying a little bow on the back of his hand. When she finished, her fingers lingered, and he took her hand in his.

Her eyes fluttered and he looked at her with what appeared on the surface to be animosity. But knowing him, this was just the way he looked at her, even if he was staring at her with admiration. While she had seen him smile several times now, it was still a rare occurrence. She wanted to grin at him, but her heart was racing so hard in her chest as he studied her, she couldn't manage. "I'm not good at this," she mumbled abashedly.

"You're beautiful," he all but whispered.

The embarrassment heightened, her face turning red. "Even like this?" she joked, her appearance worn, blood still coating parts of her body.

"Especially like this."

She shook her head, her eyes darting from him under the pressure. She opened her mouth to deny his statements, but his hands were faster, gripping either side of her waist and pulling her properly between his legs. She was only slightly taller than him standing when he sat, making it easy for him to drag her mouth to his.

He kissed her softly at first, then he tugged her so she had to straddle his lap, his lips moving more violently against hers. "There was nothing worse I could have ever done," he mumbled against her. He had thought he had lost her. He had thought she died at his hands.

He kissed her with all his force, his feelings radiating around them, trying to squash out his pruning thoughts. Her hand slid up his cheek, caressing his beard, and he held back a groan. "Don't think I'll get used to this."

"What?" she whispered.

"Being touched this softly. This sweetly."

His hands slid under her shift, and she squeaked, their lips parting fully. "I should clean first," she said embarrassed. She hadn't believed him when he called her beautiful, and she didn't feel it now. Her hair had been ruffled, her arms stained with blood, her forehead sweaty.

"I'm still at war with how breathtaking you are," he admitted. He tucked her hair behind her ear then slid it to the back of her neck. "I have never wanted anyone as badly as I want you right now."

She silently gasped, blushing at his confession, possibly not believing her ears. How could she, a bratty little princess, make the esteemed captain fall to his knees like this? She hoped he didn't fight it. Hoped he was done fighting.

His eyes flickered between hers, waiting. When she said nothing, he gently stood, propping her back on her feet. "I can wait in your chambers while you wash if you'd like. Though, I don't think I'll be able to leave even if you ask me to. So please don't ask me to."

She couldn't hold back any longer, the tears beginning to

pour down her cheeks. His brows knitted in concern, his hand clinging to her cheek, his thumb brushing away the continuous stream.

"I'm sorry," she hiccupped. She couldn't quite pick apart why she was crying now. She was so overwhelmed with love and gratitude. With the need to know what was to come of the pair of them after all this settled. She couldn't believe that this brute had been able to speak so softly to her. How she was free of her marriage with Acastus, and that opened up all sorts of possibilities in her wake. The absence of her father and brother. It all crashed down on her at once, her body still rushing from the earlier events.

Her hands grabbed his belt, and she began to undo it. "Princess?" he asked breathlessly.

"I want you, too," she said shyly, using her free hand to wipe her face, the tears stilling momentarily.

"You're crying."

"Not because I'm upset," she said, smiling up at him.

He chuckled loosely. "Let us wait until after—"

She cut him off, taking her shift and pulling it over her head. His eyes glazed down her exposed body, his throat bobbing as he swallowed. She welled with warmth as he appraised her. Is this what love felt like?

He reached for her and she yelped. He slid his arms around her back and spun so he could place her against the wall, using his other hand to pry at his stubborn trousers. She wanted him to be gentle with her. To be slow and take his time. To love her the way they both deserved. But not right now. Right now, a feral instinct took over and she didn't want him to push it back down.

His lips ravished hers.

The captain's hand parted her hair, tugging her back so he could nip at her neck, relishing in her tiny gasps, treating them like a reward. His other hand wrapped firmly around her waist, angling her hips so they dug into his. Both of them were sore and tired, Evrardin's hands bruising as he held her like she might trickle through his fingers if he didn't pay attention. Mara's nails raked down his back.

He was quick to thrust into her, both of them gasping, clawing for air. "Don't think I'll ever get used to this either," he groaned. Each time he moved, she was squished more against the wall, her eyes fluttering, her mind reeling. He moved like he was thinking about what he had done to her earlier. Like he was punishing himself. Hoping he could grind the memories of his dagger piercing her heart through the joining of their bodies.

"Ev," she murmured, her words slurred. Her small hands caressed his cheek, making him pull back to look at her. His muscular arms held her waist in his grasp, his hips unrelenting in their mission. She looked upon him with heavy-lidded eyes. "I'm in love with you," she gasped, her voice small as she spoke.

He slammed into her, then stalled, his hand caressing her cheek, brushing his thumb along her red and swollen lips as she panted. She almost convinced herself Evrardin didn't hear her, but maybe he had just taken a moment to digest words never spoken to him before because he finally cursed under his breath. "I didn't think it possible to love someone as hard and fast as I've fallen for you, *liten rev*."

Her lips tipped up and he reflected that devastating smile she so rarely had the pleasure of experiencing. Then he pressed his mouth to hers.

Chapter Fifty-Five
Evrardin

They lounged in her bed that night, freshly washed and warm under her blankets. His arms wrapped around her, the desire to have her close overwhelming. The members of the court that could be trusted took over the clean-up transition, Lord Cofsi being of great help. There stood much to fix. Much to clean. Much to assist with. And Mara and Evrardin would do their part, but not until tomorrow.

Her eyes were heavy as she clung back to him, her head resting on his chest. "What did Acastus mean when he said you two were once friends?"

Evrardin stared at the ceiling, his hand instinctively rubbing against her exposed shoulder. "Just as he said."

She tilted her chin, narrowing her eyes.

He sighed. "We were friends before all this. Grew up together. I became captain and we drifted a bit, but he was always there. I had no other family. No one else besides the

Genoivres and Crowrot." He cleared his throat. "Cas went down a path I could not follow. It corrupted him for years."

She absorbed what he said, likely trying to process how Cas could place a subservient curse on his friend. How dark magick could break someone so intently that he'd betray the person closest to him in life. "Is it bad that I felt like forgiving him in the cathedral? That I wanted him to live?"

He shook his head against the pillow. "No, *liten rev*. I may have once thought you naive and petulant, but you're far more than that. You're caring. And you see the good in people. Something I can't do myself."

Her hand found his and he interlaced their fingers, his heart never steadying as he held her close. This feeling was new to him, something he was still learning not to be bashful over.

"Aevum is to be king," she mused quietly.

He hummed in acknowledgment.

"What is to come of you?"

He sighed. "I don't really want to think about it."

She squeezed his hand. "Ev," she scolded. "I must know. Please." He looked down, her sudden pleading concerning him. "Are you to be with me? Or is this just one of your escapes...." She couldn't finish the sentence.

His eyes darkened, rolling her onto her back, his body pressed to hers, his arms holding himself up on either side of her head. She gulped. "That is not what I mean when I say I wish not to discuss it right now. Do not be mistaken, I am to be yours, Princess. If you'll have me."

She looked like she was about to burst into a fit of giggles, but instead, she just smiled, and a tiny, strangled sob made her choke. "You look so angry before you say such romantic things," she hiccupped. "Yes. I want you. I want to be yours, too." Her chest and cheeks began to pink and Evrardin smirked in amusement.

"Then we shall not worry about the in-between. Where you go, I go."

"So you'll come with me if I leave for Wrens Reach? To return to my father and brother? I'm sure they're worried sick, not having any correspondence."

He fell back beside her. "If you'll have me, yes. I don't think I'm keen on staying in Kairth for a while. Too many poor memories." Images of the day flickered in his mind. All the years he spent bound to the prince, killing and hauling bodies. The execution of his friend.

"Yes. But also so many good ones."

"I suppose you're right."

Mara sat up and adjusted her nightgown, her stomach growling.

"But all I have to do is look at you to be reminded. I don't need these godforsaken walls for that."

He mirrored her, sitting, his shirt gone, but his washed trousers loose on his waist.

"You're quite romantic, you know that?" she teased.

He reached for her and scooped her into his arms. "Don't remind me," he mumbled. She held onto the back of his neck as he strolled across the room. "Grab that," he commanded as he stood before her wardrobe, one of her dress cloaks on display. She did as she was told but looked at him confused. "I'm taking you to eat and I can't have anyone seeing you like this." Just the reminder that Acastus had once seen her in her sheer nightgown all those nights ago stirred his chest with jealousy.

She wrapped the fabric around her, and he readjusted his hold. "And I'm supposed to be okay with people seeing you like that?" she asked, referring to his exposed chest. The faint scars were something she was sure to inquire about with time, wanting to know every little detail about his prior life, and he wanted to let her.

He stopped moving. "Would you like me to put a shirt on, Princess?" He almost seemed astonished. He didn't think he'd ever had someone jealous over him before.

She nodded timidly, her face heating at the confession.

"Cute." He placed a delicate kiss on her forehead before settling her beside him. She donned her cloak and Evrardin grabbed the shirt one of the handmaidens had left for him.

He stuck out his hand expectantly and Mara interlaced their fingers, letting him lead her down the decrepit, but no longer shadowed, halls.

Everything was so messy. The confusion on Acastus' council. Who was to lead? Where to go from here? But all he knew was that he was to be at Mara's side. The rest they could figure out later.

THE END

Epilogue
Mara

Wrens Reach, September the Fifteenth, 593 A.G.

MARA'S EYES shut briefly as Evrardin lifted her from his horse, his hands tight on her waist until she stood firmly on the ground.

She could sense Evrardin's eyes on her and her lips ticked into a grin. When her eyes fluttered open, the captain watched her expectantly.

"It feels so weird to be back. To be standing in Wrens Reach again," she muttered softly, peeking out behind Evrardin and soaking in the sight of her home.

Many of Venmore's guards met the two as they trekked through the slowly lightening Sandwoods. And they had been surprised to see the princess emerge from the depths, all falling to a knee, associating the widespread lightness with her. She tried to correct them, but Evrardin had shushed her.

She asked the knights about the prince's whereabouts, and after a few odd looks between the men, they told her he went back to Venmore to aid the council with the shroud that threatened the kingdom. Pride made her stand tall; how very kingly of him.

She hadn't realized her hands were shaking until Evrardin intertwined their fingers, calling her attention back to him. "I'm right here," he reminded her.

Her face fell to a frown, not from being upset, but because she had craved those words for so long and she didn't know how to react. To have someone on her side. Someone there to catch her and help her up. Always. While she had her friends and family, her relationship with the captain felt different. Evrardin was *always* there, he even slept in the same bed as her, clutching her close, afraid to let her go even in sleep. She initially worried he'd find her presence too overbearing, too used to sleeping alone. But he had been the one to insist they share a bed, not liking the idea of leaving her alone in her rooms. He told her with a slur in his speech one morning that he had never slept quite as well as he did when she was curled against his side.

She nodded and Evrardin stepped aside so she could approach the castle. Before she made it two steps, a male voice shouted her name. Her knees threatened to buckle. Evrardin dropped her hand so when Azor came barreling toward Mara, he was able to scoop her off the ground and hug her closely.

She quickly wrapped her arms around his neck in return, clutching him closely, something she had never done before to her brother. By the gods, she missed him.

"You're okay," he mumbled in her hair.

She nodded, tears threatening to spill down her cheeks.

"Gods, Mara. I've been worried sick."

She pulled back and Azor set her straight, his hands resting on her shoulders. "I hate to say it, but you were right," she began.

He subtly removed one hand from her shoulder and

pretended to wipe something off his face, but Mara could tell his eyes were watery. "About?"

"I did miss your antics. Not right away, though, of course."

He chuckled as she shook out of his grip and began to walk toward the castle. Azor matched her pace, peeking over his shoulder at Evrardin who had his mare tied at the stable and was now following behind them.

"New guard dog?" Azor asked, giving his sister a sidelong glance.

"Something like that," Evrardin mumbled, and Mara tried her hardest to contain her smile.

Azor had barely left her side as they came into the castle, taking her to her rooms, and letting her clean up while talking to her through the door. He had so much to fill her in on, so many crazy things with her father that she had missed.

"Are you to stay here now?"

Mara rolled on the balls of her feet. She didn't know what she wanted to do now. "I haven't thought that far ahead, yet." She hoped her brother wouldn't push her for more when she still hadn't let her mind adjust to the shift, and she was glad when he didn't.

She opened her bedroom door and Azor pushed off the wall and turned to her. "Ready to see father?"

She swallowed; her throat tight. She went to speak, to tell Azor that she wasn't sure she was ready yet. She still had no idea what she wanted to say to him. But he cut her off, grabbing her arm. "What in the gods happened to your hand?"

She winced as he turned it over and inspected it. "Maybe it's time I finally tell you what happened in Solstrale these past few weeks."

Azor's eyes trailed back to her face solemnly, the pain beneath them bright, disquieted by the notion his sister had been treated poorly in his absence. That he should have fought harder for her to stay.

He nodded and walked into her room, falling to sit beside her on the bed.

After rehashing all she had dealt with in Solstrale—from Acastus slowly becoming more threatening, to the execution of Crowrot, and the sun goddess' reappearance—she realized she was ready to speak to her father. She knew exactly what she wanted to say, even if it was just a feeling. The rage and nerves fluttered down to her burnt fingertips.

"Will he join us at dinner?" Mara asked Azor. Maybe she should meet with him before dinner, so as to not cause a major scene in front of their food. Yet, the idea of Azor and Evrardin being present as she let her feelings slide off her tongue, the hurt she kept nestling inside her chest at her father's abandonment, set her at an odd form of ease. Knowing they would validate everything she went through and wouldn't let her father excuse what occurred.

Azor rubbed the back of his neck as they entered the throne room. "That's the thing," he said nervously.

She glanced at him with a brow raised before following his gaze to the courtiers and noblemen in the throne room. All except for her father.

"Father hasn't been well. Once you left, he…" Azor swallowed, pausing to turn toward her before they could make it within hearing distance of the council. "His skin started to ashen. He felt sick. Couldn't get out of bed."

Mara's heart began to race. "His skin...?" she asked aghast. Her palms warmed and she rubbed them on her dress. She hadn't realized Evrardin was in the room, intermingling with the king's council, until he shifted beside her. Her face must have been stricken with something similar to fear because his hand found her side, forcing her to look at him.

In a silent exchange, he let her know he was right there. Here for her.

When she looked back at Azor, he raised a brow. Before he could say what was on the tip of his tongue, one of the councilmen approached. "My King, if you're ready?"

Mara's head shook. "King?"

Azor nodded at the councilmen then gave Mara a cheeky grin. "Oh, forgot to tell you that one bit." He flushed slightly, biting his lip. "Father has relinquished his position to me."

She laughed, astonished. "Oh my stars."

She giggled at the fact that her brother—her annoying, frustrating, irritating, self-absorbed, caring, funny, and loving older brother—was now king of Wrens Reach.

"I didn't even know Father could do that."

Azor pursed his lips. "Neither did I." He took a deep breath, his chest relaxing when he realized she wasn't mad at him. "Come." He gestured his head toward the roundtable where the councilmen were getting seated. "You'll understand everything that has happened in your month away at this meeting."

Her face warmed at the idea of being so easily included in her brother's affairs. She looked at Evrardin whose face was stoic.

"You can bring your... *friend*, too," Azor added, and Mara definitely turned red. She could hear it in her brother's voice that he knew something was going on between her and the captain.

"Don't worry, *liten rev*," Evrardin muttered in her ear as they made their way toward the rest of the party. "You'll know when the time comes exactly what to say to your father. And you'll know what to do next."

"How do you know that?"

He gave her a coy grin. "You're stronger than you think, Princess. And you've got us here. It will come to you in the moment."

She wanted to sob at his encouraging words. Instead, she held her head high and sat at the unusually tall table, Evrardin standing behind her.

"First order of business," Azor began. He quickly fell into his kingly role and that made Mara glad. They discussed the darkening and now lightening of Wrens Reach. The state of her father. The economic welfare of their army. The plans to assist the outer farms.

Mara was surprised when her brother asked Evrardin for his thoughts on certain matters, even addressing him as "Captain."

Evrardin had leaned forward so he towered slightly over her, his hand tracing her side as he spoke, no one able to see from the shroud the table provided. His hand absently grazed her curves before halting on her stomach as he rumbled some response out to one of the more inept councilmen, making everyone around laugh. Mara glanced at him and he shook his head at the older man who clearly should be removed from the council. His fingers drifted, lightly feathering over her stomach as he moved to stand taller, and Mara's cheeks warmed. She shook her head, trying to shake the thoughts of her body round with the captain's child—his hand protectively on her belly.

The idea of bearing children had always sounded burdensome; when she imagined taking someone's hand she wasn't particularly romantically interested in, having their children always felt like a duty. Just another requirement of a wife. But when the idea fought its way into her mind as Evrardin towered behind her, a weird explosion of butterflies surfaced to her chest.

She wondered if Evrardin even wanted babes of his own. Perhaps his childhood scarred him too much to want to risk raising children.

When the council concluded, the hall erupting into separate conversations, Evrardin raised a brow. "Why are you so flustered?" He almost sounded angry, like he might be worried someone here was bothering her even though he stood guard the entire time.

She shook her head. "I'm not."

"Mara," he chided. Gods, he wasn't going to let this go until she told him what he wanted to hear. He could read her so easily that it bordered on frustrating.

She should have lied, told him she had been feeling claustrophobic, needed to step outside to cool down, or anything else. But instead, she told him the truth. "Your hand..." she said softly, the pair of them the only ones still standing at the table.

"My... hand?" He held his hand out before him, appraising it, looking for the source of her worry.

She twirled her rings. "When you stroked my stomach... I just, well, I didn't mean to. But the thought came on its own accord, I really had no say in the matter. I wasn't purposefully trying to—"

His hand fell to his side. "Out with it."

She glanced around to make sure no one could hear them, still a bit unsure of how her relationship with the captain would be taken by those who felt they held more power over her. Those who thought it wrong for a military captain to court a princess. That thought it was Mara's duty to take a new husband, one that would benefit Wrens Reach politically. "It made me think of what it would be like if I was with child." She paused before adding, "Your child."

She had to avert her gaze, too embarrassed. This would scare him off. She should have kept her mouth shut. They had only accepted their feelings for one another a measly fortnight ago—

"You'd want to have *my* children?" he asked her, astonished. His hand found her chin, forcing her to look at him. His thumb stroked across her bottom lip.

"I don't know," she trailed, dancing between him and somewhere in the distance. "I didn't hate the idea."

He studied her for a beat.

"Am I frightening you?" she asked timidly, hoping she wasn't overbearing as he often thought her.

"Quite the opposite."

Her skin flushed and her mouth parted in surprise.

Someone cleared their throat from behind and Evrardin's eyes met the person interrupting them. She turned to face her brother, thoroughly embarrassed now.

"You know," he began, and she worried he might lecture her. "Now that I'm king, I get to decide—however unfair it might be—what's to come of your marital status."

She tilted her head. "What?"

He nudged her shoulder. "I'm saying, you don't have to marry anymore. It's not required of you to marry to settle alliances—or whatever else it might be that we'd use your marriage for." He smiled, nodded at Evrardin, then strolled away from them. "Come find me when you're ready to visit Father. I'd very much like to be with you." A hint of a blush dusted Azor's cheeks. "I think I'd like to hear what you have to say to him. You're braver than me, Mara. I still don't dare to stand up to him."

Mara nodded and Azor seemed to like that answer, leaving the room fully, two councilmen shadowing him.

She looked back to Evrardin, the room becoming empty, and he stared at her. "What now?" she asked him.

"Whatever you want."

"Does it bother you if I wish for people to know... about us?"

His face remained flat, but his voice gave way to a softer tone. "No. I think I rather like the idea of people knowing you're mine."

She bit her lip and Evrardin laced their fingers together. "It's quite scandalous, don't you think?"

His free hand pushed a stray tendril of her hair out of her way, his fingers tracing through her hair like wading through water. "Not if we're to be married."

Mara almost choked, shocked at those words on his tongue. She laughed. "Marriage?! You want to... marry me?" She tried to hide the tears of love from her eyes.

"Well, you wouldn't want to have children out of wedlock, would you? Now that would be quite the scandal for a princess." He turned to leave before looking over his shoulder. "Come, *liten rev*," he cooed as if he hadn't just said the most devastatingly romantic thing she had ever heard.

Mara didn't know what was to come of her life. No idea what would happen after she visited her father, or accepted Evrardin's hand, or what she'd do after feeling like she got what she came to Wrens Reach for. Nor when she'd want to set off to Throneskeep to visit Jessamine. But what she did know was that Evrardin was going to be right beside her as the chapters of her story continued to unfold.

She scurried after him and he extended his elbow for her to hold, placing a kiss on the top of her head.

Author's note

Thank you so much for reading my debut novel, and I truly hoped you enjoyed it!

These silly, little, goofy characters came to me after I watched season one of House of the Dragon, subconsciously writing fanfiction about Rhaenyra and Harwin—it's not my fault we didn't get enough screen time with them. I literally sat back one day, several chapters deep, and the realization hit me. If you were upset at that time jump in the show too, I hope this story helped scratch that itch.

And I just want to thank my biggest motivator: my stunningly amazing and talented best friend. It all started when she confided in me that she was also writing a book. I almost fell out of my chair screaming. We proceeded to share chapters with each other one by one, leaving mentally-unwell comments and little love notes throughout the shared document. It made me want to finish my book because even if no one else would ever read it, or even if no one else ended up liking it, I was doing it for her. And my god was it funny when we both realized how our stories were so similar. Is it because we're unoriginal? Or because our minds are linked energetically? I'm leaning toward the latter.

If you liked *Glass Hearts*, hopefully you'll stick around to see what's next! (Un)fortunately, each book after this may become more and more unhinged... I haven't known power like this since the day I discovered AO3.

❤ Lore

To stay up to date on my future projects, get links to bonus chapters, and see character art, follow me on Instagram @loreolesya or sub to my newsletter via linktr.ee/loreolesya

Printed in Dunstable, United Kingdom